# LION'S WAY

## Rita Ariyoshi

Savant Books and Publications
Honolulu, HI, USA
2022

Published in the USA by Savant Books and Publications LLC
1545 Ala Mahamoe St.
Honolulu, HI 96819 USA
http://www.savantbooksandpublications.com

Printed in the USA

Edited by Vern Turner
Cover images from www.canva.com
Cover by Kenny Simmons

13 digit ISBN: 978-1-7376431-2-8

First Edition: June 2022
Library of Congress Control Number: 2022941434

# Dedication

To Joe

# Acknowledgements

I wish to thank the judges of the James Jones Literary Society for selecting LION'S WAY (then titled The Black Confessor) as a finalist for a James Jones First Novel Fellowship, and specifically Kaylie Jones for her transformative critique. The following people read all or parts of the novel on its path to publication: Jodi Belknap, Mary Bell, Carol Catanzariti, Thelma Chang, April Coloretti, Jocelyn Fujii, Kaethe Kaufman, Sheree Lipton, Clemence McLaren, Kaui Philpotts, Kent Reinker, Vicki White. Lynn Seth prayed for the book every step of the way. Suzan Forbes and Henry DeButts of Cyberzone never hesitated to come right over and solve any tech problems. And here's thunderous applause to my editor, Vernon Turner, a wise, witty storyteller in his own right.

# Chapter 1

IN THE BEGINNING

The old lava crackled beneath the feet of the tall man and his small dog as they walked across the obsidian desert at the south end of the island of Hawaii. His gaunt silhouette moved against the towering blue sky; his shape in the distance belonged to another landscape in the peculiar way that a human form distinguishes one place from another more certainly than a topographical feature.

The man's elongated head with a high, smooth forehead rested on a remarkably long neck. His face, gleaming with perspiration and the radiance of mission, was as black and iridescent as the lava around him. He held an ebony walking stick as tall as himself and covered the ground in long, absent strides, the dog scurrying at his heels to keep pace.

The sun blazed as intensely and cruelly over this southernmost tip of the island as it did over his native Sudan.

The dog began to whimper. The man bent and picked it up. "Ah, Dear Friend, you have no shoes, do you? And the lava is almost as hot as when the Earth first belched it out. My apologies, Little Brother, for you have not sinned and deserve no penance." The dog settled into the man's arms, its sides heaving in the heat, its tongue dripping great, lively drops of saliva. It licked the perspiration on the man's face and the man laughed aloud.

He continued to converse with the dog, reciting a litany of the animal's virtues, the exuberance of his whiskers, the jaunty set of his perky ears, his loyalty, intelligence, noble carriage and mysterious genealogy. "You are what Hawaiians call a 'poi dog,' a great honor which takes into account not only your astonishing chop-suey heritage but your sweet disposition."

The man was a priest, although it was not apparent by his clothing: surfer shorts and a plain white T-shirt. The only clues were a small wooden cross on a leather cord about his neck and the cross carved into the walking stick. His name was Kor Majok, named after his grandfather, a Dinka herdsman. Since Kor translates to Lion, he was known in Hawaii as Father Lion. The dog's name was Michael, named after the archangel.

He walked on. The stark landscape was devoid of life except for the occasional fern shoving itself obstinately toward the sun from a chink in the lava where some drop of moisture, mote of soil or iota of hope had lodged.

In the immense quiet, Father Lion prayed the rosary on the animal's toenails, since he had only four fingers on each hand, a legacy of his time in slavery. In the distance, on his right, lay the soft haze of the sea. To his left, the lava desert stretched to high green mountains that had at their heart the raging fire that formed all the land of Earth. On this island, that fire was still making and remaking the land in cataclysmic echoes of the original chaos.

The priest's greatest desire in life was to be alone with God, to have his very breath rise as incense to touch the hem of the Divine Presence, but he found himself saddled with a gift for the Sacrament of Reconciliation, for listening, comforting and chastising in a way that set people on the path to peace clothed in new compassion and courage. Recognizing this extraordinary gift, the Catholic bishop of Honolulu sent Father

Lion to parishes throughout the Islands to bring back into the fold the lost sheep; to harvest souls as doctors save kidneys, livers and eyes. To this end, Father Lion sat in the dark of the confessional for hours on end listening to whispered sins until their weight and shame bowed him down.

He thought of Jesus hanging on the cross accepting all the sins humanity would ever commit, imagining God had abandoned him.

The priest knew abandonment well. As a child, he had been kidnapped and sold into slavery. The memories clung to him like a second skin, deep and close to the bone.

*Am I carried high on my father's shoulders? Is he singing? Are we laughing? I remember being happy. I am seven years old.*

*It is morning. Milk fills my belly and my mother's kisses linger on my cheek. The long-horned cattle shamble before us bawling toward the river. My younger brothers herd our goats, but as the eldest son, I am allowed to assist our father with our precious cattle, our wealth.*

*The early sun lies upon the bush, gilding the dust. The air still embraces remnants of the night's chill as the deceptively complacent calm of the African morning fills my heart with the beloved predictability of my life.*

*My father stops. The muscles of his shoulders tense hard against my thighs. He pulls me down, close to his chest. He cradles me as he runs, but he cannot outrun the horses that encircle us. There is ugly laughter, choking golden dust. Then blood. My father's warm blood bathes me. That is all I see. Blood. Not my father. I do not see my father.*

*I hear myself cry. I think it is me. I do not know.*

*I am dragged by my arm, pulled up onto a horse. We thunder away, cross the Bahr el Ghazal into the land of the Northerners. We stop for the night. I see more men, more horses, more captured children. We*

3

*want our mothers. We cry for our mothers. Someone shouts at us, fires a gun at the sky. "Any child who cries will be killed," A man grabs a small, wailing girl by the hair. A long knife flashes in the firelight. "Here, play ball!" He throws something. What? I do not see. I am blinded by tears of terror.*

*My father always told me that God is good. God is always with me. I am God's child, the son of the king of Heaven and Earth. Where is God now? My father's blood is dark and stiff on my clothes. I want only my mother.*

Father Lion found cleansing in solitude, so whenever possible, he walked, rather than drove, from parish to parish. The loneliness imposed when he was young had penetrated his innermost being, becoming an intrinsic element of himself. In his deepest chamber of quiet, God dwelled in utter simplicity. The quieter he managed to be, the more he felt God expand within him, at once apprehended and eternally unknowable. He had come to believe that words, with all their nuances, interpretations and ambiguities got in the way of his exchanges with the Divine. The communication between the man and the Great Mystery flowed without words, bypassing his keen, intuitive mind, linking essence to essence, spirit to spirit-source in strange melodious groans akin to the primal song of a whale roaming the liquid plains of the ocean.

He had been carrying his dog for an hour through the rosary's joyful and sorrowful mysteries, through his memories and musings, when he saw, almost as a mirage, six coconut palms sprouting from the black expanse. Palms meant water.

# Chapter 2
## THE DISCORDANT SONG OF THE LAVA MADONNA

As he approached the palm trees, Father Lion heard music; wild, discordant, off-key but oddly interesting piano music. He picked up his pace, peering intently into the heat.

A girl was playing a piano under a tarp in the middle of the lava desert. As he got closer, he noted that the tarp extended from a rude shelter built into a crevasse. A small distance away, a garbage heap rose. American civilization, he thought, requires as much room for its waste as its goods.

The girl paused in her playing. The angry, frustrated cries of a baby split the air. The girl turned toward the shelter, saw the priest, and froze, shading her eyes with her arm. She was young, fourteen or fifteen, with honey-colored skin and long, brown, wavy hair pulled back off a thin rodent-like face. She thrust out her receding chin and crossed her arms at her bare waist, just above her skimpy denim shorts.

Father Lion set Michael down and waved.

Tentatively, the girl waved back, then resumed her defensive stance.

"Aloha," he called out.

"Hi," she answered, still wary.

"I enjoyed your music."

She did not respond.

"Do you mind if my friend Michael and I rest?" When she looked beyond him, he explained, "Michael's my dog."

"Well, okay, I guess. There's a pond over by the coconut trees with good water you can drink without boiling. "

"*Mahalo*. I'm Father Lion Majok on my way to Sacred Heart Church in Na'alehu."

"You some kine priest?"

"A Catholic priest."

"My tutu and grampa are Catholics. They stay Kona side." Then, as if confiding too much, she said, "Na'alehu's pretty far you know."

"I like to walk. Is that your baby crying?"

"She's my baby sister." The girl then unleashed a string of expletives describing her mother and her mother's boyfriend. "My mom leaves me out here to watch the baby when they go Hilo."

She disappeared into the dim interior of the shelter, an affair cobbled together with scrap lumber and sheets of old corrugated tin. The absurdity of the weather-beaten piano in the middle of the old lava flow made Lion smile as he proceeded to the pond. He slid his backpack off his shoulders, scooped water into his bottle and filled the collapsible bowl he carried for the dog.

The girl, with the baby on her hip, joined him at the pond.

"What is your baby sister's name?"

"Anela."

"Angel. That's' a beautiful name."

"I named her. My mom was too stoned.'"

"And what is your name?"

"Tori."

"I like that name, too."

"Well, I like your name. Lion's way cool."

"I come from Africa."

6

"Wow. That's like far away, right?"

"Shouldn't you be in school, Tori?"

"I'm home-schooled."

Father Lion kept silent, deliberately creating uncomfortable space in the conversation. If one waited long enough, people always filled the silence with their yearnings and secret shames, things they never told another soul. It was part of his gift.

As expected, Tori filled the pause. "Well, I'm supposed to be home-schooled. My mom keeps promising to crack the books with me but she doesn't know what she's doing. My tutu brings me books from Kona when she visits, but my mom hates the sight of her, says she has her nose so high in the air she'd drown in the rain — not that it ever rains out here. She's my dad's mom, obviously."

"And where is your father?"

"Dubai. That's like far away, too. He works construction. There's no work here right now. My mom made my dad move out and then Sapman moved in, and pretty soon here we are out here because my dad stopped paying our rent. My mom's gonna take him to court and make him pay, and she's gonna say that Anela's his kid, too, even though she's not, so my dad'll have to pay more child support. I mean legally, I suppose she's his kid because my mom and my dad are still legally married, and my mom says that's what the law says. It's not Anela's fault that Sapman is her bio-dad." She addressed the baby, tickling her chin, "Is it, huh? Not your fault you got a worthless, disgusting dad."

The delighted baby gurgled, kicked, and waved her tiny arms.

"I conclude you don't like your mother's boyfriend very much."

"If my mom only knew that Sapman loves me more than her. He always tries to get his hands on me. 'I love you, Baby. I love you, Baby.' Oh, da stink breath. His teeth are so rotten."

"Does Anela's father have a name other than Sapman?"

"Yeah. Sometimes I use another word that rhymes with Sap. His name's Trapman. Garrett Trapman. He comes from THE Trapman family but they cut him off. He's such a druggie loser. He told us he has a million dollars in a trust fund, but they got it all locked up. He can't touch a penny. In his mom's house they even have this big Koa bed that King Kalakaua slept in when he came Hilo. The king liked to play cards with Sapman's great-great-grand whateveh. Like I'm impressed. He's still Sapman loser."

"Do you mind if I call him Garrett? We priests can't always use the more colorful, perhaps more accurate name."

"Call him whatever you want. Like I said, he's still Sapman loser. He wanted me to sell my piano when we moved out here."

"Won't it get ruined?"

"'At least I'll have it for a while longer. My gramma wants me to live Kona side with her and go to school, but my mom needs me here for Anela and for the welfare check."

"What do you want, Tori?"

"I want..." She paused, raised her face to the blue sky. "I want hip-hugger jeans." She shrugged in resignation. "I used to want to go to music school, but I already gave up on that one."

"Would you like to live with your grandparents?"

"You're kidding, right? Who would want to live here? But Anela's here. They won't take care of her if I leave. I thought about it."

"What's your grandmother's name?"

"Wanda Tamsing."

"And your grandfather?"

"Sharmain."

Michael turned his head, ears alert, and stood up, nose twitching.

Only then did the priest and the girl hear the sound of a motor. The girl said, "That's Sapman's truck. He won't like it that you're here."

A gleaming black truck raised on huge tires bounced slowly over the lava toward them. Lion got up to face it. Michael stood next to his left leg, quivering.

Tori cuddled the baby. "Here comes your din-din. Shh now." She kissed her.

The instant the driver cut the engine, he leaped from the truck, grabbed a shotgun from the backseat and racked a shell in the gun as he swaggered toward the priest. His jeans rode so low on his gaunt torso, he was in danger of losing them. A chained pit bull barked from the bed of the truck.

Michael did not flinch and neither did Father Lion.

A deep, permanent sneer distorted the man's face as he let loose a withering barrage of vulgarity that included asking who Lion was and what he was doing here.

Tori spoke up, "He's a priest, Daddy." Her "Daddy" bristled with sarcasm.

"Father Lion Majok's my name. I'm on my way to Na'alehu, saw the trees and stopped for water. That's a beautif —"

"Water? I know you priests and what you're up to. You stopped for a little piece of something else from this slut. Right?"

A woman climbed down from the truck, yelling, "Shaddup!" to the lunging pit bull. She was a dried-up, frizzy-haired version of her daughter, whom she addressed in the same tone she used on the snarling dog. "You're supposed to be taking care of your baby sister not entertaining strange men." She had bad teeth, sallow skin and quick, sly eyes.

Tori defied her. "There's no food. What am I supposed to do?"

The mother slapped her, "Don't you sass me. And you..." She turned on the priest. "Get outta here. Scram-ay voo!."

The driver leered. "The lady means what she says, pree-vert. Move or I'll sic my dog on you and your mutt."

Father Lion bowed toward Tori. *"Mahalo* for the water. God bless you. All of you."

He turned and walked away while Garrett Trapman ranted after him and fired the gun into the air. Father Lion continued south toward Na'alehu with the snarls and barks of the pit bull at his back. Michael nervously glanced up at him. "It's all right, little friend. They're all in chains of their own making."

He prayed for each one of them, especially the girl who played an out-of-tune piano, and named her baby sister Anela. Lion thought she had just enough hunger and eccentricity to make some headway in life. But she would likely be derailed by misfortune and slip unnoticed into unhappiness. Her life story was outlined on her eager face, and in her crude language. Only the unpleasant details remained. Yet there was that piano…

Lion thought about how easily she was persuaded from hostility to openness, and her wily courage in facing down the mother's boyfriend. "Tamsing," he said aloud to Michael. "Sharmain and Wanda Tamsing. Kona."

# Chapter 3
ALMOST HOME

Father Lion sat behind the confessional screen reading his breviary in dim light. The door to the small room behind the altar stood open. It was Saturday evening at Sacred Heart Church in Na'alehu, and he could hear the ocean whispering among the lava rocks at the shore. The trade winds teased the *hala*, the coconut palms, and the round-leafed *kamani* trees. The priest prayed and waited, humbly aware that he was standing in for, or, more accurately, sitting in for God and Saint Peter. He held in his hands the power to forgive sins.

This power had been passed down through generations of priests in an unbroken chain stretching back two thousand years beginning with Jesus, who said to his apostles, "Whose sins you shall forgive, they are forgiven, and whose sins you shall retain, they are retained." This miraculous power to restore a man or woman to life, to put their sins as far from them as East is from West, and enable them to begin anew, was lately and largely neglected. The current generation did not believe in sin or moral absolutes. Sin, to them, was old fashioned.

Father Lion harbored no regrets about devoting his life to the equally old-fashioned notion of service. He believed in bringing comfort to the weary, hope to the hopeless, joy to the sorrowful and mercy to the cruel. He bestowed these gifts as if he possessed them in abundance. In truth, the priest's only comfort was in offering comfort. His only hope was to die in a state of grace, and his only joy realized in communion with the Father. Mercy, however, he had received in abundance, and waited to share it. He prayed to the Holy Spirit for wisdom. He prayed that someone would come to confession and avail themselves of the grace that had traveled through the centuries from the Divine Master, grace that had endured through persecution, corruption, indifference, and now waited here in a tiny church beside the sea in the middle of the vast Pacific Ocean.

He felt that if people truly understood the power of the sacrament they would be lined up for miles to unburden themselves. He amused himself: Hey folks, step right up to the spiritual dump and recycle your clunker life. Throw away the Prozac and vodka, cancel your appointments with the shrink and plastic surgeon. Look at yourself in the mirror and see what the Lord sees: Beauty.

Just outside the church door, Michael heaved a sigh. Confession nights were long and lonely for him and he had already sniffed and sampled everything rank around him.

Father Lion heard footsteps on the wooden floor of the church . The floor creaked then creaked again. Someone had knelt to pray, then rose. The footsteps approached the light of the open door, hesitated, then a man plunged into the room.

As he entered, Father Lion invited, "Welcome. Please feel free to talk in privacy behind the screen, or there's an extra chair on this side and we can talk *he alo a he alo,* face to face. It's up to you."

The man stepped around the screen, his countenance twisted in a private agony. He appeared to be in his early fifties with a full head of grey hair, pale eyes, and the kind of splotched, sun-damaged skin Caucasians developed in the Islands.

"I don't know why I'm here, Father."

"God does."

"I'm so full of hatred, Father, it's like I'm choking on my own guts. It's gonna kill me and I can't let that happen. I have responsibilities. I gotta keep going. I can't rest until..." He stopped, unable to continue.

Father Lion gestured toward the chair.

The man threw himself at it, doubled over, his face smothered in his hands.

The priest waited, leaning attentively toward the afflicted man, offering no comfort but his presence, praying silently.

Horrible wrenching sobs erupted, and still Father Lion waited and prayed.

"My daughter's old boyfriend is getting married." The statement had jagged edges. "He had the nerve to invite us to the wedding. We're Megan's parents for god's sake. She should be the one walking down the aisle with him. How does he expect us to feel? What are we supposed to do? Buy the happy couple a toaster?"

Judging by the degree of the man's distress, Father Lion suspected a much larger problem than a jilted daughter.

Anger spewed from the man in waves. "Greg never loved Megan. If he did, how could he just walk away. He's as bad as the others. Oh God, oh God, they killed my baby girl. They raped and murdered my Megan and threw her away like garbage."

There they were, the words Father Lion had been preparing himself to hear. He became aware of the Holy Spirit, light as a feather, hovering, fanning the room with white wings.

"I am so sorry," the priest said. "Your heart must be broken."

"Broken? Ha! I'd like to smash it myself. My heart is so full of hatred it's consuming me. It's been three years since Megan died and nothing's better. In fact, everything is worse."

13

"There is no time limit on grief."

"I'll never get over it. The police still don't know who did it. Or if they do, they're not saying. They're bumbling the case or covering up. A pack of local incompetents. See how my hatred expands. Now it's the cops, too. And the locals. God help me."

"Would you like a glass of water?"

"Only if it's big enough to drown myself in."

Lion said gently. "Begin at the beginning. Tell me what you know. I remind you that I have taken a sacred vow to maintain your privacy. Nothing from the confessional is ever repeated to anyone. I'm here to help you."

The man straightened up in his chair, took a deep breath and began, "I'm Charley Roy." He proceeded to tell how his daughter had been brutally raped and left to die along a country road.

Father Lion said, "I wish I had words to comfort you, but I don't."

"I knew that ahead of time. I didn't come for comfort. There is none. I just don't know what to do with my hatred. I even hate the hate. It eats at me. I let it keep me company in the night. It owns me. I reek of it and I'm sick to death of it. I don't know how to live anymore. Will I ever be myself again, Father?"

"No."

"Thank you for your honesty."

"You have the heart of a father. It beats for your children. You are the protector of the family, their shield. You feel you have failed as a father. You are overwhelmed by guilt, and the person you hate most is yourself."

Tears streamed down Charley Roy's face.

"My dear brother, you would have given your life for your daughter. You know this. God knows this. Let our father in Heaven, who saw his own child, hang on a cross with a crown of thorns upon his bloodied brow, let this divine father-heart grieve with you."

Lion placed his long, bony hand on Charley Roy's head and felt tension drain from the man as his body surrendered to the priest's touch. He urged him, "Put your heavy burden of guilt and hate in a sack and hand it to Jesus. Be a free man."

"How?" He cried.

"You must forgive Megan's killers."

"I can't. I won't."

"Forgiveness is demanded of you by Jesus. It's not an option. You think that by forgiving your daughter's killers, it somehow makes what they did to her okay? You're afraid that by forgiving them, the terrible deed will come to mean less and less, that maybe someday you'll be able to bear it, and that will be the ultimate betrayal of Megan."

"Yes, yes, yes. All of that."

"I know it is not humanly possible to forgive such a thing." Lion waited, knowing Charley Roy's next statement would come as a whisper.

"Help me." The words were barely audible.

"I will share the road to freedom with you. First, you must make the intellectual decision to forgive. Your emotions won't be there, but you can decide to do it, in your mind, while your heart and guts rebel. 'Don't give evil any ground to stand on. Evil done to you that remains festering in your heart is evil strengthened exponentially." Lion continued, "Deciding to forgive is only step one. There is more demanded of you.

"Step two: Once you have made the decision to forgive you must begin to conform all your thoughts and words and actions to your decision. When you think of Megan's killers, pray they are brought to justice so they have a chance at salvation. Pray for their families. Remember when our gentle Jesus hung on the cross, he forgave the men who tortured and killed him."

Charley snapped, "He was God."

"Which brings us to step three: Once you have made the intellectual decision to forgive, and you begin to conform your thoughts, words and actions to that decision, God steps in and, one day, as a gift, he gives you what you cannot attain on your own: the gift of a forgiving heart, and the peace that comes with it."

Charley exhaled. "How long will it take, Father, before I find any peace?"

"I don't know. We're free for as long as we are vigilant."

Charley Roy leaned against the back of his chair as if he had just set down a piece of heavy furniture. "Thank you again for your honesty."

Father Lion heard Charley Roy's footsteps as he left the church, faster, surer than when he entered. He knew the profound relief and startling rush of happiness of the recently confessed man. It wouldn't last in this case. The man had much struggling ahead of him. But perhaps he would remember how hopeful he felt walking out into the night.

# Chapter 4

THE CALL

"You da Black Confessor?" The man's voice on the phone had a typical Island lilt to it.

The call came in the middle of the afternoon, just as Father Lion was settling down with a tall glass of cold water in the guest house at Holy Rosary Church. "I understand that's what I'm called."

""Da priest what come from Africa?"

"Yes. How may I help you?"

"You going Saint Joseph Hilo?"

"Yes."

"When you be dere?"

"I'll be there in ten days and I'll stay nine days."

"Tanks, Faddah. I come see you dere."

"Whom shall I expect?"

"What?"

"What's your name so I may look for you?"

"Nevah mine da name. I fine you." The man hung up.

A chill passed over the priest as if a swiftly moving cloud had briefly eclipsed the sun. He could not be sure, but he thought he heard the faint scratchy laughter of the Adversary, the seducer who once offered him the fatal comfort of despair, the patient one who waited, watching for the faltering step, the sprouting seeds of ego, or even just a little complacency, to take up residence in the soul. It was only for an instant. It might have been the breezes in the bamboo or, Father Lion smiled, breezes in the brain. He crossed himself just the same. The chill passed, but perhaps the Adversary lingered in the form of discontent, for Father Lion complained, "You know, Lord, I find the confessional a burden. You are aware of my yearning for a monastery, yes, even a hermitage. A cave. Please whisper to Bishop Carroll about me and mention a monastery with the Angelus bell calling at noon, simple labor, the chanted psalms, the night prayer, and a small cell with a narrow bed for me." The vow of obedience weighed heavily on Father Lion.

Seventeen people came to the evening service. Lion counted them. He supposed it was a good turnout for a small rural church with elderly demographics. The Adversary has made such fine use of technology, employing television and computers to introduce spirits and visions into cozy homes that were best left outdoors. Murder, sadism, rape, forensic dissections, maggots, flies, blood. These are the last visions of the day, carried from television into sleep, corroding the soul.

But a Luddite sermon was not what these people came to church to hear. They were so accustomed to their big-screen calamities that Father Lion decided to speak about modern slavery, a subject which might pique their desensitized sensibilities.

He began: "In 1863 President Abraham Lincoln issued the *Emancipation Proclamation*, freeing the slaves. Slavery was so profitable at the time, that to preserve the demonic business, those slave states permitting the sale of human beings, men, women and children, those slave states tore their own country, the young America, in two and almost ended the greatest experiment in self-government the world has known." He left the pulpit and paced across the altar. "Well, I am sorry to tell poor Mr. Lincoln that slavery has not ended, and it is still profitable. It is estimated that there are between thirty and forty million slaves in the world today. Does that shock you? Why have you not heard this before? Because, my dear people, these millions of your fellow human beings have no voice. Eighty percent are women and children, most of them sold into sexual slavery. According to the United States State Department and the Central Intelligence Agency, approximately fifty thousand women and children are trafficked annually into the United States for sexual exploitation and as slaves in the garment and agriculture industries. In the U.S. alone, human trafficking yields nine billion tax free dollars a year. If they sold stock in slaver enterprises, it would be a hot offering. Tell me, my good people, should a human being be sold as a commodity, like wheat or soybeans? Or is a human a long-term investment? Is a woman blue-chip stock? Or is she like investment property to be dolled up and flipped for profit?"

Father Lion then brought his message closer to home: "The rugs you walk upon, the chocolate bars you eat, the diamonds you wear on your fingers to signify love may very well be the products of slave labor performed by children just like your children and grandchildren. But these children live in unspeakable conditions. I was that slave child." He paused to lend gravity to his words. "And now I am a priest among you, by the grace of God. It is a miracle. Do we believe in miracles today? Yes, my brothers and sisters, we do." If the parishioners thought they were in for a happy ending, they were mistaken. Father Lion pressed on.

"We have read sensational headlines about an abducted eleven-year-old girl, rescued after eighteen years. The newspapers yipped and bayed about how she was forced to be a sex slave. We are all properly horrified, but we console ourselves that these terrible crimes are rare. My dear people, I regret to report that the crime is repeated every single day. Yes, slavers lurk outside California high schools, and like beasts of prey they select the weakest in the crowd, the immigrant girl whose parents are illegally in the country. They threaten to harm her family, report them to the government. The average age for such a child to enter prostitution is twelve or thirteen. If they are picked up by the police, they are treated as criminals, not victims, and the slaver moves on to another school, another child. Where is our outrage? American outrage is for the price of gasoline."

He caught himself shouting, pounding the pulpit. He smoothed his hand across the pulpit's surface. Perspiration beaded his furrowed brow. He breathed deeply to control himself.

All the things about forgiveness and serenity that he'd preached to Charley Roy, he found difficult to follow himself. He thought he had forgiven his slave master, but the fury lurked beneath the surface. His two kidnapped brothers were still missing. He did not know what else he might be called upon to forgive. He looked out upon the startled faces of his small congregation and saw they had great compassion for him.

In the end, these good people would put money in the collection basket to ransom slaves. Afterwards, they might talk about slavery to their neighbors or family, while recounting facts to startle them. But most will just forget those facts and think of something else.

Wearily, Father Lion returned to his room to discover that he had not locked the door. His first thought was his dog. As he pushed on the door, a lovely fragrance greeted him. He heard the dog's tail swishing in the dark just before a muddy nose inserted itself into his hand. He flicked on the light and Michael leaped to greet him. "What have you done, little rascal? Hmm? What have we here?"

The room was filled with flowers, fragrant gardenias, showy heliconia, wild yellow ginger, a bowl of pink plumeria, and strewn on the floor a lovely orchid on which Michael had been munching.

"Ah, but you missed the food. Or maybe you saved it for me. Of course, that's it. You are an angelic animal." Crowded on the small table against the far wall were a sushi platter wrapped in plastic, a bowl of fresh fruit, brownies, a bag of mochi crunch, cookies and a small loaf of what smelled like banana bread. Beside the bread rested a cellophane bag of dog treats neatly tied with a bow from which dangled a plush toy bone.

The priest opened a white envelope propped against the fruit bowl and read, "We love you dear Father Lion. Aloha from your friends at Holy Rosary Church."

He felt remorse for scolding these good people when they were truly living as God intended, in beauty and peace. They labored, gardened and baked brownies. They tended their small part of the planet and cared for each other.

He thought of the man who had telephoned, the one with the lilting voice and mysterious burden, and sat down inexplicably disturbed. *Lord, how can I meet the needs of every human being who comes to me? It is too much to contemplate. With the best of intentions, we humans fail each other time and time again. It is not enough to be good. I must do as much good as I can. With your help, Lord, I will carry on and do my best. But you must know how weak and unreliable I am. I beg you, please have the bishop order me to a monastery to fast and pray on my knees, besieging the heavens twenty-four-seven. Or whisper in His Excellency's ear that maybe I belong back in Africa. Instead, Lord, you have sent me here to a too comfortable calling. People bring me mochi crunch. My head rests on a clean pillow. Please reconsider...*

Michael needed a walk so the two set off briskly into the night. The love songs of the coqui frogs soothed Father Lion. The thick vegetation loomed close to the road whispering to him of Africa. The only thing missing in Hawaii was danger. He thought again of the man who telephoned. Danger, that is what he had sensed in the call, the short breaths, the abrupt departure, the withholding of the name. It was like a distant storm advancing on him. His old wariness surfaced. For the first time in ages, he had the feeling of being hunted.

When he returned to his room, he allowed himself two brownies and acknowledged that sometimes homemade baked goods were as fortifying as prayer. Why is that? Because of the heavenly taste? Because of the love.

# Chapter 5
ABEED

Father Lion looked out upon the expectant faces crowding Saint Joseph's Church in Hilo. For most of them, life was not easy but neither was it dire. Americans, even these most remote Oceanic Americans, have no idea what it is like to have nothing, absolutely nothing. They construct acres of storage facilities to hold what their huge houses cannot. Even the poorest homeless people own shoes and require purloined shopping carts to haul about their pitiful possessions.

For the most part, the people attending Saint Joseph's did not have much money, and their opportunities on an agricultural island in the middle of the sea, were limited. Yet most of them were rich in what they fondly called "aloha," love for one another and the place in which they lived. This night, they sought riches that could not be heaped in a shopping cart or stowed in a storage facility. They wanted an encounter with God followed by refreshments. They came to hear a slave's story and meet the Black Confessor. They desired to be better people, more considerate of neighbor, gentler with the very young and very old, more heedful of the commandments.

As one who has known and experienced the depths of human depravity, and personally met the cunning Author of Evil, the basic goodness of the average person continually astounded and cheered Father Lion.

If his reputation drew people closer to God tonight, he welcomed it.

All the glory was God's. His primary job was to listen to their sorrows and sins until his ears hurt, his heart ached, and his soul weighed a hundred thousand pounds.

When it was helpful, when he was up to it, he shared his own story, sometimes employing embarrassing theatrics. The bigger the crowd, the more need for drama. Perhaps that's why Jesus, while preaching to the multitude on a hillside in Galilee, turned five loaves of bread and two fishes into food for thousands before their very eyes. Jesus was a showman, and held his audience in the palm of his hand. They listened and remembered when he told them that the poor in spirit will inherit the kingdom of Heaven; the meek possess the land; mourners find comfort; seekers of justice have their fill. The merciful shall obtain mercy; the clean of heart will see God; the peacemakers will be called children of God; those who suffer persecution for justice's sake, will attain Heaven.

Father Lion became aware of people shifting in their pews, coughs, throat-clearings. At times he was terrified, fearing he had nothing to teach these good people. After listening to his tale, they would be more generous than wise in their offerings, because it was all going to the Catholic missions in Africa. He knew that after he finished talking and the donation baskets collected, he would enter the anonymity of the confessional. One by one, people would file in, kneel in the dark, make the sign of the cross, and empty themselves of their sins, whispering them away.

In the sacrament, he would first assure the penitents of God's care and forgiveness, then send them back into the world to forgive one another.

Standing at Saint Joseph's lectern with the eyes of the waiting people upon him, the unworthy messenger, Father Lion prayed. He breathed deeply. It was never easy, no matter how many times he told his personal tale.

In the uneasy quiet he began, "I come from Sudan, Africa, from the tribe of Dinka. I was baptized as an infant into the Catholic faith. The church was a very long walk." He smiled. "In those days I was not such a walker."

The congregation smiled back. They knew he walked everywhere. He had even been written up in the *Hawai'i Catholic Herald* with a photograph of him and Michael, his dog. He continued: "In our humble home of thatch and clay, we had one book, the Bible. I didn't know my mother couldn't read because she would open the book and turn the pages as she told us from memory the stories of Noah and the flood, Daniel and the lion.

"I had two younger brothers and a little sister. Our parents loved us very much. When I was seven years old, my father was murdered, and I was kidnaped and sold into slavery. The slave raiders took me and dozens of other captured boys and girls north of our home. They put us in a low, squat building behind the souk and sold us. I have since learned that the price of a black child in the Sudan slave trade today is between fifteen and forty dollars. I stood on a block of wood, naked, trying not to cry, while a man inspected my teeth and my genitals before purchasing me. My buyer took me farther north, farther away from my family. He said I had a new name, '*Abeed*,' which, in Arabic, means 'filth.'"

The congregation shifted uneasily. They needed some levity. He smiled. "I was a child with a sense of justice, and I made up a secret, very unkind name for my new master, *Ali El Mum Nhom*, which translates as Ali The Insane." The people smiled, a few laughed nervously. Father Lion continued, "At his cattle compound, Ali El Mum Nhom shoved me off the horse and herded me to a goat shed. Now many of you, being country people like me, know how pungent goats can be. My new home, if I can call it that, was quite aromatic.

"Ali El Mum Nhom bellowed, and an old, very dark, very wrinkled man emerged from the stinking shadows. On his forehead, I recognized the distinctive Dinka scarification. Scarring a boy's face is both a rite of passage to manhood and a sort of ID card, signifying his clan. This old man was not of my clan, but of my people. He hobbled in a most hideous fashion and groveled piteously while my new master shouted and cracked his rhino-hide whip. The old man scurried to a gate leading to the master's compound, opened it, and Ali El Mum Nhom rode through, leaving me with the old man, whom he called Hinzir, Pig.

"To me, he was Michael the Archangel in clever disguise. He told me he would speak to me in our Dinka language only this once and that I must never speak it again or Ali El Mum Nhom would beat us. He told me I must learn Arabic. He asked me my true name. When I told him Kor Majok, he smiled, 'Kor is lion. Never forget your name. Say your name to yourself every day or you will forget it as I have forgotten mine. Let them call you Abeed. Answer to Abeed. But your name is Kor Majok. Do whatever they tell you, whatever it is, no matter how difficult or degrading, so you may live.' He asked if I was Christian and when I said I was, Hinzir warned, 'He will want you to worship his god. Do it. Talk to Jesus in your heart. Talk to his god with your lips. Jesus is sweet. He will understand. If you refuse to convert to Islam, as I foolishly did, our evil master will cut your tendons in your feet, as he cut mine, and you will be like me.'"

Father Lion's voice rose oratorically, "I confess to you, my brothers and sisters, to all the angels and saints, that I denied my God. When Ali El Mum Nhom produced a picture of Jesus Christ, a wrinkled dirty picture of Our Lord, threw it on the ground, and ordered me to step on it, I did. I am like Peter denying our Lord. I was like the crowds in the streets of Jerusalem spitting on and reviling our dear Savior as he carried his cross toward Golgotha. For me, for you."

Lion stopped, drained by his memories, and asked the congregation to pray for him. "We will say ten Hail Marys while meditating on the resurrection of Jesus."

The power of all the prayers sweetening the air around him filled Father Lion with renewed strength. Back and forth he paced as he spoke, "Ali El Mum Nhom was a family man. He had two wives and eleven children, four sons and seven daughters. He gave them each a stick. They ran happily toward me and they beat me and kicked me and called me by my new name, Filth."

Father Lion paused, letting the enormity of the violence and humiliation fill the church. "When they finished, I lay in the dirt, unable to move, crying for my mother. At dusk, Hinzir returned from herding the cattle. He led me to his own bed, a pile of straw with rags, and washed my wounds with his ration of water while speaking once more in forbidden Dinka. He told me, 'This is your life now. It will not always be your life. You will escape. When you are older, faster, and smarter, you will escape and go home. You must stay alive until that day comes, and it surely will come.'

"Hinzir became like a father to me. We worked the cattle together. I already knew much about these animals from my own father. Hinzir showed me all the grazing places in the wadi and where the water was. He taught me to count in Arabic. We counted all day long, making sure that as we moved, we did not lose a single animal, for we would be severely beaten if we did. The inevitable evening came when we made a mistake in counting. A cow was missing. Ali El Mum Nhom flew into a fury. He summoned his children and dragged me to the middle of the compound where there was a tree stump. He sent his eldest son for a saw. 'Which finger do you want me to cut off? Tell me, or I'll cut them all off, one by one.' I was terrified, as you can imagine. I could not speak. 'Is it to be all of them, then?' He thrust my little hand on to the block while his eldest son held me down.

"'The smallest finger, Master, the littlest one,' I cried out. The children laughed and clapped while he sawed off my pinky finger." Father Lion held up his right hand. He heard the collective gasp. He was never comfortable with such theatrics but if it meant more funds in the collection basket for Africa, he would do it.

He continued, "Then, because it was such a small finger, he sawed off the pinky of my other hand also." Father Lion held up his left hand. "Hinzir bandaged my fingers with rags from his bed. That was the last time I saw him. When I woke up, he was gone. Perhaps they killed him. I didn't dare ask.

"Now I was truly alone. Ali El Mum Nhom's second son became my supervisor on the daily cattle rounds. He was a cruel young man and berated me and beat me without provocation. I wanted to die, but more than that, I wanted to see the beautiful face of my mother once more." Father Lion hung his head in sorrow, omitting, as he always did, the second's son's sexual abuse. As with most victims, it was he who bore the shame.

"After approximately a year, the second son tired of his sport, and I was left alone to tend the cattle. I spoke to the animals in the Dinka tongue so I would not lose the voice of my soul.

"It was in my loneliness and littleness that I met my true father, your true father, a terrifying and compassionate father, the source of all life, the source of all love. I met the maker of the wind, the scorching sun and the parched desert. I met the maker of cool fresh water and the great rivers, the maker of my mother and father. I was as dense as a river stone in matters of the spirit, but since my father had told me God was always with me, I began to talk to God. 'Sir God, this is your little son, Lion Majok, and I need your help.' Before I knew him, before I comprehended his magnificence, God pitied and protected me. I prayed perhaps a hundred times a day, and a hundred times at night in the fetid squalor of my goat shed. I fell asleep with the name of Jesus on my lips.

"I became a model slave, trusted by my master. I bowed toward Mecca. By the time I was thirteen, Ali El Mum Nhom trusted me to stay overnight with the cattle during the dry season. He knew I had found grazing and water far enough away from the compound that driving the animals home in the same day was impossible. At first, he sent one of his sons on horseback to check on me and warn me that if I tried to escape, they would cut off one leg. I began to fast and drink little water, training myself to do without.

"Always, I talked to God. I knew he heard me because he sent me signs: a red bird flying overhead while I prayed; an aura around the sun or the moon; two leaves fallen in the shape of a cross at my feet. One night when I was sixteen, I was out with the cattle and fell asleep beside a tree under a dazzling starry sky. In my dream, a very ugly man with a head like a lion walked upon the waters of the Nile. From that horrible face, contorted and festering with sores, the man's eyes shone with love, and he said to me, 'Lion Majok, prepare yourself to return to your own people. It will be soon. Do not be afraid.'

"So, I began to run. I ran circles around the cows as they grazed. I ran all day. I lifted stones for weights. I became my own twenty-four hour fitness club.

"In a second dream that came to me back in the goat shed, the ugly

29

lion-faced man came to me again, walking on the Nile. He was dressed in rags, like mine, but his eyes were shining with inner light, the way a flower glows before you pick it. I didn't know it then, but I now know that man in my dreams was our own Father Damien of Molokai, and he said to me, 'It is time, Lion of the Dinka. Behold, your boat awaits you.'

"I almost laughed. A boat? I was far from the river. But I knew my father in Heaven sent this holy and fearsome saint to help me find my way home. At dawn I set out as usual with the cattle. After I had walked for three hours, I abandoned them and fled. Not only could I run without tiring, I felt as if I had eagle's wings lifting me. My years working with the cattle served me well; I knew how to find water. I feared nothing, for God was directing my path. After many days, I reached a small town along the great River Nile and saw a dilapidated ferry moored at the quay. It was my boat, the one foretold by my beautiful, ugly friend. It was my Princess Line Cruise Ship, my Love Boat."

Father Lion looked out upon the congregation expectantly. They didn't laugh, but they smiled. "How was I to present myself to the captain? I was dirty, ragged and had no money. While I was hiding in the shadows of an alley, a peddler with a donkey came by. He greeted me, *'Salam,'* and I returned the greeting, afraid for the first time since I left Ali El Mum Nhom. I was so close to my goal, I almost fainted with fear and hunger. The peddler offered me milk and honey from a jug, and a well-worn but clean garment. When I protested that I had no money to pay him, the man said, 'Allah cares for us through one another. Take the gift and go in peace to do the same.'

"I found a private place beside the river, buried my rags, bathed and dressed. I then presented myself to the captain of the ferry and begged passage. He spoke to me sharply and shooed me away, but I had not gone far when he bellowed for me to come back. A man had arrived with several camels to unload, and I was promptly put to work. Rather than pay me, the captain offered me a corner of the deck, back by the noisy, smelly engine.

"I was on my way home at last. How my heart rejoiced in the flow of the Nile, the chugging and coughing of the engine carrying me south. When the ferry docked in the evening, I feared going ashore, afraid I would not be allowed back aboard, afraid Ali El Mum Nhom or his sons would somehow find me and chop off my leg. I was very hungry and survived on the kindness of other passengers. I began to wonder if I would even know my mother's face. Would she know me? It never occurred to me that she would not be there.

"It turned out that our village had been burned years ago, the men killed, the women and children captured and taken away. I approached a Dinka man watering his cattle. 'My name is Lion Majok. Do you know my family'?"

"I knew the Majok clan very well. Most are in their graves. But some escaped and fled to the Imatongs." He pointed to the mountains.

"My mother's name is Tereze."

"Ah, Christian. Then she may be with the Christian holy man hiding in the hills." The man gave me a bowl of milk and wild honey and sent me on my way with two bananas.

"I wandered for days in the mountains, almost despairing. I scolded God. How could he bring me this far only to be lost? I fell to my knees, pleading, 'Help me.' And that is how the militia found me. Crying. Needless to say, they were not impressed with me. They didn't even bind me, as they led me to their camp.

"Miraculously, I saw my mother right away. I knew her instantly. She was carrying an armload of twigs. She looked at me, but it took her a moment to recognize me. After all, she had not seen me since I was seven. I towered over her. 'Ma.' She hesitated, then dropped her kindling and ran to me, praising God for me, the boy who had been called 'Filth' and was now Lion again."

It was time to wrap up his talk. "My mother lived in a large encampment of Dinka refugees from destroyed villages and sundered families. Bishop Desmond Binda, not of our tribe, but one with us, lived half of his time in our camp, and half in his residence in Khartoum. He had a laptop computer and sent out e-mails about slavery to reporters and television stations around the world. The government of Sudan still keeps claiming there is no slavery.

"My mother still doesn't know what became of my two younger brothers, Kintu and Mayom. They were both kidnaped. Only my little sister, Eulalia, then ten, is still with her.

"Bishop Binda had set up a school in the camp, so at age sixteen, I began my formal education. Tucked in a package of clothing from an American charity was a book, *Holy Man*, by Gavan Daws. It was the story of Father Damien, servant to the lepers of Molokai. As soon as I saw the portrait of the blessed priest on the cover, his face ravaged by leprosy, I knew he was the ugly man who had come to me in my dreams. Gradually, and I admit a bit reluctantly, I came to understand that God was calling me to continue following Damien, right into the priesthood.

"However, pursuing higher education in Sudan would be too dangerous for me, an escaped slave. And I had no funds to go abroad.

"On a trip to Rome, Bishop Binda learned from our Bishop Carroll of Honolulu that his diocese needed priests and would finance seminary education for a few young men willing to serve in Hawaii. I was overwhelmed to think I might follow in the actual footsteps of our beloved Damien."

Father Lion paused, drained once more, but needed to finish his story. He leaned on the lectern. "Indeed, my first parish after ordination was Saint Sophia on Molokai. I began my priesthood there, in the shadow of Damien, but Bishop Carroll had other plans for me. So I stand before you, a former slave, not from the past but from the shameful trade that still flourishes today, even as we speak.

"It costs about twenty dollars to ransom a child out of slavery. Many people oppose such purchases, saying it encourages the slavers to kidnap more children and sell them off to Christians for a fast dollar. I say that even if thirty percent of the current trade is a result of this practice of ransom, then seventy percent represents children who have lived in conditions of unspeakable cruelty for many years. I have seen their joyful faces when they are set free from bondage. I ask you to please help Bishop Binda in his efforts. Please pray for the slaves and pray for those who enslave women and children, for it is an evil thing they do and God is watching them. They are breaking God's heart. Thank you and God bless you."

Exhausted, Father Lion sat down and hung his head while the collection baskets were passed. He reflected that when bad things happen to adults, they walk through bad the times and come out the other side, but when bad things happen to a child, those things become a part of who he is. Abeed. Filth.

He looked to the crucifix. *I am Lion, the beloved son of the King of Heaven and Earth.*

But little Abeed still lived among the roots and weeds of his being.

Lion's Way

# Chapter 6
## THE GOOD FATHER

The next morning as Father Lion prepared to set out from Hilo for Saint Theresa's in Mountainview, the phone rang. He glanced at his watch.

"Hello, Faddah. It's me what call you at Holy Rosary. From my iPhone. I wait for you in church, in a confession boot."

The soft pidgin, the tension between the words...Lion had almost forgotten the mysterious man who had promised to call again. He experienced a rare moment of annoyance at this detour on the pathway of his day. He looked at the crucifix on the wall and smiled ruefully. Sometimes one lays down one's life for others, not in a hail of bullets, but ten minutes at a time, listening to their woes. "I'll be there right away, my brother."

"Tanks, eh. You had your breakfast, Faddah? If you no eat, I wait."

Lion heard the man's nervousness, his desperate hope for reprieve. *"Mahalo,* but I've eaten, praise God. I'll be right there."

He hung up the phone and turned to his dog, "Sorry, Michael, it's another confession. Be a good dog while I try to be a good servant."

Lion unpacked his priestly stole, the one his mother had made for his ordination, embroidered with a sleek lion, bold African flora, and a bright gold cross.

Michael gazed at him with soulful brown eyes. He knew that stole meant a long delay.

"If dogs pray, please pray for me, the man who feeds you."

On the short walk from the rectory to the church, Father Lion prayed for the penitent he was about to meet. He asked that the Holy Spirit guide the man to a good confession, and that he, acting as God's humble priest, could bring the man God's love and forgiveness without the slightest hint of impatience.

He entered the confessional, kissed the cross on his stole and placed it about his shoulders.

From the dark penitent's chamber, the man cleared his throat. He was wearing shorts for Lion heard one knee peel away from the vinyl kneeler as he shifted his weight. Keys rattled. Lion slid open the little screened window and waited. The man shifted on his knees again. A rubber slipper hit the floor.

"Bless me, Faddah, for I have sinned. I am one screw-up guy, but today I no talk 'bout me. I wanna talk bout what anudda guy do."

Father Lion was tempted to remind the man of the scripture admonishing him to remove the plank from his own eye before noting the splinter in the eye of another. He said, "Perhaps it is that other person who should be seeking reconciliation."

"Two."

"Two?"

"Two a dem. Maybe tree what involved. This is official confession now, right? You no can tell what I say no maddah what?"

"The seal of the confessional is sacred unto death."

"Dey waterboard you, still no can?"

"Cannot."

The man took a deep breath and audibly exhaled. "Okay, 'kay. I got tree sons, two a dem rotten. So bad I wan kill em. Drugs, drink alla time. Da maddah *ma-ke* five years. I do my best on my own, Faddah. I no take sass. They sass me, I geeve-'em dirty lickins, but dey rotten buggahs and dey try corrupt da baby. Good ting my wife wit da Lord, so she no see em now. She spoil our boys, treat em like little kings. Dis would kill her more dan da stroke." The man strained to maintain composure, fencing his words with small grunts of dissatisfaction.

Father Lion asked, "How can I help you?"

"I no know." Anguish broke through. Any moment the torrent would gush. "Dey killed someone, Faddah. I heard em wit' my own ears. Da two beeg ones treten da little guy. 'Faddah, dey killed dat *haole wahine,* Megan Roy, da one on da TV couple years back."

Lion gasped as if all the air had been sucked out of the confessional.

"'You dere, Faddah?"

"Yes, yes. I know that crime well. It was all over the newspapers."

"Da two beeg ones rape and kill her, da small guy no do it, but he in a car wit' 'em. Oh Faddah, why dey li dat? Why dey do someting so bad? My own keeds. How dey be so rotten to da core? We raise 'em up right. Why dey do dat? Why I still love 'em? Answer me dat, Faddah. Why I still love 'em?"

"You have a father's love for them, the same love our father in Heaven bears for his wayward children. That is a good and holy thing. Nothing we do can ever separate us from the father's love. God himself has set the example for you."

"What I do now, Faddah? Turn in my own keeds?"

"You have to ask yourself what the best way is to help your sons."

"I raise em right, Faddah. Discipline em, make 'em go church."

"And now you must discern what is right for them at this time in their lives. How long have you known about this?"

"From da begeening almos'."

"And you have kept their terrible secret. Has that helped them? Are they better men now because you protected them?"

The "No," eased out very quietly.

"And your youngest son what's his name?"

"Enoch, Faddah. You no tell."

"How old is Enoch?"

"Fifrteen, Faddah. Twelve when it happen. He was dere, but he no do notting."

"That's a big burden for a child to carry by himself. How is he doing?"

"I no know. He da quiet one. Nevah say notting."

"Do you want to save your sons?"

*"Ae.* Yes."

"Then you know what you have to do."

"What—I lose all my keeds?"

"Your kids are already lost." From his experience in the confessional, Lion recognized this as the moment to be direct, even to shock. "My dear brother, the way things are, your poor sons are damned."

The man moaned as if flames from Hell had just shot up and scorched him where he knelt.

"Your sons need help. They will never have the opportunity for salvation or to become good men while they have such poison inside them."

"I turn 'em in, dey go prison for life."

"Two of them will, yes. But perhaps you can save Enoch."

"I know dey deserve it, but how a man do dat to his own keeds? I wait and wait for da police to discover 'em, but no can. Dey too clever, my boys."

Father Lion noted the pitiful trace of pride. "Many men turn to our Lord while they're in prison and save their immortal souls."

"Oh, da shame. How I gonna live wi dat?"

"How are you living now? How is your son Enoch living?"

"Not so good. Smart boy but no more school."

"God has a perfect plan for Enoch's life, but Enoch can't find it right now. And God loves your two older sons and wants them to live with him in Heaven someday. If they were the only men on Earth, Jesus would have died just to save them."

"Dat's it, Faddah. God no make junk."

"If Jesus died to save them, what will you do to save them?"

"Faddah, I gotta go now. Tanks, eh." The man rose abruptly, rattled his keys. "You no look see who I am. You stay dere till you hear da church door close—I slam 'em, kay?"

"I will stay here and pray for you and your sons and for Charley and Ellie—the mother and father of Megan Roy."

"You lucky you have no sons, Faddah." The man left, his rubber slippers slapping the floor in retreat. He slammed the church door.

Father Lion hung his head. He had failed. He should not have mentioned damnation. People do not take kindly to Hell these days. And he had prodded the man to do something so painful that he ran off without blessing or comfort.

Lion prayed: *Well, Lord, see how I let you down again. In the clinches, I am not your man. I would be much better in a Trappist monastery with a vow of silence. You will have to work on that poor man now.*

There were times, and this was one of them, when Lion regarded his gift for the sacrament of confession and reconciliation as an affliction. In an ironic sense, the diocese of Honolulu had purchased him and he had become a slave for Christ.

Lion's Way

# Chapter 7

A SUNDAY STROLLL IN HELL

On Sunday morning, the little church in Mountainview rocked on its timbers as a choir, more enthusiastic than talented, twanged its guitars and happily bellowed about majesty and salvation. Their leader's loud nasal voice hit every note with painful accuracy.

Father Lion gathered them all into his heart, embracing their hopes and sorrows as he bent over the bread and whispered the sacred words, "This is my body which is given up for you." He raised the bread high and saw in the thin translucent wafer the face of Christ bearing the crown of thorns. It was not distinct, but it was there when you sought it.

After mass, Lion decided to borrow the parish car and pay a visit to Hawaii Volcanoes National Park. He had never seen Kilauea's red-hot lava.

He parked where the road ended in hardened lava. The awesome volcanic devastation sprawled as far as his eye could see. Ahead, towering clouds of steam marked the place where Kilauea bled seething magma into the ocean.

Near the park ranger's trailer, a bouquet of anthuriums and ti had been left for Pele. People still offered tribute to the goddess of fire on this island of five volcanoes: Mauna Loa, massive enough to contain the entire Sierra Nevada range; green Kohala; slumbering Hualalai; fiery Kilauea, erupting continuously since 1983, and snow-crowned Mauna

Kea, the world's tallest mountain, if measured from its base on the ocean floor.

He had been warned that if he met a woman with a white dog as he walked about the Big Island, he was to be polite for it might be Pele. He liked it that the goddess traveled with a dog. He wondered how Michael would react to a spirit dog, should they meet.

Drivers traversing the lava desert of the island routinely reported picking up a beautiful female hitchhiker and her dog, then having the woman and dog inexplicably vanish from the car while traveling at fifty miles an hour. Before every major eruption, people see Pele and are warned of the coming event. Homeowners driven away by advancing lava flows graciously acknowledge, "This land is Pele's. She wants my house, she takes it." Pele also took an entire subdivision, great swaths of forest, the village of Kalapana, the famous Kaimu Black Sand Beach, a visitor center in the park, Wahaula Heiau, an ancient temple and a Protestant church. She would have gotten the Catholic church, too, but the parishioners jacked up their historic little church and moved it out of Pele's fiery path.

Lion leaned now on his walking stick. The lava terrain was treacherous, and it was four miles from where the road ended to Pele's scalding chamber. This newer hardened lava was nasty, fragile stuff, shattering beneath his feet.

He paused to survey his path toward the towering clouds of steam. "Are you okay, Michael?" The dog stepped nimbly while Lion carefully picked his way along the broken surface. The priest's eyes burned from unseen particles in the air as he walked among the tourists in candy-colored clothes scampering along to catch a glimpse of Hell.

He planned to stay until after sunset when the eruption appears most spectacular. He carried water, a flashlight, dried apricots for himself and beef jerky for Michael. As he approached the eruption site, its heat assaulted him. A few people stood transfixed as swollen orange toes of lava oozed slowly toward them. Father Lion stopped, praised God silently for the majesty and power of his mighty hand, then put Michael on his leash.

Near the major active flow site, park rangers had set out orange traffic cones to mark a safe path to a small cove of gritty black sand at the shore. A photographer had set up a tripod trained on the sea cliffs.

Awestruck, Father Lion sat down on a basalt shelf to watch flaming cascades tumble over black rocks into the turquoise ocean, sizzling, crackling, boiling the water, creating a tempest of steam. Flames were visible even beneath the waves. Rocks yawned open. The Earth's blood spewed from the maw of the planet, spilling, mounding and birthing new land. He had secured a grandstand seat at the act of creation.

The sun sank low toward the horizon. In the brief tropical twilight, when the sky and sea turned magenta and gold, more lava became visible. High in the mountains, flaming rivers snaked and oozed through the forest blackening the land, torching trees in their journey to the sea. It was humbling to witness.

The photographer turned briefly in Lion's direction, then ignored him, intent on the fussiness of his vocation.

Lion took out his cell phone and called Lilinoe. "Hey, Little Sister. You'll never guess where I am." Of all the Kamana family, his *hanai* or adopted family, Lilinoe was his favorite.

"I'm always telling you to go to Hell. Are you there yet?" she teased.

"I am. That's why I called. I'm at Kilauea Volcano and the hot lava is flowing. It's awesome."

"I went there on my sixth-grade class trip. Lion, I can't talk now, okay?"

He heard an unexpected exasperation in her voice. The phone connection crackled and went dead. A weight rolled into the pit of his stomach. Something was wrong. He pounded out Lilinoe's number again. This time it went to voicemail. "Lili, it's Lion again. Call me back. I love you."

He waited while lava tumbled into the ocean and people ebbed and flowed around him exclaiming into their cell phones. Michael whined. He gave the dog water then pulled him close, hugging his furry warmth.

Now, with the glow of Hell all about him, he felt it was as good a time as any to call Bishop Carroll, his mentor, confessor, friend and thorn. Without mentioning the name of Megan Roy or any specifics of the case, Lion confided to the bishop that he could shed light on a certain notorious murder but for the restrictions of the confessional. He asked the bishop, "Is there anything at all I can do without breaking the seal of the sacrament? Could I write an anonymous letter to the police?"

He knew the answer before the bishop spoke, but the matter so haunted him that he had to raise it. As expected, Bishop Carroll said, "You know you can't do that. All you can do and it's the most powerful action you can take, is pray for justice. I trust you are doing this."

"Your Grace, I'm so troubled by this murder. I've met the victim's family. They're good people and they've waited years for justice." He sighed deeply, smelling the volcanic, eggy sulfur. "It's so difficult not to be drawn into the proceedings."

"When we cannot deflect the arrows of injustice and indifference, we take them into our own hearts. It's not a pen and an anonymous tip you need, Lion, you need to be on your knees."

The reprimand was typical of the bishop. He was a master of theological cliches and doctrine. Until Lion met Bishop James Carroll, he had never met a man who had not experienced suffering, his own or another's. This American bishop seemed to enjoy consistently good fortune. He walked through life always well groomed and well fed, unmarred by either quotidian trials or great calamity. If sorrow dared to cast its shadow upon him, Lord Jim, as Lion secretly called the bishop, would march right over it perfumed in clouds of incense and English after-shave lotion.

Lion said, "This situation eats me up, to think of murderers walking freely about while the victim's family is devastated for life. I am constantly drawn to the issue of human suffering, why a merciful God seems to require it."

"Our father in Heaven didn't plan for us to suffer. He placed us in Paradise. It is we who invited evil with our disobedience and inordinate pride, wanting to be God, to know everything, both good and evil." He paused. Lion could picture Bishop Carroll, getting impatient, his neck stiffening. The man continued. "We want to know even those things that will bring about our doom because we're not wise enough to handle them. Take atomic energy, for example." He asked, "You do keep a daily holy hour, don't you, Lion?"

"Most humbly, Your Grace, I try to keep my whole day holy. And I will attempt patience while waiting on the Lord's perfect timing."

"Good. Good." The bishop was clearly anxious to get away, his quota of tolerance spent. He quickly, absently, said good night and hung up, leaving Lion alone on the lava flow.

From the hot flames and shadows, the wheedling voice of the Adversary whispered, "Abeed. Abeed too still waits for justice."

Justice can be a terrible, inflammatory thing, searing the hands that mete it out and the soul demanding action, even useless self-destructive action. Lion cried out, "How long do we wait, Lord, for you to act?"

There was no answer he could discern from Heaven, but the Adversary, right at home in the brimstone, cackled, "You'll wait forever for Mr. Big Upstairs to do something because he doesn't give a damn about justice. He tells you to turn the other cheek. I say, an eye for an eye.' He says 'Do unto others as you want others to do unto you. I say 'Go for the jugular. Do unto others what they did to you only a hundred times harder.'"

"Jesus," Lion prayed. "Deal with my enemy." He got up, brushed himself off and walked away, heat and flames at his back and a cold darkness before him. The way across the black lava was more difficult at night, even with his flashlight. Michael picked his own way, sniffing and mincing. Fortunately, park rangers had laid out reflectors as guides across the dangerous terrain.

Lion considered his own death. He thought that if his death were to come in this moment, he could surrender with no regrets. It was a liberating feeling. Freedom bloomed in his chest and he picked up his pace. When he got to the car, he raised his hands and did a little Dinka dance in the dark. Dancing for joy is merely fun. Dancing in grief, doubt, and dread is exhilarating.

# Chapter 8
ABSOLUTION

Nothing in this windless, quiet morning prepared Father Lion for the events that would soon unfold. He was working quietly, polishing his retreat sermon when the telephone rang. He ignored it until he heard Bishop Carroll's commanding voice scorching the answering machine. He lifted the phone, his eyes still on his sermon, and heard the bishop, without preliminaries, demand, "Have you read the morning papers?"

"No, Excellency, I haven't seen any newspapers since I've been here."

"You haven't in any way compromised the seal of the confessional, have you?"

"Of course not, Excellency."

"No anonymous tips to the police? A well-placed word? Because if you have…"

"Please. What are you getting at, Your Grace?"

"It's in the paper today, that an anonymous tip led to the arrest of three brothers for the murder of a young girl a few years back on the Big Island."

Cautiously Lion asked, "What young girl?"

"Megan Roy."

Lion uttered a silent prayer of gratitude.

"Are you there, Lion?"

"Yes, yes."

"I won't ask if this is the murder you spoke to me about, although I suspect it is. As your confessor and superior, I need to know that you did nothing to violate the sacred bond of the sacrament."

"Nothing, I assure you, Your Grace, except that which you advised: prayer. May I please have the names of the men arrested?"

"The last name's Rossman. Let's see—Seth, Paul and Enoch Rossman"

Lion thanked the bishop, hung up the phone and wrote the names on the phone pad, drawing a small cross above each name and retracing the crosses, deeper and deeper, until the paper tore. He sat for long minutes, then jumped to his feet. "Come on, Michael."

It was a forty-minute drive to the Roys' home.

As he pulled into the yard, Charley Roy burst from the house like a man pursued and looked down on Lion. Immediately his anger softened to relief. "Oh, Father Lion, I'm so glad you're here. It's Ellie, my wife. I don't know what to do with her. She's hysterical. You heard the news?"

"Yes." He rushed up the steps and into the house behind Charley.

Ellie, in a fury, though confined to her rocking chair, was throwing books, a paperweight, a frying pan. She turned on her husband as he tried to restrain her arms. "Don't touch me. It was your idea to move to Hawaii. I did it for you. If we had stayed in California…"

Only now noticing Lion, Ellie went limp.

Lion eased her down to her rocker while Charley stalked from the house.

"I know who you are. Charley told me. You heard the news?" she asked weakly.

"I came immediately."

"You know how we heard?" Her voice rose to a shrill cry. "We read the newspaper. That's how. Nobody called us. Nobody. "

"You have every right to be upset."

"I should be rejoicing," she said bitterly.

"What is there to rejoice about?" Lion said. "You still have your grief. It didn't go away because someone was arrested. And now another family's tragedy begins."

"I don't care about that other family." She thrust out her delicate chin in defiance. "Those men are animals."

"Justice will be done now."

"And I will sit in that courtroom every day of the trial if it kills me. They will have to look at me, Megan's mother." Her hands on the rocker trembled

"May I pray with you?"

"I can't pray. I just don't have it in me. You pray. I'll agree. But please don't pray for them, the killers, or their family. I can't agree to that."

Lion thanked God for the capture of the young men. He prayed that justice would be served. He prayed for Megan's soul and then for the Roys, that they would have enough strength to get through the long ordeal of the trial. Ellie looked up at him, her eyes welling with tears. When she lowered her gaze, the tears - just two of them - trickled down her ashen cheeks. He passed her a tissue. "What can I do for you, Ellie?"

"I need to apologize to my husband. I was horrid just now. You saw me at my worst. Well, maybe not my worst. My aim used to be better."

"You've suffered a great loss."

"Why me, Father? God is supposed to be my friend. Ah, but there it is. His friends suffer, don't they? Persecution, ridicule, decapitation. So why would anyone choose to follow God, when it clearly is not in their best interest?"

"As with any other love relationship, we enter into a relationship with God knowing the perils, the small and great surrenders, a chipping away of our precious selves and our most cherished little attitudes and attachments. What seems like organic extinction, a breaking down of the smallest molecules of our corporal selves, is, in reality, the evaporation or immolation of all that stands in the way of our union with the Divine, our entry into eternal sublimity."

"I love how priests talk. You can't argue with them because you can't understand a word they're saying."

"I'm sorry. I…"

She interrupted, "No, I get it. I just couldn't explain it to anyone else without sounding abysmally holy or just plain full of beans." Her rocker moved in short little beats. "Please ask Charley to come in."

Lion found Charley sitting on the porch steps and sat down beside him

"You got here just in time, Father. She was spinning out of control."

"It must be awful, hearing about the arrests this way."

"You know, you go along, you make your adjustments. I was doing okay, taking your advice, working on forgiveness—and now I know their names. Now I want to kill those men. I want blood on the floor, and I want it now." A low guttural grunt escaped him. "We're living it all over again. I dread the trial."

"Is there anything I can do for you?"

"Pray for us."

"I do. I will."

When he got to the general store in Na'alehu, Lion stopped for coffee. He had a difficult time feeling any sympathy for the killers. He didn't know if the father of the Rossman brothers would be angry with him for suggesting he go to the police, or even if the father suspected him of leading the police in their direction.

Everyone inside the small store was talking about the Rossmans. They were well known in the neighborhood. Lion identified himself as a priest and got directions to the Rossman house in Puna. "Dey trouble, Reverend," one man said. "We geeve dat place a wide bert."

The man behind the counter muttered, "Dey come here, I lock da place."

"No can come," the first man said, pulling the cling wrap off a Spam musubi. "Rossmans all lock up." He bit into the rice with obvious pleasure.

Lion found the Rossman house easily. It was small and well-kept, surrounded by fruit trees, ginger and palms. Several cars were parked out front in the grass. A dog barked and lunged on its chain. "You better stay here, Michael." Lion rolled down the car windows for Michael. He poured water for him into his collapsible bowl. He was stalling, hesitating. The door of the house opened and a heavy woman in black shorts and a T-shirt proclaiming "Titas Rule" appraised him with distrust, standing truculently on parted legs.

"I'm looking for Franklin Rossman," he said, approaching the house. "I'm Father Lion Majok, a Catholic priest. I've spoken to Franklin before."

She shouted over her shoulder to the interior of the house. "It's okay, Frankie Boy, it's not a reporter. It's that *popolo* priest." Her pale brown eyes remained hostile. "Aloha, Father. I'm Franklin's sister, Betty Jean Lowery."

The small house was crowded with large people. The cloying smell of malevolence clung to them. Betty Jean introduced Lion to her husband, Clayton, her sister Mona, Mona's husband, Saji, and finally, Franklin. Everyone rose to greet him except Franklin, who sat crumpled into a black Barcalounger.

51

In a broken voice that Lion recognized immediately, Franklin apologized for not struggling out of his chair.

"It's okay," Lion assured him.

"Sit down, Father," Betty Jean urged, indicating the end of the sofa closest to the Barcalounger.

"I cannot believe you come see me," Franklin said, his mouth twisted with the effort of not bawling.

"He's taking it pretty hard," Betty Jean said with unsavory sympathy. "I don't know how those boys could do that to their father. He's a good man. If my Alfred ever did something like that, I'd kick his *okole* all over Puna, then I'd kill him myself with my bare hands."

At that, Franklin sobbed aloud. The other men drifted outside and Mona slipped into the kitchen. Betty Jean patted her brother's shoulder and joined her sister where she could listen to every word.

From the depths of his chair and his grief, Franklin groaned, "I got nobody now, Faddah. Donna wit' da Lord, and tree sons in prison. How it happen li' dat? One day you got a happy family, keeds all over da place, next day notting. You work hard all your life to put food on a table and one day for no reason your own keeds dey kill someone. How it happen li' dat? I do my best wit' deese boys. I no spoil 'em."

Lion thought the saddest part was that this man really did do his best. "God loves your sons. He sent his own son to die for your sons."

"Enoch, the small one, he no do it. I know it. I tell da udder two, you tell da cops your small brah stay in da car."

Softly, Father Lion said, "Franklin, my brother, they collected four DNA samples. Enoch's, too. And there's still one man missing."

Franklin shook his head in denial. "Not Enoch." He lowered his voice to a whisper. "I confess, I'm da one what turn em in, Faddah, and now I'm sorry."

"You did the right thing. It took courage."

"Dey start growing da *pakalolo* out back and selling da crystal mett. I lose da house, Faddah, da feds catch em. Dey no listen. I rip out da kine plants and my son, da beeg one, Sett, he punch me out. His own *makuakane*. So, I call da police. Da rest, as dey say, is history. You do somting for Enoch, Faddah? Go see im?"

"I will."

Betty Jean came back in the room carrying two plates. "Shoyu chicken and rice. Gotta keep up your strent, Franklin." She gave them each chopsticks and napkins, then retreated. She and Mona joined their husbands drinking beer at the picnic table outside.

Franklin nodded toward the window. "Widdout dem, I don't know what I do. What folks do widdout family?"

Lion thought of the Roys sitting alone with their grief.

The grim old prison was secluded down a country road. Lion prayed aloud for the Rossman brothers as he drove. "I know, Lord, that you don't want to lose a single sheep, and neither do you want to swell the legions of the Enemy with these recruits."

The two older brothers refused to see Lion. Only Enoch came shuffling out to the visitation room. His squat body could be sketched in rounded lines, nothing straight or strong. The young man scrunched into the metal chair, sitting sideways so he didn't have to look at the priest he had agreed to see.

Lion introduced himself and said, "I was a prisoner once. I know what it's like, so I came to see how I might help you."

Enoch glanced at him out of the side of his eye without turning toward him.

Lion waited.

Grudgingly Enoch asked, "You one prisoner? Whatchu do?"

"I was born black."

Enoch glanced again, his lazy, hooded eyes not quite masking a faint spark of interest.

"I was once a slave," Lion said.

"We still got 'em? Slaves?"

"Yes."

"Not in dis country."

"Yes. Here."

Enoch turned around, faced Lion, and spoke vehemently. "I didn't do it. I no kill that *wahine*. And I no rape her like dey say."

"Your father believes in your innocence."

"I hate him."

"He believes in you even though he knows you were there."

"Look at me. Do I look like a keed what has a father believes in 'im?"

"Enoch, you know who the fourth man is. Don't protect him. Tell the police. Make a deal. Save yourself."

"I no rat."

"Nobody else can save you. Do you want to live the rest of your life as a prisoner?"

"I got no life. My life *pau.*"

"I thought that once, too."

"How you bust out?"

"God sent a priest to me just as he sends me to you."

"You bring one saw?"

"No, I was terrified that I would be a slave my whole life. I lived in fear and filth." In a whisper Father Lion said, "Filth was my name. But I prayed, and once I got the courage to take the first steps toward my freedom, many people helped me, surprising people. A man I thought was my enemy fed me and put clean clothes on me.

"The police, the courts can help you, Enoch. But you need to tell them who the fourth man is. Save yourself and bring some justice to Megan Roy's family. Do this one good thing, Enoch. Take one step down a different road and God will help you. He is reaching out his hand to you. It's what your mother wants."

"Hey, you no talk my maddah."

Lion persisted, exploring the soft spot. "Your mother is standing beside the Lord, waiting to help you take that first step, like she helped you take your very first baby steps."

With one finger Enoch wiped the eye that was broadside to the priest. His voice sank to a dull, monotone. "I was there. I seen it all. I cried. They call me one girl. 'Do it, do it,' they tell me. I was twelve years old. I never do it before." He began to shake with silent sobs. "And since that one time, I never do it again. Every time I get close to a babe, I see that *wahine* looking up at me, and no can. Every minute I breathe, I hate myself. I hate my brothers because dey make me. I hate my faddah 'cause he not dere for me. 'Sorry,' I say to that *wahine* in my head, like one song you cannot forget. Round and round in my head. Sorry, sorry, sorry 'til I wan' shoot myself. Like I tell you, my life *pau*. I just no fall down yet." Lion waited in prayerful silence.

Enoch took a deep breath. "It was my cuz, my cousin Alfred Lowery. Numbah four guy."

"Please tell the police, Enoch. Take that step."

"I no rat. You want? You rat da cops."

"Thank you, Enoch, with your permission, I will. God bless you. Do you want me to hear your confession?"

"Sorry. Dat's all I gonna say. Sorry."

"That's all you need to say. Your sins are forgiven." He made the sign of the cross before the grill separating them. "In the name of the Father and of the Son and of the Holy Spirit. Amen."

"I going to Heaven now?"

"Yes, but I'll be back to see you before that."

"My brothers kill me if dey know."

"Is Alfred Lowery your Auntie Betty Jean's son?"

Enoch nodded, then suddenly got up as if he couldn't stand another second with Father Lion. The guard in the far corner of the room sprang to attention. Enoch walked away without a backward glance.

Lion spoke to the warden and gave him the name of Alfred Lowery. He also suggested that Enoch Rossman be placed on suicide watch.

The next day, Alfred Lowery was arrested. That evening, the prison warden telephoned Franklin Rossman to report that his son Enoch had hung himself in his cell. Franklin then called Father Lion to give him the news.

Lion was curiously detached. He felt he should be anguished. He had gotten Enoch to confess, given him the sacrament, yet a vast sense of futility haunted him. "This day thou shalt be with me in Paradise," Jesus had said to the good thief who hung on a cross beside Him.

He told Franklin Rossman he had visited Enoch in prison. "I heard his confession and gave him absolution. Your son is with the Lord, Franklin."

"He no go da udder place?"

"No."

"Den he wit' his maddah."

"Yes."

"When I get him back, you say a funeral Mass for Enoch, Faddah?"

"I will."

Lion let the Roys know he would be saying a Requiem Mass for the soul of Enoch Rossman.

After the service, Lion went with the Rossmans to the cemetery. He noticed a car parked under some hala trees across the road. He recognized the car but did not see Charley Roy himself.

Later in the day, he saw the same car pulled up to the shoreline where the wind-whipped waves lashed the rocks. Charley Roy sat in the driver's seat. Seeing Lion pull up, he got out of the car and leaned on it facing the ocean. "I thought it would make me feel better to see one of those monsters go in the ground." He regarded the waves a moment, then wearily turned to Lion. "But all I saw was the father, a man as broken over his loss as I am over Megan." He turned back to the turbulent sea, then laughed. "I think God is working me over. I never thought I'd feel one iota of sympathy for that gang. But you know what? God is like an incurable disease. Once he gets hold of you, he gets in your marrow and holds you up when it might be kinder to just let you die."

"I know."

# Chapter 9
## LITTLE BROTHER

After Enoch Rossman's funeral, Lion had begged the bishop for a little time to visit his *hanai* family. He needed the kind of rest that only family can offer. Besides, ever since Lilinoe's call, he harbored a feeling that something was dreadfully wrong at home.

Carrying a box of manapua and mooncakes, Lion walked inland from the bus stop on Kalanianaole Highway. Fallen plumeria blossoms littered his path. Barking dogs hailed his passing. It was a long walk to the Kamana farm, and, as always, Lion welcomed it. He passed fields of corn, an orchid nursery, papaya farms and gleaming taro *lo'i;* the flooded fields that make taro the most beautiful crop on Earth. If Lion hadn't believed that mankind came directly from the hand of God, he would choose to believe the early Hawaiians' story that the first people came from the taro plant and that the human heart is a small version of the large, velvety, heart-shaped leaves of the taro. This, they claimed, made mankind taro's little brother.

When he rounded a bend, Lion stopped in the middle of the road to take in his favorite view, the weathered, red Kamana house dwarfed by the sheer green palisade of the Ko'olau Mountains. A generous lanai wrapped around three sides of the house and a green lawn spread from there to the edge of the *lo'i*. Two horses, Brownie and Coco, grazed near the house, and a striped cat, Popoki, slept curled in a saddle resting on the porch railing. This was as close to a home as the African priest knew in this world. His visit was intended as a surprise, for he knew he was always welcome at the Kamanas'. He loved his *hanai* family and raised his hand in blessing as he approached.

Bishop Carroll of Honolulu, true to his promise to Bishop Binda of Sudan, had found a devout Catholic family to sponsor Lion, his newest seminarian. Pops and Iris Kamana had welcomed the overwhelmed young Lion into their hearts and home. They explained that *hanai* meant embracing someone as a true member of the family forever, and added him to their own four children. David, the oldest, who now went by Kawika, the Hawaiian translation for his name, was an attorney with a consuming interest in the rights and grievances of native Hawaiians. He was six and a half feet tall and had the finely chiseled face and arrogant demeanor of royalty. His brother Moses looked like a clone of Pops, heavily set with short legs and heavily muscled calves. Moses worked the farm beside his father and wanted nothing more in life than to care for the land and raise good food and a good family. But his girlfriend, the voluptuous, sweet Momi with the flawlessly lacquered fingernails would not consent to live on the farm.

Both Kamana daughters, Pohai and Lilinoe, were beautiful by any standard. They had similar golden faces with high strong cheekbones, hair the color of rich mahogany, and large brown eyes. Lili, the younger, however, had put on some weight, and strutted her pounds as if they were dearly won.

Even the dogs welcomed Lion. Nalu, the black Labrador retriever, and Thatcher, a fierce little terrier mix who bore a resemblance to the former British prime minister, bounded to greet him, barking extravagantly. Thatcher was Michael's mother, his father a mystery.

Iris Kamana came out to survey the commotion, spotted him, clapped her hands to her mouth and called to the interior of the house, "It's Lion. Praise the Lord, Pops. It's our Lion."

Strangely, Pops didn't amble out to greet him. Iris, however, had enough enthusiasm for two. With her arms outstretched and a smile straight from Heaven, she folded Lion into her warm bony embrace, and whispered, "Pops is sick, Lion. He got the cancer."

"Oh my."

"We didn't want to tell you on the phone, Son. We didn't want you to worry when no can do notting."

"I can pray, Mom."

"We know you do that awreddy, pray for each of us every day. We know our names are written on your heart, as you are on ours." Her hands went to her breast.

Lion waved to Moses in the distance, up to his thighs in muck, pulling taro, a job Lion loved. "I'll *kokua*," he called, setting the dogs to another round of barking.

Moses stood up straight, waved a muddy arm in return and bent again to the taro.

Iris scolded the dogs, then put her hand on the screen door, momentarily preventing Lion from entering. She whispered, "Pops looks bad. Chemo. Don't let it show your face. No matter the look, that man coming through. The Lord is taking care of him. Come."

Even with the warning, Lion was unprepared for the change in his beloved *hanai* father.

The man sat in his usual brown stuffed chair as if shrinking into it, rather than occupying it. His head of peppery grey hair was reduced to a few scraggly wisps hanging limply over his ears. "You are medicine for my sore eyes, Son." Pops bumped fists with Lion, grinning up at him.

"Eh, whatchu tink my new hair-do? I always wan' try da comb-over."

"You look like a bank president, Pops. How you feeling?"

"Wit' da Lord's help, I gonna lick dis ting."

A toilet flushed in the back bathroom and a minute later Pohai sailed into the room with a smile as warm as her mother's. "Hey, what's all the racket?" She hugged Lion tightly. "I thought I heard you, Brah."

He feasted his eyes on her lovely expectant face. The nice thing about Pohai was she was as beautiful inside as she was outside. He fist-bumped her. "Howzit?"

"Top of the charts," she sang. "How's the God game?"

"Sky's the limit."

Iris sat down on the arm of her husband's chair and gazed fondly at Lion. As a young African student, he had been a nearly perfect fit in her family. Initially, Kawika had expressed his opinion that they should be helping their own kind when there were so many needs in the Hawaiian community. He disagreed with reaching out to a *popolo,* a total stranger from thousands of miles away. Once he told his parents how he felt, however, Kawika went on to welcome Lion warmly, and even made a decent surfer out of him.

"Pohai, show your brother your new CD," Iris said. It was her talented daughter's second album and already a hit.

In the cover photograph, Pohai wore a tank top, cut-off jeans and her trademark head lei of *palapalae* fern. She was looking up from her ukulele as if the photographer had just surprised her. Lion read the song list, raising his eyebrows, nodding his head in approval. "Looking good, my tita."

"Sounding good, too, I hope." She laughed. "I'll get us some juice."

"Watch out your head," Pops said, "Any bigger no fit trew da kitchen door." His love and pride glowed in his eyes.

Pohai leaned over and smooched his balding head, intentionally leaving a lipstick imprint on the scalp.

When she left the room, Pops said, "I wait for dat kiss, my love tattoo. I know I look like rubbish, but da lipstick show da world, one *wahine* care bout dis ole man. I walk wit' pride."

"He's such a rascal," Iris said, putting her arm around her husband, then calling into the kitchen, "Pohai, there's a white box there from Lion. Bring that, too, when you bring the juice." She was hoping for Maunakea-Street manapua and was not disappointed.

"What's Kawika up to these days?" Lion asked.

"He got one big case now," Pops said. "Hooo da big."

Iris said, "You know that trouble with Kamehameha Schools? You read about it?"

"I haven't been keeping up with the newspapers, I'm afraid."

Pohai came back with a tray of juices, saying, "One *haole* chick sued the school because they wouldn't admit her *haole* son because he's *haole*."

Pops said, "They stole our nation, they stole our land, they build hotels on our beaches, and now they want our school what our Princess Pauahi geeve us. What more we can geeve 'm? Our *koko* out our veins?"

"I take it that Kawika is representing the school?" Lion pressed the cold glass gratefully to his forehead before drinking.

"*Ae*," Iris said. "I feel sorry for that little boy. They letting him attend class while the case goes through the courts. The school told the teachers and students to treat him with aloha. He's only a child and it's not his fault."

"Good, good." Only after everyone had finished their manapua, did Lion bring up the youngest Kamana daughter: "And how's Lili?"

Iris and Pops exchanged glances. Pohai carried their manapua plates to the kitchen. Pops shook his head. He looked gnomish with his wisps of hair dangling limply. "Dat *wahine* running wild, I tell you."

"Maybe you can talk to her, Lion," Iris pleaded. "She respects you. We're only her parents. What do we know?"

"I'll do my best. Where is she?"

"She no come home two nights now," Pops said. "Sixteen years old and out all night. I geeve her to da Lord. He love her more dan I do."

"Do you know where she is? Is she all right?"

"She's with the boyfriend." Iris said "boyfriend" as if the word left a strong, sharp taste on her tongue.

"Japonee guy." Pops added. "He got one souped-up Harley." Lion detected trace amounts of admiration if not for the boyfriend then for his bike.

"I don't like that thing," Iris said. "It's dangerous."

"So's Lili." Pohai said as she plunked down on the other arm of her father's chair."

"Let's go help Moses," Lion suggested. He changed into swim trunks and a stained old T-shirt, and he and Pohai went out to the taro patch. They brought Moses a glass of iced guava juice.

Harvesting food was as much God's work as harvesting souls and Lion believed the tasks were entwined. You can't discuss theology with a starving man, you must feed him first. Barefoot, he stepped into the *lo'i* and sank in mud almost to his knees. It felt so good he curled his toes in pleasure.

"It's like chocolate," Pohai said. "Can you imagine. They do chocolate body wraps at the Hilton spa in Waikiki—and charge big bucks for it."

Lion pictured fleshy pink tourists wallowing in chocolate, squealing to each other in glee. "Yes," he managed to say, "mud has the same viscosity as chocolate."

Pohai teased, "Is viscosity a sin, Lion? It sounds like it should be one of the deadly ones."

He turned a smiling face to them, knowing the teasing and laughter were because he was their brother and they loved him. He bent down into the water pulling weeds from around the luminous young taro shoots, tucked the weeds into the mud just as Pops had taught him, then stomped them down deep to become the only fertilizer for the taro.

They finished weeding and moved on to the next *lo'i,* which was ready to be pulled. Done in good company, pulling taro was like playing in the mud.

"Hey, Willie Wonka," Moses called out as they cleared the last taro. "We *pau,*" and with that he pushed Lion backwards into the mud. Lion grabbed Pohai on the way down and she pulled Moses in with her, all of them laughing, covered in mud from, head to foot. It was tradition. When they staggered out of the muck, they saw that Pops had come out on the porch and was propped in the old wicker chair in the corner, looking out on them with wistful happiness.

Now that they had harvested the taro, an unharvested soul roared in on the back of a huge motorcycle bristling with chrome. The bike sped to the Kamana gate and slammed to a stop in a cloud of red dust, engine revving. Lilinoe jumped off, sauntered through the gate, and made directly for the house with neither a backward glance to her biker buddy nor a wave to her mud-caked siblings. She paused briefly, said something to Pops that made him shrink, and went inside.

The biker, as might be expected, was a brute of a man with a long, black braid dangling from beneath the red bandana knotted about his skull. It probably took him hours at the gym to build and maintain the bulging, heavily tattooed arms resting on the handlebars. For a moment, he watched the space where Lilinoe had been, then made a wide and showy U-turn, and roared away in another dust tornado.

Lion and Moses looked at each other and shook their heads. Moses said, "Pops no need da kine."

"I'll talk to her."

"Good luck," Pohai said. "You'll need it."

Later, after bathing, Lion knocked lightly on Lilinoe's bedroom door. When no one answered, he opened it a crack. "Lili?" The ceiling fan whirred.

She was in bed, her back to the door. In a voice muffled by her pillow, she said, "Not now, Lion. Go away, please." She hunched up tighter, then sighed ornately. She was in no mood for a sermon, but turned to face him, knowing he would not leave until he had tried to save her immortal soul yet again.

He waited for her to speak.

She sat up, her mascara streaked from crying.

He passed her the box of tissues from the dresser top.

Lili wiped at her eyes and examined the black smear on the tissue. "I'm a mess." She grabbed at her long gleaming hair and twisted it into a knot on the back of her head. "You do that on purpose, don't you?"

"What?"

"Nothing. You stand there and say nothing. It's a tactic. You make people uneasy so they spill their guts."

"I'm sorry to cause you grief. I admit that silence is sometimes provocative." Lion leaned against the doorjamb. "I guess I spent so many years afraid of being beaten for daring to speak at all, silence has become my nature."

"Sorry. I keep forgetting you were once a slave." She begrudged his misfortune. It always gave him a moral edge.

"Can I help you with anything, Little Sister."

"No. I handle."

"I'm a good listener."

"I just need some sleep, okay?"

"Mom and Pops are concerned about you."

"Don't lay a guilt trip on me. I know we're all supposed to tip-toe around because Pops has the cancer, so you won't see me bothering him. I'm hardly ever home and when I am, I stay outta his way."

"Well, if you ever want to talk, I'm available."

"Tanks, eh, Lion. Love you."

"Love you, too, Lil."

She immediately flopped back down into her pillows, face to the wall.

The family begged Lion to stay for dinner, but he excused himself. "I have to have dinner with the bishop and then it's back to the Big Island tomorrow morning. And I have to rescue Michael from the bishop's secretary tonight."

Iris took his arm. "Please bless us before you go." She called to Lilinoe, "Your brother leaving." That brought her out of her bedroom.

He gently put his hand on his foster mother's head and prayed for God's will in her life. He did the same for each member of the family. With Pops he pleaded for mercy, for a return to health. When he came to Lili, she lowered her head. He quietly prayed that the Blessed Virgin would comfort her in whatever troubles had descended upon her. She hugged him for a long minute.

Lion blessed the house in parting, "May all who dwell within these walls dwell in peace and may all who enter know the presence of the Lord of Love."

He was almost to the gate when Lili called to him, "Lion. Wait. Walk you to the bus stop."

Dusk gathered about them as the evening sky bent softly to the land. She looped her arm through his. "I'm pregnant, Lion."

He stopped in the middle of the road. "Oh my, Lili. Oh my." He tried to hug her but she pulled away. They stood there looking at each other. He reached for the right thing to say to express his love and concern, to hide his shock. "Oh, Lil, you must be frightened. How do you feel? Have you seen a doctor? We'll figure this out. It will be fine."

She didn't answer but briefly leaned into him while he stroked her hair. They walked on in silence. Finally, Lion asked, "Who's the father?"

"Lance."

"On the motorcycle?"

"Yes. Worse yet, Lion, it's twins."

"Two babies. Oh, Lili, you're going to have your hands full."

"Lance wants me to have an abortion."

Lion stopped. In the distance a dog barked. "You realize that's something I can't condone. But I will always love you, no matter what. Nothing can change that. There's help for young women in your position. It's not like the old days."

Lilinoe kept walking. "Me and Lance get to decide this. No one else."

"God has already decided. He gave those babies life." Lion caught up with her, imploring, "Tell Mom. She'll stand by you."

"She got enough on her plate with Pops and all."

"Lili." He tugged on her arm. "Our Father in Heaven chose you to be his instrument to bring these gifts into the world."

"I'm a junior in high school."

"Our Blessed Mother was fifteen when she gave birth to the Savior of the World."

"And look how that turned out for her." She pulled her arm away from his. "I'm going back to the house."

"Lili, give Mom a chance. Tell her. As for Pops, maybe God in his wisdom is giving him something to think about besides his illness. It brings new life into the family and takes the focus off dying."

"Bye, Lion." She turned toward home, then came back and kissed him on the cheek. "I love you."

"I love all three of you."

"Don't you say a word to Mom, or anyone." She hurried away into the dusk.

It was dark by the time Lion reached the bus stop. While waiting, he continued to pray for Lilinoe and her children, for Pops with his cancer, for each member of his *hanai* family. He prayed for his own mother and sister, for his missing brothers, Kintu, and Mayom. He prayed for the Roys, and for the killers of their daughter, especially Enoch Rossman. He prayed for the father who handed his sons over to justice, and for that whole tragic family.

*Are there really people in the world untouched by misfortune and sorrow?* He thought of the elegant Bishop Carroll, secure in this world and the next. *Is there ever enough money to buy happiness or enough power to buffer grief?* He suspected there was.

# Chapter 10
FEAST FOR FAMINE

Bishop Carroll was that puzzling mix of holiness and ambition. He was lean and self-focused, spending as much time on his treadmill as on his knees. He envisioned himself wearing the crimson cape of a cardinal and perhaps holding the staff of Saint Peter as the first American pope.

The bishop paid great attention to food, and had made reservations for himself and Lion at Alan Wong's, President Obama's favorite restaurant in Hawaii. He ordered the wine and reminded Lion that his credit card bill went straight to his brother Wills, "the Wall Street Wonder," so they could order what they pleased. The Carroll brothers had worked out a scheme when Lion first arrived in Hawaii with his tales of poverty and persecution. In addition to paying the bishop's charge account in full, Wills now sent double the amount of every one of Bishop Carroll's restaurant tabs to Bishop Binda in Sudan for his charities.

"I know the deal," Lion said, "The more we eat, the better off the starving are. But I still find all this food disconcerting. It's so—unfair. I can't help thinking of people foraging in dumps while we gorge ourselves."

"Please, Lion, I know you have a point, and you never let me forget it. I have to admit, I often imagine what our esteemed Protestant brethren must say when they see the Catholic bishop of Honolulu driving a brand-new Mercedes every year. Or what the people in this restaurant think when they see two princes of the Church dining so extravagantly. In addition to what he does for Binda, my dear brother Wills also floats a number of my own charitable pet projects. I think Wills feels he can pursue whatever godless schemes he concocts in business so long as he shares the plunder with the Church. If anyone can schmooze Saint Peter and bribe his way past the pearly gates, it's my brother Wills." Bishop Carroll expertly swirled the wine, sniffed it assiduously, then tasted and pronounced it *"magnifique."*

"Now if you have no objection, Lion—and even if you do—I'll just order the five-course chef's special menu for us. Think of it as a means to an end."

Lion slumped into acquiescence.

Bishop Carroll prattled on, "We think of a man's conscience in terms of moral absolutes." His voice was strong and measured, his face so readable. "We imagine conscience as a scold hurling bolts of lightning if even our eye should stray. But conscience is a fickle thing, really, and easily mollified." He inhaled the bouquet of his wine once more, in pleasure rather than appraisal. "I do believe Wills imagines himself leapfrogging his way through purgatory on this little dinner scheme, jumping ahead of common adulterers, pickpockets and corrupt politicians. Now there's redundancy for you."

Lion lifted his wine glass. "To your brother Wills. May I find a little more room in my stomach for his charity."

Bishop Carroll smiled. "That's the spirit." He reached inside his jacket and pulled out a battered letter. "I almost forgot. This came today, from your sister, I believe."

The delicate airmail paper crinkled as Lion took it. He recognized the stamps, the crisp lightness of the foreign airmail paper, Eulalia's clear hand. He held on to the letter as if he was able to read right through the envelope. He sat back slowly, already absorbing the coming blow. *How do we sense death whispering in the crinkle of the paper? Or is it in the ink that flows from the hand of one who loves us and must deliver the wound?*

He carefully wiped his knife clean on his napkin, then slit the envelope, praying as he did so. His eyes devoured the contents, then rested, unseeing, on the paper.

"Bad news?"

Lion's voice was barely audible. "My youngest brother, Mayom, is dead. Has been dead for years. Nobody knew."

"I'm so sorry, Lion. God rest his soul."

"My other brother, Kintu, has been found alive. Apparently the men who kidnaped him made him into one of those boy soldiers. He was in something called The Lord's Resistance Army in Uganda. He's in police custody now and they may send him to the Hague to stand trial as a war criminal."

"But he's a child."

"He was a child when they took him. He's twenty-two now."

"I see. That is most distressing."

"Eulalia and my mother are going back to our family land. They're leaving the refugee camp."

"Is it safe?"

"Who in this world is safe?"

With considerable and visible effort, the bishop suppressed a belch. When he saw that Lion could no longer eat, he performed an act of mercy, suggesting they take their desserts to go.

Back at the rectory, Lion gathered his dog in his arms, and fed him some coconut cake. He then walked him through the dark streets of downtown Honolulu, deserted except for the homeless sleeping in doorways and on benches, everywhere except Waikiki where tourists might see them.

He thought of his brothers, Kintu and Mayom, whom he would not have known had he met them on the street this night. Lion wondered what he should be feeling, for he felt nothing but empty. He had lost his brothers years ago, yet his ears rang with Eulalia's closing words: "You are Ma's comfort. She has one son who made it to safety." He cringed at the obligations that simple sentence put upon him. He didn't yet know what they were, their shape and texture. Just their weight.

Bishop Carroll was on his treadmill when Lion returned to the rectory and said he wished to receive the sacrament of confession.

They sat down together. "Bless me, Father, for I have sinned," Lion began. He first confessed to loneliness, discouragement, and willfulness. "I have this great desire for solitude, all my own desire, I suspect, and not the prompting of the Holy Spirit. I sometimes feel imprisoned in the confessional and must pray away my resentment."

"Ah, your familiar cross. Dear Lion, embrace this gift for the sacrament, embrace it as the cross that the Lord has fit precisely to your shoulders. The cross we each bear isn't necessarily the one we would choose. More often, our cross is one we must quietly pick up each morning and carry through the heat of the day."

"Is that what you do, Your Grace?"

Bishop Carroll appeared startled. His back stiffened. "I used to, but I've become so comfortable with my cross, I hardly consider it a burden now."

"May I ask what your cross is?"

"Numbers. Business acumen. I had a calling to become a priest and I've been transformed into my banker brother; Wills, in clerical drag. I know it doesn't sound much like martyrdom to you, a former slave, but my sanctified vision of myself I see as a grave loss."

"You could still realize your vision. Give up your office. Run from it into a monastery."

"You're projecting your dream onto me, Lion. And it's too late for that. I've been nipped by ambition. First American pope comes to mind."

"With God's help, it could happen."

"God alone knows what's in store for me. In the meantime, I'm being a good steward of the resources entrusted to me. Including you." He squirmed uncomfortably. "I'm sorry about your brothers. Let me know if I can help you regarding your family."

"Perhaps I could visit them, Lion suggested." He closed his eyes, fearing the answer.

"In time, perhaps. I can't spare you right now. You know how short-handed we are in this diocese, and we have all those retreats you're scheduled to conduct. May I remind you, that's why you're here in Hawaii, and not in Africa."

"I see." Lion's relief was so great it startled him.

"However, if you feel you must, I suppose I can juggle things a bit; borrow a Jesuit from the Mainland."

"No, no. I understand." His fear of going back to Africa shocked him. Until this moment of choice, he had not suspected its presence lurking in the shadows, now jumping out to remind him of his past helplessness and degradation.

He barely heard the bishop ask, "What do you think of, Lion, while you're walking from place to place?"

He composed himself. "I imagine that it is not me walking, but Christ, so every step blesses the ground."

"Hmph. But whose feet are tired at the end of the day? Yours or

Christ's?"

Meekly he said, "My time alone on the road is necessary to nurture the grace I need for the confessional. If I'm to save my own soul by offering Christ's salvation to others, I need silence to hear the Spirit. This world is so full of alarms and distractions—and food."

"I understand." Groaning under the weight of his dinner, the bishop said, "I really do."

Lion was overcome with pity for this man who enjoyed his brother's riches to the point of making himself sick. The cross the bishop carried was covered in gravy; his own in blood.

# Chapter 11

## THE HOTHOUSE

The change from lush pastureland to lava desert did not appear to be gradual as Father Lion and Michael walked from Waimea in the Kohala Mountains to Puako on the Kona coast of the Big Island. The change from one environment to another seemed to happen in one step. He thought that life was like that. It changes swiftly, randomly. A step is taken. The world is suddenly different. Years ago, in one moment, Lion went from the elation of being on his father's shoulders to the abject despair of being hurled into his captor's goat stye. Now he was a priest in Hawaii, knowing it could change again, without warning.

His step quickened in the heat. He consulted Michael about the landscape they traversed. "Look at this." His arm swept across the empty volcanic devastation. "It's like someone fried the night itself. I grasp small crumbs of wisdom, and just when I think I finally have a grip on something, the vague foggy shape of a larger truth looms, humbling me yet again. Is that not so, Michael?"

Clouds hung back in the hills leaving the coastal sky a vivid, merciless blue as the priest and the dog descended to the lowlands.

The key to the rectory at Assumption Church was right where it was supposed to be, under the pot of bougainvillea by the door. The house was spare, swept clean, every surface gleaming.

A note from the pastor said, in part, "I hear from Bishop Jim that you're a surfer, so I inveighed upon a parishioner to lend you a board for the duration. It's in the garage. You'll find the best waves down at the end of the paved road. My sources, however, cautioned me, that Puako is not the greatest surfing spot. So, I've left mask, fins, and snorkel, too. I can vouch for the snorkeling." The note also advised that a parishioner named Gigi Balubar would call for him and bring him to her home for dinner.

Lion barely had time for a swim and shower. With Michael, he sprinted to the beach across the road and dove in, gratefully feeling the chill along every inch of his body as he stretched out upon the water.

Gigi Balubar's husband, Ferdinand, called for Father Lion at five o'clock. He was an older man, slight, taciturn, and deeply tanned. "Dog's okay," he said as Michael jumped into the cab of the truck and sat on the floor between Lion's legs.

The prim, barnyard-red Balubar house had several greenhouses stretching out from its rear. Ferdinand explained, "We grow hothouse tomatoes. I ship out a thousand pounds a week, reds, yellows, Tiny Tims." He spoke with pride. "I order the seeds from Holland, the Ozark Mountains. All over. Mostly heirlooms, not genetically altered."

Gigi stood in the doorway, a thin sixty-ish woman with muscular arms and an air of barely suppressed mirth. She proudly held a tray of drinks with stalks of celery sprouting in them. "Don't worry, Father, they're virgin marys. No liquor, only lots of just-squeezed tomato juice. Of course, I can sneak in a little something if you like."

The interior of the Balubar house was small and crowded with large pieces of ornate furniture polished to a high gloss. Vases of plastic flowers, fussy birdcages holding fake birds and a legion of ceramic Chinese people inhabited every spare surface. Gigi had set the dining room table with a lace cloth, stemmed glasses, gold-rimmed china and a centerpiece of garden flowers. A crystal chandelier winked overhead. Gigi was as proud of her dining room as Ferdinand was of his tomatoes.

After a dinner of pork adobo, fried rice, roasted tomatoes, and lumpia, Gigi brought out a pineapple upside-down cake. "You're lucky, Father," she chirped, holding the cake aloft. "It's not tomato upside-down cake."

When they finished, Ferdinand invited the priest out to the greenhouses. "I got plenty of water for the tomatoes," he explained. "People don't realize it, but we got so much freshwater springs under this lava. I don't know where the water comes from. Maybe the snows on Mauna Kea. But sometimes I think that the middle of the Earth is not fire, but water. You get past the magma and deep at the core of the planet is this giant dark pool of cool fresh water."

"I like that thought. I'm going to hold on to it."

They walked the rows of tomatoes. "These are the Tigerellas, my favorites. Here, try a bite."

Lion crunched into the warm fruit. "Mmm. This packs a lot of flavor."

"I don't grow much of these. They taste good but don't sell. People think there's something wrong with them because of the splotchy skin, but that's the way they are. Over here, I got Brandywines, great for slicing. And this one I'm just trying out. The seeds come from the Ukraine. It's called Cosmonaut Volkov after a Russian astronaut. Supposed to be productive in hot weather. So far so good."

Lion complimented his host on his tomatoes, and was promptly handed a bagful.

Gigi offered to drive Lion home.

"It's a nice night and the moon is almost full. Michael and I will enjoy the walk."

"Then I'll walk you out to the road."

As they strolled down the driveway, Gigi said, "You know, Father, I came here from Luzon when I was eighteen. My brother came first and saved his money to bring me up. I will never forget the first time I went into a supermarket here and saw all this food, beautiful food, all wrapped and displayed. I thought of people I had just left back home who had so little to eat and I burst out crying. Right there in Safeway."

On Sunday morning Lion delivered a fire and brimstone sermon:"My dear brothers and sisters," he began, "as I walk around the islands, I meet many young people. I have noticed that they often speak a different language. I don't mean Hawaiian or Japanese or Chinese, but an impure dialog that is vulgar, lazy and mean. Why is this bad? Impure language releases all the passions. One immodest or unseemly word can start a thousand evil thoughts, a thousand shameful desires, and can introduce innocent souls to evils of which they had previously been happily ignorant.

"Have you listened to the lyrics of today's popular music? You may think, 'Oh Father, it doesn't mean anything. It's just a stupid song.' I say no. We cannot afford to laugh or make light of conversations, music, films which God wishes us to detest with all our hearts. We cannot swim with impunity in the sewer. We catch a disease.

"We prefer to think of Hell as a state of mind rather than an actual physical place. But, my friends, the children of Fatima were given a vision of Hell that terrified them. They described a pit of fire with men, women and loathsome beasts writhing in the flames.

"Today, I beseech you to put out the fires in your own lives. Take charge of the public discourse and the type of speech allowed in your homes. Correct the young. If your children persist in their errors, devise appropriate consequences. The moment the television brings vulgarity into your living room is the moment you grab the remote and turn it off. Write or e-mail your local television and radio stations when they indulge in degrading and demeaning broadcasts. Write to advertisers who sponsor such impurity and violence. Save our youth from Hell on Earth in terms of wrecked lives, wasted intellects, needless sorrow. Save yourselves in the process. Hell is real. Its maw is wide open and the impurities it spreads across the ground are slippery. Beware."

He started to leave the pulpit to continue the Mass, then returned, "I will hear confessions immediately after Mass. I know this is unscheduled. But last night I sat in the confessional and very few came. So this morning you have another opportunity to confess your sins. Tell the Adversary to go to Hell and mean it."

Monday morning, in his early prayers, Father Lion thanked God for the number of souls who had lined up after Mass for the sacrament.

Without eating breakfast, he went to the ocean. Michael ran ahead and doubled back before he got to the shoreline. The dog swam beside him as he snorkeled at the edge of the cove marveling at the streaks of color shooting through the water, the wriggling manini, the bored *humuhumunukunukuapuaa*, the canary yellow tangs. A moray eel peered from its coral nest, almost invisible.

Two calls awaited him when he returned to the rectory: Bishop Carroll and Lili. He called the bishop first, to get it out of the way so he could spend as much time as needed with Lili.

"My spies tell me you ranted about Hell in your Sunday sermon," the bishop scolded.

"Your spies?"

The bishop laughed robustly. "I don't have spies. But I did get a few complaints."

Lion was crushed. "I thought it went very well. People lined up for confession afterwards."

"Because you scared the hell out of them."

"How many complaints?"

"Actually, one. It's just that hellfire and brimstone is the bad old way. People don't buy it anymore. We don't have the influence and power we used to. People are too affluent, too educated. We have a most beautiful philosophy of love to offer. That's where your emphasis should be."

"Fifty-seven confessions."

"A word to the wise, my good friend: I don't want complaints. We're in the midst of a fund-raising drive in a bad economy. I don't want that sort of thing going to hell in a hand basket, so to speak."

"With all due respect, Your Grace, I hope that the only accounting we have to do in the end is the number of souls we saved from damnation."

After a moment of silence, Bishop Carroll said, "In the final analysis, you are right, of course." He paused again, then said wearily, "I wonder how many bishops you'll find in Heaven when you get there?"

"It won't be Heaven for me without my dear friend, the Bishop of Honolulu." Lion surprised himself with his unctuous diplomacy.

He poured himself a Coca-Cola before sitting down to make his next call. "Yeah, Lili, Lion here."

"What? You think I don't know your voice? Anyway, thanks for getting back to me."

"No thanks needed, little sister. Howzit?"

"Sick as a dog most mornings. And Jerko is history."

"You mean your motorcycle man?"

She was scornful. "Idiot. He was pressuring me to have an abortion. He doesn't want to spend his Saturdays at Chuck E. Cheese's for the next eighteen years, or pay child support."

"So, you have decided not to have an abortion?"

"I think so."

"I'm so happy."

"Well don't be. The truth is, Lion, I went to the clinic to have one and I got on the table and I couldn't do it. I got up, put my clothes back on and just left. Jerk-o was so mad. That's when I told him to go eff himself."

He heard her sniffling. "I know this is hard, Tita, but it will all work out. You'll see. Have you told Mom, yet?"

"No. I run the shower so she doesn't hear me puking my guts out. God, what timing, she's so worried about Pops. She's got a full plate and then I come along pregnant with not one but two babies."

"Mom has enough room in her heart for your babies. And you are already enthroned there. Nothing can dislodge you from her heart."

"The one I can't stand to find out about it is Pohai. She's so perfect. She's going to think I'm such a screw-up."

"From the beginning of time, God planned these babies. Their names are written on the palm of his hand."

"How? I don't have their names, yet."

"You will. They will come to you." Lion spent the rest of the day in prayer, meditation, and reading his favorite scripture passages from the Book of Isaiah: "Let the islands keep silence before me, and the nations take new strength. Everyone shall help his neighbor, and shall say to his brother: Be of good courage. Fear not, for I am with thee: turn not aside, for I am thy God: I have strengthened thee, and have helped thee…even to your old age I am the same and to your grey hairs I will carry you. You will keep in perfect peace him whose mind is steadfast, because he trusts in you."

When the heat of the day had passed, Lion walked out on the lava among the famous petroglyphs of Puako where thousands of figures were incised into slabs and domes of hard lava. Ages ago, people had chanted and prayed and then patiently chipped away at the lava to leave a message.

Was it altruism or a hunger to endure beyond the corruptible body, to find some permanence as days changed to years and years to eons, to beg, "Remember us."

# Chapter 12
## THE LONESOME ROAD TO KONA

He set out walking to Kailua-Kona in the evening when the long, flat road was cooler and his eyes could no longer feast on Puako's soft beauty. He hoped to shield his heart from the pull of contented life at the edge of the great obsidian desert of the Kohala Coast.

He wore a neon-orange traffic vest with a flashing dog collar for Michael, so they would not be mowed down by speeding cars on the dark stretches of Mamalahoa Highway.

Amusing fantasies often decorated Father Lion's long walks and troubled neither his soul, nor God. His daydreams were comic relief from his rosaries and mortifications. They helped to keep his view of himself in perspective: He was a sinful man aspiring to an impossible perfection.

He imagined himself settling down as the Monk of Puako, a holy man whose very gaze set men on "The Way."

The Monk of Puako would likely be invited to conduct self-actualization seminars at Hawaii's resort spas, which specialize in perfumed water cures and hot stone massages. He would deliver riveting lectures on healing the inner child, stress-busting with Jesus and burning fat through centering prayer. He might even write a best-seller, *The Way of Golf: A Holy Man's Guide to A Hole in One* or *Apostolic Anorexia: Be a Joyful Loser.*

A pick-up truck blazed dangerously past Father Lion. He tightened Michael's leash. As the truck pulled ahead, he heard cans clatter on the lava rocks, then saw the moon-glint on aluminum as more beer cans sailed in the air, barely missing him.

The nighttime traffic surprised the priest. Probably tourists with too many mai tais under their belts, or hotel workers heading home, weary, and sleepy. He was not enjoying this walk. He was nervous, more for Michael than himself, and it was a long way to St. Michael the Archangel Church. Shortly after midnight, a Honda Accord pulled to the side of the road up ahead. It was a middle-class, middle-ager's car, perhaps a parishioner from Puako recognizing him and wanting to offer him a lift. He hurried toward it, relieved. The electric window rolled down as he approached and a young woman leaned her head out of the passenger side of the car, "Hey, want a ride?"

"I've got a dog."

"Yeah, I see. Does it bite?"

"Only miscreants."

"Jeez, I don't want the mutt taking a chunk outta me."

"I understand. We're fine with walking. It was kind of you to offer."

"No, no, it's okay. The dog's okay. Climb in the back. I can hold your stick up here. Just in case."

When Lion opened the car door to get in, he found, in addition to the woman, and the man driving, there was another man in the back seat. The latter was thin and hunched, his mood as dark as his clothes. This was the moment Lion knew he should back away. But courtesy, mistrust of his own judgement, fear of giving offense, all conspired to have him lift his foot and step into the car. He slid into the seat, Michael in his lap.

The man next to him sighed elaborately, as if this hitchhiker was the latest in a series of private persecutions. The driver, whose head sprouted such a crop of ratty coils it blocked the view, didn't turn to look at him. He smelled sour, like old milk.Michael's back-hairs stood up at rakish attention. As soon as Lion closed the car door and he heard the lock click, he knew Michael was right, something disagreeable was afoot.

The woman turned in her seat to face him. He guessed she was in her thirties and accustomed to spontaneous address changes. "So," she said, "where you from?"

"Do you mean now, or originally?"

The other passenger muttered to his window, "Christ, a simple question turns into the Spanish Inquisition."

"Both," she said, glaring at the mutterer.

"I just came from Puako," Lion said, "and before that Hilo. But I was born in Africa."

"You and our president," the mutterer said to his window.

The woman sneered, "Shut your face, Willis. For your information, Barak Obama was born right here in Hawaii."

"Have you seen his birth certificate? No one has seen his actual birth certificate. No one, because he was born in Kenya. He's a goddamn illegal alien and he's got the keys to Fort Knox jingling in his pocket."

The woman ignored Willis and asked Father Lion his name.

He withheld his clerical affiliation, not sure if it was an asset or liability in this company. "Lion Majok."

"Lion. No way." She poked the driver with her elbow. "Did you hear that, Haji?"

The driver kept his eyes on the road.

She apologized for him, "Don't worry, the guy's not a terrorist. Haji's not his real name. He's really Kevin but he's always coming home with good stuff—like a magician. So we call him Haji Baba. My name is -- Sophia." Her pause made it obvious she had just made up her name.

Lion attempted chatter to mask his escalating fear with small talk. "I'm pleased to meet the three of you. However, I must inform you that I'm not named for the jungle beast, but for my father's favorite cow who was the color of a lion. My dog is Michael, after the archangel."

Willis continued his conversation with his window. "Now we get a genealogy tutorial." He rolled his eyes as Sophia began to sing, "Michael, row the boat ashore, ah-lay-loo-ya."

"And a golden oldies hit parade."

Finally Haji the driver turned on the car radio and began to punch the buttons, growing angrier by the second. He finally found music that sounded like pots and pans crashing and that seemed to mollify him.

With reckless suddenness, the car veered off the highway and headed up a slope on a barely passable road. Alarmed, Lion leaned forward, addressing the driver, "You can let Michael and me out here, please. We'll get to Kona on our own. You've been a great help."

No one responded. The car lurched and strained and finally stopped with nothing around but an old van parked in the moonlight on the side of the deserted road. Casually, Haji reached under his seat, drew out a gun, and ordered Lion, "Outta the car."

Lion opened his door gingerly, and swung his feet out, Michael still in his lap.

Haji was already out of the car and standing in front of him. "The dog stays."

"You can't keep my dog."

Willis grabbed Michael, threw him back in the car, knocked Lion to the ground and slammed the car door. The dog began to bark frantically, lunging at the window, his traffic collar flashing.

88

"Please, the dog is my companion. He's not a pedigree, he's not worth anything to you."

Willis echoed, "He's not worth anything to you," in a high mocking voice. "For all we know the mutt's a rare Nepalese temple spaniel." He spat while Sophia unzipped Lion's backpack and rummaged through it methodically.

When she came across Lion's priestly stole, she held it up. "Hey nice. Look at the lions on it, will you?"

"My mother made it for me. She embroidered—"

Sophia interrupted him, "Tell your mom thanks," and she threaded it through the belt loops of her jeans tying it on the side. She went back to inspecting his bag. "Nothin in here."

Haji shoved the gun to Lion's temple. "Where's your money?"

"The little I have is in my wallet, in my back pocket. You're welcome to it. Just let me have my dog."

Willis laughed, imitated him again and added in utter contempt, "Listen to him bargaining. Whada ya think this is, a flea market?"

Haji held out his hand, "The wallet." He swung his gun around, pointing it at the barking dog.

"Here, here, take the wallet. Take anything."

"Now he's pleading." Willis spat again from a seemingly inexhaustible supply of phlegm and contempt.

Sophia took the wallet, shrugging in a parody of winsomeness. "Sorry."

Haji threatened, "If you've got less than a hundred bucks, we're wasting you and the dog," He asked Sophia, "How much?" .

She counted quickly, "Thirty-seven dollars."

Haji went stiff with rage, fired his gun at the car, missing it. Michael stopped barking and whimpered. "Where else have you got money?

Strip."

When Father Lion hesitated, Haji again turned his gun on the car. "Now. Or I kill the mutt."

Quickly Father Lion undressed, handing his clothes to Sophia.

"Nothing," she announced.

"Turn around," Haji ordered.

Instead, Father Lion looked directly at him and said, "Jesus loves you and Jesus loves me, and Jesus doesn't want you to hurt me." Quietly he added, "I have so little money because I'm a priest."

Willis shook his head. "Jesus. All the random targets and we pick a priest."

"In the Honda, both of you," Haji barked at his companions. "You're driving," he ordered Sophia. "Get outta here. You know where to meet me."

Willis threw Lion's walking stick out the window as the Honda drove off, Michael barking frantically, jumping at the back window, the red lights of his traffic collar winking small alarms.

"And you, on your knees." Haji prodded him with the barrel of the gun.

Father Lion knelt, expecting to be executed. *So, this is how it ends, in violence after all.* He prayed aloud, "Father, forgive Kevin for he doesn't know what he's doing to himself. Watch over Michael, have mercy on me a sinner and welcome me home."

Haji turned abruptly, climbed into the parked van, and drove off. Lion, trembling, quickly dressed, gathered his things, and set out toward Kailua-Kona on foot. Anguished, he prayed for Michael and apologized to his mother for the loss of the stole.

*All the suffering in the world, Lord, and I'm asking you to watch out for a dog. You can handle it, Father, the wars, genocides, terrorism, and*

90

*a missing mixed-breed dog, without one distracting from another.*

Just after dawn, on the fringes of Kailua town, where the dive operators and luau vendors advertise in luridly colored signs, he saw the Honda abandoned on the side of the road. He ran toward it, hoping to find Michael asleep on the seat. He was Abeed again, running for his life, terrified and expectant, relying on God to save him, to save Michael. Dogs die quickly in a closed car.

Michael wasn't there.

Utterly exhausted, the priest arrived at St. Michael's parish. Before greeting the pastor or calling the police to make a report, Lion slipped into the dim light of the airy old church beneath the tall trees. He had no words with which to pray. He just knelt before the altar, hunched over the pew, and let his spirit pray for him in groans and sighs and incomprehensible sounds. Lion couldn't be sure how long he prayed, perhaps moments, maybe an hour, but he found he had been crying.

Father Simon, the pastor of Saint Michael the Archangel, was an elderly Irish priest, who in better times for the Church, would have happily retired to a life of Gregorian chant and intercessory prayer, perhaps visited by widowed sisters bearing cakes and invitations to Sunday dinner. His hair was stark white, his entire face rosy. He had a ready smile and perpetually wet, startled blue eyes. He persuaded Father Lion to report his experience not only to the police but to the Humane Society so they could be on the lookout for his dog.

That evening, they dined at the Kona Inn on the bay. Across the water, at the mouth of the harbor, the restored temple of Kamehameha the Great loomed, oddly unsettling even today, with its carved god images and the prayer tower holding fresh tribute. After almost two centuries of Christianity, Hawiians still brought temple offerings of taro or fruit tied in ti leaf bundles and leis that dried in the sun. Tourists in vivid new muumuus and aloha shirts were paraded past the temple on the way to the King Kamehameha Hotel's luau grounds. The tourists probably never realized how close they were to ancient ceremonies and old spirits.

"Sad in a way, isn't it?" Father Lion said.

"Humph, some things are best left behind." Father Simon's wet eyes never quite overflowed into tears. "I heard tales that my own people copulated with horses before Saint Patrick showed up. And thank the Lord for the good saint. I wouldn't want to hear a confession like that." He swirled his whiskey. "I imagine you've got your share of voodoo gods in Africa demanding all manner of dark rituals, killing bats and virgins and chickens. For the first time in history, the Muslims now outnumber the Catholics. Of course, if we include the bloody Protestants, we're still ahead of them."

Lion suspected the dinner and conversation were all to distract him from the loss of his dog and his own narrow escape. He blamed himself for the situation. "I was so naive to set out at night. I just wanted to avoid the heat of the day."

"We've got some crazy people on this island, that's for sure. Dog fights, cock fights. Chop shops. Drugs. The cops turn a blind eye."

"Dog fights?" Lion choked. .

"Yeah. They kidnap small dogs, little pets. Use 'em for bait to train the pit bulls."

"I should have paid attention to my dog. Michael didn't want to get in that car. He knew it was trouble. I knew it, and still I got in. Why?"

"I'd have done the same. Always trying to be Mr. Nice Guy, Mr. No Offense. Is your dog microchipped?"

"Yes."

"Thank God for that. I'm an incorrigible optimist despite all evidence mitigating against sunny outcomes."

"Then maybe you can help in another matter. Do you know parishioners named Sharmain and Wanda Tamsing?"

Father Simon's face lit up with gratitude to be off the subject of the dog. "Salt of the earth. Good people. Mrs. Tamsing's in charge of the altar guild and he's an usher."

"I met their granddaughter, Tori. She's living with her mother and the mother's boyfriend under a tarp on the old lava flow near Manuka."

"Yes, I heard about that. Bad scene."

"I believe she's in grave danger. I'd like to talk with the grandparents."

"We can call on them tomorrow. Wanda's been a wreck over the whole thing, but there isn't much she can do. Lord knows she's tried. She even got a lawyer. No dice." He sipped his drink. "Where do you go from here? Saint Benedict's?"

"Yes."

"When the time comes, I'll drive you."

They continued their dinner in the long shadow of ancient deities, listening to a faint thunder of drums from the luau grounds.

Lion's Way

# Chapter 13

## A TRICK OF THE EYE

Amidst the miniaturized splendor of the great cathedral of Burgos, Spain, Father Lion knelt and prayed for his dog. He tried to purge himself of whimpering self-pity: *I don't ask for much, Lord, just my dog.* And the bargaining bravado: *I'm your servant Lord. I signed on for life. You owe me.*

He just wanted his dog back, and he wanted God's will to bend to his own. *Saint Benedict's my last church on this island, Lord. I'm ordered to Maui after this. Am I to leave Michael behind in the care of thieves or worse? Please, at least, make sure Michael has food and water and don't let him be thrown to the pit bulls.* Lion again apologized to God. Guiltily, he added prayers for all the children, orphans and slaves, who went to bed hungry every night. He knelt for a long period, unaware of the passage of time.

Slowly, Father Lion got up from his knees and turned on the lights. He noticed the details of the splendid *trompe l'oeil* cathedral painted on the walls of this tiny church in Honaunau by Father John Velge, a Belgian priest as obscure as himself. In the light of the waning day, the painted palms on the columns went from green to black. Saint Francis of Assisi knelt in his grotto receiving the stigmata. Jesus rose in full Biblical glory, poised on a cliff, casting Satan down into the abyss. Daniel stood before Belshazzar, king of the Chaldeans, explaining the mystical handwriting on the wall. No wonder the Chaldean king was baffled, the writing was in Hawaiian. *"Ua Emi Loa Oe Aupuni; Make no ka Pono.* The remaining three murals adorning the sides of the church depicted Cain murdering Abel, the horrors of Hell and the delights of a good death. In happy contrast, the statues of Jesus and Mary were draped in fresh flower leis.

Headlights in the church's driveway announced the punctual arrival of his dinner. A wiry woman bristling with energy introduced herself as Ola and handed him a tray holding a steaming hot, covered casserole dish. "You carry that, Father. I manage the rest."

She quickly set the table in the rectory, put a pot of orchids in the middle and spread broad, shiny *laua'e* fern around it. She offered mochiko chicken, choi sum, spinach salad with star fruit, dried cranberries and toasted almonds, and finally, "This, Father, is special for you, African Rice Salad. I found the recipe online."

Father Lion had never tasted anything quite like it, tangy with peanuts and parsley. "It's delicious," he said, truthfully.

"Like your mama used to make?"

He dabbed at his mouth. "My mother had no computer to go online and find such a wonderful recipe. But if she could have Googled, I'm sure she would have prepared a dish just like this."

They both laughed.

"Your mama still around or she with the Lord?"

"She's in South Sudan with my sister. They were in a refugee camp for years but now they're going home."

"Life is so hard, yah?"

Lion heard an old sorrow surface in her voice and sat back, prepared to listen.

"I had a little girl, Father. Her name was Anuhea." Ola savored the name as she said it. "Anuhea was one of those *punahele* children, nothing but joy. She made my heart glad just to be with her. I melted when I watched her curled up in sleep. She was the apple of her daddy's eye." Ola smiled, shaking her head.

"Then she got the meningitis, not the spinal kine, but cerebral meningitis, and in two days she was gone, before we could even say goodbye. Just like that. I looked at her lying there on the hospital bed, so perfect, just like she was sleeping. I kept waiting in terror for her next breath."

"You know you will see your child again."

"I know that, Father. I believe it." She laughed loudly at herself. "And that's why I'm so darn good, cooking for priests, cleaning the church, doing all I can for the Lord because when he calls me, I want to be sure I'm going straight to where there's a little angel named Anuhea waiting for her mama."

"How is your husband doing?"

"He's fine, but no more my husband. Not his fault, Father. He just couldn't handle. Every time we looked at each other, we saw only sorrow. A man cannot live like that. A woman is better at grief. He found someone who made him happy again. He has a nice family with her now. He's a good man. And I know, Father, that if I ever need him, I just call and Harvey be right there for me. But Father, I'm an independent woman. And I have Jesus. My life is full of music and love and friends. I write songs, you know. *Himeni,* the sacred songs in Hawaiian."

She launched into a lesson on Hawaiian music, how in ancient times it had beat but no melody. "Then the missionaries brought their hymns. That's why everyone converted to Christianity. The missionaries were smart, they didn't start out with catechism class, they organized singing schools. The people would have followed Jesus anywhere as long as they could sing." Suddenly excited, she begged, "Father Lion, come to the church now."

They turned on all the lights, lit the votive candles and climbed to the small choir loft. Ola uncovered the organ and began to play. Her fingers flew over the keys, the music rising and swirling, then sighing and whispering. Her rich, strong voice belted out, "*Ma'ke a la hele o Iesu...*" She moved effortlessly from song to song, flooding the church with passion. Then, with an intricate prelude, she sang, almost in a whisper, Gounod's *Ave Maria.* Her range was impressive, her "Amen" holy and clear.

"That was beautiful," Lion said.

She covered the organ. "Oh, I was just showing off." She took his hand momentarily. "Let me be your tour guide." She led him down the narrow stairs and around the church, telling him about the murals. "They're famous. They're in a book, *Angels Over the Altar.* It says, and I quote, 'Here on a hillside in Hawaii, we beheld a little corner of medieval Europe, not approached through artifice or sophistication, but surviving in a direct, incredible line of descent.'"

She then translated the Hawaiian inscriptions painted on the supporting columns in fanciful banners. "This one says, 'May the holy cross be my light. Let not the dragon be my guide.'" She ended with *'He poine kou mea ininini mai ai. Nau no e inu kou poino.* Never suggest to me thy vanities. May you drink your own poison.'"

As she turned out the lights and snuffed the candles she said, "I think about that one a lot. It sounds harsh, but I see mean people do that all the time. They hurt someone else, or they hold anger in their hearts, and pretty soon they poison their own selves. They're dead. Maybe still walking around, but *ma'ke.* You know what I mean?"

"It can be collective poison, too," Lion said. "Whole societies, nations, can poison themselves. They develop a taste for destruction."

"That's right, Father. You know. You've seen the worst." She lightened the moment with laughter. "But now you lucky come Hawaii."

"I sometimes feel I have no right to be here. I should be in Africa doing something to alleviate the suffering and hardship. But I have taken a vow of obedience, the hardest vow of all. Poverty and chastity are, as you say, 'a piece of cake' compared to obedience."

"Obedience is not an issue with me, Father. No one is my boss. And chastity gets easier with age. But poverty? That gets harder with age." She hugged Father Lion in parting. "I left cereal, papaya, and banana bread for your breakfast."

"You are most kind. And *mahalo nui loa* for the concert."

"You're a good *hanai* Hawaiian. I see you tomorrow night. The place going to be packed."

"Will you sing your *Ave Maria* before I speak? You'll give me courage."

"Praise God. I will be happy to do that. But it's you they want to hear. You famous, Father." She laughed. "God's rock star."

In the morning, Father Lion again telephoned the Humane Society, to no avail. He then set out down the mountain to visit Pu'uhonua O Honaunau, an ancient place of refuge where the gods of old Hawaii are kept in a park, like dangerous wildlife.

Michael's absence was keenly felt as Lion walked in his long, ground-devouring lope. At the park, he strolled among the massive stone remnants of the old temple complex and marveled at its size and complexity. Every island once had such a place, where criminals and anyone in danger could flee, where women and children sequestered themselves for safety in time of war. Once inside the walls, they were untouchable. When the men stopped fighting, the women and children went home. When the criminals repented and were rehabilitated, they were free to leave the sanctuary and live unmolested in their communities.

Gazing at the carved wooden *ki'i,* Father Lion understood a little better Father John Velge's passion to create a magnificent place of worship. *Look at the competition,* Lion thought. *Look what the poor priest was up against. These do not appear to be gentle spirits. Father Velge knew he had to conjure something impressive to win the souls of people accustomed to such awesome deities.*

The Belgian missionary had feverishly painted every available surface in his little church, doing his small part to redirect these deeply spiritual people to the good news of the gospel.

Lion wiped his brow and wished he could remain at Pu'uhonua for the sunset, but he had a sermon to deliver.

That evening, three hundred people crowded into the parish hall to hear Father Lion speak, then trickled in afterwards to confess their sins. One by one he sent them home assured of God's love, regardless of what they had done. He prayed long after they had gone. *"Have pity on us, Lord, we are so helpless, our bodies so vulnerable. We lose dogs, car keys, people we love. Shine your light on our path as we stumble toward you."*

Ola arrived in the morning to drive Lion to the airport for his flight to Honolulu. Just as he was telephoning the Humane Society one last time, a car pulled into the driveway. Ola tugged the curtain aside. "That's the Tamsings' car. Aloha, Wanda," she called through the screen.

"Oh, good," Lion said. "I can ask her about her granddaughter."

Ola grinned. "No need. There's a girl with her and, sweet baby Jesus, Lion, is it...?"

A dog bolted from the car, quivering and whining, pawing the rectory door.

"Michael." Lion opened the door and the dog flew at him, jumping off the floor, crying and licking in paroxysms of slobbery happiness.

Ola said, "If only everyone we love was so happy to see us."

Wanda Tamsing, her heavily sprayed bouffant hair standing up stiffly, put her arm around her granddaughter. "I'm just as happy as that dog to get my hands on this girl. If I wasn't so old, I'd do flips, too."

Tori put her hands on her hips, distancing herself from her grandmother's embrace. Radiating tough confidence and relishing her role as dog-rescuer, she said to Father Lion, "Some druggies came to see Sapman. He wasn't home. They had your dog with them. I remembered him, so I told them, 'I give you ice, you give me the dog.' Hey, no contest. Sapman beat me up when he got home, so I got even. I told my mom about how her lover boy was always after me. She grabbed the baby and told me to get in the truck right away. I took Michael with me or Sapman woulda shot him." Tori's swagger crumbled. She bit her thin lips. "My mom drove me to Hilo. I thought she was breaking away from Sapman, but she gave me some money and told me never to come back."

Wanda again put her arm around Tori and this time the girl bent into her grandmother's shape as Wanda stroked her hair. "Honey, I know it's harsh, but that's the best thing your Mom ever did for you, besides giving birth to you."

Lion knelt on one knee, alternately hugging Michael and fending off the dog's enthusiasm. "Thank you, Tori, for bringing my dog home." He stood up and turned to Ola, "This is the girl I was telling you about who had a piano in the middle of the lava."

"You like to play?" Ola asked.

"More than anything. But I'm no good."

"Let's see just how bad you are." Ola led the girl into the church. They all climbed to the choir loft. Carefully, almost reverently she removed the cover from the piano, ran her hand along the bench and invited, "Play whatever you want, Tori. Anything."

Tori sighed deeply and sat down with a lowered head. Her hands grazed the keys making no sound, then in barely perceptible movements she began to play, rambling over the instrument, releasing airy melodies that rolled into substance then back to ephemera. There was no conclusion. She just stopped.

Ola sat beside her on the bench. They could have been mother and daughter captured in a moment of intimacy. "That was lovely. Will you help me with the choir, Tori?"

"Me? How?"

"I need someone to help with the music on Sundays. In return, I'll work with you on the piano, give you exercises, lessons. Tori, the good Lord has given you a gift. He picked you out and blessed you with music. I will help you make the most of it, and when you have learned all I have to give you, I will pass you along to others with more talent than me. What piece was that you played? I didn't recognize it."

"It's nothing. I just made it up as I went along. It's what I played on the lava. Some of the keys on my piano were out of tune so I had to work around them. It's my own song."

# Chapter 14
FLAME

Lion waited in the reception room of the diocesan office. The bishop's secretary, Carlene, asked, "You want something to drink? Tea? Passion orange?"

"Water would be nice, thank you."

"The dog, too?"

He nodded.

Carlene, short, wide and matronly beyond her thirty-five years, moved with alarming energy. She was from Brooklyn and quite belligerent about it, maintaining that the poisons in the city's air pollution had given her super powers. She just hadn't found out what they were yet. She returned with a bowl and glass, huffing in elaborate annoyance, and complained, "His Graceship has someone in there. A woman. Looks like trouble to me. She wouldn't give me her name. I told her that His Magnificence was busy, and she'd have to make an appointment. But no. She just parked herself in a chair like she owned the joint and said, 'I'll wait.' She said she knew him. Humph. Money, money, money written all over her." Carlene whispered conspiratorially, "Expensive blond hair. A Chanel bag."

"Maybe she's family."

"She's something, that's for sure." Carlene arched her tweezed and penciled brows in disapproval. "She called him Jimmy. His Holyship turned white as my stationary."

The door opened. Normally fastidious in his appearance, the bishop's Roman collar hung loose, and perspiration stained his shirt. The woman was attractive for her years, well-groomed, and wearing a yellow linen dress with gold sandals. Her toenails glittered. The bishop towered over her. She tilted her head slightly and smiled tentatively as the bishop, in his best magisterial voice, introduced her, "Patsy, may I present our resident conscience, Father Lion Majok of Africa. Lion, this is Patsy Barrett."

"Maccia," she corrected him, smiling more uncertainly.

Lion stood and gently took her proffered hand as if it were made of glass. "My pleasure."

"Is your dog from Africa, too?"

"He's a Waimanalo poi dog."

The bishop explained, "A local mutt."

"He's adorable. Did anyone ever tell you he looks like Margaret Thatcher?"

"His mother is a dead ringer." Lion laughed. "Father's known only to God."

The bishop blushed and swept his arm expansively, "And this is the woman I can't live without, my secretary, Carlene O'Donnell. I believe you've already met."

"Chawmed, I'm sure," Carlene said, oozing hospitality. "Do you need parking validation, Mrs. Maccia?" She stamped the ticket as if killing something.

Patsy Barrett Maccia turned to the bishop. "I know you're busy, so I'll be on my way."

A faint trace of expensive perfume lingered in her wake. Carlene sniffed. "Shalimar. In the daytime." She rolled her eyes.

The bishop asked, "Do I have any more appointments for today?"

Carlene glanced at her appointment book. "Father Blanchard at three."

"Call him and reschedule."

"We've already done that twice."

"Alright, alright. I suppose I have to swallow that frog, so it's best not to look at it too long. Move Blanchard to four o'clock and I'll be back in time. Come, Lion, we're going on a little drive." He handed him his car keys. "You're driving." When Lion glanced at his dog, the bishop said, "Carlene will watch him," and swept out of the office as if to thunderous applause.

Carlene rolled her eyes again. "I wonder what bee got into His Pomposity's bonnet. Good luck, Father. Your mutt will be fine. Won't cha, boy?" She patted him roughly.

As they snaked up the mountain past multimillion-dollar estates with their gaudy electronic gates, guest houses, swimming pools and statuary wedged into the rainforest, Bishop Carroll asked Lion about Kintu. "Heard any news about the trial?"

"Nothing yet."

"Well, I've interfered in your life once again. I had Wills wire money for a defense lawyer to your Bishop of Sudan. What's his name?"

"Binda."

"Bishop Desmond Binda, of course. How could I forget?"

Bishop Carroll had astounding recall for names and numbers. Lion knew this lapse was an indication of the degree of the man's agitation, which he strongly suspected had something to do with Mrs. Maccia.

"Wills has agreed to pick up the tab to fight any indictment and/or extradition, and if all that fails, he'll be sure your brother is accurately represented in the Hague. Apparently, he's already gotten Kintu into a secure rehab facility."

Lion was overwhelmed and when he tried to thank Bishop Carroll, the bishop cut him off with an inquiry about the Kamana family.

Lion said. "Pops seems to be holding his own with the chemo. He has a lot of spirit."

"Good man, good man. The best."

"I am very grateful to you for what you're doing for my brother, and I'll always be grateful that you arranged for me to be part of the Kamana family."

"Did I ever tell you how it all came about?" The bishop then launched into the story Lion had heard many times before. "It was quite the evening, that first night I heard about you." The bishop turned up the air conditioning, fiddled with the vents, and straightened his Roman collar. "I took the good Bishop Binda to my favorite restaurant in Rome, La Pergola. We were in Rome for the Papal Conference on Persecuted Christian Minorities. Binda was the principal speaker. Fascinating talk. Fascinating. Did you know, Lion, that in the two thousand years of our faith, approximately seventy million people have been killed, simply for following the gentle teachings of Jesus Christ?"

"Yes," Lion said, braking for a hairpin turn. "And most killed since the beginning of the twentieth century."

"The bishop continued, "I believe the figure is sixty-five percent, which is about forty-five million murdered Christians, give or take a few poor souls."

Lion glanced at Bishop Carroll sitting so comfortably next to him in his air-conditioned Mercedes and said, "In my country of South Sudan plus the northern Sudan, more than a million and a half Christians have been butchered by the Janjaweed since 1984."

"Janjaweed?"

Bitterness crept into Lion's voice, "Janjaweed is a radical Muslim militia who indulge in genocide as sport. They've taken more than two-hundred-thousand people, mostly women and children from my tribe, Dinka, into slavery. That is to say nothing of the rape, mutilation, torture, and murder, including the murder of my father and my youngest brother. My mother and sister had to flee to a refugee camp. And the world does nothing." Lion pulled to the side of the road to compose himself. The bishop cleared his throat, lifted a hand as if to pat or embrace Lion then let the hand fall back into his lap and stared straight ahead. Finally, Lion, with great weariness, said, "The world does nothing and neither do I."

"Well, I do, Lion. Or rather, I make sure good old Wills does."

"It doesn't excuse me."

Bishop Carroll sighed deeply in either compassion or annoyance. Lion couldn't be sure which. "I'm sorry for your suffering, Lion. You may blame me for not releasing you back to Africa, if you like, but guilt doesn't become you. Guilt is not of the Spirit." Looking out the window at a showy wrought iron gate mounted with security cameras, the bishop concluded rather absently, "I'm afraid the world looks on Africa as a basket case." He glanced at his watch. "And you are not the Messiah."

Lion pulled back out on the upward bound road, hating the Mercedes, hating his cushioned life. "Yes, Africa is a basket case, but a basket of the world's own weaving."

The rebuke hung in the air like an unpleasant odor until the bishop said, "You're doing all you can, Lion, all those doubled dinner tabs are going straight into Binda's account." He straightened himself, somehow inflating his presence. "I remember the night we made the deal for you. Across the entire U.S., the number of Catholics has increased by thirty-two percent to more than sixty-four million faithful, while the number of priests has declined by twenty-two percent. There are more priests in America over ninety than under thirty. In Hawaii, we've been recruiting priests from the Philippines for years and we're still short. We've got doddering priests managing huge parishes, priests who should be retired but there's nobody in the pipeline."

"America's not hungry enough. Poor nations produce priests."

Ever the diplomat, Bishop Carroll said, "I don't think it's the hunger so much as the fact that the developed nations have low birth rates. When a family has but one son, they don't want him in the priesthood. He must carry on the family name, that sort of thing."

"And so you poach young seminarians from poor countries."

The bishop dipped his head, froggishly doubling his chin. "I don't think of it as poaching. We offer young men like yourself an education they otherwise wouldn't have, in return for serving here as priests. My brother Wills finances our seminarian program, including your tutors."

As intended, Lion felt chastened.

Bishop Carroll continued, "Do you know what your Bishop Binda said when we were walking across Saint Peter's Square, in the shadow of Michelangelo's dome and Bernini's two hundred eighty-four Doric columns?" Without waiting for an answer, he continued, "Your amazing bishop said, 'I can't help wondering what poor Jesus would think if he happened to wander through the Vatican in his sandals. I rather doubt he would be at home there.'

"Binda has a point. You'll have to come to Rome someday, Lion. Yes. You have a brilliant future ahead of you." He added, "One day, I'll take you to La Pergola. Binda was so impressed with the vermeil tableware, the tapestries and Dresden porcelains, I thought for a moment he was going to genuflect right there in the restaurant."

They had reached the park at the top of the mountain, emerging from damp greens into sunshine. Without prelude Bishop Carroll got out of the car and commanded the hilltop looking out over the city of Honolulu, all its concrete canyons blinding the eye. "Look at this," he said as Lion joined him. "Here we are on a little mote of land in the middle of the ocean, and we've got skyscrapers and freeways." He swept his arm theatrically across the vista. "Let's sit down."

They retreated to a bench in the shade. The bishop looked around, making sure they had the park to themselves. "I have a most grave matter I need to discuss with you in the utmost confidence."

Abruptly he got up from the bench. "It's too hot, too sunny. I'm breaking out in a rash. Let's go back down. We'll talk in the cathedral."

"It's not anything about... You haven't had any bad news from Sudan, have you?"

"No, no, nothing like that. This is all about me, I'm afraid."

They rode in silence, each man praying for the other. As they pulled into the underground garage of the diocesan building, Bishop Carroll said, "What sealed the deal for me, when Binda and I discussed the possibility of bringing you here, was your apparition of Father Damien. And I want you to know that when we had worked out all the details, Binda said I would never be sorry for choosing you. And he was right."

"Thank you."

They entered the dim interior of the historic cathedral to find an old woman kneeling before the Blessed Virgin statue rubbing the plaster toe, and a homeless man napping in a pew. Nodding toward the man, Lion whispered, "He certainly picked a nice safe place to sleep it off, didn't he?"

"They urinate on the floor, spit in the holy water fountains and help themselves to the candle money. I'm considering locking the church when there are no services in progress, but I'm hesitant to do that, because many people enjoy stopping in for a few quiet minutes."

"Perhaps you can work out a schedule of volunteer monitors."

"Good idea. Well..." Bishop Carroll gestured toward the confessional. "Best done this way."

"Do you need time for examination of conscience?"

"I'm quite clear, thank you."

Lion sat in the dark and waited, praying he would be able to hear without obvious shock, the sins of a bishop, which must, of necessity, be more grandiose than those of the average penitent.

The formal confession began with the ritual prayers, then the bishop said, "I have fathered a child."

After a long pause, the startled Father Lion cautiously asked, "Excellency, you broke your vow of celibacy?"

The "No." was emphatic. "It happened a long time ago, before I professed my vows. I was in high school as a matter of fact. I took a classmate to the prom. The woman you met in my office, Patsy Barrett. Well, we were both ignorant kids and after the prom we had too much to drink at a nightclub in Manhattan, and, well, I never knew she got pregnant. Nobody told me. I didn't see her again until today when she informed me that I had a son and that he wanted to meet me before being deployed to Afghanistan. He's stationed at Schofield. Married with three children. It seems I'm a grandfather too, although that is a much more difficult admission due to the sin of vanity, to which I must also confess."

"You have carried this sexual sin on your soul all this time, throughout your priestly life?"

"No, no, no. I confessed it before ever entering the priesthood. But finding out that my transgression resulted in a child seems to cry out for some further clarification or chastisement or wisdom. I'm not sure what

I need, but I needed to tell someone, to confess it aloud."

"Thank you for trusting me."

"I trust the sacrament." The bishop quickly amended. "I chose you because God has gifted you for this particular ministry. People come to you burdened and you free them from their yokes. I get the reports all the time. It's a true calling, Lion. Not to be lightly dismissed. Oh, I know you think you should be a Trappist monk with raw knees. That or Africa. But I know something else that you don't. I know that you really don't want to go back to Africa even though you think you should want to."

Lion was startled. "I have to ponder that, Excellency."

"Do."

"But it is you, Excellency, partaking of the sacrament today. There is no sin here, but I think you need to advise your superiors about this development."

"You are entirely right, Lion, but I'm not ready. Do you realize that any elevations I might have politicked for are now precluded?"

"Perhaps it's time for you to step back, relinquish control, leave decisions concerning your future up to your superiors and God. And leave issues of your relationship with your son up to your son. He has asked for you before he goes into battle."

"Yes, it's his needs that are important, not mine."

"Are you going to meet him?"

"Yes, but I'm not sure where. It should be on neutral ground, public but not too public. Certainly not at a meal. Too much of a commitment, too awkward. We might be seen."

Lion thought a moment and suggested, "The Byodo-In."

"The Buddhist temple in Haiku?"

"You won't meet any of your flock there. They've got a nice garden."

"Lion, will you come with me?"

"I will if you want, but I think it would be better if it were just the two of you."

"I don't know if I'll be able to drive."

"I'll drive you then, and I'll disappear. I'll bring a book and sit in a far corner of the garden so you can have your privacy. You can take all the time you want."

The bishop's head scraped against the confessional screen as he bowed it. "I am so full of sorrow, Lion. I'm grieving for missing my son's youth and his mother's ordeal, and I'm ashamed to say, I'm grieving for my own future. For the first time in my life, I feel mired in the common human morass."

Lion was moved to pity. "A son is a gift from God. That's something my own father said to me every day, including the day he was murdered. Since that fateful day, I have been blessed with many fathers, including you, Your Grace."

"Thank you, Lion. I look on you with the concern of a parent."

Lion ritually blessed the bishop and concluded the sacrament. He opened the confessional door and watched the bishop make his way uncertainly toward the altar and kneel before the tabernacle. Lion thought about Africa. The bishop was right. He was afraid.

# Chapter 15
## SQUARE PEGS

Michael, wearing a lei of silk flowers, greeted Lion in the bishop's office. The dog's breath smelled of tuna fish.

Carlene knelt and hugged Michael to her ample bosom. "I shared my lunch. Right, boy? I can well afford to miss a meal and you're such a nice doggie. You love tuna salad on rye, don't you? Tell your daddy you love tuna on rye but hold the pickle." She asked, "Where's Lord Bountiful, the slave driver?"

"Still at the cathedral," Lion answered.

"Is he okay?"

"What do you mean?"

"I'm an RN, for crying out loud. I can see that something, and I mean something major, has really upset him. He came out of his office like a bird on a hot wire."

Lion nodded. "You're very perceptive, Carlene. And what, may I ask, is a nurse doing working as a secretary when there is such need of healing in the world?"

Carlene struggled to her feet. Her hair had the grey hue of a nuisance bird. "Ooh, ooh. Do I hear a moralistic scolding?" She leaned on the desk a moment, narrowed her eyes to slits and retaliated: "Well, let me lay the truth on you, Father. I'm a pediatric nurse by training, and I got burned out. I had it up to here." Her hand met her several chins. "I cared for sick and dying children, praying for and with them, then over their dead bodies, while dealing with their parents' grief. Go ahead, call me unprofessional, but I loved every child in my care. Then one day I asked myself, what kind of a God does this to innocent little children? Huh? Little children bald from chemo, dying with sweet smiles on their ravaged faces, trying to console their parents. And what about you, Father Lion?" She emphasized Lion. "What are you doing in nice cushy Hawaii when there's so much suffering in Africa? And while we're on the subject of Africa, how does God explain all the pain over there? He is a miser with the rain while crops dry up and people and animals starve. Father, I am a survivor not only of a career crisis but a faith crisis. I'm here because I needed a break from death. This job came up. I got recommended and here I am."

"Forgive me," Lion said. "I didn't mean to offend you. Suffering wouldn't bother you so much if you didn't have a big heart."

She turned away, stiff with the effort of not crying. When she spun back to face him, she put her hands squarely on her hips. "Well, you're right about the need for healing in the world. That's the thing of it. I know you're right. But I still say, God made this mess, or perhaps more accurately, God sat back and did zilch. He allowed us to make this mess, the wars and genocides, so, let him do something about it."

"He did."

"Yeah?" She raised her chin in challenge. "What?"

Softly, Lion said, "He made you."

She paraded past him. "You really know how to hit a girl, Father."

The door closed behind her none too gently, leaving Lion alone in the bishop's office. "Well, Michael, I guess I'll never be the ambassador of anything."

As he let himself out, Lion saw Carlene had nested back at her desk.

She looked up at him. Her weepy eyes, her weight and her oily grey hair reflected the whole condition of her life. She pleaded, "Please, Father, don't say anything to the bishop about how unhappy I am. I have to figure out what to do with myself, but right now I really need this job to pay my rent."

He asked, "Do you have family in the Islands who can help you?"

"Code for am I married? No. I never married. Probably never will. I'll certainly never have kids. My biological clock already ran down. Thanks for that, too, God. My father still lives in Brooklyn, but he's a nasty old drunk. I refuse to have him in my life. I have a sister in Connecticut and two brothers in New Jersey, all of them cold-hearted. So, the short answer is no, I don't have a family."

"Sometimes we have to step out in faith, make a risky move to open ourselves up, free ourselves for whatever good things God has in store for us."

"I thought I was doing that when I quit my position at the hospital and took a job with the Church. And look at me now: more miserable than ever."

"God is not finished with you, yet."

"Well, he better hurry up and get busy before I'm finished with him."

"I could recite some platitudes such as 'God's time is not our time,' but you deserve better. I promise to pray for you every day because I know what it's like to be doing your best and wondering if it's the true work to which you are called."

"You know what?" She stood up defiantly. "I'll pray for you, too, Father." She hurled the offer at him as if it were a weapon. "I'll pray for you every day, because this sick world not only needs nurses but Africa needs priests."

Lion put out his hand. "We've got ourselves a deal."

Carlene softened immediately, ignored his hand and hugged him.

The bishop cleared his throat to announce his presence. "I thought you'd be off with your dog by now." He was clearly uncomfortable facing Lion so soon after confessing he had a son. He leafed through his phone messages and asked Carlene, "Are the monthly financials on my desk?"

"They are, Your Grace. You'll note a paw print on the first page. Michael's seal of approval."

Bishop Carroll was all business, no smiles, but he had an uncharacteristically disheveled look. He turned to Lion before entering his office. "I'll call you as soon as I set the appointment we discussed." He closed his door behind him.

The meeting with the bishop's son was set for the following day. Lion drove, leaving Michael again in the care of Carlene. As he drove over the Pali, Lion said, "Carlene seems to be doing a good job."

"I'm sure Saint Francis loves her. She feeds feral cats." Bishop Carroll then called attention to the rainbows, three of them vaulting across the mountains. "A hopeful omen, Lion. I don't know how to behave as a father. I don't know what's expected of me. How am I to love this son I've never met"?

"Tell him some family stories. Tell him about your mother and father, his grandparents. Tell him about your gift for numbers."

"He's a captain in the army. West Point graduate. He distinguished himself in Iraq. He's been here at Schofield Barracks almost a year, but Patsy, his mother, said he didn't have the nerve to call me. That's why she flew out here from New York to break the ice."

"It must have been very difficult for her all those years ago; pregnant, unmarried."

"There's my position to consider, too, Lion. Wouldn't the press just love to get their hands on this. Can't you see the headlines: *Honolulu Bishop Fathers a Child.* Nobody would bother to read that it happened before I became a priest. I'm finished, Lion. Any ambitions I harbored have detonated."

Lion made the turn off Kahekili Highway into the Valley of the Temples. "As we approach, shall we pray that your heart is prepared to receive your son and give to him whatever it is that he needs from you, and that his heart be prepared to receive you?"

"This is why you're so good for me, Lion. You don't oil the tongue. You get right to the heart of the matter. Lead the prayer, please."

The two men prayed as they passed the rolling hills of the Catholic portion of the temple's burial grounds and rounded the curve to the Buddhist section with its black marble gravestones inscribed in gold *kanji.* The bishop commented, "The dead, it seems, are excused from ecumenism, to sleep comfortably as tenants among their own tenets."

Lion stopped a moment as the vermillion temple came into view, set like a brilliant jewel against the sheer green palisade of the Ko'olau Mountains.

"It's beautiful," the bishop said. "I can't believe I've never been here."

"I used to come here often when I was in seminary. I never found my answers here, but I believe the Buddha taught me to ask the big questions." He drove on to the parking area.

"Well, I did some reading since you suggested this place, Lion. Did you know the temple is an exact replica of a nine-hundred-year-old temple in Uji, Japan? That the Buddha is eighteen-feet high? And supposedly there's a seven-ton bronze bell somewhere."

"You're supposed to ring it to add years to your life."

"Why would anyone want to do that?" the bishop asked. "I mean, if we really believe in Heaven as we say we do, we should be anxious to get there as soon as possible."

"It's just over the bridge."

"What? Heaven?"

"The bell."

"That's where I'll wait for my son, by the long-life bell. He's going to Afghanistan in a few days. I'll have him give it a few extra gongs."

A long arched footbridge led to the bronze bell, the ponds, and the huge statue of the Buddha. "I'll wait in the upper garden," Lion said. He walked up the slope, past rushing streams and quiet pools filled with koi until he found his favorite bench. He looked back down. Through the shrubbery he could see the bishop, pacing, waiting, scanning the bridge, and the little clusters of tourists chatting, taking pictures, waiting for straggling spouses. Then Lion saw a young man stride tensely over the bridge. He had the same ginger colored hair as the bishop, even parted on the same side. The bishop recognized his son in the same instant and took a hesitant step forward. The man stopped a moment, glanced about as if for reinforcements, then thrust out his hand in greeting.

"Please," Lion prayed aloud with urgency, "Please give Bishop Carroll the grace to hug his son. Shove them into each other's arms if you must, Lord."

The bishop held out both arms and the two men embraced roughly, stiffly, as Lion watched the mysterious pull of blood to blood take over and the men hug tightly, thumping backs.

Lion looked away as if caught spying on something intensely, beautifully intimate. Tears fell on his prayer book and he ached remembering his own father's thin, ebony arms enfolding a little boy, kissing his soft, tight curls. There were times when Lion walked about the Islands, in the heat of the day, thinking he detected his father's particular scent in his own perspiration. It would be only momentary, but it always stopped him.

When Lion dared to look for the bishop again, he and his son were standing beside the great bronze bell, the son tugging on the thick rope to strike the bell. Its resonance vibrated in the air and echoed against the *pali* of the Ko'olau. Father and son smiled at each other. Lion could almost hear the bishop urging him to ring it again. The son lustily hauled back on the rope, giving the voice of the bell added depth and volume as it reached the mountains and returned in a shimmering blanket of echo.

The bishop gestured toward the gravel path leading to the temple. The two men appeared to be exchanging pleasantries as they walked. They did not fall into step. It wasn't natural. They bent to remove their shoes before entering the sanctuary, accidentally bumped heads and laughed nervously.

Lion lost sight of them as they entered the incense-laden temple. The bishop emerged first, perhaps uncomfortable. Ecumenism was one thing. Obeisance to an eighteen-foot Buddha quite another. The son came out with bowed head. They retrieved their shoes and strolled over a little bridge, pausing to watch the koi swim in their kaleidoscopic mosaics. At the gift shop and snack stand, they took a table, drank from cans and talked. They were too far away for Lion to discern anything so he retreated to his prayer book, checking on them occasionally. They were examining a cell phone, probably looking at photographs.

About twenty minutes went by before Lion looked again. The bishop had his right hand extended over his son, lightly touching his hair, obviously blessing him. A peacock's raucous shriek pierced the air. The son rose, rather formally, shook his father's hand, turned and walked away. Bishop Carroll called after him. The son appeared to pause momentarily. Perhaps he hadn't heard the bishop's words over the shrill din of the peacocks now screaming from several corners. In any event, he did not look back. He walked like a leader of men, confident and burdened.

The bishop looked bereft. Lion hurried to join him. He sat across from him and waited.

In a dull monotone, Bishop Carroll said, "Did you know there are ten thousand koi in these ponds?"

Lion waited without comment.

"Do you know what my son's first words to me were? He said, 'I'm sure I'm a bit of an embarrassment to you.'"

"How did you respond?"

"Inadequately, of course. Why are we priests always so wise in dealing with everyone else's situations, but when it comes to our own, we're as dense as fog? I jauntily said, 'Embarrassment? Shock is more like it.'" Bishop Carroll elaborated, "After all, he's had a few years to get used to having a bishop for a father. I've had two days to absorb having a son."

"He looks just like you. I spotted him instantly."

The bishop smiled, overcome by highly suspect biological pride. "He's a fine man. Patsy told him about me on his eighteenth birthday. The bishop reached into his shirt pocket and handed Lion a photograph of his three grandchildren. This one's Billy. Dan described him as eight, going on twenty-eight. And guess what? He has an amazing gift for math."

"I wonder where he gets that from?"

Bishop Carroll preened. "And this is Betsy, the eldest, just turning twelve and a bit on the moody side, Dan says. Although she looks happy enough here."

Lion said, "She looks like she'll break a lot of hearts someday."

"Or discover the cure for cancer. She's a budding genius, according to her father." He added, "The baby is Emma. I think she looks like my mother, God rest her soul."

He pocketed the photograph. "Dan's wife and children will be staying here in Hawaii while he's gone. They're in military housing at Schofield."

"Will you visit them?"

"No. Dan's wife, Leslie, knows about me, but the children don't. They might say something outside the house, and Dan doesn't want to cause me any grief or scandal." The bishop abruptly stood. "We should be getting back to the office."

As they drove up to the tunnel through the mountains connecting the windward side of the island with Honolulu, Bishop Carroll said, "Daniel told me he almost backed out at the last minute."

"Understandable."

"I never imagined I would have a son. It was something, a happiness, I gave up for God. And now I am acutely aware of my loss in not being a part of my son's life. I'm glad he had a loving stepfather. And his mother, it goes without saying. What a grand and good character she is. At the same time, I'm suddenly, unreasonably jealous of all the Little League games his stepfather attended, every shoe lace he tied." He sighed deeply. "My son didn't even know what to call me."

Lion smiled. "He could just call you Father."

"I deserve no special designation, either clerical or filial. I told him my friends call me Excellency."

"You didn't."

"I'm afraid I did. We didn't settle on anything. He asked for my blessing and left."

They drove in silence until they reached the parking garage. Before they got out of the car, the bishop said, "I have a great favor to ask of you."

"Anything."

"When you're on Maui, I want you to look up Lehua Nii for me. Do you remember her?"

"Your former secretary?" Lion remembered her as a large Hawaiian woman with hair in a bouffant style unseen in decades, and anchored with enough flowers to represent the floral diversity of several Island ecosystems.

"She moved to Wailuku with her twin granddaughters; they're just babies. The mother's a heroin addict. Lehua inherited a big old house. Now she has cancer. See if she needs anything."

"That terrible disease. Of course, I'll call on her. I hope it's not urgent because I planned to spend a couple of days with my family in Waimanalo before I go to Maui."

"Give the Kamanas my regards."

When they reached the diocesan center, Bishop Carroll went directly to his office without greeting Carlene, and closed the door behind him.

Carlene rolled her eyes. "That man. I sometimes think Lord Jim is my penance for a youth of debauchery." She grinned at Lion, as if delighted with remembered wickedness, and held up her hand. "I know, too much information."

It amazed Lion how many people thought sin added to their luster. "Don't forget our prayer pact." He let himself out followed by his lei-bedecked dog.

Carlene called after him, "I'm praying that you go back to Africa. So there."

"I'm praying for God's will in your life, Carlene, that it will be revealed to you and that you follow wherever it leads. Have your spiritual bags packed."

"God's will is it? Okay. But you better dust off your leopard cape and safari helmet just in case it's *sayonara* to you."

Lion's Way

# Chapter 16
## THE BANQUET

Lion and Michael walked the long scenic way to Waimanalo to visit his family before flying to his duties on Maui. They spent the night at Holy Trinity rectory in Niu and set out before dawn. Hugging the bike lane of Kalanianaole Highway, they passed Kuliouou, Hawaii Kai and Koko Kai.

By sunrise, the priest and his dog reached the overlook to Hanauma Bay. It was impossible to see the lacy coral reefs beneath the waves because of the way the morning sun blazed across the water. Lion would have gone down for a swim with Michael, but dogs weren't allowed in the marine sanctuary. "It's okay, Michael, Ka Iwi is up ahead. We'll soak there."

They pushed on to the most beautiful part of the walk, the dramatic lava coastline snaking around Koko Crater. The ocean assaulted the black cliffs, combusting in magnificent white plumes and great sprays, pulling back in aqua curls then rolling in for the next assault. At Sandy Beach, Lion veered off the road to walk along the shore where he could let Michael off the leash to run. He didn't swim because the dog might follow him into the water and get killed in Sandy's notoriously powerful shore break. The wind came up, refreshing his face, his lungs, his spirit as he walked in long, sure strides across the flat land. He looked forward to seeing his family, how Pops was doing with his cancer, if Lili looked pregnant yet with her twins, whether Moses had finally convinced Momi of the splendid fingernails to marry him. He'd miss Pohai, who was away working a show in Las Vegas, but Iris always had a warm smile for him..

Lion and Michael trudged up and down the dunes and over the old bridge across the first lagoon, then walked through the tall grass skirting the other inlets toward a small cove at the base of Makapu'u. They had the little beach to themselves and swam about with great pleasure. After swimming, they rested on the warm, black sand. Lion had a strip of *pipi kaula* for Michael and an energy bar for himself. As they stretched out on the beach, a low moan came to them from across the water. It had an unearthly quality, liquid and longing. He climbed up on the rocky promontory of Makapu'u and shaded his eyes with his arm to look out to sea. And there in the morning calm about a hundred humpback whales were migrating north, swimming and singing to each other in mysterious harmonies that changed every year but were known throughout their leviathan tribe. Their great ponderous shapes darkened the sun-splashed waves. The pod of whales filled Lion with unspeakable joy. He had seen the cetacean skeleton in Bishop Museum and marveled that the flipper bones of the whale were the shape of a human hand. He envied their freedom, their song.

When I die, I shall see all that is veiled. I will see the first man emerge from clay, watch the migrations of tribes and herds going forth to multiply and fill the Earth. He smiled, imagining the day after Judgement Day to be a vast cinematic extravaganza, outdoing even the works of Akira Kirosawa.

The Kamanas, except for their dogs, were expecting him. If rowdy little Thatcher recognized Michael as her puppy, no one would guess it. She gave him no quarter, barking and nagging at his heels all the way from the gate to the house.

It was strange that no one rushed out on the porch at his approach. That was not a good sign. Before Lion could knock, his brother Kawika came to the door and embraced him. "Everything okay?" Lion asked.

"Everything's rubbish. Glad you're here."

A hospital bed dominated the living room, a wizened shape propped on it. Pops looked up at Lion, his eyes luminous. "Soon I gonna see da Lord face to face."

Lion smiled despite his alarm, and fist-bumped Pops, afraid of breaking him in an embrace. "Suppose Saint Peter won't let you in?"

"I tell him I'm your friend, Lion."

"You're my Hawaiian father."

Tears rolled down Pops' desiccated brown cheeks. He grunted in disgust. "You come into dis world naked and bawling and you go out dat way, too. In dis life, you cry enough tears to float your canoe."

Kawika said, with the formality of an attorney, "That's very profound, Pops, because, ultimately we each have to launch and paddle our own canoe out beyond the protective reef and into the breakers to get to the open sea."

Iris came swinging into the room on crutches. "What's all this talk about crying? This is a happy day when our Lion comes."

Lion rushed to her side and kissed her on the cheek. "Mom, what happened?"

"I fell and I got osteoporosis, so my darn leg broke. And my hip. They put an eighteen-inch titanium rod in there."

Kawika put his arm around his mother. "How about that? Mom's a bionic babe." He, too, kissed her on the cheek and she beamed.

"You got my smile spot," she said, touching her cheek.

Kawika didn't have to explain but he always did. "All you have to do is kiss that spot and Mom grins from ear to ear, no matter what: The Ko'olaus fall down, the atom bomb gets dropped, she can't help smiling."

Lion helped ease her into the chair close to Pops. "Where's Lili?" he asked.

"Costco," Iris said. "I don't know what we'd do without her, with Pohai up in Vegas working the show and all."

Cautiously he asked, "How's Lili feeling?" He sipped water.

From his pillows, Pops said, "Lili really coming tru for us, dat girl. Day and night she help us."

Kawika said, "I came over today to give her a break to go shopping, get a pedicure. Who would have guessed, Lili would be the rock of the family?"

"I always know she's a good girl," Iris said. "She's finishing school at night, get her G.E.D."

Lion sat forward, leaning on his knees. "You know, I should be mad at you guys. You got all this going on and you don't even tell me."

"We no want to trouble you, Lion." Iris patted his arm. "You do the Lord's work. We're family, so we hang back."

"As a member of this family, I want to know what's going on."

"Relax, Lion," Kawika said. "They haven't told Pohai either. They're afraid she'd be on the first plane home and blow her career. She's got a big break with this Vegas gig. This is how they want to do it, so we have to respect that. And it's good for Lili to grow up and have some respon-sibility."

Pops said, "We got the hospice, too. Dey come every day, wash me, powder my butt, roll me over. Nice folks."

"And Moses keeps the farm going," Iris said. "We got chickens now, too. We're expanding."

Pops laughed. "Pretty soon we be one agricultural conglomerate."

They heard the old Dodge truck pull up to the gate. Lion looked out to see Lili jump down to open it. He hurried out to close the gate after her and help with groceries.

"Hi, Brah." She did not seem happy to see him. Her hug was perfunctory, her body stiff.

*"E, Tita."*

She opened the back of the truck and grabbed a twenty-five-pound sack of dog food.

"Let me," Lion said. "You shouldn't be carrying stuff like that." She glared at him with a look approaching hatred, and in that moment, he knew she was no longer pregnant. He stumbled back and let her pass with the sack of dog food.

Kawika came out to help, too. "Boy, she's in a mood. I thought it would help her to get out for a while."

"She's under a lot of stress," Lion said. "And she's young." He felt as if he'd been kicked in the stomach. Moses came in from the *lo'i* with taro tops under his arm. When Lili censured him with her eyes, he assured her, "I'll clean 'em and cook 'em. No worry."

"Good. This is supposed to be an easy meal," she said. "I got two barbecued chickens from Costco, a thing of macaroni salad, and a carrot cake. I made poi this morning. You want luau leaf, you do 'em."

They held hands around the hospital bed while Lion led the prayer before dinner. Sometimes he got carried away, as he did this evening; the needs were so great. After the "Amen," Lili said sullenly and with a false smile, "Lion believes in long prayers and cold food."

They dined in the living room, plates in their laps. Pops dozed off and awakened several times. "I don't want to miss one minute wit' da family. My time grow short."

Kawika teased him, "Oh come on, Pops. You're gonna live so long we'll have to take you out in the *lo'i* and club you to death."

At the end of the meal, as Lili cleared the dishes, Lion offered to help, hoping to corner her in the kitchen and talk.

Instead, she said, "Good, you take over. "I'm going to put my pampered feet up and admire my red hooker nails. I'm exhausted."

After he finished the dishes, Lion took Pops' ukulele out to the porch. He sat on the steps in the moonlight, leaned against a post and strummed nothing in particular. He'd made his own adjustments, learning to play without his pinky fingers. He played softly, falling into "Hi'ilawe."

Kawika joined him. "So much pain in there."

"More than we can know," Lion said.

"Funny, you go along in life and everything's fine, then overnight it turns to mud. Then sooner or later you come out of that, too, and you almost forget how bad it was." He reached for the ukulele. "Let me?" Kawika began playing an utterly sad song, so full of longing it was sorrow itself set to music. "Queen Kapiolani wrote this love song for her king when he was away in San Francisco. It's almost as if she knew she'd never see him again. I can picture her on the upper lanai of Iolani Palace watching for his ship to round Diamond Head and sail for the harbor. Then she sees the ship draped in black and softly begins to sing her love song, her back straight, head high, while everyone around her wails." Still playing, Kawika asked, "How long you gonna be here, Lion?"

"Just the night. The bishop's got me scheduled to go to Maui and make the rounds of the parishes there."

"I'll be on Maui, too. I've got a water rights trial." He played a little riff then said, "Lion, I'm worried about Lili. She's the smartest one of us all and she should be in school. The strain is showing."

"I'm worried about her, too. How long do the doctors give Pops?"

"A couple of months maybe. If we're lucky. I try and stop by almost every day. It's hard sometimes with trial preps and all." Kawika's swiftly darting eyes filled with tears. "I've got to squeeze in as much of Pops as I can. This is it."

"I'm glad Moses is here, too."

"Momi is *hapai.*"

"Momi's pregnant?"

"Yeah. She and Moses want to get married but it's obviously not the time to move Momi into the house, so they're waiting."

"Does Lili know about Momi's baby?"

"No. Don't say anything. They'll tell everyone soon."

Iris announced she was sleeping in the living room next to Pops. "Thirty-nine years sleeping with this man." She laughed and took her husband's withered hand. "I'm addicted."

In the deep of night, Lion awoke and thought he heard someone crying, the sobs muffled by pillows. He lay very still but didn't hear it again.

*Oh God, we are corrupted by the evil whispering from within and broken by the blows which befall us from without. Let us not be diminished. Let us resist with every fiber of our being, with the steel of our human will until you prevail, and when you take from us that which we hold most dear, let us praise you still, and hold to the task you have set for us, for in your realm we are renewed and transformed. Let us cast light into the abyss of evil, deeper down than fear.*

Lion awoke again at dawn, roused by Moses' new roosters reaching incendiary heights of exuberance. With Michael trotting beside him, he went along the *lo'i,* hearing the trickle of water, the cooing of doves as the rising sun burnished the land. The night's chill breathed out from the plants onto his ankles as he walked.

Lili hurried across the grass to the new henhouse, rushing as if she hadn't seen Lion, when she couldn't have missed him. When she emerged with a basket of eggs, he was waiting.

"I got nothing to say, Brah."

"I love you, little sister."

"I'm too damn busy."

"I can help."

"You're stalking me, Lion. Leave me alone. I mean it." She wouldn't look at him.

"Call me when you're ready."

She marched away. "Don't hold your breath."

For breakfast, Lili fixed taro pancakes with coconut syrup, spicy Portuguese sausage and wedges of papaya. Pops said, "If I'd a known what a good cook Lili is, I'd a broken her mother's leg years ago."

Lili's smile was a grimace as she shoveled in stacks of food. She ate almost as much as Moses.

"Broke da mouf," Moses said, wiping his hands with a paper napkin. He cleared his throat and said, "I got one important announcement." He winked at Kawika and began, "Pops, you gonna be a grandpa."

Lion glanced at Lili who was bent over her food, motionless.

"Momi gonna have my baby."

Pops smiled softly, "That's good news, son."

Iris demanded, "When is the wedding?"

Before Moses could answer, Lili rushed off to her room, slamming the door.

"What's with her?" Moses asked.

"She's probably thinking of more work, poor ting." Iris patted Lion's hand. "And she broke up with Lance, good for her, but I know that girl and she's hurting. Go talk to her, Lion. She thinks the world of you."

Reluctantly, he followed Lili. When he knocked on her door she bellowed, "Leave me alone." He stood a moment, helpless and embarrassed at being so useless, then put his hand on the door and traced a cross with his thumb. He returned to the others and shrugged.

Moses said, "Don't worry. We not making more work. Momi's going stay home wit her folks and da baby. No wedding yet, Mom. We gonna wait to save up."

Iris said, "Lion, tell your brother to get married. He's got a baby on the way."

Smiling, Lion turned to Moses. "Get married, Moses."

"When I do, you marry us, 'kay?"

"I'd be honored."

"When da baby due?" Pops asked, probably calculating whether he would live to see his first grandchild.

"August."

"Bout time you told us," Iris huffed. She crossed her arms and said, "Grandmother. I'm going to be a grandmother, praise the Lord. Pops, we're having a baby."

Nobody but Lion seemed to pay any attention to how extraordinarily empty Lili's chair was.

He wished he could stay and help, but the bishop had his months mapped out for him. *Foxes have their dens, lions their lairs, bears their caves. Can I call this my home? My nest? My home is not in this world. This I must remember.*

He paused, his hand on the gate and looked back at the fluted mountains gathering mist about their green peaks, horses grazing, the taro glowing emerald in the sun, and the little red house with so much sorrow inside.

# Chapter 17

## THIS WAY TO PARADISE

The Wailuku house was big and old, and of no particular style, sprouting additions, odd windows and a witch's hat turret. It sat behind a high lava rock wall surrounded by large trees, giant ferns, and tall heliconia that hung down in red claws; so that the house, big as it was, looked oddly grateful to be allowed tenancy. Finding no bell by the gate, Lion and Michael let themselves into the peaceful Maui garden. Michael, unmoved by the loveliness, sniffed avidly about, seeking just the right foliage to irrigate.

The inner door of the house stood open and inviting, but the screen door was locked. Lion peered inside at a high ceiling, gleaming wooden floors and a staircase with dark polished railings. "Aloha," he called. Getting no answer, he waited a few moments and tried again, louder.

From the upper regions he heard someone stirring about and then saw Lehua Nii, a bald woman he barely recognized, inching her way down the stairs.

As soon as she saw him, she grinned broadly. "Father Lion." She walked slowly toward the door, flat-footed, toes pointed outward. The cancer, he heard, had gone from her breast to her spine.

The air inside the house was cool, and the living room, which Lehua primly called "the parlor," was tastefully crammed with Hawaiian artifacts and big pots filled with ferns. Dead leis draped several old photographs, and an antique pig platter holding a collection of Japanese green glass fishing floats dominated a koa wood coffee table.

"You used to find these all the time washed up on the beach," Lehua said as she motioned him to a comfortable old sofa. "Now the Japanese use plastic floats. Rubbish." She sat down in a rocker opposite him. "Would you like some iced tea, Father?"

"Yes, thank you, and a bowl of water for Michael, if you would."

"The tea is in a pitcher in the refrigerator and just use any old bowl for the dog's water."

When he returned with two glasses of tea, she said, "Forgive me for not getting up. This is my chemo week. I nap when the twins do."

"I awakened you. I'm sorry."

"It's okay as long as you didn't awaken them." Lehua's pitiful condition, the hairless head, sallow skin, distorted spinal curve was purgatory itself to behold. Her lively, intelligent eyes only made her appearance more heart-wrenching.

"I don't know how I'm going to manage," she continued, "and I can't say anything or apply for assistance because I may lose custody of my grand-babies. As soon as my daughter Raynette heard about my illness, she filed suit to get the twins back. I can't let that happen. I don't know what I'm going to do. I need a new lawyer and I can't afford one. Between the twins and the cancer, I can't work. The lawyer I had before won't take the case because I still owe money from the last two go-arounds. Thank God for this house or we'd be living in the park. My Auntie Marie went home to the Lord just in time and left this nice old house to me." Lehua raised her arm to Heaven. *"Mahalo nui loa,* Auntie Marie."

"It's a comfortable home."

"I'm blessed," she said with no irony, her smile shining, her baldness haloed in light. "But sometimes I ask myself: why do we have to suffer? What's the point? Why is there cancer in the world if there is a good God?"

"That's the age-old question: why do bad things happen to good people? Pain, unexamined, is pointless, a deadly poison. It can make us bitter, self-centered, and cruel. As Christians, we learn that since suffering is an unavoidable part of our human condition, we can use its power to transform."

"Then I got a lot of high octane transformation power, Father."

"I never felt as close to Christ as when I was a slave. I had no choice but to completely abandon myself to him so that he was as real to me as my pain. Strangely, I never felt more alive than I did in those days."

"That's because when we're suffering, we're looking the alternative right in the face and we know which side we're still on."

Lion smiled grimly. He thought of Pops. And Iris with her heart breaking, yet patiently enduring.

"What will happen to the twins if I die? They're only ten months old. I could surrender to God's will if it weren't for the twins. But I'm all they have. Without me, Raynette will get them back and her boyfriend will be burning them with cigarettes again. I'm not ready for Heaven yet. I'm still battling Hell, right here."

"You're right where God wants you to be at this moment and you are succeeding against those things that resist you."

She leaned forward, turned an ear to the stairs. "I thought I heard them, the twins."

"Me, too. Definitely."

"Come." She put her finger to her lips. "Be quiet. It's fun to surprise them."

They crept up the stairs and paused before a dim room. The twins sat in separate cribs, gurgling to each other.

"They have their own language," Lehua whispered. "It's almost spooky."

Lion smiled, intrigued. "Identical twins?"

"Yes." She marched into the room and opened the blinds. "Hello my sweet *mo'opuna* babies. Did you have a good nap?" Sunlight flooded the room, igniting the rosy walls, pink crib sheets, blankets, and shaggy rugs.

The babies fell silent at the sight of Father Lion. They were beautiful honey colored children with large eyes, slightly downturned brows and sparse, wispy brown hair. They were obviously wary and looked to their grandmother for reassurance. Lehua smiled at them. "This is Tutu's friend, Father Lion. I know he doesn't look like a lion, but he can growl."

Lion imitated a kitten mewling, making the twins laugh. He asked Lehua, "How do you tell them apart?"

"Easy. By their scars."

She held one twin's arm. "This is Shy-Anne. See, her cigarette burns are almost in a straight line." She went to the other crib and gently took the other twin's arm. "Shoshona's scars are all over the place, arms, back, legs. She's the noisy one. These innocent babies have been through so much in their young lives, I just pray that Jesus clouds their memories so they have no recollection of the abuse."

"The courts would never return them to such a situation, would they?"

"The newspapers are full of stories of kids returned to their parents and they end up dead or missing. Raynette's in rehab again. I've been through this since she was fourteen." She pulled two disposable diapers from a box. "Here. You do Shoshona. I've got Shy-Anne. Here's a wipe.

There's the powder."

He had never diapered a baby before. "How do I?"

"Peel back those tabs on the side. That's it. You got it. Make it nice and snug. Hey, you get A-plus in advanced diapering."

Lehua let the twins crawl backwards down the stairs, staying in front of them in case they tumbled. "I had to teach them. No can carry sometimes." She gave them each a bottle of juice and collapsed in her rocker. "I read in a John Steinbeck book, *Cannery Row*, I think, where the old grandmother who babysits the daughter's children, would cook up a pot of beans and strew them on the floor. Then, she could sit down while they crawled around and ate the beans, one by one. It was her only peace. I think I'll get a crock pot."

"You need help, Lehua."

"Tell me about it. I have friends who come over a couple of times a week and I'm so grateful. But it's never enough." She straightened up. "I tell you though, I'll go through hell and high water to keep those babies safe." She changed the subject. "Tell me how Lord Jim is doing these days. That *wahine* working out?"

"Carlene?"

"That's the one. I liked her, but you tell me what a nurse is doing working as a secretary. And I'm the one who recommended her for the job. I met her in the Renew program. Father Terry asked me to befriend her, so I did. Hoo, she's a tough one. But she has a heart of pure gold."

It was as if a comic strip light bulb flicked on over Lion's head, his idea was so sudden and brilliant. "Do you have an extra bedroom?" he asked.

"I got enough bedrooms in this house to run a brothel." She laughed.

"Not what I had in mind, but what would you think of a nurse moving in to help you?"

"It would have to be an angel nurse because I can't afford to pay a human one."

"May I use your phone?"

Lion reached Carlene at the chancery office. "Have you got a minute?"

"It's not like I'm filing my nails," she answered. "Are you calling to tell me you got the call back to Africa, because I'm praying for you and I hope you've been praying for me. We have a deal, you know."

"I have been praying for you and I believe our good Lord has led me to a radical proposal for you."

"Hey, it's a proposal. I'll take it." When Lion didn't respond, she added, "Just joking, Father. What radical proposal do you have in mind? I'm all ears."

"It would involve a job change."

"Now you're really talking."

"And a move to Maui."

"That's a bit of a problem. You see, I've got a boyfriend. A new one. And it's nice."

"I see."

"I assumed Tex was the answer to your prayers for me. So tell me what else you and Jesus have in mind."

"You remember the bishop's former secretary, Lehua Nii?"

"How can I forget her, and that hair-garden piled a mile high on her head and always pinned with flowers, ferns, tree limbs? I even suspect-ed there was a bird or a monkey in there on a few occasions." She laughed heartily.

"She's in a desperate situation."

"Oh no. What'd she do?"

"As you may know, she's taking care of her twin granddaughters—

and she's developed cancer, spine and breast. The good news is she inherited a nice big house in Wailuku, lots of room. But she's afraid of losing custody of the girls because of her illness. They've been badly abused."

"I'm not a lawyer."

"I know. I've got an idea on that one, too."

"I get it. You want me to move there and help her with her cancer and her kids?"

"She can't pay you, but you can live at the house, rent-free, of course."

"Maui Memorial Hospital is in Wailuku. I could get a part-time job there."

"If she had a nurse living with her, she probably wouldn't lose custody."

"Tex—my boyfriend—drives a tour bus. Maybe he could transfer to Maui." She quickly added, "Don't worry, Father. We don't live together, not without the sacrament and a diamond."

Lion hadn't anticipated a boyfriend. "Do you want time to think this over?"

"Father, nobody ever needed me before. I'll do it. I'll have to give notice to the bishop and pack up my place and talk to Tex."

"What if Tex won't go along with it?"

"Good-bye, Tex. I can't explain it, but the minute you mentioned moving to Maui, I was sure it's the right thing for me. I can't wait to get my hands on those twins. I'll be their Auntie Carlene. I'll go to their First Holy Communions, their graduations. I'm going to open a savings account for their college. Thank you, Father Lion, mucho *mahalos*."

"I'm the one who should be thanking you, praise God."

"Actually, Father, I have an ulterior motive. My drunken father wants to move here and have me take care of him while he self-destructs from cirrhosis and emphysema. I now have a great excuse to say no."

"Carlene, if you have family obligations…"

"I don't owe that man a damn thing, excuse my French. The only thing he ever gave me was lessons in how not to live. My sisters and my brothers live a lot closer to him than I do. Let them deal with him. No way, Jose. So, thank you, Father Lion. You've given me a clear conscience to just say no. Is Lehua there? Can she come to the phone?"

Father Lion heard only half the conversation between the women, but he heard crying and full-throated laughter.

The bishop would hate having to train another new secretary. Lion next called Kawika Kamana's law office in Honolulu only to be told that Mr. Kamana was off island but he could leave a message.

"This is his brother, Lion. Please tell him I need to speak with him. Tell him it's urgent. Here's a number on Maui where he can reach me."

The secretary was suspicious. "I didn't know he had a brother named Lion." She must be new, but it hurt anyway. "I'll give him the message when he calls in."

A friend of Lehua's came by with a big pot of *jook* for dinner and a *haupia* pie. "White stuff when you're nauseous," she said. "My gastro guy told me that."

"That was Tammy," Lehua said. "She's got a bunch of teenagers and she still finds time to bring me meals. I don't know how she does it."

Just as they got the twins into their highchairs and were sitting down to feed them, the phone rang. "Can you keep two spoons going?" Lehua asked.

"I am Lion," he said, clowning for the twins. "Lion strong. Lion can do anything."

Lehua answered the phone and passed it to him. "For you."

It was Kawika and he was on Maui. "With a friend," he explained.

"I need to see you," Lion said.

"Got a pretty full schedule, but my friend and I are going hiking tomorrow. Want to join us? We can talk then."

"Hold on." He turned to Lehua and asked, "Will you be okay on your own tomorrow?"

"It's Saturday. My prayer group is coming over to help me clean."

"You're on," he said to Kawika."May I bring Michael on the hike?"

"Why not? And I know you've got good walking shoes. We're hiking Makamakaole Trail in the West Maui Mountains. It's pretty strenuous."

"I'll be fine, brah."

When Lion told Lehua where they were going, she said, "I heard on the TV we're supposed to get heavy rains tomorrow. Be careful of flash floods."

"If it rains, I assume we won't go."

"How many brothers you got?" she asked.

Lion briefly closed his eyes then carefully answered, "Four. Two biological brothers in Africa. One is deceased. I've got a sister, too. And my mother is still alive. And I have my two *hanai* Kamana brothers in Waimanalo, Moses and Kawika, along with parents and two sisters."

"You're lucky you got the Kamanas. Nice old family."

"Bishop Carroll set it up when I first came to Hawaii as a seminary student. My brother Kawika went to Punahou with Barak Obama."

"Not."

"They were both on scholarship."

"You got friends in really high places. You and me, we're blessed, Father."

Lion said grace over the dinner. The *jook* was rich with rice, ginger and turkey. Lehua's friend had brought along little packets of crushed peanuts, chopped Chinese parsley and a can of mirinzuke for garnish.

As he ate, Lion reflected that God's original plan for the world was Paradise. It was our pride and disobedience that introduced suffering and mortality. *All our lives we seek that return to Paradise, but sometimes we must settle for just a bowl of warm rice gruel from a friend.*

# Chapter 18

## WITH FRIENDS

Sunshine McAndrews had a disposition that matched her name. "*Makamakaole* means banishment, punishment. Where we're going today is a place of punishment, and you'll soon see why." She kept her eyes on the narrow twister of a road, ambitiously called Kahekili Highway, as it skirted dramatic coastal cliffs and climbed into dense verdure. Clouds sat low on the brow of the West Maui Mountains.

Kawika, sitting next to Sunshine in the front passenger seat, corrected her, "The name *Makamakaole* means 'without friends.'"

"Well, duh, when you're banished, you don't have a lot of friends. In ancient times on Maui when you broke the *kapu* you were exiled to that valley."

Lion sat quietly in the back of the jeep with his arm around his dog. The success of his mission, persuading his brother to take Lehua Nii's custody battle to court for free, depended on Kawika being in a receptive mood, tranquilized, perhaps, by natural beauty and strenuous exercise. But Lion could almost see steam coming out of the top of Kawika's head. His brother didn't like to be corrected, especially by a *haole* blithely making assertions about Hawaiian culture.

Kawika's back straightened, and his torso lifted as he became the *mo'i*, imperiously issuing edicts, "I spoke with our *kupuna*." Kawika was staking territory. "You don't know the *kaona*, the hidden meaning. I

was told that the valley got its name from the fog, that the fog is so per-
vasive you cannot see your friends two feet in front of you and therefore
you feel abandoned and without friends."

She persisted, "I've never run into fog there and I've hiked that sucker
a gazillion times and mostly the weather's been fine." Sunshine, who
billed herself as a naturalist, worked as a guide for Take A Hike Maui,
an adventure tour company, and this was her day off. "There are two
waterfalls. You climb up a rope and some rocks to the second cascade.
It's really beautiful. In fact," she said, "Don, my boss, got married at the
top waterfall last year. "

Kawika elbowed her. "Don't get any ideas just because I brought
along my own priest today."

"Give me one good reason why I would even want to marry you."

Judging by the electricity between them, Lion suspected Sunshine
and Kawika were sleeping together, and knowing his brother, felt sorry
for Sunshine. Kawika might sleep with a *haole,* but he'd never marry
one. Lion spoke up to dilute the tension, "I heard we're supposed to get
rain today."

Undaunted, Sunshine said, "I checked. We're supposed to get rain,
but not until evening. We'll be *pau* long before then." She then launched
into a cultural dissertation on rain, "The old Hawaiians had hundreds of
names for rain." She didn't know when to stop. Predictably, Kawika's
scorn was majestic but she defended herself admirably, further dooming
any lasting romance.

Lion attempted peace. "I'm impressed with how you've embraced
Hawaii. Where are you from, Sunshine?"

"You know, I get so tired of that. Everyone assumes because I'm
*haole* that I'm from the Mainland. Well, I'm a Maui girl, born in Haiku."

Lion, contrite, ventured further, "I wonder which rain we'll get today."

"Rain? Look at that blue sky." Kawika rolled down the jeep window. "Once in a while the weatherman should just look out the window."

They pulled off the road next to a chain-link fence bearing a sign: *"Kapu.* No trespassing. Private property." The fence had a hole as big as a man.

"We have permission," Sunshine said. "Not that the sign stops anyone, obviously." She took three backpacks from the rear of the jeep and handed out two. "Lunch, water, poncho." She hoisted her own pack on her shoulders and set out on sturdy, tanned legs. Lion bent through the hole, followed by Michael, then Kawika.

Immediately trees closed around them, plunging them into rainforest so dense it blocked the sun and so quiet they could hear their hearts drumming in their ears. A thick blanket of leaves carpeted the damp ground.

Sunshine held back tree branches so they didn't whip the men behind her. Michael scampered ahead, racing back and forth, drinking in the scents, checking on Lion. The day grew darker, the terrain rougher, the hikers more silent and determined. They came to a wide stream. "We have to cross it," Sunshine said. "Are you game? There are thirteen stream crossings on the trail. It's a mile to the waterfall and plunge pool."

Lion appraised the rocks. They looked like ankle breakers.

Kawika was all for proceeding. "I can do a mile in my sleep."

"It's not just the distance," Sunshine said. "I don't like the sky. The rain may be earlier than forecast."

"We're here," Kawika said. "By this time tomorrow I'll be back in a stuffy courtroom wearing a jacket and tie. Let's go for it." He took the first step into the water, which didn't even come over the tops of his sandals.

As soon as Michael saw the direction in which they were proceeding, he bounded into the stream climbed on a rock and stood nobly like a shepherd until all had safely passed.

A bit of a wind came up and played the thick bamboo like chimes. Sunshine went into guide mode saying, "The first Polynesian colonizers of Hawaii brought bamboo with them from their home islands of Tahiti and the Marquesas."

Kawika glowered.

By the sixth stream crossing a light rain began its ghostly descent. Sunshine lifted her face and put out her tongue. The water in the stream beds quickly rose to shin deep. They slipped on their ponchos. By the twelfth crossing, the widest, the rain was coming down heavier and the stream ran much faster. Sunshine peered out from her hood, rain dribbling onto her face. "I don't like this."

"We're almost there," Kawika said and strode purposefully into the swirling water.

Lion leashed Michael for the crossing, afraid the dog might be swept away.

"You baby that dog," his brother called over the roar of the water.

"I think he's cute," Sunshine shouted.

"Lion or the dog?" Kawika was already on the opposite bank.

"Both." She paused midstream, looked up at the grey flannel sky through the clear spot in the forest canopy and said, "I really think we should turn back."

"Go on back, *hohe*," Kawika challenged.

"Don't you call me a coward," she yelled, then shook her head and said to Lion, "This is so stupid, but I can't let him go on alone. He thinks he's mister Hawaiian macho man, but he could get lost, especially if the rain washes out the trail. If you want to turn around, I think it's the smart thing to do."

With grave misgivings, Lion stooped, dipped his hand into the stream and made the sign of the cross. "He's my brother. I'll stick with him."

"Your moron brother. And we're just as dumb to follow him."

In sullen silence the three hikers and the dog crashed along the trail in the pouring rain. Michael looked woeful. His fur hung in wet clumps and his tail curled beneath him.

As they approached the last stream crossing just before the waterfall, a loud clap of thunder cracked, vibrated, and echoed against the mountain walls "That's it," Sunshine called out. "We're all going back. I've got the car keys and I swear I'll leave you, Kawika."

He ignored her. She caught up with him as he hesitated at the bank of the stream which was now a raging brown torrent carrying tree limbs and plant debris. "You are a fool if you try to cross that. And we better get out of here as fast as we can—and I mean turn and *run* before we get caught in a flash flood. This is a very narrow valley."

Kawika glared at her as if she had personally opened the calabash of rains and poured them out on him.

Lion nodded toward the direction from which they had come and gently urged, "Come on, brah, let's listen to the expert."

He stormed back down the trail.

The twelfth crossing was now almost impossible to recross. The rising water eddied around rocks and roared past them. Michael whimpered as Lion dragged him in. They were almost across when a large tree limb swept past, snagged the leash, yanked it from Lion's hand and carried Michael downstream, the dog paddling furiously. Lion cried out; Sunshine screamed. Kawika hesitated only a moment then raced through the brush and over rocks to a curve in the water, dropped his backpack and plunged in, heedless of his own safety. He lunged at the tree branch and held it, trying to untangle the leash but couldn't.

Lion jumped in behind him and grabbed the panicked dog, who continued to paddle even when his front feet were out of the water. "Unhook him," Lion yelled.

Kawika let go of the branch to grab at the leash. The force of the water almost tore Michael from Lion's arms. "Hold him, hold him," Kawika bellowed over the roar of the water. He struggled a moment then unhooked the leash.

Lion might have fallen except for Sunshine clutching his poncho in her fist.

"Thank you," Lion gasped, depositing Michael on firm ground.

"No time for that." Sunshine raced away. "This whole valley could go. Come on."

At each stream crossing, they had to carry the dog through the torrent. By the time they reached their original crossing, the water that hadn't reached their shoe tops now swirled around their hips. They plunged in, helping each other. They made it safely then ran the final leg of the trail. Drenched, exhausted, and grateful, they collapsed in the jeep.

"Thanks for saving Michael," Lion said, clinging to the wet dog.

"It's the least I could do," Kawika said in a moment of humility. "I should have listened to the expert."

"I'm no expert," Sunshine said. "It's just that I've hiked Makamakaole so many times."

"But this time you were with friends," Kawika said.

"Yeah." She grinned.

"Want me to drive?" Kawika asked.

She handed him the keys. "I'd like to stretch out in the back if you don't mind. Lion, why don't you sit up front with your brother."

As they climbed over each other and settled into their places, Lion noticed Kawika pinch Sunshine's rump as she passed by him. Michael could not be persuaded to stay in the back but cried and pawed until Lion took the shivering dog and placed him in his lap.

Sunshine checked the backpacks. "Lunch is ruined. We've got apples, bottled water and turkey-brownie soup."

On the drive back to Wailuku, Kawika apologized for pushing them onward into the storm.

Lion grinned. It was the perfect moment to spring his request. "Brother, I have a big favor to ask of you."

Kawika smiled and shook his head in resignation. "Lay it on."

"There's a woman in Wailuku who had to quit her job because of cancer and now she has no money and is afraid she'll lose custody of her granddaughters, identical twin babies."

"Where's the mother?"

"She's the one suing for custody. She's a drug addict with a rap sheet and a boyfriend who tells the babies apart by scarring them with cigarette burns. Even if the mother doesn't get the kids, they may end up in foster care."

"Maybe they'll be better off under the circumstances."

"I've arranged for a registered nurse to live with the grandmother. Now I just need a lawyer, *pro bono*."

Kawika sighed deeply, while the windshield wipers thwacked furiously.

"They're Hawaiian," Lion added, his voice laden with petty triumph.

"I was going to say yes, anyway."

Sleepily, from the backseat, Sunshine said, "You know, Kapalua Resort and the West Maui coast get about twenty to thirty inches of rain a year. Guess how much the mountains get?" She quickly answered her own question. "Three hundred to four hundred and fifty inches a year."

Lion said, "I think we got at least half that today, right Michael?"

The dog was as sleepy as Sunshine and sighed as deeply and with as much resignation as Kawika. They stopped for pizza and ate it in the jeep rather than leave Michael alone. Lion was quite pleased with how the day had gone. They survived. He had a free lawyer.

# Chapter 19

MAUI WOWIE

"I'm not a Catholic." Sylphide stated firmly. "And I'm not converting. I'm eighty-seven." The tiny, truculent woman had been towed into the office of Lahaina's Maria Lanakila Church by her friend Darlene Young, a parishioner, who was surprised to find the pastor away on retreat and a substitute priest sitting in. And an African named Father Lion at that.

"If I can, I'll be happy to help you," Father Lion replied, "no matter how or if you worship God."

"Goddess. It's a she: Gaia." Sylphide had probably been a beauty once. Her features were delicate, her eyes a vivid, mocking blue.

"Ah," Lion sat back. "Gaia. The Creatrix."

Sylphide flashed him a coquettish smile.

"I wanted to inquire about Catholic Charities services for the elderly," Darlene said. "I understand they are quite comprehensive, and my friend Sylphide will be needing housing in three months."

"I don't need charity," Sylphide sniffed. "I just need a place to live. I can pay for it. I have means."

"She needs some form of assisted living," Darlene said. "She does have social security and a widow's pension, but unfortunately she has no savings left and has lost her home."

"I didn't lose my home," Sylphide said. "I know right where it is."

"Tell me what happened, and we'll see what we can do."

Darlene spoke for her friend, "Sylphide has two daughters, Glenn-Anne and Jillie. Glenn-Anne is married and living in Makawao. She's been managing her mother's money and frankly, Father, I suspect she's been helping herself to it on a fairly regular basis."

Sylphide defended her daughter. "I think you're wrong, Darlene." She turned to Lion. "Why, right now she's on a Mediterranean cruise."

"On your money." Darlene explained, "Sylphide gave Glenn-Anne a hundred thousand dollars six months ago."

"A gift." Sylphide smiled. "I wanted her to have her inheritance while I'm still around to see her enjoy it."

"I'm afraid, Father, that Sylphide's generosity has been her undoing. You see, when she bought her house in Lahaina, she and Jillie bought it together."

Sylphide interrupted, "I put in three quarters and Jillie put in one quarter. That way we could pay cash and not worry about a mortgage. I thought I was so smart. I thought I could trust my own child."

"The problem is," Darlene continued, "Sylphide put the house in Jillie's name so Jillie won't have to pay estate taxes when Sylphide passes away. Now Jillie wants Sylphide out of the house."

"The whore." Sylphide's thin mouth curled in delighted disgust.

"Jillie has a new live-in boyfriend," Darlene explained.

Father Lion listened to the facts and the tone of what was said.

"It's very clear to me," Sylphide argued. "The boyfriend is always sniffling and agitated and so easily offended. He's a druggie. I know the signs. I wasn't always this old—or this ladylike. Why, when I came to Maui in the seventies, it was pot island. Maui Wowie. You could get anything on Front Street—drugs, crabs." She sat back smugly. "Still can."

"Perhaps we can find a nice rental and a companion to live with you," Father Lion suggested. "I just had a happy conclusion to a situation in Wailuku. I'm sure we can work something out."

Darlene shook her head. "It gets worse, Father. As soon as Jillie owned her mother's house outright, she marched straight down to the bank and mortgaged it to the hilt. She then used the money to buy thirty acres of land near Haiku."

"My daughter the slut and this—this Juan Valdez—think they're going to grow coffee. Hah," Sylphide sneered. "My daughter can't even grow a philodendron"

Darlene plunged on, "Jillie just gave Sylphide three-month's notice to get out of the house. She's selling it and evicting her own mother."

"I don't understand it. I gave my children everything. I lived for them. Now they're throwing me out in the street in my old age. I'll be sitting on the curb with my cats."

Darlene pleaded, "I was hoping, Father, that our pastor, Father Ing would talk to Jillie, but since he's not here, will you ? "

"Do you think she would pay any attention to a priest?" Lion asked.

"We already went to a lawyer and what Jillie's doing is perfectly legal. I thought maybe someone with some moral authority could mediate a just solution." Darlene, in a rising voice, exhibited more indignation than the evictee "This is wrong, wrong, wrong."

Sylphide looked quite pleased to be the center of a drama. She smiled and patted a large and colorful enamel butterfly pinned to her shirt.

"I'll talk to Jillie," Lion promised.

As he drove the winding road to Haiku, Father Lion turned to Michael, whose head was hanging out the window of Father Ing's Toyota, and said, "I'm glad I've got you along, boy, and I see you're glad the air conditioner is broken and the windows wide open."

Jillie currently had no telephone and he had heard that Haiku harbored a colony of aging hippies, crystal healers, California Hindus, and various druggies, drop-outs and cultists, all steeped in a thriving marijuana culture. Some lived in ecologically-conscious houses while others squatted in shacks and under tarps in the jungle. Lion watched the mile markers slip by.

"Ah, here's the dirt road, right on schedule." He proceeded very slowly as the twisted lane descended into dense vegetation. Unkempt, wind-torn banana plants lined both sides, hitting the car as it inched along. There was something ominous about the snap of the thick leaves as they thwacked the windshield. The dark shadows, sliced by brilliant shafts of fierce sunlight abruptly brought him back to Africa, to that long-ago morning when he rode his father's shoulders and horses came thundering upon them, tree limbs snapping like gun fire. Lion gripped the steering wheel, and stopped the car, completely unnerved, breathing as if running; the terror as real as if he were seven years old again. "How long do old fears last, Michael? Does fear embed itself like a computer virus? Is it a warning? Is fear mocking me, telling me that I can't run far enough?" He rubbed the dog behind his ears. "I'm safe, Michael. I believe in a loving God. I dwell in peace and plenty in a country of laws where people stop at traffic lights even when no one else is about, and yet that unreasonable fear of mine is always just below the surface."

He eased the car forward again, and said with false cheer, "They're going to have to do a lot of clearing if they intend to grow coffee here." He rounded a curve in the dense jungle and a man with a machete stood in front of the car, barring the way. Lion hit the brakes.

A huge gold crucifix gleamed against the man's dirty, sweat-stained shirt. Michael growled with impressive menace.

"Easy, boy." Lion focused on the cross as the man belligerently approached.

"We got nothing today," the man snarled, gripping the machete.

Lion knew immediately the man was not talking about a bag of coffee beans . More calmly than he felt, he said, "I'm here to see Jillie Spivak. Is she around?"

"I told you, man, we got nothing. Nada. Beat it." The accent was Spanish.

"I'm not buying. I'm a priest. I came to see Jillie about her mother."

The man stared a moment then grudgingly stepped back. He nodded for Lion to go on, then spat on the ground as the car passed.

A pack of barking dogs charged the Toyota as Lion cautiously approached a small clearing. A woman, hard at work building a shack, paused to yell at the dogs. Her rude dwelling slouched nearby. It had one solid wall, but open shower curtains made up the other three. Inside, Lion could see an unmade bed, a makeshift table piled with pots, big jugs of water and various plastic bowls. Beside it, a line of tables under a screen held neat rows of potted marijuana plants. Old lawn chairs were strewn about outside in the weeds.

The woman was as hostile as the man with the machete. She clutched a hammer and said nothing.

Lion got out of the car, leaving Michael inside. "You Jillie?"

"Who wants to know?"

"I'm Father Lion Majok, a Catholic priest. I came to talk to you about your mother, Sylphide."

She removed her work gloves as if settling down for a tasty snack. "You mean Betty?"

"I'm sorry. I thought you were Jillie."

"I am. But she's not Sylphide. Her real name is Betty. Sylphide is her Maui name." The woman's greying blonde hair straggled from a long ponytail. Her skin was taut and tan with fine lines etched about the

157

eyes." I could tell you tales about my dear, sweet mother that would shock your holy ears." She nodded toward the Toyota. "Better let your dog out of the car. It's hot. My dogs are okay."

Michael gingerly stepped down, then with cautious enthusiasm joined the romping pack.

"You want some organic lemonade? I make it with Meyer lemons, ginger and honey. It's quite nice."

"Thank you."

"Here, sit in the shade." She righted an upended chair and brushed it off with her hand. As Lion sat, she retreated to the shed, still talking. "I suppose Betty sent you here about my house. The law didn't work, so now comes the church."

"I'm here at the behest of a concerned friend who brought your mother in to see me."

Jillie emerged with two plastic glasses, one yellow, one purple, and sat down in the flattened grass near him. "Betty cries on everyone's shoulder about her horrible daughters and everyone feels so sorry for her. Well, let me fill you in on a few inconvenient details I'm sure she forgot to mention."

The lemonade had a nice peppery taste.

Jillie sipped deeply and began her tale, savoring it as she spoke. "I was nine when my parents got divorced." Then my mother up and moved me and my sister from San Franciso to Maui, and my Dad married someone else, had more daughters and, well, basically forgot about me and Glenn-Anne. We lived out of cardboard boxes and went to five schools in one year. I know my mother looks like a sweet little old lady but don't let appearances fool you. She may be sweet as cotton candy in her dotage, but she was a rotten mother. At night she rode her bicycle to bars. Then she started bringing guys home and she was so stoned she had no idea what these creeps did to her and to me and my sister. She has the nerve to call me a whore. I bet Betty didn't tell you any of this, did she?"

"You certainly paint a very different portrait of the woman I met."

"You don't believe me, do you?" Jillie leaned toward Lion as if she might upend his chair. "I want that woman out of my house and out of my life."

Startled, Lion pulled back. "I didn't see any evidence of drug abuse in your mother."

"Yeah, well, she got in with the holistic crowd, did colonic irrigation, sweat lodge, yoga, self-actualization campouts, dream workshops and suddenly she's Sylphide, and she says she's our mom." Jillie settled back down.

"Sylphide baked nine-grain bread, made her own granola and acidophilous yogurt and even got a dog. Well, it was too late for me and Glenn-Anne. Then she gets lucky and meets a techie dude from New York, and they get married, and we all move into a condo at Wailea and pretend to be a normal family. The new dad makes a new will and in a burst of bonding includes me and my sister. Then he has the decency to drop dead. So my mom, the grieving widow, talks me into putting my money in with hers so she can buy her dream house in Lahaina—and, stupid me, I do it. Have you been to the Lepidoptera Villa?"

"I beg your pardon?"

"My house. The one she's living in."

"No. I met your mother at the church."

"Well, all I'm going to say is that when I sell the place, anything with a butterfly motif is going, too."

Lion asked, "Do you think we could work out some compromise that would allow your mother some dignity and security in her last years?"

"What's with the 'we?' What's in this for you?"

"I assure you I have no interest except to hope for peace and security for all concerned."

"Well, I assure you I, for one, will be fine. I have no intention of living like this forever. Look at this dump, will you? I'm selling the Lahaina house so I can build a new one here; with no Sylphide and no butterflies."

"What's to become of your mother?"

Jillie spoke forcefully, almost spitting the words. "When I was a powerless little kid, my mother didn't protect me. Why should I care about her now? What goes around, comes around. Don't you just love karma?"

"I prefer charity."

"I'm free of that woman. That's all I care about."

He got up to leave. "I'll do what I can for your mother. Catholic Charities has services for the elderly. But Jillie, you won't be free of your mother until you forgive her."

"Oh yes I will. Just watch."

"Was that your boyfriend I met back there on the road?"

"Hermon?" She pronounced it Her-MON. "He's clearing land for our coffee crop."

Lion walked over to the screened shed. "Which will be a cover crop for your marijuana enterprise?"

She inserted herself between the priest and the plants. "Not that it's any of your business but we don't sell weed to kids. We're raising this for the legal medical marijuana trade. Think of me as a pharmacist not a drug dealer."

"I think of you, Jillie, as a precious child of Jesus, who is waiting for you to come in out of the anger."

"You don't have to think of me at all, Reverend. I am just fine. God didn't care about me when I needed him, when some pervert had his hands all over me. Just pray for Betty." The name was vinegar on her tongue. "She's the one who's going to need prayers, and a roof over her head."

Hermon swaggered into the clearing. "You okay?" he asked Jillie.

"I was just leaving," Lion said. He whistled for Michael. The dog came crashing through the brush and jumped happily into the car, filthy and panting.

As Lion drove away, he fought to drive carefully, so great was his impatience and his pity. *These people, Sylphide and her daughters, have food, clothing, shelter, money, and each other. They are free from want, free from disease and oppression, and yet they are so angry and unhappy. What does it take to satisfy an American?*

He blushed with shame for he was as judgmental as Jillie.He glanced at the couple in the rear-view mirror. Jillie and Hermon stood comfortably next to each other, contentious survivors, gleaning the leavings of happiness from a banquet where they had no seat. Betrayal and possibly great tragedy could be foretold in the unyielding set of their shoulders, the way their legs formed "A"s.

# Chapter 20
## ONE NIGHT ON MAUI

The jacaranda trees wept lavender petals over the meadows and hills of Maui's Upcountry. They carpeted rooftops and roads, adorned cattle and drifted in the drowsy trade winds, masking the dormant, raw power of Haleakala, Maui's huge volcano. It was early morning and rainbows vaulted everywhere, two and three at a time, sometimes dancing down in a curtain of vivid mist. The beauty was almost too much to bear. Father Lion smiled as he walked, though the road was steep and the weather warm.

"Now isn't God just the grandest, Michael? All this and tonight we'll have wiener-schnitzel or sauerbraten, one or the other. We can count on that when we stay with the Chings. And a cold beer." He could already smell and taste a home-cooked dinner.

The priest and his dog walked the back road to Kula, avoiding Haleakala Highway with its impatient traffic and speeding streams of "bike down a volcano" tours. Instead, Lion and Michael faced acres of sweet Maui onions, fields of carnations, and protea farms with their huge African flowers. "Hello, landsmen," he called out to the blooms. Their magnificent, lunaresque faces were bigger than his own and stood regally on stiff unbending stems. Three horses lazed in the shade of a jacaranda tree, unaware of how lovely they looked with lavender blossoms tangled in their manes and dusting their haunches.

When they got to the Ching's sprawling mountainside home with its wall of windows looking down over the island and the ocean far below, it was late afternoon with long shadows in the meadows. The air at that elevation was cool and Laila Ching grew temperate-zone flowers all around the house: hollyhocks, hydrangeas, geraniums and roses. In the back, she maintained an orderly kitchen garden with regimented rows of tomatoes, lettuce, strawberries and herbs.

Heidi and Hans, the Chings' German shepherds, raucously greeted Lion and Michael. In the midst of the commotion, Laila came bursting out the door, waving madly from the deck. She was a handsome woman with vibrant rosy skin, curly yellow hair and a full, ripe figure which she carried not only proudly, but ostentatiously. "Velcome, velcome, Father Lion." Her German accent came out only on certain words. "Quiet, children. Enough barking. You know this nice man by now." She rushed forward, embraced the priest, and kissed him loudly on the cheek. "We've been waiting all day for you, right, children?" Laila loved her dogs, but her husband had allergies, so no animals were allowed in the house.

The first thing Father Lion noticed when he entered the house with its familiar, imposing pieces of dark furniture, was the absence of cooking aromas. His disappointment must have registered on his face, for Laila said, "Sherman is away, so I thought it would be a treat for us to eat out tonight." She brushed her hands together, quickly, loudly. "So, I made reservations at Ferraro's at the Four Seasons. That should do very nicely."

The ornately carved cuckoo clock chirped five o'clock. Lion groaned inwardly.

Laila assured him, "Don't worry, dahlink. In the morning I will make my notorious orange pastries just for you. People beg but I will not share my recipe. No. It's my secret. Oh, and I left a little gift for you in your room. Wear it tonight, yes?"

A new, obviously expensive aloha shirt and knife-pleated khaki trousers decorated his bed. He fingered the silken fabric of the shirt and shook his head in resignation. The shirt was a rich dark blue imprinted with gold medallions. *We can be so easily corrupted by luxurious garments. We put them on, preen admiringly before the mirror and imagine that at last we will be recognized for who we truly are.* He thought of Jesus in sandals and homespun tunic, Mother Theresa with only two saris, and of his beloved Damien administering the sacraments in threadbare soutane. He dropped the shirt back on the bed, almost in revulsion. *Why can't I escape riches? The more I yearn for a monastery, a brown robe and the Angelus bell calling me from the fields, the more I am deluged with epicurean dinners.*

He showered and, with grave misgivings, slipped on his new clothes. He straightened his shoulders and imagined his mother, so far away in Africa, seeing him now. She would be so proud. He thought of the daughters of Ali El Mum Nhom and wondered if they would still call him Abeed, Filth. He concluded that they would.

Lion had never been anywhere with Laila except church. She slipped her arm through his, pulled him closer and, laughing prettily for show, paraded through the lobby of the hotel. He didn't know where to rest his eyes, for the cut of her dress was quite revealing from his height. It came as a great relief when they were finally seated at Ferraro's.

Their outdoor table overlooked the beach, violin music drifted through the air, and just a sliver of the Maui moon sailed above the ocean. He was grateful for the presentation of menus large enough to hide behind.

Since Laila had no Bishop Carroll-like deals with the bishop of Sudan, Lion felt free to eat simply and ordered a bowl of minestrone.

"Is that all? You will starve to death." She turned to the waiter and ordered, "Bring this handsome man also a veal shank and some risotto." She selected a German Riesling and when Lion declined a glass, she had one poured for him anyway, leaning toward him, lips pursed. "To a wonderful evening."

He raised his glass in salute. "It's a shame Sherman isn't here to enjoy it with us. It's a lovely wine, crisp and just a little sweet. My compliments."

"It's from Hattenheimer Schutzenhaus. Sherman will faint when he gets the bill." She shrugged provocatively. "But I'm sure Sherman is having a good time at the plant in China. You know how much fun those dreary communists are." She laughed gleefully, mockingly, perfect white teeth gleaming. "I don't go on the business trips with Sherman because all they eat in China is Chinese food. Imagine. I despise Chinese food, all skin and bones. Sherman, of course, adores it, being Chinese. He's fifth generation American and he still can't look at a pig without seeing *manapua* pork hash."

Lion asked about Laila's business, a fashionable boutique called Ooh-La-Loha in Makawao. "Ah, my little shoppe, it does very well and keeps me out of trouble. I bring everything in from Europe. Saint Tropez, Dusseldorf, Paris, Corfu, Capri. I am proud to say I don't carry one thing made in China, not a tote, not a shoe. Everything from Europe. In fact, dahlink, you are a lucky man to find me on Maui. I leave next week for a month-long buying trip. So la-la. Enjoy"

"What about your dogs? Who will care for them?"

"Oh, Sherman will be back." She dismissed her husband with impatient eyebrows and a raised shoulder. "Tell me something about your Africa, Lion."

"What would you like to hear? It's an enormous and remarkably diverse place."

"Anything. Tell me anything."

Lion thought a moment, scanning his mental images of Sudan and could find nothing, except his mother's shining face, that did not cause him pain. To entertain Laila and live up to her expectations, he sat back, smiled and said, "My father named me for his favorite bull. It's traditional."

"You had a bull named Lion? And what did you call a lion? Moo-Moo? Ooh, wait. That's what Hawaiians call a dress."

He laughed. "The bull was the color of a lion. My grandfather had the same name after a different bull. In Dinka, Lion is Kor."

"Kor. I like that."

She began to pour herself another glass of wine when the waiter pounced and took over. She continued, "So you are really named for your grandfather."

"My father always insisted I was named for the bull, not the man. It was better luck, he claimed, since cattle are wealth. I never knew whether he was joking or not."

"Tell me, Lion, do you have any jewelry connections in Africa?"

"I beg your pardon?"

"African jewelry is so original. I've seen gorgeous tribal pieces. I'd love to bring some authentic items to Maui. Nobody else is doing Africa, and I predict with our Black president, we will see an upswing of interest in African art and jewelry." She tilted her head and raised her glass. "I'm good at predicting retail trends. It's my great strength."

"I'm afraid I can't help you. Jewelry was not part of my African experience."

She sipped more wine, closed her eyes. A tear escaped. "My world is so superficial. I know that. Here you are, a former slave now living in Hawaii and dedicating your life to helping others, and what am I doing? Selling dresses and sandals to people who have more money than God. You must think me a very foolish woman."

"I think you are a very brave woman."

She laughed suddenly, harshly. "Brave? Me? Why?"

"I don't know why, but I've always had a feeling that you have overcome some great tragedy in your past. We survivors recognize each other. We can smell each other's wounds."

"I thought I smelled like Chanel Allure Eau de Parfum."

"Do you want to tell me about it?"

Glass raised, she clicked her tongue. "Someday, maybe, but tonight we are having too much fun, dear Kor." In the course of the dinner, she finished off the bottle of wine.

When the valet brought her Mercedes, she slipped into the passenger seat and slept on the way home, head thrown back, mouth open, emitting sweet little snores.

In the middle of the night, surfacing from dreamless sleep, Lion thought he felt the dreaded weight of the enemy on his chest. He expected the usual stench of sulphur but instead was enveloped in a fragrance of lilies and roses. He sat bolt upright and saw in the dim moonlight leaking in the window, not the enemy, but Laila sitting on his bed, her pale, shimmering robe fallen open.

"Shhh," she said. "Please, Lion, I need you." She reached out and lightly placed her hand on his bare thigh.

He leaped from the bed as if stung and stood trembling by the window. "Please Laila. Leave me."

She rose from the bed and padded toward him.

He glared out the window into the dark, sweat dewing his brow, and commanded, "Don't touch me." His neck throbbed. "I beg you."

She drew back and collapsed limply on the bed, every line of her body portraying rejection.

He should comfort her, yes, he heard the sibilant whisper: *You are a priest and this woman needs Christ's comfort. What would Jesus do? Comfort her, of course. Nothing more.*

"Oh God, oh God." The words were torn from him. He couldn't afford to comfort her, to smell her, to be close to her and embrace the shimmering robe and the luminous body beneath it.

"Making love is not an evil thing, Lion," she softly argued. "David loved Bathsheba and God understood David's passion even when David had Bathsheba's husband, Uriah the Hittite, killed. God still sent his son to be of the house of David. So who does it hurt if we love each other?"

He could not look at her but focused on a dark tree rising against the stars beyond the window. "I don't know why Jesus was celibate," he said, "or why it's so important, but I have chosen to follow him in his way. I've taken vows and I take them most seriously."

"Look at me, Lion. God made me. Tell me I'm bad."

Anguished, he turned to face her, his body trembling. Hoarsely he whispered, "You are beautiful." The admission broke the enchantment as if he had snapped his fingers. He shrugged. "And I'm flattered by your attention."

"Don't condescend."

"Laila, if you care for me, you'll leave this room." He pleaded, "I am still a man."

She pulled her robe tight, knotting the sash. "You said I was brave. I'm not." She composed herself, and continued, "When I was fourteen years old, my family lived in Garmisch-Partenkirchen, a beautiful town high in the Bavarian Alps. Oh yes, everybody loves Garmisch. The

American soldiers based in Europe take holiday in beautiful Garmisch. I was on my way home from school one day, and one of those soldiers grabbed me. He dragged me into the woods and raped me. I was then a virgin."

He instinctively took a dangerous step toward her.

"No," she ordered. "You stay there." She fled to the doorway and paused, the hall light making a halo about her tousled head. "I had a baby girl." Her voice fell to a whisper, her shoulders rounded to shelter her heart. My parents made me give her up." Tears streamed down her shadowed face. "I don't know where she is."

"God planned your little girl from the beginning of time. Her life is an integral part of his great plan of creation. He has not abandoned her."

"He should have figured out a better way to get her born."

"God seems to have trouble in this area. Look what he put his own mother through."

"Please forgive me, Father." The honorific was pointed. She backed into the hall. "Ack, I've probably just had too much Hattenheimer Schutzenhaus." She turned away, then paused. "I was using you, wasn't I?"

"That occurred to me."

"I'm sorry. Does this count as confession?"

"I imagine it does. Yes."

"I am truly sorry."

"Are you okay?"

"Yes."

"We'll talk in the morning."

"Thank you Father." This time she said it gently.

Lion closed his door. He climbed into bed and lay awake for a long time, overcome with monumental loneliness.

Before the sun even cleared the mountain, Laila had two horses saddled. She and Lion rode into the silence and chill of the eucalyptus forest above Olinda with Michael, Hans and Heidi tearing ahead and racing back. The horses snorted, impatient to run, but since Lion was not much of a rider, Laila set a plodding pace.

As the trail wound out of the forest and into upland meadows, Laila suddenly gave her horse free rein and raced ahead. Lion had all he could do to keep his own mount from speeding after her. As it willfully picked up its pace, he bounced in the saddle, jarring his teeth and brains.

Laila came galloping back, her face flushed and happy, hair wind-blown. She dismounted, unpacked a picnic breakfast and spread out orange cinnamon buns and sliced pineapple on a red and white *palaka* print tablecloth, then poured hot chocolate. All of Maui basked in morning sunshine. Below them, the resorts of Wailea and the wall of holiday condominiums in Kihei lay softly on the lip of the land where the ocean tasted it. Tiny surfers paddled out for the first waves of the day and small boats etched their way across the morning's blue sea, heading for Molokini. Finally Laila said, "My lost daughter would be thirty-nine. Imagine me with a thirty-nine-year-old daughter."

Lion smiled. "No one would believe it."

"Her birthday is February twelfth. Every year on her birthday, I go to Mass and ask God to let her know that her mother sends her love. I think of that girl every day and I don't even know my own child's name."

"What do you call her in your prayers?"

"Marlena." Her face lit up at the saying of the name. "My little Marlena. I held her in my arms. I visited her in the orphanage every week until she was adopted by an American military couple. It was all very hush-hush."

"Have you ever made any attempt to find her?"

"I don't want to interfere with her life and I'm afraid. What if she had a horrible childhood? What if her parents didn't love her? She will ask about her biological father. What do I tell her? Your father raped me? What if she hates me? You see, I am not a brave woman at all. You misjudged me." She began to pack up the picnic things, snapping lids shut.

"I think not. Does Sherman know?"

"Yes."

Laila briskly waved the tablecloth, shaking out crumbs. She leaned into her horse before mounting, eyes on the stirrups and said, "Thank you for rejecting me last night. It would have been a terrible mistake."

Just as quietly, he answered, "How could my inner turmoil be construed as rejection of you? My 'no' was an affirmation of the life I have chosen to give to God. It had nothing to do with rejecting you."

That evening when Laila drove Lion to the tiny white Holy Ghost Church in Kula, the crowd was already overflowing, all waiting to tell him their sins. He would have to return to Honolulu before he could confess his own lust to the bishop.

*The body is such a betrayer, seldom on the side of the spirit, warring, waiting with its urgencies, needing only a word, a glance, a fragrant moment to seize power.*

# Chapter 21
DAWN PATROL

Onshore winds fueled the power of the fifteen-foot waves as they surged ashore at Hana, Maui, thrashing and crashing on jet black sands. Lion lounged on his board out beyond the breakers. It was dawn and three other surfers had braved the early morning chill to catch the first big surf of the winter season. A skinny wasp-waisted boy of about thirteen with gleaming brown skin and the surfer's well developed shoulders fearlessly, expertly dropped in from the top of a wave, rode its wild foaming face, all grace and grit, and veered into the tube, emerging with bellows of joy.

Sudden, acute pain pierced Lion as he sat astride his surfboard. It lasted just an instant, but he saw with terrible clarity his own youth. These little windows of memory were beginning to open with a disturbing frequency, sneaking up on him and mocking his happiness when he least expected them. He dipped his hand in the salt water, blessed himself, and thanked God that in this place a boy could enjoy the bounty of creation and grow happily into his manhood with a reasonable expectation of long life. Earlier, Lion had seen the boy's school books piled on rocks safely back from the reach of the sea, not far from where Michael curled up under the coconut palms. Lion watched the horizon for the next set of waves. He had given an appreciative "shaka" salute as the boy paddled back out. Now the boy grinned widely and returned the salute, arm exultantly high in the air.

Rugged little Alau island loomed behind the surfers while the soft benevolent greens of the Maui countryside spread out before them, burnished in golden morning light. Haleakala, the House of the Sun, rose into mist-veiled heights robed in verdure. A splendid peace sat on Lion's shoulders even though all was wet turbulence around him.

*If you keep your eyes firmly on goodness you will remain calm though wave-tossed and cold. More than that, you will learn to embrace the storms, because all of it is necessary to bring you to this place, for you to have this moment.*

What was the pull of surfing for the boy? He didn't sit still long enough for contemplation but took four waves for every one of Lion's. No wonder he was so thin.

They were both straddling their boards looking out to sea, Lion crouching, the boy on his stomach, legs bent up, toes twitching, one arm on the nose of his board, the other dangling in the water, poised for the next "right" wave. Lion saw everything so clearly it was as if his mind snapped a photograph, perfectly exposed, sharp, arrested in time. Something bumped his board. In the same instant, a mammoth sinister shape passed beneath him, speeding right for the boy. In a rush of exploding water, a huge shark came up, its horrible maw open. It grabbed the boy's arm, violently shaking him from his board.

Lion yelled as he raced toward the attack, heart drumming, legs and arms made of iron, moving anyway. "Be gone! Be gone!" Curling waves, white water. Faster. "In the name of Jesus, I command you, be gone."

The frothing waves blushed with blood. He continued to roar like the beast of his own name as he pulled the dazed boy from the roiling water onto his board. His right arm was gone, along with a jagged piece of his board. Lion paddled away from the attack, trailing blood. The fifteen-foot shark, with a bellyful of fiberglass and bone, disappeared. Lion ripped off his surfboard leash, tied a hasty tourniquet and caught the next wave, crouching on his knees, holding onto the boy.

The other two surfers had seen the attack. One was already ashore, grabbing a cell phone from his backpack. The other stood chest deep in the water to assist them onto the sand.

The boy slipped in and out of consciousness while they covered him in every article of clothing they had. The surfer with the cellphone ran up with a blanket.

"You're going to be okay," Lion told the boy. "What's your name?"

"Kimo," he whispered.

"Jesus loves you, Kimo, and he will bring you through."

His eyes fluttered closed. He was deathly pale.

Lion made the sign of the cross on the boy's forehead, his lips, his ears, the shoulder from which the arm had been torn.

"Thank you." Only his lips moved. There was no sound.

"Jesus is right here with you, Kimo."

He lost consciousness, a small smile on his bloodless lips.

Lion kept saying his name, "Kimo. Kimo, stay with us," as he knelt over him.

The ambulance sirens roused the boy. Weakly he whispered, "My arm is gone, isn't it?"

"Yes, Kimo," Lion said. "But you are here, safely in the arms of Jesus. Do you hear the sirens Kimo? It's the ambulance, Kimo. Hold my hand while we pray: Our Father who art in heaven..."

The boy slipped away again. His lips fell slightly open.

The emergency medical team took over, cutting off Lion's blood-soaked leash from the stump of the arm and applying a tourniquet band.

They called for a helicopter to get him to the hospital in Wailuku, quickly put him into the ambulance and raced for the Hana airfield.

Lion gathered up the abandoned schoolbooks and clothing. The boy's name was in a notebook, Kimo Sing. One of the surfers said, "I'll show you where he lives."

Fortunately, the Sings lived right in Hana town. It was a small, cheery house with a well-tended garden, one street back from the bay. He rolled down the car windows. "You'll have to wait here, Michael."

"I'll wait with him," the surfer said.

A little bronze gong called to the interior of the house. "Mrs. Sing?"

"Yes." The woman was wary, her plain oval face alert to inconvenience or a sales pitch.

"I'm Father Lion Majok, a Catholic priest. I have news about your son, Kimo."

Her hands went to her mouth as she fell against the doorframe.

"He's been taken by helicopter to Maui Memorial Hospital in Wailuku."

"What happened, tell me, tell me." The woman clutched her ribs.

"He was surfing. A shark attack."

"It's someone else. Kimo's in school. His surfboard's in the carport." The woman ran outside and saw the empty rack. "Oh my God. Oh no."

"Let me call someone for you. I have his books in my car. Apparently, he cut class."

The mother walked in small tight circles wringing her hands. "Call the hotel." She gave him the number "Ask for Calvin Sing. Please. He's a waiter, breakfast shift. Jesus, Jesus, Jesus."

"Let's go inside," Lion urged.

When told that Mr. Sing was unavailable, Lion said. "Page him, please. It's a family emergency. I'm a priest." He waited for the anxious hello. "Calvin Sing? My name is Lion Majok"

Mrs. Sing grabbed the phone from him. "Calvin, please. Come home. It's Kimo. He was attacked by a shark. They flew him to Wailuku to the hospital. Hurry, please. We've got to go." She listened, then pleaded, "I don't know, I don't know. Just hurry." She slammed the phone into its cradle and began to gather up her purse. "My phone. My cell phone. Then I have to pack a little bag. Please call our pastor. Brother Nelson. There. In the Rolodex. Ledbetter, Nelson and Alice Ledbetter." She flew into the bedroom, opening doors and drawers in a frenzy of motion. Lion made the calls for her.

The minister promised to come immediately and, indeed, arrived at the same time as Calvin Sing. As soon as she saw them, Mrs. Sing collapsed in a chair and began to weep piteously. Her husband knelt to comfort her, taking her hands in his. "Our son is in God's hands. We need have no fear."

When Lion introduced himself to their pastor as a Catholic priest, the pastor stiffened almost imperceptibly. A moment passed before he recovered his charity, and a little too jovially clapped Lion about the shoulders. "We're all on the same team." Brother Nelson then took charge and gathered the Sings into an exclusive huddle. Calvin opened the circle to include Lion, reaching for his hand. Brother Nelson's imploring prayers were loud, and dramatic with anguish and authority, demanding divine attention, dictating the outcome. He shivered and shook, turned red with fervor, pulverizing the hands he held.

Calvin Sing withdrew and directed Lion into the kitchen. "Can you tell me, quickly, what happened."

"I was surfing. Your son was on his board a few yards from me."

"Oh that one. Cutting school again."

Lion continued, "A large shark attacked. I was able to pull Kimo onto my board, but I'm afraid he's lost his right arm. I tied a tourniquet, but I'm sure he lost a lot of blood. The medivac helicopter flew him to Wailuku. He might be at the hospital by now. You could call."

"Thank you." Calvin took the phone into the bedroom and closed the door. He emerged as if beaten, and announced, "They're rushing Kimo into surgery. They're doing everything they can. He's lost his arm, as you said, and a lot of blood."

Mrs. Sing went as pale as if her own blood had been drained. "We need another helicopter. We've got to get to the hospital."

The pastor hit the keypad of his phone. "I'm calling our prayer warriors."

Calvin put his arm across his wife's shoulders, squeezing her. "Stay calm, Irene. You have to be strong for Kimo."

"I know. I can't doubt. We have to be of one accord. No weak link in the prayer chain."

Brother Nelson quoted: "Ephesians six, verse thirteen. 'Therefore put on the full armor of God, so that when the day of evil comes, you may be able to stand your ground, and after you have done everything, to stand. Stand firm then, with the belt of truth buckled around your waist, with the breastplate of righteousness in place, and with your feet fitted with the readiness that comes from the gospel of peace. In addition to all this, take up the shield of faith, with which you can extinguish all the flaming arrows of the evil one. Take the helmet of salvation and the sword of the spirit which is the word of God.'"

Lion wanted to tell Irene Sing that if she was weak and could not stand and carry a sword, Jesus would carry her in his arms, shelter her in the shadow of his wing, but he saw that this was no time to indulge in sectarian dissection of scripture. This family needed the strength of their familiar rock.

"Kimo will be in surgery for a few hours," Calvin said. "We'll drive to Wailuku and be there when he comes out of it."

His wife said, "We'll pray the whole way. We'll cover the doctors, the nurses, everyone touching our son."

Brother Nelson grasped his own hands in prayer, looked to the ceiling and cried out. "Lord, we claim the victory. We come against all the powers of the evil one, in the precious name of Jesus." He dwelled on the name as if it were delicious. The Sings chorused their amens, then Calvin said, "We'll take our car, then we'll have it there when we can drive Kimo home. I guess we'll be in Wailuku for a few days. I better call my boss. We'll have to get a room in Wailuku."

Brother Nelson insisted on going with the Sings. His wife would make the three-hour drive to the hospital later and pick him up.

Lion volunteered, "I know someone you might be able to stay with. She has a nice big house right in Wailuku. Let me make a call."

The practicalities of dealing with tragedy asserted themselves, and became almost as salutary as prayer, distracting everyone from panic and despair. The Sings and their pastor donned their helmets, belts, swords, all the clanging armor of their beliefs and set out on the winding road from Hana, crossing the fifty-four one-lane bridges on the way to Wailuku.

Father Lion had no doubt that the trio would pray the entire way, never once faltering in their conviction that Kimo would live, claiming the victory, putting God on the spot so that he had to perform or lose face. Lion smiled. God, of course, would see right through their manipulations and be filled with compassion for them. They were, after all, poor creatures of his own design, coping as best as they could with their powerlessness and mortality. He would rain down his love on them as they drove into the nightmare.

Lion thanked the young surfer, got into his car and began to shake violently. He found, to his dismay, that he could not drive. He had not faced death in all its pitiless implacability in a long, long time. If death can come so swiftly, unexpectedly, randomly, on a sunny Hawaiian morning, then there is no place of safety in this world. Finally he said to Michael, "That shark was a beautiful creature, superbly designed for its purpose, which is, simply, to kill, to eat." He remembered the rows of teeth, the cavernous maw.

# Chapter 22

## THE PROMISED LAND

Television crews crowded the room, jostling for position, rearranging the parents into pleasing tableaus around the bed, making sure they kept Kimo Sing's bandaged stump in their digital crosshairs. The boy, propped with pillows, was perfectly composed in the midst of the media blitz, answering inane, inappropriate questions in a voice as clear and sure as a sunlit wave. His mother couldn't keep her hands off him, smoothing his heavy hair, tugging the hospital gown, fluffing the pillows, pitifully rubbing his only arm.

Lion had just arrived and hovered in the corridor. The voraciousness of the media crowd made him want to turn away and head for the hospital cafeteria, but Calvin Sing spotted him and rushed toward him, cameras swiveling to capture the action.

Taking Lion by the arm and proudly displaying him to the reporters, Calvin announced, "This is the man who saved my son."

Microphones were thrust at Lion. "Tell us what happened. Did you see the attack? How big was the shark? What's your view on global warming and shark extinction? How did you feel seeing his arm gone?"

"I was there. I did what anyone would have done. That's all."

Seizing the moment, the doctor ordered the news crews out.

Calvin Sing gripped Lion's hand. "I never really thanked you."

Mrs. Sing placed his other hand against her cheek. "Without you, I would be grieving with the worst sorrow a mother can know."

Kimo beamed. "Hey, Dude, I saw you catch some waves. Good styling."

"Not nearly as good as you."

The boy's eyes filled with tears. "If I can't surf, I don't think I can live."

Lion cited scripture because Kimo obviously knew and treasured the Bible. "Saint Paul reminds us to worry about nothing and pray about everything."

Kimo jumped in with the attribution: "Philippians four, verse six." He glanced at his hugely bandaged shoulder and quickly looked away. "I've always sought God's will. Thy will be done on Earth as it is in Heaven."

Lion responded, "Seeking God's will in all things is admirable, wonderful, especially in one so young. Most people are never able to get that far on their spiritual journey, but after the surrender of your will, God requires one more thing of you. You won't like it, Kimo, but it's the ultimate thing necessary for serenity."

"What's that?"

"The surrender of your heart's desire."

The boy gasped, "Give him my surfing?"

"Yes."

"But it's my life."

"Precisely." Lion drew closer. "Give it all to him. You may find that surfing is exactly what God has in mind for you. If so, he will guide you and help you get back on your board to surf again without fear. But you must be open to other paths, paths perhaps not of your own choosing."

Lion thought of his coveted monastic cell and felt hypocritical asking this child to do what he had not yet been able to do himself: surrender desire. With less certainty, he advised, "Honor God with what is dearest to you and he will not be outdone in generosity."

Kimo sank deeper into his pillows. "You know, I'm trying to be up-beat. I can't do any more. How can God ask me to give up surfing?"

"Nobody is forcing you. I am just pointing the way to peace." Lion added, "A peace I myself have not yet achieved. Just be honest with God. Keep talking to your Abba Father who loves you." He turned to the parents. "I'll see you this evening at the house."

Calvin thanked Lion for arranging for them to stay with Lehua Nii, then Irene walked into the corridor with him. "I'm glad you said what you did to Kimo. I hope he never goes in the water again."

As Lion walked back to Lehua's house in the heat of the afternoon, his own words weighed him down. *Surrender your heart's desire. It sounds so noble and profound and you think, "Of course. That's it." But how do you stop desiring?* How could he turn off his yearning for soli-tude and prayer? It was a good and holy desire. Surely he must be al-lowed that shred of who he really was. *You will have to rip my desire out of me, Lord, and when you do, my very soul goes with it.*

And that, Lion knew, was the essence of his life's issues. Solitude can be a terrifying thing. It is not always tranquil. The inner soul is stirred. The deepest fears may rise to the surface. Many people, in pursuit of the spirit, without the fortification of companionship or accountability lose sight of the rational.

Lion saw himself alone in a cell, on his knees. He might become a man of hair shirts, self-flagellation and spiked belts. He didn't think that would happen, but one never knew. Possibly he'd just creep away and become nothing special, just another struggling, sinning human taking up space on the planet, contributing nothing of value.

Three days later, Kimo Sing was released from the hospital and the Sings spent their last night at the big old house in Wailuku.

Lion was glad to see his brother, Kawika, who had come back to Maui to present Lehua's petition for permanent custody of her granddaughters to the court in the morning. The bishop had also come to speak on behalf of his former secretary.

"How's Sunshine McAndrews?" Lion asked Kawika.

"I suppose she's fine. I haven't talked to her."

"I liked her."

"Me, too. That's the problem. I could have gone for her in a big way, but I promised myself that I'd marry and have kids only with a Hawaiian woman."

"Organic eugenics."

"Hey, we Hawaiians are an endangered species and I believe we have a lot to contribute to the world."

"Is it so important, Kawika? Isn't it more important just to live a good life?"

"A so-called good life isn't good enough for me. I want justice. I want to know that my story doesn't end with my passing." He turned to see Lehua gingerly making her way down the stairs and sprang up to help her. He sat her next to himself and offered her a bowl of rice.

Calvin Sing said, "I never thought I would be breaking bread with the Catholic bishop of Honolulu." He laughed. "I was always told the Catholic church was the whore of Babylon."

Irene Sing gripped his arm in alarm.

Father Lion, with a twin perched on each knee, said, "To quote your pastor, Calvin, 'We're all on the same team.'" He handed Shy-Anne to the bishop and Shoshona to Mrs. Sing, then retrieved an *ukulele* from the living room. He had tuned it earlier in the day, and he began to strum. Everyone relaxed. Now they could smile. Lion looked around the table at Lehua in her wig, Kimo with one arm, Kawika of the bad attitude and good heart, Bishop Carroll with his secret son, Carlene stoutly shouldering the hurts of a lifetime and the twins with their cigarette burns and uncertain fate. All of them had been invited to stand closer to the cross. He looked at the happiness and food spread out before them and could have wept with joy.

He began to sing: "Now there's a little baby her name is Carly Rose. She is the sweetest thing no matter where she goes..." He sang it in English and Hawaiian to rousing applause, Kawika joining him for the Hawaiian verses. Lion then turned to Carlene. "That was for you. Thank you for the beautiful meal and for your beautiful spirit."

Kimo lifted his glass of milk in salute. "Reverend Lion, you rock as good as the Ka'au Crater Boys. And here's to Miss Carly Rose."

Lehua said, "Carlene, that's your name from now on. Our precious Carly Rose. I couldn't do this without you."

Carlene abruptly left the table. Lion heard her sniffling in the kitchen, heard paper towels unrolling from the rack. She needed a moment to compose herself. She came back in with a pot in each hand. "More coffee? Tea anyone?" When she sat down, she pulled the twins into her lap and said, "Now I know what a real family feels like."

Lion, still strumming, said, "God keeps giving us families, sometimes when we least expect them. They are for our comfort and learning. And most of all for our loving." He did not look at Bishop Carroll, who was blushing furiously.

"Lilinoe." Lion said her name aloud as he awoke the next morning. His last dream before waking centered on his *hanai* sister. He dreamt of her sitting on a little stool in the middle of some grass; a pile of dark lava rocks beside her. On the perimeter, a stone wall was under construction, and he saw that stone by stone, Lili was tightly walling herself in. Any parlor prophet could interpret that dream.

Lion talked to Bishop Carroll on the porch after breakfast. "I know someone who's had an abortion. I understand and agree with the Church's uncompromising position on the subject, but in this case, the mother is only a child herself, and she's grieving. I have to find a way to help her. What can I do, as a priest?"

The bishop looked up from the *Maui News*. Doves cooed in the trees. "Hear her confession, of course, Lion." He glanced back at the page he had been reading and added absently, "And bring her the Lord's forgiveness. That's why we have the sacraments."

"She won't confess. She's not ready."

Resigned, Bishop Carroll put down the paper. "Have you heard of Project Rachel?"

"Vaguely I remember hearing something."

"When you get back to Honolulu, access my secretary's computer. There's a nun in Kaneohe who's involved in an abortion recovery ministry. Her name is Sister Felicia Jenkins. I've gotten nothing but good reports about the program." The bishop looked out on the dewy garden. "These women need a way back."

"Thank you."

"By the way, how's Kamana doing?"

"Not well at all," Lion said. "Iris broke her leg and hip. After the Saint Augustine retreat, I hope to spend a few days at home with them."

"It's fortunate they have so many children to help out. If I can do anything, let me know." The bishop picked up the paper again, and said with studied nonchalance, "I haven't heard from Dan Johnson since he left for Afghanistan."

Lion sat back down and asked softly, "Did you hope to?"

The bishop hit the newspaper to straighten it out and kept looking at it. "I wondered. I suppose I'm just a curiosity to him. Let's see what the old boy looks like. Well, he got a good gander at the paterfamilias and that was apparently enough. Can't say as I blame him."

Lion noticed an uncharacteristic trace of self-pity and decided not to indulge it. "Have you told anyone else about him yet?"

"I'm aware that I'm procrastinating. There are going to be severe consequences, as you can well imagine, to such a revelation. In a very selfish way, I'm relieved not to have heard from him." With a grumpy harrumph that stiffened his spine, the bishop folded the paper neatly and put it aside. "I wish I had brought a camera the day Dan and I met, but I didn't want to seem intrusive; forty years late with the baby pictures. He's a fine looking man, I'll say that. I suppose I could write to his mother and ask for a photograph."

"Perhaps if you ask anyone for a photo it should be your son himself."

The bishop glanced guiltily toward the door to see if anyone had eavesdropped. "Of course," he whispered. "But that's more fraught with potential rejection."

The screen door whined on its hinges and Kawika, in suit and tie and carrying a briefcase, came out onto the porch. Lion had never seen him dressed for court. He looked like a stranger.

"Sorry to interrupt," Kawika said to the bishop. "But we don't want to be late. Your support for Lehua will carry some weight."

Bishop Carroll sprang from his chair. "If you have any difficulties with that website, Lion, call me. We have to have dinner soon. They're having a special menu to celebrate the new burgundies at Chef Mavro's."

"I'm inviting myself to that one," Kawika said, "But right now we've got a custody case to win." He turned to the door as Lehua carefully let herself out. "Right, Tutu?"

Lehua forced a smile. "God is good, and our cause is just. We going to win. *Imua* Kawika."

# Chapter 23

## ALOHA 'OE

Back on Oahu, Lion stopped at Zippy's in Kailua for a big tub of chili. Its rich aroma perfumed Saint Augustine's parish car as he and Michael drove through Enchanted Lake, past the riding stables, and on to Waimanalo. The sky promised rain and the Ko'olau Mountains were already festooned with mist.

He got out of the car to open the Kamana gate, and as he did, he gazed fondly at the tranquil farm and the rich greens of the orderly crops. Coco and Brownie grazed beside the *kalo lo'i*. There was the old red house with the generous porch, the cat asleep in the saddle on the railing, as usual. It never changed. And yet, inside that house, a man lay dying and a young woman despaired.

*Help me, Lord, to bring comfort. Give me your words.*

Nalu and Thatcher ambled over, wagging their tails, not barking, even when Michael jumped out the window to join them.

Lili came out on the porch looking thin and haggard, aged beyond her tender years. She hung her head. Her long hair parted, baring her neck. "I'm glad you're here, Lion. I got your old room ready. Pops is real bad. I called Pohai last night to come home from Vegas. Kawika knows." Her posture defied embrace. "Oh," she said, "Kawika said to tell you he got his decision on the Maui case. Lehua got the kids."

Lion wanted to hug and hold Lili, but it was as if an electric fence hemmed her in. "Praise God."

"Praise Kawika," she said, not meeting his eyes.

Lion held out the tub of chili as an offering. "Thought I'd give you a break. No need cook."

A trace of her old sassy self leaked through her fatigue. "Right. The house is crowded and you bring beans for everyone. Good thinking, Lion."

He laughed. "What other brilliant thing can I do to help?"

"Right now, just be with Pops and Mom. Moses took the taro to the poi factory. Pohai's flight gets in at three. You can pick her up at the airport."

"Will do. You okay, Lili?"

Her look was murderous. "Lay off, okay, Lion. I am getting through with white knuckles. Don't stand on my fingers."

She marched into the house announcing brightly, "Hey, look what the cat dragged in." The whole house was hushed and hunkered down, as if the floors and walls and everyone within awaited the awesome arrival of Death.

Iris, sitting by her sleeping husband's bedside, her leg still in a cast, reached up toward Lion. "You bring joy to my aching heart."

He kissed her, smelling coconut in her grey hair. "How is he?"

"We got the morphine drip going. Soon, Lion, his suffering be over."

Lion had seen the film *E.T.* and that's who Pops looked like, dark and wizened and so small in the white sheets, the shape of his skull pronounced against the white pillow. Lion bent over and kissed him on the forehead. His shallow breathing continued undisturbed.

Iris said, "That Lilinoe is one saint. She's taking it real hard, Lion. Real hard. I worry 'bout her."

"How you holding up, Mom?"

"This darn leg. I feel so helpless, just making more work for everyone."

Lion reached for her hand. "You're usually the one taking care of everyone else, standing in the kitchen, making sure everyone is fed and happy. You're not used to receiving care, are you?"

"Sometimes it's harder to receive than give."

Pops stirred, licked his dry lips. Iris immediately offered him the straw in the bedside cup. "Lion's here, Pops. He came to see you. He gonna stay with us again, got his old room back."

Pops lifted a trembling hand. His eyes fluttered open. "Son." He slowly, painfully breathed it out. He fell back asleep with a small smile. Iris smoothed Vaseline on his lips.

The family, one by one, tip-toed into the kitchen where Lilinoe had cooked rice and heated Zippy's chili. Moses brought home a custard pie. It was a somber meal drenched with love's guilt for eating amidst such sorrow.

Afterward, Lion swept the porch, shook out the chair pillows, then turned to the cat in the saddle who had been watching his industry with a wary and insouciant eye. "Sorry, Popoki, but this is a coup." He chased the cat, who landed in the grass, grumbling. Tail high, Popoki pranced off with great and mincing dignity. Lion wiped down the saddie.

Pohai walked from the airport terminal with such confidence and good posture that she stood out in the arriving crowd. She immediately spotted the Kamana Dodge parked at the curb and hurried toward it, trailing her luggage.

Lion greeted her with a kiss and a plumeria lei. "Mom made it," he said. "Moses picked the flowers."

She held it to her nose. "Plumeria, the best. I smell plumeria and I

191

know I'm home. How's Pops?"

Lion heaved her bags into the back of the truck. "Not so good. It won't be long."

"I'm glad I got here in time. I was worried I'd be too late to say good-bye."

"Lili's been the rock of the family."

"It's about time. She still with that Heck's Angel?"

"You can say Hell's Angel. I won't be offended."

"That guy's not man enough for the title. He's a Saturday rider."

"He left her. So go easy on her."

"Everyone always goes easy on her. That's her problem. At her age, I wasn't allowed to get away with half the stuff she does. How have you been?"

"Just finished up a circuit of Maui and a retreat at Saint Augustine's."

"Did you give 'em hell, Lion?"

"I hope I gave them Heaven."

"God, I'm glad to be home." Pohai leaned her head toward the open window and let the wind rake her hair.

"Mom broke her leg."

"What? When?" Pohai sat up indignantly. "No one told me."

"They didn't want you to give up your show and come home from Vegas."

She shook her head. "You can't turn your back on them. You never know what you're going to find when you go home. Cheech."

When they got to the house, Momi came out on the porch and waved. She was a voluptuous young woman with dark skin, full breasts, and delicate features. Her enormous sparkling eyes radiated an exceptional life force. A T-shirt stretched tightly over her ballooning stomach.

Pohai said, "And there's something else nobody told me. Moses has obviously been busy." She jumped down from the truck, rushed up the porch steps and hugged the expectant mother. "Hey, congrats. When's the big day?"

"Not soon enough," Momi said, all aglow. "Got one rascal in there."

"Boy or girl?"

"Boy. Hi, Lion." Momi kissed him on the cheek.

"God bless you and your little son." Lion hadn't seen Momi in a while and hadn't realized she was this far along in her pregnancy. He ached at the thought of Lili.

Pohai gasped when she saw Pops and bent over to cry into her mother's embrace while Pops slept. Moses and Kawika came over to put their arms around her. When she composed herself, she asked, "Where's Lili?"

Iris said, "Napping. Twenty-four-seven that girl taking care of us."

"She should be in school," Kawika said. "She's losing a whole semester."

"I'm home now," Pohai said. "I can take over and she can get back to school."

"How long you home for?" Kawika asked.

"As long as it takes. I'm in no hurry." She added defensively, "I don't have to go back to Vegas at all."

"We'll talk about that later," Iris said. "Momi brought dinner, didn't you, Momi, dear."

"Kalua pig and cabbage," she said.

"My favorite." Pohai hugged her again.

"I know. Moses told me. And mac salad and poi."

"God, I am home."

Lili and Pops slept through dinner. Momi set out paper plates so clean-up was easy. Pohai unpacked her ukulele, sat beside Pops's bed and began to sing softly, *'E Ku'u Pua Mai Ole.'"*

After a few bars, Pops opened his eyes. "You're here."

"Yeah," she smiled.

"I waited for you."

Pohai stopped playing and kissed him on his forehead.

"You leave your lips dere?" His eyes were exceptionally clear, as if already seeing beyond his physical surroundings.

Lion had often witnessed such a rally before the end.

Pohai grinned. "Bright red Lady-Gaga lips, Pops."

"Den I'm almost ready. No need da long faces. Where's my sweetheart?"

Iris leaned closer. "Right here. I'm always right here, Pops." They held hands. "Forty-two years wit' this man." Tears rolled down her cheeks.

Momi passed her a tissue.

Pops asked, "Lion, you gonna give me last blessings?"

Softly he answered, "Sure, Pops. Give me a minute to get ready." He went outside, cut a ti leaf from the plant at the foot of the steps, quickly de-ribbed, washed, and dried it. He poured water into a calabash and blessed it. He then got out his Bible, the little round case holding the consecrated bread, and the precious vial of Jerusalem olive oil the bishop had given him. He draped his stole about his neck, acutely missing the stole his mother had embroidered for his ordination. He was ready.

He walked into the room, waving the ti leaf to sprinkle everyone and everything with blessed water. Pops asked to sit up and Kawika pushed a button to raise the head of the bed while Iris resettled his pillows.

Lion then asked everyone to leave the room for a few minutes while he heard Pops' confession. As they filed out, Kawika grinned. "Hey, Pops, no change your will now. I get all the recycle cans under the porch, right?" Kawika, as an attorney, must have seen and heard many deathbed dramas where families fought over the goods while the corpse was still warm.

Pops' confession was sweet, like a child's. He smiled. "Can't get into much trouble deez days. I guess my numbah one sin was doubt, but I worked on it. You know what, Son? Even if I get da udder side and I find out it's all one big crock, I still okay wit' it because my fait in Jesus helped me live one good and peaceful life. I do believe dat dis day I will be wit' our Lord in Paradise, like da tief what hung wit' him on da cross."

"All your sins are forgiven, Pops, in the name of the Father and of the Son and of the Holy Spirit." He anointed Pops's head and hands with oil, making small crosses with his thumb. After a few minutes of quiet meditation, Lion invited the rest of the family back in. "I have communion for all who want it." He approached Pops first and was about to give him the wafer of bread when Iris interceded, whispering, "He can't handle. Just break off a tiny piece. I'll receive the rest of his."

Lion bent over and placed a small crumb on the man's outstretched tongue, saying, "The body of Christ, Pops."

"Amen."

He then did the same for each member of the family, noting Lili's continued absence. When he came to Momi she said, "I'm Pentecostal, Lion, not Catholic."

Moses spoke up, "Yeah, but you eating da bread for da little guy inside and he one Cat-lick."

Everyone laughed, glad for the lightness of the moment.

Lion said, "Momi, Catholics believe that this bread, while it looks and tastes like bread, is really and truly the body of the living God, Jesus Christ. If you can accept this mystery, let me put the bread in your left hand. Then use your right hand to put it in your mouth."

She glanced at Moses who nodded encouragement, then put out her hand, smiling.

Lion found himself curiously detached and gave everyone a few minutes for private prayer.

Pops broke the silence, his voice quivering and raspy, "Hey, you folks gonna sing me out?"

Choking up, Pohai asked, "What you want us to sing, Pops?"

"*Puamana,* den *Hi'ilawe,* den whateveh."

The family began to sing together. Midway through the first song, Lili came out of her room and joined them, wedging herself between Pohai and her mother.

The pace of the music picked up with "Hi'ilawe." Kawika took an *ipu* from atop a cabinet and gently tapped out the beat. Pops whispered, "I just resting my eyes. Keep singing."

On the second verse of *"Kanaka Waiwai"* Lion noticed Pops shudder slightly and exhale. He did not take another breath.

Iris noticed, too, and pulled in her lips and looked up at Lion, her eyes brimming. "Pops gone."

Pohai hesitated with the music and Lion said, "Keep playing. Keep singing. His ears still hear. It's the last sense to close while the soul is departing."

They sang louder, filling the room with their grief and music. Pohai rolled seamlessly into "Aloha Oe," the beloved song of farewell.

It was too much. Lili threw her arms across her father's body, "Pops, don't go, don't go."

Her mother pulled her gently away. "Let Pops be, Lili Girl. Let him go."

The others kept singing while Iris rocked Lili like a baby.

Lion fingered his priestly stole, feeling for a pride of embroidered lions, knowing they weren't there. This was a beautiful death. He thought of his own father, hacked to death as he struggled to hold and protect his son, his blood warming the boy, his father's body left in the grass, meat for hyenas. Overwhelming grief and shocking resentment assaulted him, causing him to gasp aloud. Pohai leaned into him, saying, "I know, I know." But she didn't know.

# Chapter 24

REQUIEM

Pops' funeral was the kind of party he would have loved. The whole *ohana* gathered for the event: siblings, cousins, uncles, aunties, and friends who might as well be family they stick so close.

The ladies of the Altar Society festively decorated Saint George's Church in Waimanalo with banners, flowers, ferns, palm fronds, and entire flowering limbs of trees.

The musicians played a mix of Hawaiian favorites and hymns, seamlessly riffing from one to the other. People stood up and danced in the aisles when they heard a hula they knew, sometimes a dozen dancers at a time, all dancing for the man everyone knew and loved as "Pops."

The only somber note intruded when a phalanx of young men wheeled in the casket. A barefoot elderly cousin on Iris's side, Kaleo Aiona, draped in *kikepa kapa,* chanted an ancient lamentation, as he led the procession. The cadences rose and fell, as the beloved Hawaiian language began at the *piko,* the navel, rolled across the tongue and flowed out on the breath. It was so visceral, so raw and beautiful that the chant shredded hearts and deeply satisfied at an elementary level, older than memory, needier than doubt. It came from the beginning, before the first tree, before birth, when all was embedded in God

The bishop himself, in full regalia with pointy hat and crooked staff, offered the Requiem Mass, his very presence an honor.

Lion gave the sermon and chose the theme of fatherhood, a disquieting subject in modern America. His *hanai* family sat in the first row beside the casket. He began: "I am blessed in this life to have not one, but three fathers." Suddenly choked up, he struggled to tell his story, "I was born to Jawara Majok. His name means 'lover of peace,' but when I was a child, my father was murdered by men who proclaim peace with their lips yet regard war as holy." He paused. "Later, as a terrified youth from the African bush, a student and stranger in these Islands, I was welcomed as a son by Jacob Kamana, known to everyone as Pops. I don't know if I ever heard Pops utter the word peace, but peace was his whole life. When he stood on his porch and looked out on his *kalo lo'i* with the green leaves drinking the rain, the look on his face was pure peace. Just being in his presence was peace. You sat with Pops and your heart calmed down, no matter what. Pops' father in heaven is my third father. He is also your father, so we are all brothers and sisters."

Lion went on to say how necessary fatherhood was to society and families, how fathers were not merely larger, hairier moms. They had a different, unique role in the raising of a child. "A child at the edge of the ocean is told by its mother, 'Be careful. Watch where you put your foot. Never turn your back on the surf.' The father, on the other hand, urges, 'Swim, son. Ride the wave. You can do it.' The child needs both messages."

Lion urged the men in the congregation to be good fathers like Pops. "Take in the fatherless child. Be a father beyond your blood. God knows there are enough children missing their fathers today."

As the eldest Kamana son, Kawika, dressed in a charcoal grey suit with white shirt and deep blue tie, began the eulogy, he apologized for the grandness of his outfit saying, "I wore this suit for Pops. All his life he worked hard and faithfully with his hands and bent back, so I could go to work in this monkey outfit."

Friends and family laughed, cried and sang their way through the service, then feasted afterward in the church hall at a buffet prepared by the joint church committees of hospitality and bereavement.

When the bishop deigned to stay for the lunch, Lion hovered by his side introducing him to everyone so he felt at ease. In the buffet line, the bishop whispered to Lion, "I don't know what half these dishes are. Will I like this?" he asked, nodding toward a tray of something swimming in rich thick gravy.

"Pig's intestines."

"I'll pass"

Moses laughed and enunciated in self-conscious non-pidgin English, "We Hawaiians don't eat until we're full—we eat until we're tired."

All through the meal, people got up, grabbed the microphone and told stories of Pops. Lion asked Kawika, "Do you think I should tell them about the coffin?"

"Oh da good one," Moses answered.

Lion walked slowly toward the microphone. "This is the story of another funeral," he began. "Mine. It was the day before my ordination and who pulls up to Saint Stephen's Seminary but Pops and Moses in the old Dodge truck. 'We need some muscle here,' Pops says. In the truck he's got this huge piece of furniture wrapped in an old quilt. The minute I saw the shape, I knew what it was and it made me go pale." Hearing ripples of cautious laughter, Lion went on, "White as a ghost."

Moses ambled up and stood beside him, "So white he look one *haole*." Loud laughter erupted.

Lion continued, "I touch the thing and I cannot take my hand away. All of a sudden I know what it is to be a priest. Like I was zapped. Then my brother Moses, here, put that big arm of his around my shoulder and says, 'Pops made it hisself.'"

Moses put his arm around Lion again. "Took Pops one month make da ting."

Lion continued, "My brah here climbs up in the truck and takes off the blanket and Pops is standing there waiting to see what I'm going to do, because the gift Pops has made me is a coffin." He heard the collective gasp.

"If you one vampire, you need da ting," Moses laughed uproariously at himself.

"That coffin was the most beautiful gift I've ever received. The love shone all over it. Now, since I am not a vampire, I have to tell you why Pops made me a coffin."

Moses interjected, "Pops read that Father Damien *moe-moe* in a coffin the night before they make him one priest. Weird, yah?"

Lion didn't point out that Pops had erred. Rather than sleeping in a coffin, Damien, as all his priestly order did, slept in a mortuary shroud the night before ordination. Lion continued, "It was to signify that Damien was dead to his old life, his old desires, and that when he awoke in the morning he would be a new person living only for God. He would be a priest."

"Awesome." Moses shivered. "So we bring dis ting to Lion's room. Lucky his room on da first floor."

"And Pops said to me, 'Dis da real ting, Lion. Tomorrow you be one priest forever.' That night, I briefly considered sleeping in my comfortable bed instead of that hard, narrow coffin, but I couldn't do that. I had to honor Pops, so I climb into the coffin and then I think I should get my pillow. What harm will a pillow do? But I resisted because I didn't think Damien would get a pillow for his head. Remember how he slept under a *hala* tree on Molokai until all the lepers were housed? And let me tell you, that coffin was mighty uncomfortable. I felt the wood in every knob of my spine."

Moses leaned into the microphone, "Good ting da dead no beef."

"That night the devil himself visited me. A wave of frigid air descended on me, like sleeping in a freezer. The thing sat on my chest and its breath was *pilau*. I prayed all night long and then I actually shouted the name of Jesus. And that's when the weight lifted and all of a sudden I could smell plumeria again and the mock orange. I tell you, I didn't get much sleep that night. But by morning, I had died to my old life and was privileged to begin anew with the help of Christ and Pops."

Moses embraced Lion, "We love you, brah."

Later, Lion thanked the bishop for officiating as he walked him to his car. "It means a lot to me. You brought honor to the family."

"It was quite the feast." He took out his wallet, and for a moment Lion was afraid he would degrade the hospitality with an offer of payment, but the bishop extracted a photograph and handed it to Lion.

"Dan Johnson?" Lion looked at the tense face under the helmet and shuddered at the sight and size of the gun on his shoulder. "He really looks like you in this photo."

"Do you think so?"

"Look at that determined jaw. Definitely you."

"I'm a coward. I still haven't told Cardinal McCarthy."

"You don't need to be fearful. You haven't in any way violated your vows. Your son was born before you became a priest."

"It would be a terrible scandal if it came out. Anti-Catholicism is the last fashionable prejudice in America, the thinking man's anti-Semitism. It's actually politically correct, in some circles, to ridicule and hate Catholics. Unfortunately, the Church has fed the cannons of the Catholic haters and Church baiters with our grievous sins against children, and worse, covering them up. Unfortunately, due to these terrible deeds, the Church has lost its moral authority at a time when society most needs it." He laughed ruefully. "The media will have a field day with this one. They'll descend on my son's family and harass and humiliate them. Sometimes I feel like running away. I could have a magnificent life in Belize or Costa Rica living off my brother. It has immense appeal."

"Run away? Your Grace…"

"Don't worry. It's an idle thought. I'm a priest forever, for better or for worse." He got in his black Mercedes, looked up at Lion and said, "I may have an opening for a pastor at Saint Anthony's in Kailua later this year, but for now, I'm sending you to Kauai. Sooner or later, I'll have to let you settle down with a parish of your own."

The next as day Lion prepared to leave for Kauai, he saw Lili alone near the horses. It was a beautiful morning complete with a *mauka* rainbow. The horses shuddered at his approach and Lili turned away from the rainbow to greet him. "Beautiful, huh? Like Pops sent the rainbow to tell us he's okay."

"You've been a rock, Lili, an angel through all this."

"I'm just the one who's here. That's all."

"That's plenty." He patted Coco's haunches, feeling the horse's skin quiver with pleasure. "How are you holding up?"

Lili leaned into Brownie, and the horse nuzzled her, draping its gentle head over her shoulder. "No sugar, Brownie. Sorry." She looked at Lion directly and said, "I know what you're leading up to and I'm not ready to talk about it. I'm not sure I ever will be. But I'm dealing with it myself, okay."

"When you're ready…"

"If I'm ever ready, you'll be the first to know."

"Promise?"

She shrugged. "Promises aren't worth the words they're spoken with."

"There are people waiting to help you heal. There's even a church ritual…"

Angry, she interrupted, "The church needs to stay out of my pants." The horse snorted, shook its head, and pulled away. "Sorry, Lion. But I told you, I'm handling. Okay?"

"I love you, Lili."

"Love you, too."

They embraced under the rainbow.

Iris come out on the porch and waved to them.

They knew they made a beautiful image for her and it lightened the moment. Arm in arm they walked toward the house. "I'll make coffee," Lili said.

Lion's Way

# Chapter 25
LOST WORLD

The last time Father Lion visited Kauai, he had been a young seminarian, and Steven Spielberg was on the island filming *Jurassic Park*. The sylvan Nebula waterfall in the opening sequence of the blockbuster was really Kauai's Manuwaiopuna Falls, and the ferocious storm that unleashed the dinosaur rampage was the very real Hurricane Iniki that devastated Kauai, September 11, 1992.

Now, Islanders went about their routines, blissfully unaware that another hurricane was about to descend on them. Lion had celebrated daily Mass, heard confessions at Saint Raphael's Church, and was just closing up when a distraught young mother approached him. She carried her sleeping infant in a portable car-seat contraption.

Desperation vibrated in her every brusk gesture and harried word. Seething with emotion, she begged him to hear her confession. She insisted on going into the confessional and leaving the baby asleep in the first pew. Her breathlessness bordered on panic. "Father, I have a terrible secret and I don't know what it is. It's like buried so deep, I can't get to it. All I know is, it's something awful and it makes me afraid for my baby."

"Afraid for your little baby?"

"Yes," she whispered. "I'm afraid I might hurt him." Her voice rose in vehemence and fear, "I hate his breathing. I'm responsible for his breathing for the next twenty years. I have a bad memory of some kind. It involves a baby. I don't know if I'm that baby. Maybe in another life I hurt a baby. Maybe I just watch too much Oprah."

From outside the confessional, the baby began to cry flogging the mother into further agitation. "Oh, there he goes again. See? He's always crying. I can't tell my husband how much I hate his crying or he'll think I'm some kind of freak. Sometimes when Kavin's not home, I have to walk out of the house when Tyler cries. I'm afraid I'll drop him accidentally on purpose, or smother him with a pillow or throw him against a wall to make him stop. Help me, Father, please, please help me."

The young woman burst from the confessional to soothe the child. "There you are, my little Tyler Tater Tot. There, there. Mommy's here." She looked up desperately, "The only way I can get him to sleep is to put him in the car and drive him around. Sometimes I drive all night. Hanalei, Waimea. I'm exhausted."

Father Lion watched her tenderly lift the baby from its carrier. "See, Father, I want to be a good mother. I love my baby. I'd kill myself if I ever hurt him." She began to bounce him against her chest, patting his back none too gently.

Lion invited, "Let's sit down and talk about all this, shall we?

"Here?"

"Anywhere you like. In the rectory, the garden."

"I feel safe here in the church, like the devil can't get to me as long as I'm here." The baby grew red in the face, bracing himself to howl again.

Lion gestured for the woman to sit in the first pew. She was so frazzled, he wished she'd put the baby down. "Tell me something about your family. Beginning perhaps with your name. I'm Father Lion."

"I'm Chris Higa. I know I don't look like a Higa. It's my husband who's Japanese. And he's a really nice guy. He deserves a sane wife.

He's handsome, too, not that that's everything but it sure helps on difficult days. He's like a samurai version of the Marlborough man, but very sensitive. Sometimes he sees me getting frustrated with the baby and he takes over. But he works, of course. Front desk manager at the Tradewinds, so he's not home a lot at night. I wanted to nurse Tyler, but he won't nurse from me. He shoves my breast away. Kavin keeps telling me I'm a good mother. But I'm not. If he only knew. Father, where do these dark urges come from? They can't be natural. Am I possessed?"

"The devil can't enter anyone without their permission."

"But it's like I have a shadow inside me; a thick, liquid shadow. I'm swimming in dark waters crying for help. I keep yelling, but no one hears me. I should be so happy. I have everything I want. I love my husband and my baby. Why is this terrible thing surfacing now? Is there really some awful memory stalking me?"

Father Lion leaned toward her. "Have you heard of post-partum depression? The baby blues? Have you talked to your doctor?"

"I thought about that. Raging hormones. But I don't want anyone to think I'm crazy and take Tyler away from me."

"Post-partum depression is a clinically recognized condition. We can call on your doctor, right now, together. I'll go with you."

She jumped up, setting the baby to crying again. "You can't tell anyone. You're bound to secrecy. This is still confession, right? Even though we're not in the box."

"I can't do anything without your permission." He sought to divert and calm her. "Tell me a little about your home life as a child."

She began to pace, jiggling the baby, who grew more violent in his protests. "I grew up on Long Island in New York. You know what this weather feels like today, Father? It's like Long Island when a hurricane is approaching. Everything would get deathly still and so quiet, like even the birds are making shelter plans. I put on the TV this morning, but there's nothing about a storm on the news. Well, I've lived through hurricanes and this feels like one's coming."

"There's a hurricane hundreds of miles south of us, traveling west. It's no threat to the Islands. Of course, that was Hurricane Iniki's path, too."

"Maybe it's my hormones."

Lion held out his arms. "Here, let me hold the baby."

"Take him, please." She shoved the angry infant at him.

He cradled the child and talked to him in a cooing voice, "The distant hurricane is probably affecting our weather system, isn't that right, Tyler? Hmm? There. Do you know how much God loves you? Hmm?" He was a beautiful child with large black eyes and a full head of black hair as rebellious and obstinate as his protests.

The baby stared at the priest, sniffled and breathed deeply, calming himself.

"See how he quiets right down when you hold him, Father. He hates me."

"Perhaps the baby senses your fear of harming him. A baby's most deeply rooted fear is being dropped. Chris, tell me about your parents." Lion paced about, the infant draped on his shoulder.

"My mother moved from Long Island to Arizona a year ago and re-sides in a retirement community where she rides around in a golf cart, plays cards and does amateur theater. I hear she dances the can-can. God help us.

"And your father?"

"He died five years ago. Do you think perhaps my secret is some-thing that happened to me as a child?"

"We often repress experiences we can't deal with and they surface when we're older, wiser and more powerful."

"Powerful. Interesting word choice."

"Are you an English teacher?"

"Writer. I'm a spa writer, which is a more debased subspecies of travel writer. Well, there's no repressed childhood sexual trauma because I remember losing my virginity in high school out behind Mary's shrine. Don't worry, I confessed that a long time ago. God, I can't breathe. Doesn't this weather bother you?"

"I'm from Africa." He shrugged. The baby was falling asleep.

"That's right. You're used to this equatorial torpor."

"I'm genetically equipped for it, yes."

She appraised him and smiled for the first time. "Me? My family's Irish. I mean way back. They came during the famine. My dermatologist tells me I was bred for the rain."

"Have you talked to your mother about how you're feeling? Perhaps she can shed some light on what's troubling you."

"She phoned yesterday and, get this, she tells me, 'You have a very liberal mother. I'm having sex with a widowed architect in my bridge group.'" Chris shouted, "Too much information, mother."

Startled, the baby opened his eyes and, mercifully, fell asleep again. "I can't let her near Tyler. She's a chain smoker. I could almost smell her dragon breath right through the phone, all the way across the Arizona desert express to my nostrils. Between that and her booze, which she delicately refers to as her 'old fashions,' thinking it makes her drinking a sort of charming affectation, she's a liability to have around. My scent memory of my mother is not talcum powder or toll house cookies, it's booze and cigarette butts."

"She managed to raise you to adulthood. Maybe a short visit. She can visit and give you some respite so you can do some things for yourself.

Get out of the house. Go on a date with your husband."

"And leave Tyler with her? I'd rather leave him with the Taliban." Chris grunted in frustration, arms stiff, hands curled into fists. "This isn't just post-partum stress, Father. There's something there. Something horrible. The baby knows it. He senses danger, like you said."

"Would you like me to pray over you?"

"Will it make the darkness inside me go away?"

"Do you want to release it?"

"That's an interesting question. It puts the responsibility on me rather than you or God. Very clever. But if you drive whatever it is away, or I release it, I'll never know what it is."

"You don't have to."

"Okay. I'll try." She bowed her head, quivering with agitation. "So, pray."

Lion put the baby gently in his carrier then laid his hands on Chris's soft pale hair. He remained silent until he felt her grow still, until her breathing slowed.

He prayed aloud, "Dear Father in Heaven, we come before you in great distress. Our sister Chris believes she has a terrible memory that she can't retrieve. Please lift her burden so she can lovingly care for her baby as she yearns to. Bless little Tyler with serenity. Cast out all spirits that are not of you. We thank you, Father for this great healing, believing it is already accomplished even as our desire leaves our lips and rises to you." He trailed off repeating, "Praise you, Lord. Praise your name."

Chris arose with tears in her eyes and thanked him.

"Promise me you will call your doctor," Lion said.

Immediately her panic returned. "I believed in your prayers. For five whole seconds, I believed that I was healed, but I see you don't." She picked up the baby and marched out of the church, slamming the door.

Lion listened helplessly as the car started and peeled away in a screech of engine and tires. "Forgive me, dear Lord, for I am your lowly servant, the weakest of the weak. Without you, I am nothing." He then prayed for Chris and her family, losing track of time while his sadness morphed into quiet repose. He gazed upon God and felt God gaze upon him.

When he took Michael to the beach later, the ocean was so calm, that Lion could see fish flitting and sea cucumbers curled in their coral niches even without a snorkel and mask. The dog swam in happy circles around him.

That night, the oppressively still air resurrected an early memory of the African jungle when the night was so deep, dark and quiet he could hear insects walking about on broad leaves and rustling in the thatching. In his dreams that night, he heard a baby crying and couldn't find it in the dark. And then it stopped, as if something else had found the child and silenced it.

In an eerie repeat of the 1992 hurricane disaster, civil defense sirens wailed Hawaii awake at five-thirty in the morning. Momentarily confused and touched by fear, Lion sat bolt upright in bed. He fumbled for the light, got up and began switching on lights in the rectory. Michael followed him closely as he made his way to the living room, and turned on the television to hear: "...this is a hurricane warning. Overnight, Hurricane Ehu'ehu changed course and is heading directly for the Hawaiian Islands with winds of one hundred sixty to one hundred eighty miles an hour. All residents of the coastal zones and areas prone to flooding, and all people living in single-wall construction homes are urged to begin evacuation to your designated shelters immediately. The eye of the storm is expected to pass through the Kaieiewaho Channel between the islands of Oahu and Kauai at approximately two o'clock p.m. This is a potentially deadly category five hurricane. We repeat..."

Lion peered out the window into the dark morning while sirens wailed and the television blared. Lights flickered on all over Kauai. He calmly brewed coffee and checked rectory supplies. The pastor, Paul Ronkowski, had compiled an impressive inventory of Dinty Moore beef stew, B&M baked beans, packages of dried ramen, and tins of sardines and tuna fish. Half a dozen five-gallon jugs of bottled water sat lined up beneath the grocery shelves. "Nothing here for dogs, Michael, but if worse comes to worse, I'll share the Dinty Moore."

The sky outside lightened as Lion filled every vessel he could find with water then filled the bathtub. With a mounting sense of excitement, an exhilaration he did not understand, he efficiently checked for flash-lights and batteries and found a battery-operated radio on the top shelf of the pantry.

Following the advice of the television commentators, he walked the perimeter of the church and rectory looking for potted plants, garden furniture, anything that might become a projectile in the storm and brought it inside. The morning sky turned beach-day blue, but already the early harbingers of the coming winds whispered among nervous palms, hissing sibilant threats. The birds did not sing. They already knew, in their thin avian blood, that disaster was approaching and had found their hiding places.

Lion paused in his labors to check out the waves at Brennnecke's Beach. "Come on Michael." Crazy surfers, not nearly as wise as the mynahs and doves, streaked down the monster curls. The ocean, now in league with the wind, roared at the land, breaking and rising in white, rabid foam. The winds grew stronger, gritty with salt from the scoured sea. While Lion and his dog watched, the sky went from luminous blue with a smear of white clouds to an opaque grey, dense and circular. He had never seen such ominous magnificence.

He rushed back to the rectory to complete preparations. Just as he got there, a car and a pick-up truck pulled into the church lot. Three men introduced themselves as parishioners, Masa, Kaleo and Jeff. Jeff's two dogs stood in the bed of the truck. "We came to help, Father," Kaleo said. "Looks like you been busy awreddy."

Masa, a spidery old man who claimed to be the church's volunteer landscaper, noted the stripped Fatima shrine. "You move 'em?"

"The potted plants are inside the church already."

Masa commenced his own tour of the perimeter, carrying a chain saw from the garage into the church. "Might have to cut your way out."

Jeff whistled and the two black Labradors jumped from the bed of his truck and bounded over, Michael with them.

"Nice dogs."

"They're my best buds," Jeff said. "This one even likes a little brews-ki." He patted the dog's head. The sun had bleached out Jeff's hair, and surfing had built the young man's shoulders into powerful bulks. He said, "I grew up on the East Coast near Cape Hatteras. We got hurri-canes all the time, real beauts."

"I was right here during Iniki," Kaleo said. "We got work to do."

"Right on, brah." Jeff followed him to the garage, where they pulled sheets of labeled plywood from storage.

Kaleo said, "Last time, we cut 'em so they fit over the church and rectory windows. Just gotta nail 'em."

They spent the next two hours boarding windows while the wind grew in intensity. Coconuts started flying about like missiles.

The phone in the rectory rang insistently. It was Bishop Carroll. Lion had forgotten he was on the island for a wedding, staying at the luxurious Tradewinds resort, courtesy of the bride's family. "I want you to ride out the storm over here at the hotel," the bishop ordered. "I have a suite. You'll be more than comfortable and I think it will be safer and you won't be alone."

"I was planning to stay with the church and the blessed sacrament."

"Is the church secure?"

"Some parishioners came and helped me board it up. We're ready."

"Good. They say this storm is going to be bad. I'm going to need you here, Lion. They've got over a thousand guests in the hotel right now, plus two hundred and forty employees. And a film crew shooting yet another sequel to *Jurassic Park.*"

"I can't come. What about Michael?"

The bishop sputtered, "You and that blasted dog." His tone was tinged with some affection. "Tie him up. Leave him with someone, a parishioner. You can't bring him here. It's just a dog. They're not allowed in the hotel."

"With all due respect Your Grace, may I remind you of Saint Francis and his care for the animals?"

"May I remind you, Lion, I've been very patient in the matter of this dog. Every pastor in the state has been patient while you drag that animal around with you. Now, we're losing valuable time here. Secure your noble beast, pray to Saint Francis, and get yourself over here before they close the roads. I need you." He hung up, not suffering further argument.

Lion exhaled. Reminded of his priestly vow of obedience, the cornerstone of his vocation, he apologized to God for his insubordination. Still feeling rebellious, he muttered, "If Spielberg needs an actor to play *Tyrannosaurus rex,* I've got just the man."

Another car pulled into the church parking lot, and Saint Raphael's pastor leaped out. Lion rushed to greet him. "Paul, glad you're here."

"Came back from Honolulu soon as I heard the hurricane news. Got the last flight in. They've closed the airport." He noted the boarded church. "Good work." Father Paul Ronkowski had lost his chin to excessive weight and had pale, sickly skin, but moved with surprising agility. He sped through sentences as if he had a pending appointment. He called out to the men who had just boarded the last window, shouting over the mounting wind, *"Mahalo nui."*

Kaleo invited the priests to come with him to the civil defense shelter.

"We're staying right here," Father Paul announced. "Church is solid, rock and coral. Go home to your families while you can."

Masa and Kaleo left, but Jeff lingered by his truck.

Lion apologized to the pastor, "Our bishop is at the Tradewinds for a wedding tomorrow. He's ordered me there to help him. They've got more than a thousand guests at the hotel. Why don't you come, too?"

"I heard the big man was on island. You go. I rode out Iniki in the church, I'll do the same this time. I've got food, water, batteries. With any sort of luck this thing will be over in a few hours and we'll all be fine. Better leave your dog. They won't let him in at the hotel."

"You don't mind?"

"He'll be good company. Now off with you. Take my car. I drove here in that rental."

"You know I'd rather be here than at the resort. I'm not entirely comfortable in such rarified circles. Don't forget, I grew up talking to monkeys."

"You were probably in better company."

Lion leashed Michael, ruffled his ears and handed him over to the pastor. He didn't turn around when the dog barked after him but kept walking toward the car, still smarting from the bishop's little tantrum, his casual use of power.

Jeff stood by his truck, his labs sitting and grinning beside him. "I'm gonna stay with the padre." He shrugged. "Got no family here but these guys, and they'll keep your dog company."

"God bless you, Jeff."

"I'll watch your dog like he's one of my own."

Ehu'ehu made landfall at three-thirty p.m., slamming ashore at Keka-ha, churning and devouring the entire island in its howling maw. "God, it's magnificent," Bishop Carroll said. "Look at those coconut palms bending and dancing. It's like a courtship with the wind." He turned away, pleased with his metaphor and drew the heavy drapes closed. "So we don't get decapitated if the glass breaks."

Lion thought the wind was like God. We know not where it comes from or where it goes.

The phone rang. A recorded message announced that the hotel's general manager, Wolfe von Gelden, was ordering everyone to pack a small bag, bring a pillow and blanket, and head for the ballroom. The wind roared, growing stronger by the second, rattling the sliding lanai doors in their frames, shivering the heavy drapes. Lion and the bishop needed no further urging.

In the ballroom, guests accustomed to room service, spa treatments and orchids on their pillows huddled together on chaise lounges and the floor. The musicians who normally serenaded poolside at sundown, sang every song they knew dueling with the howling wind. The electricity sputtered then plunged everyone into darkness. Now they could really hear the wind, roaring like a locomotive, speeding for them. All communication lines went down, cutting Kauai off completely from the rest of the world. The storm moaned and howled and screamed in high-pitched glee like a demented woman, determined to get in and tear everyone and everything to pieces with talons and fangs of cold, biting wind. Water cascaded down the walls of the ballroom and chords of wind, almost like music, sang in the darkness, frenzied, growing toward crescendo.

Using flashlights, von Gelden and his staff, fearing the collapse of the ballroom, moved a thousand people into the service tunnels deep in the hotel. The people walked meekly, quickly, helping one another.

The *Jurassic* film crew, using their generators, set up lights. Bottled water, platters of sushi and wedding cake were served as the eye of the storm moved over the island, bringing mere minutes of terrible, oppressive calm, then renewed fury with winds from the opposite quarter.

Lion moved among the people, inquiring after their comfort, fetching water, calming fears with quiet prayers. He was energized and shockingly happy.

"Remind me to head for a resort any time there's a natural disaster," the bishop quipped, amusing those huddled near him who had no idea a bishop could quip. "I prefer to have my natural disasters catered,"

Lion said, "I hope Father Paul and that young surfer are all right in the church with the dogs."

"Saint Raphael's was built in the 1850s when they knew how to build a church. I'm sure your blasted dog is fine."

Finally, hours later, the hotel manager confided to Bishop Carroll that the storm was abating and soon he would organize the staff to see the guests to their rooms, all but those in the lower oceanfront sections, which were in ruins.

The bishop urged Lion, "Lead the people in a hymn. We've been spared and we need to say thank you."

Quickly formulating his thoughts, Lion told von Gelden, "How about a non-denominational song? Everyone knows, *Amazing Grace*." He spoke to the musicians, who sprang to the task. After the first bar, everyone stood. Tears streamed down their faces and they hugged each other. Several made the sign of the cross.

Lion said, "I'm going outside. I need air."

Bishop Carroll offered, "It's dark. You shouldn't go alone, and I could use some fresh air, too."

A bearded man from the film crew introduced himself as Doug and asked, "Mind if I tag along?" He had a camera and a huge spotlight. "Should be some dramatic footage of the wreckage."

The darkness outside was dense, brooding, the wind not quite spent. They needed the cameraman's powerful light. The beam slowly swept across the landscape revealing utter destruction. "My God," Doug said, "It looks like a nuclear attack. This is fabulous footage. We couldn't pay for this kind of wreckage."

"Quiet," Lion snapped. "Do you hear that? A baby?"

They all listened, then quite distinctly, from the direction of the ocean, a baby cried. They raced for the shoreline, dodging jagged parts of buildings and broken trees. Doug shined his light out to sea, and they saw a woman waving from a tangle of tree branches. "Help," she called, "help me."

Lion kicked off his shoes and waded into the turbulent water.

Doug put his camera down, handed the light to the bishop, and followed Lion while the bishop kept the light trained on the woman.

Debris churned in the waves. Heedless of his own safety Lion swam out toward the desperate woman pinioned in light. With one arm she clung to a tree branch, the other clutched a Styrofoam cooler. The baby's cries came from inside the cooler. The woman was Chris Higa. She was too exhausted to speak as Lion and Doug dragged her and the

220

cooler to shore following the stream of light. By now a small group had gathered on the sand. Both Lion and Doug emerged with nasty gashes in their feet. As soon as she touched the shore, Chris collapsed in the sand, her shoulders heaving in silent sobs. She was clad only in her underwear.

Lion ordered, "We need blankets. Someone get Kavin Higa from the front desk. This is his wife and baby."

A woman slipped off her cardigan and draped it around Chris. Lion lifted Tyler from the cooler. Bishop Carroll removed his dry shirt and gave it to Lion to wrap the infant. Lion gently stripped the baby's wet clothes, wrapped him in the shirt and handed him to the bishop. "You hold him. You're dry."

Awkwardly, the bishop stroked Tyler's back. The infant, with one great sigh and a few shudders, fell asleep. Lion noticed the prelate's pride. Yes, he was human at times.

Neither Lion nor Doug could walk unassisted because of the wounds to their feet. Once back inside the hotel, a guest who was a doctor cleaned and bandaged the two men. He gave Chris a tranquilizer.

Chris, clearly feeling the medication, said, "Father, I saved my baby. I saved him. He was crying and crying and I couldn't stand it so I got in the car to drive around, even in the storm, stupid me. On the road in a hurricane. Roofs and tree limbs flying all over the place. Then I got scared so I tried to get to the hotel. I wanted to be with Kavin. We were almost there when we were taken by a wave. I managed to get out of the car with Tyler and grab that tree branch. I don't know how long I could have held on. Thank God that cooler came floating by, and I got him into it. I saved my little baby's life, didn't I?"

Father Lion took her hand, "You did. You're a good and brave mother. Chris, the terrible thing you thought was in your past, was in your future and it was the hurricane. Now it's over, gone. You never have to deal with it again." He squeezed her hand and smiled. "If Tyler hadn't been screaming his guts out, we'd never have known you were out there in the surf."

"He can cry all he wants from now on."

Back in their suite, Bishop Carroll and Father Lion opened the drapes. There was no moonlight, only inky blackness and the crashing cannonade of the ocean. Bishop Carroll said, "I was insensitive about your dog and I'm sorry."

"Thank you."

"But I can't have disobedience. You can't disobey me and I can't disobey the cardinal and the cardinal can't disobey the pope and the pope can't disobey God. Our whole structure is built on obedience, for better or worse."

Meekly Lion said, "If I had had my own way, I wouldn't have been here, and maybe no one would have heard the baby cry and we would have lost them. I was meant to be here."

Sunrise came in a brief showy extravaganza of golds and pinks, then the sky turned a brilliant, heedless blue. Survivors crept cautiously from shelters and from under mattresses and wept. Not a leaf nor a branch remained on a tree. Many of the tall, graceful coconut palms had lost their heads. Grasslands and cane fields were stripped bare. The storm surge had flooded the beaches and piled them with debris. Seventy percent of the homes on the island were destroyed or damaged beyond repair. Ehu'ehu's fierce winds had surpassed two hundred miles an hour.

Bishop Carroll flew back to Honolulu on one of the first flights out, but Father Lion and Michael remained on Kauai for five months, staying with Father Paul at Saint Raphael's. They worked with the Red Cross, the National Guard and Catholic Relief Services providing comfort, support and showers. It was an oddly wonderful time when people helped each other. Without electricity, neighbors sat under the stars and talked to each other.

Lion went to bed each night exhausted and happy. He began to re-think his dream of living in quiet contemplation removed from the world. Perhaps his role was one of service. His thoughts turned to Africa, where the suffering was so enormous and the relief efforts stretched so terribly thin.

He prayed confidently. After all, God had gone to great lengths to set a slave boy free and get him safely to the opposite side of the world. Surely God had his hand upon him still and would, in his perfect time, reveal what was to come next.

# Chapter 26

THE DOOR

"My whole life, my existence, is one big sin." Tears ran down the woman's dry, dust-caked cheeks as she sat in the dirt at the edge of a precipice overlooking Kauai's Kalalau Valley. "But don't worry, I'm not going to jump. I'm not going to throw away this life and the next one, too." She sniffled and wiped her nose with the stranger's handkerchief. "That's what they say in the near-death-experience stories. If you die by suicide, you can't get to the light."

Lion, who had come upon the woman near the start of the Pihea Trail, sat beside her, Michael's leash wound tightly around his hand. Wind swirled up from the ocean and the depths of the green wilderness below. As mist drifted across the fluted valley wall, the ghost of a rainbow grew stronger, brighter and more dazzling.

"That's what I come here for," the woman said. "The rainbow, the promise." She began to hum, "Somewhere Over the Rainbow," and then she sang it. Her voice had the strength and richness of a bronze gong. The notes and words hung in the air with such resonance that they could have fallen as rain, drenching the now.

When she finished her song, Lion silently clapped his hands, reluctant to make a sound or to speak and break the spell.

"Thank you," she whispered, tears streaming again. "Today's my birthday. I'm sixty."

"Well, happy birthday."

"I can't believe I made it this far, especially since I started out as a mistake."

"God doesn't make mistakes."

"Maybe not, but my mother did. She had to get married because of me. Today, I'd have been aborted." The woman's eyes were a striking, vivid green with brown flecks. Her hair may have once been blonde, but was now streaked with gray, and hung in long, thick waves. She hugged her knees, which were draped in a voluminous skirt soft with age. "Maybe that would've been best."

"Then you would not be here today amidst such beauty, crowned in rainbows on your sixtieth birthday," he gestured dramatically, "gifting me with song."

She smiled.

When he first saw her perched on the edge of the cliff, Lion immediately recognized her fortress of solitude, and had no intention of violating it. He seated himself at a small distance, looking at the view, being available should the woman need his counsel.

She was so lost in her sorrows that at first, she failed to notice the man and his dog. Eventually, she had turned to him and asked if he had a Kleenex.

That's when Lion gave her his clean handkerchief

"I haven't seen a real handkerchief in years," she said. "But I don't want to give it back now that I've blown my nose in it."

"It's okay. Keep it."

"I'll count it as a birthday present." She smiled in resignation at what would probably be her only gift. "You're so polite. You're not trying to hit on me, are you? Because I'm telling you up front, you're wasting your time."

"I'm Lion Majok. I'm a Catholic priest."

"Well, well, well. A priest. How provident, that I started by telling you my whole life is one big sin."

"I think perhaps our spirits recognized kin. I was drawn to your aura of solitude."

"It's a defense," she said.

"I know."

"Loneliness is my homeland."

"I'll defend that homeland with my life." Lion sighed deeply. "I yearn for solitude with all my being. It's why I hike in the wilderness at every opportunity and walk everywhere else. I can't get enough of it."

"You know how I got to my homeland? I used to see this door in my mind. It was a big brown metal door, you know, the kind they have in institutions? And I knew that if I walked through that illusory door, nobody could touch me ever again, I would be so alone. I might even stop talking and lose my ability to speak. I was terrified of that door, and at the same time, fascinated. It was an ugly door, but on the other side I knew complete freedom waited. All I needed was a little courage. It's amazing how reluctant we are to seize our freedom. But one day, I just opened that door and the light that poured on me was pure gold and I walked through and there was no ground beneath me, but somehow I could stand. And here I am."

She was so strangely touching, it was Lion's turn to tear up. "I love you, my spirit sister. You and your song are a gift to me today."

"You better not be hitting on me."

He wanted to ask her name but knew he shouldn't. "You must have experienced a lot of hurt in your life."

"You, too, Mr. Lion." Using his name with the "Mr." was a distancing move. She shifted, hugged her knees again and rested her head on her kneecaps. For a long time she didn't speak. Finally she said, "My father loved me too much the wrong way." When Lion opened his mouth to speak, she put up her hand. "No. Don't say anything. Just let me talk now that I've gotten started. This is my birthday present to me. Speaking the truth. I'm sixty and I don't care who it hurts anymore. Poor you. You're my dumpster."

"Dump away. Finding you here today was no accident. I'm right where God wants me to be."

"You must have disgusting karma."

"Karma, as I understand it, is getting what you deserve, good or bad. Well, we don't always get what we deserve of the good or the bad."

She pulled in her lips and refused to speak until Lion urged her, "Please continue. Give yourself the gift of laying down your burden."

She took a deep breath and exhaled, shaking her head. "My younger sister and I shared the same bedroom and even she doesn't believe me."

"I believe you."

"I know." A coldness crept into her voice, her face hardened. "The first time my father came into my bed, I was six. Six. Just a little girl. In the middle of the night, he'd climb quietly into my bed and pull the covers gently over us both. He started out just touching me. He said it was because he loved me best. He said he didn't want to touch my sister, that she wasn't pretty like me. It was our secret, he said, and if anyone found out, my mother would be jealous and make him leave the family.

"When I was nine, I told my mother, 'Daddy comes into my bed at night.' I can still see her face, the way it snapped shut like a trap. She said that was a terrible lie and the next time I opened my mouth with such filth she would clean it out with oven cleaner."

When Lion gasped, the woman shrugged. "My mother stopped talking to me after that. She'd answer direct questions. That's it. Sometimes it seemed that she left me alone in the house with my father on purpose. My father said he loved me more than my mother, more than anyone in the world. He said I was special. I believed him. By the time I was in high school, we were drinking together and I was having sex with the football team, the basketball team, and him. Don't ask me how, but I made it into college, with a scholarship. When I told him I was going to board at school, he was devastated. I was so glad to be out of that house I vowed I'd never go back. But Christmas came around and I was so lonely I went home. I didn't appreciate the strange, exquisite comfort of loneliness in those days. When I got home, my father and I made love again. I'd missed him. I went back to school, and he hung himself in the basement. Shh. No sympathy. Please.

"After that, I stuck it out at school and never again slept under the same roof as my mother. As soon as I graduated, I left California to go backpacking in Asia, and ended up in Kathmandu. I met Franz on Freak Street. He was from Switzerland." She noted that fact with a small trace of pride. "We were high all the time on primo quality stuff." She hugged her knees tighter and sighed over her memories. "Oh, those were the days."

After a long pause, during which Michael settled down next to Lion, she continued, "There was a whole colony of Westerners living in Kathmandu back then. We were all there for the cheap drugs and, this may shock you, the spirituality, the non-judgmental spirituality. I loved the little bells, the prayer flags, even sitting in a painful position." She glanced at Lion. "Most of the locals avoided us, except when they wanted to sell us something. So we freakers helped each other out, you know with food or whatever. But Franz kept getting sick all the time, one bug after another. So we left.

"Somebody told us that in Hawaii you could live on the beach for free, so that's where we went. When we got here, we made easy money with our drug connections. We had a regular pipeline going. The best smack. But once we had kids, we started getting uneasy about getting caught. By then, we had squirreled away a little of our drug money, and we opened an art gallery in one of those vintage buildings in Hanapepe. We called it Aquarian Dreamscapes. Super original. It was right next to the feed and grain store. We painted the outside bright sunflower yellow. I hung white eyelet curtains in the windows and he painted rainbows on the glass. We were doing okay with the tourists, selling his work and the work of other Kauai artists, potters, woodworkers. Then Franz got heavy into acid; to release his creativity he said. His paintings got crazy. But the crazier they got, the better they sold. Meantime, I fell apart. I was drunk or stoned all the time. CPS took both our kids."

"Where are they now?"

"Shh." She might have been talking to the dog, she was so stern and dismissive. "One day I paid a surprise visit to Aquarian Dreamscapes. I usually didn't go there. It was his space. The door was locked. I knocked. Franz came to the door all testy with a paint brush in his hand and there was this horrible smell about him. I can't describe it. Sharp and rotten—old—like he needed to be buried. He was not happy to see me. Of course I barged in, positive I'd find some surf doll naked in the back studio. He slammed the door to the studio and planted himself in front of it. We yelled at each other til I thought it would come to blows.

"Then he says, 'Now that you're stark raving mad, you're in just the right zone for what you're about to see.' He opened the door and stood back like, ta-dah welcome to the big top. I looked around the studio and here were all these paintings of demons, disgusting creatures dripping green slime from their fangs, eyes hanging out of sockets. Evil, evil, evil. Then there was that stench coming off him. I couldn't get out of there fast enough. I ran and kept running but the smell kept following me. I ran into the ocean, clothes and all. I stayed there till I couldn't smell the evil stink anymore. I don't know what happened to Franz. He might be dead or back yodeling in the Alps, I don't know. The gallery's gone. It was a long time ago."

"Are you all right now?"

"Face it. Some people are seriously damaged goods and can never be all right. I'm one of them. Look, you were probably heading for the Pihea Trail. I don't want to hold you up anymore. Thanks for listening to my random birthday ramblings."

"Why don't you come hiking with me?"

"I'm not exactly dressed for a hike." She shrugged and straightened her back. "But what the heck. It's my birthday. Can you wait while I get shoes from my car?"

She chattered like a child on an excursion. "*Pihea* means lamentation of many voices. Don't you love the smell of the *mokihana*, sort of like Italian Christmas cookies. I get a rash from it, though." Her breath came in gasps and after about a half-mile she announced, "I better turn back. You go ahead."

Lion didn't want to leave her by herself with such labored breathing. "It's okay. I'll go back with you. Michael got a bit of a run and that's what he needed."

They returned to the overlook and she offered him a ride back to Waimea town. Her car, a beat-up, rusting old Chevy was piled with bedding, clothes, a frying pan, hibachi, water jug and bulging plastic bags. She obviously lived out of it. She swept some clothes off the passenger seat to make room for him. "Welcome to my rolling closet. The dog will have to sit in your lap. No more room. Oh, and the seatbelt doesn't work. You can walk if you want."

"Michael and I are grateful for the ride. As for the seatbelt, I'll put myself in God's hands."

As they drove down the winding road skirting Waimea Canyon, the woman said, "I'm camped at Polihale Beach. If you need a place to stay, there's a whole bunch of us homeless there. It's beautiful - so far, knock on wood," she rapped the side of her head, "the county is leaving us alone. I've got room in my tent, no hanky-panky included. Or you can sleep in my car. It's a real professional opportunity for a priest—all those people to be salvaged."

Lion had a few more days on Kauai before he was due back in Honolulu, and the idea of camping on the beach had great appeal. "If you stop in Waimea," he said, "I'll pick up some groceries for us."

The cane-haul road to Polihale cut through fields of high sugar cane. "Roll up the window or we'll be covered in red dirt," she said, taking the ruts and bumps slowly and carefully. "I can't afford to break an axle."

By the time they reached the beach, the sun was low on the horizon, igniting the huge surf in shades of gold and pink. Her tent was a ramshackle tangle of tarps and beams tucked into some *naupaka* bushes. Lion guessed there must be twenty just like it scattered along the edge of the sand, set back from the beach. He unloaded the bags of groceries. "I'll start a fire."

"Use the hibachi."

A shirtless man with skin the color of bread crust, a paunch overflowing his shorts, and a wide face framed with wild grey hair, limped across the sand carrying a fish wrapped in newspaper. "Eh, Star, you want one *papio*? Just caught."

"Eh, tanks, brah. Dis my friend, Lion. Lion this is Brother Ox."

The man wiped his hand on his shorts and held it out. "Sorry, my hand all stink the fish."

"I'm pleased to meet you," Lion said, shaking the man's hand.

"Eh, Star, your friend here talks like one scholar. Where you from, brah?"

"Africa."

"Not." The Ox was awestruck.

"I've been in Hawaii for many years, but I was born and raised in Sudan."

"For real? You some kine African prince like Eddie Murphy?"

"I was a slave and now, by the grace of God, I'm a priest."

"Whoa. What kine priest? You da voodoo?"

"Catholic priest," Lion said. "Sorry no spells or magic."

The Ox said, "Oh da too bad, yah?" He winked at Star. "Be back later. I got some good *pakalolo*. We make one party tonight. *A hui hou.*"

"Would you like to stay for dinner?" Lion asked him.

"My *wahine* awreddy cooking." The Ox walked away shaking his head. "Africa."

Star lit an oil lamp. For dinner they grilled the *papio* and some pineapple slices and cooked two potatoes in the coals. Lion did not comment on the woman's name and wondered if Star was a given name or a taken name.

It was dark when Ox returned. A woman, as brown and wide as himself, came with him, trailing a small dog. She carried a bottle of beer and plopped down in the sand without introduction. Almost grudgingly, she acknowledged Lion with a raise of her chin. "Eh, aloha, Africa.

"Welcome to our fire."

A few more people drifted in from the dark and settled down. Lion noted that Star moved his backpack inside the tent and closed the flap. Michael made friends with the visiting dogs.

The Ox lit up a joint and passed it around, eliciting sighs of pleasure.

He lit another and sent that, too, on its way around the small group. Lion passed them along without smoking. A man strummed a guitar. Ox asked him, "Eh, Africa, sing us one Africa song."

Lion looked quickly around. The night was dark, the surf quiet, and the mood mellow. He reached out for the guitar. When its owner surrendered it, Lion instead of playing, began to beat on the instrument, softly, slowly at first, feeling the old Dinka rhythms creep into his hands. He heard in his mind the African wail, poignant and full of jubilation, telling the old stories of hunts, bravery, and man-woman business. It was the day of his departure from Sudan. He was dressed in a new suit and everyone had gathered in the grass to admire him, and to sing him away into the wide world.

He now sang the words of "*Aram Meleng de Judaai,*" and as the rhythm built in his body, he remembered everyone jumping for joy as they sang; up and down, up and down together. He saw the choir in white robes, his mother in a yellow and brown turban, his sister Eulalia in a prim frilly dress, all of them gathered in the grass while young men casually holding machine guns, scanned the bush, making sure they were safe in their joy.

As he sang at Polihale, Lion's heart ached exactly as it did the day he left Africa, strapped into the airplane seat, watching his world shrink and disappear.

He handed the guitar back while the little group clapped. "Thank you." He bowed. "You are truly kind, but African songs are not meant to be sung alone. Tomorrow morning we'll have church on the beach and we'll all sing."

They nodded and grunted and he thought they probably wouldn't come.

In twos and threes, they drifted off to their tents. Lion said to Star,

"Nice people."

"Yeah, well, don't romanticize this group. We're not Robin Hood and his band of merry men. Some of these guys are druggies and alkies and when they're high on meth they'd slit your throat for a french fry. That song you sang was really nice."

"I haven't sung it in years. I'm surprised I remembered it."

"I set up a blanket and pillow in the tent for you. Like I said, don't get any ideas."

"It's a beautiful night and the sand is soft. I'll sleep under the stars if you don't mind."

"Suit yourself. If you use the public restroom, bring your own water. It's not potable there."

Michael was delighted with this opportunity to sleep in the crook of his adored master's arm. Lion stretched out in the sand and lost himself in the brilliance of the heavens. He counted nine shooting stars before he fell asleep.

He awoke with the dawn, and he and Michael walked the long length of Polihale to where the green cliffs of the Na Pali Coast come down to the sea. He looked forward to saying a Mass of thanksgiving on the beach beneath the blue dome of God's own cathedral.

Returning to the camp area, he met Ox setting up two fishing poles, and told him, "Thirty minutes."

"Church here on the beach?"

"Yes," Lion shouted with open arms. "Yes. Tell the others. Come, everyone to the spiritual banquet. Receive." He was aware he sounded slightly deranged. People poked their heads out from the shelters. They could identify with madness.

A woman offered, "You need one altar, Father? Take my table." It was a crooked plastic thing set in the sand.

"Perfect."

He set it up at the edge of the *naupaka*. Someone brought a *pareau* for a cloth and draped it on the table. He had bought a box of soda crackers in Waimea—that would serve as Eucharistic bread. Wine he knew would be no problem here.

A bigger crowd than the night before straggled over. There had to be twenty or thirty people. He looked over the faces, scarred by life, but beautiful and loved passionately by God. That's what he told them, and he said it with such conviction that most believed him.

Star sang *Amazing Grace*, with everyone joining in.

When it came time for communion, he deviated from orthodoxy and said, "Catholics believe that the bread and wine actually become the body and blood of Jesus Christ. If you can accept this miracle, please come forward and receive." Most came eagerly, respectfully. A few looked around, shrugged, and shuffled forward, taking bigger sips of wine than ritual demanded.

The man with the guitar broke into the reverie with, *Go Tell It On The Mountain*. Everyone clapped and laughed. Where they knew the words, they sang. Lion was so wildly happy he shouted, "In Africa, when we sing, we move. We jump." He began to jump up and down. His elation was contagious. Everyone jumped and leaped in the air. Those who couldn't jump bent at the knees, bobbing. Their dogs barked. It was a wondrous morning.

He stayed at Polihale for three days, saying Mass each morning. He heard confessions and he baptized men and women, standing in the surf, blessing them. In the evening, they still smoked *pakalolo* and drank their wine, but they knew they were loved.

"I wish you could stay with us forever," Star said as she watched him gather up his small belongings. "But we both know that nothing is forever."

"Except God's love." He reached out for her hand but she flinched and he withdrew. "I've been so happy here. You and your friends have refreshed my soul. I wish I weren't due back in Honolulu, but I am."

"I wish I could believe in God."

"May I give you a little experiment?"

"You're going to pull God out of a hat, like a rabbit?"

"Nothing so exotic. No parlor tricks. I'm merely suggesting you pretend to believe in God for, say, thirty days."

"Ah, my parents were right after all; hypocrisy." She said it with a smile, joking.

"You have to be honest, because God knows your heart. Your prayer can go something like this, 'Hey God, if you exist, I'm saying good morning. I will be especially kind just for today. Try me out, God. Do something grand.' Tell God everything, your anger, your sorrow, your doubts. Listen for an answer. I promise you'll hear from him."

"Him?"

Lion conceded, smiling, "God is beyond gender. We use the masculine pronoun for God the way we use the feminine for ships. "

"Shim. I'll call God Shim."

"It's as good as anything else."

"And here's my good deed for the day: I'll drive you to the airport in Lihue."

"I'll buy the gas."

"You're on."

As they walked to the car, campers followed. When Star turned the ignition, more campers heard and came. Suddenly they were all singing and jumping. Deep inside something stirred in Lion, an inarticulate yearning for home.

# Chapter 27

FAMISHED

Bishop Carroll preferred to have his dinner indoors in the cool of the air-conditioning, rather than on the restaurant's balmy, beachside verandah, so that is where he and Father Lion sat. It was still light, and besotted tourists dotted Waikiki's golden sands. All along the world's dream beach, bronze young men in loin cloths lit the tiki torches around the swimming pools of all the high-rise hotels. The torches and hula dancers reminded everyone that this was Hawaii, and not Miami or Cancun.

With a wry smile, the bishop said, "I wish we could pass a collection basket among such a prosperous, carefree crowd, but we'd probably get less charity here than at a country church in a Hawaiian valley." He glanced at the menu. "Shall we order the three-course tasting menu with paired wines?"

Lion knew it was useless to protest, so that is what they ate and drank. They had finished the appetizer sampler of blackened ahi, mango shrimp cocktail, and lomi-lomi salmon, paired with a Loire Valley Sancerre, and were amiably working their way through the entree sample. He stretched his neck as if seeking oxygen, and took a long sip of wine. He was miserable. Only last night he'd been sitting in the sand at Polihale eating just-caught *papio* with his hands, licking his fingers while stars blazed in the sky and the dark ocean sang its anthems.

"You seem distracted, Lion." The bishop cracked his crab leg and probed its recesses with a small fork.

"Sorry. I guess I am. My mind keeps going back to Kauai, living among the homeless, quite happily, I might add."

"I detect a whiff of your perennial dinner guilt." The bishop actually sniffed the air.

"Gluttony guilt." Lion ate the beef first, as if his plate might be spirited away before he finished. "I realize that what I eat directly affects how much money your brother sends to Africa. Double the dinner tab, isn't it? But there ought to be a better way to Heaven than with *au jus* stains on my soul."

"Ah, you're young enough to yearn for a more sacrificial destiny, a real cross. Have you considered that the fork is your cross?"

"Yes." Lion realized he was being an ungrateful guest and that it was in his own best interest to get himself under control.

The bishop leered at a morsel of crab on his fork, and delicately ate it, reminding Lion of a fastidious cat.

"We are in a position now, as adults, as men of God, to do something about hunger in the world," Lion said.

"I'm aware of the magnitude of the problem, but you and I have developed quite different approaches, haven't we? I've set it up so that the more we eat, the more money goes to feed the hungry. Now that's a show we could take on the road, something that might appeal to our fellow Americans. Contribute double your dinner tab to the food bank. Self-indulgence as virtue.

Lion sat stiffly. "When I first came here, I couldn't believe that both worlds, Africa and America, famine and feast, existed together in space and time. There was a major disconnect. I tried to reconcile my two worlds. But the fact is, we people have drawn artificial lines on the globe. We say, those on this side of the line eat. Those on that side do not. We throw food away while others starve. Where is the justice?"

He suddenly leaped from his chair, surprising even himself. "Your Grace, if we were truly passionate about ending world hunger, it would end." He looked around, embarrassed at the little stir his antics had created, the pause in the tinkle of cutlery, the apprehension in the waiters, and he sat down, chastened.

The bishop spoke slowly, "International charities are doing amazing work. I realize it's not enough." He remembered his own youthful missionary zeal and spoke gently, "Not enough people feel any sense of obligation, much less charity, toward the least of their brothers. I believe my approach is more efficacious. The 'haves' needn't miss a single meal. They can indulge in a kind of high caloric rectitude. Make those pounds pay off." He laughed aloud to assure the room that he was having a brilliant, animated, perfectly normal conversation with an excitable young man. However, seeing that Lion was still perched precariously on the edge of his chair, he added, "Seriously, when I was your age, the issue of famine caused a crisis in my own vocation. My background is Irish. The Irish were devout people, even under the brutal oppression of the English. They risked their lives to go to Mass in the woods when the Mass was forbidden. Life was difficult and dangerous, but at least they had their potatoes. They survived. Then in 1845, the potato crop failed. It failed again and again. People on their knees pleaded with God just for a potato. They died by the thousands, whole villages. How could God not answer such a simple prayer?

"Luke, chapter eleven, verse eleven says, 'which of you, if he asks his father for bread, will be given a stone?' A potato was too much to ask? I was angry at God. But I became even angrier when I read that all during the years of the Great Hunger, Ireland raised enough food to feed every man, woman and child, but the British took the grain, the fattened pigs, the clotted cream by armed convoys to the Irish ports and loaded the larder on ships bound for England. This drove me to read everything I could get my hands on about historic famines and I could not find one that was not caused by man."

The bishop once again displayed his formidable talent for recalling numbers: "In the Soviet Union, more than five million people starved to death between 1932 and 1934, particularly in the Ukraine, during Stalin's ruthless farm collectivization. The estimates of starvation deaths in China during the failed Great Leap Forward range between seventeen and thirty million people. The famines in Ethiopia, Sudan and Somalia have been caused by war, corruption and deliberate sabotage of food production and aid distribution. India has not had any mass starvation since throwing off the yoke of British colonialism. People do not starve when their government is accountable to them.

"Who knows, maybe I carry a generational memory of hunger and this is why I enjoy food so much." The bishop swirled his wine and sipped. "Now, tell me what has brought on all this turmoil in your soul?"

"I felt so useful on Kauai. There was such need after the hurricane. I worked hard all day, every day and was truly happy. The last few days on the island I camped out with some homeless people. They made me think about my ministry. I am beginning to think that instead of being a cloistered monk, I should be a hands-on priest working to relieve suffering and injustice in the world; to finally free the slaves. I don't know how many people are dying of starvation right this minute while I convince myself that stuffing myself is a virtue." He coughed, close to gagging.

A long pause ensued before the bishop spoke: "Lion, you have a gift for the confessional. You know that. And that gift calls for you to give up your cherished little ideas about the kind of priest you want to be, and be the priest you are called to be." Bishop Carroll lifted his large white napkin and dabbed at his mouth in a mincing, unbecoming way. "Besides, the diocese of Honolulu has a sizable investment in you. We need you here."

In utter dismay Lion looked around the restaurant and couldn't help thinking that these were not the people most in need of his ministrations.

The bishop had a way of pulling back and widening his eyes, a warning that his patience was becoming frayed. "I see you surveying the room. I know what you're thinking: 'Are these heedless, indulged people worth my life?'"

Lion lowered his gaze. "You know me so well."

The bishop was genuinely fond of Lion and had great plans for his advancement in the Church. "I imagine there were moments when even Jesus might have had the same thoughts. I've asked myself this very question and the answer is a resounding yes. These people are worth my life. Each human being is equal in God's sight. One is not more valued because he is successful, another more noble because he is poor. Mother Theresa in her travels from India to wealthier countries came to believe that the spiritual poverty of the comfortable was a greater affliction than the physical poverty of the poor." He turned his attention to the lamb chop with its frilly white bootie. "When I was in seminary, I imagined heroically working in India among the poorest of the poor. Yes, yes I did, believe it or not. All seminarians go through that phase."

"I'm not a seminarian. I'm a priest mature in my vocation." This was the time to make his big request. He leaned forward. "I've had a letter from home. My sister, Eulalia, is getting married. May I, at least, have leave to attend her wedding?"

Bishop Carroll continued to cut his lamb chop. When he spoke, his manner was brisk, his eyes still on his meat. "A month. I can spare you for a month. No more. Consider your airline ticket a gift from me. I'll put you in touch with my agent."

Before Lion could thank him, the bishop abruptly changed the topic. "I haven't heard any more from Daniel Johnson since I thanked him for the photograph. I don't know where he is in Afghanistan. The whole country looks like a vacant lot to me. The only attractive parts I've seen on television are the poppy fields. None of it is safe."

"War is never the answer." Lion consciously put aside his own concerns. Wearily he began to eat again in small bites. "Your son is always in my prayers, Your Grace."

The bishop's fears, his vulnerability, his embarrassment at the approach of the waiter bearing the dessert sampler were painfully obvious.

To atone, Lion would have to suffer through a chocolate spring roll, a scoop of mango sorbet and a slice of strawberry shortcake. There was no relief in sight. *My God*, he thought. *Will I still be doing this in twenty years? Or worse, will I be pining for a cardinal's crimson cape, snatched away due to my own folly, consoling myself with food and wine, wearying some poor subordinate priest?*

"The mango sorbet has a nice cold tang to it, don't you think?" The bishop had an entirely manufactured gleam in his eyes. "As I might have mentioned before, I'm considering you for Saint Anthony of Padua Church in Kailua, Lion. It's a large parish with a respected elementary school. It would be a feather in your cap. Come to my office tomorrow morning. I'll give you some reading material about the school. It's why you were brought here, educated here at considerable expense. This is the vineyard in which you are destined to labor. Regard it as a kind of bloodless martyrdom, if that helps."

Lion closed his eyes. With great difficulty he managed to thank his superior for leave to attend his sister's wedding.

"Your Binda will be the one thanking me. Get a look at this dinner tab." The bishop, almost in glee, laid down his credit card. "Nice work, Lion. Yes indeed."

Lion's Way

# Chapter 28
## RIDING THE CLOUDS

Time droned on as Father Lion rode the clouds toward home. He shifted his long legs trying to find an angle that neither bothered anyone else nor caused him too much discomfort. He wondered how welcome he would be back in his own country, if he would fit in after so many years away. Would ties of blood and memory reach out and bind him so tightly, sweetly that he wouldn't be able to leave? Would he get out alive a second time?

From his window seat he saw the cloud-burdened Imatong Mountains as the plane began its long descent, flying low over the tawny grasslands of South Sudan. He counted twelve zebras, then a herd of giraffes gliding like sylphs across the savannah. He had been happy here, loved beyond measure. Until the morning when horsemen from the north charged across the river with guns and flashing swords and carried him away to slavery.

*The small and the slow are eaten by the swift and strong. This is Africa, this is the world. Those who survive bear scars that fester beyond a lifetime, like a genetic disease. Why does joy leave no bright tattoo to bloom forever in the chambers of the heart, seeding the genes? We nurse our wounds so tenderly while happiness evaporates like dew on sharp blades of grass.*

The plane approached the untidy urban sprawl of Juba. It screeched along the tarmac, then clumsily rumbled toward the terminal. Before it stopped, a kind of polite tumult erupted as passengers retrieved their belongings from the overhead bins, laughed, jostled, stretched, inched toward the exit. Before disembarking, Lion stood a moment in the portal, smacked with the power of forgotten heat and the particular African fragrance of earth, animals, people and the sweetness of rot, the nutrient of the future. His feet rang on the metal steps and then they touched the ground.

He cleared customs without incident and stepped into the hot tumult of the terminal. Scanning the crowd, he spotted Kintu immediately. He looked just like their father, except for a nasty purple scar close to his hairline. Lion waved. Only then did Kintu recognize him and step forward to take his bag. The brothers who hadn't seen each other since childhood greeted each other awkwardly, Kintu grunting, Lion thumping his back.

They took a taxi to the bus depot which was surrounded by the clamor of a street market. A riot of bright plastic goods, small electronics, brooms, combs, squawking chickens, fruits and vegetables was carefully laid out on cloths spread upon the ground. Women, splendidly arrayed in wildly patterned dresses, wraps and turbans, milled about in a fluid mosaic, or they sat regally like queens on upturned buckets, haggling. Lion suddenly loved each black face, basking in the disquieting pleasure of homogeneity. He smiled ridiculously at everything. Children gathered around him, holding out their hands, their eyes merry and cunning. He gave away all his coins. He was euphoric, Kintu impatient.

The coughing, gargling and roaring of the old bus made conversation impossible. The windows were long gone, so dust swirled in from the flat dirt road. They skirted small villages and family compounds almost invisible in the bush. Only the high conical thatched roofs and smoke rising from cooking fires gave them away. Lion felt as if he had landed on some other planet, for surely this could not exist in the same world as Waikiki. He passed men grooming their elegant huge-horned cattle, rubbing ash on each animal to deflect the rays of the sun and discourage insects. He remembered lovingly doing this same thing, the animal's muscles rippling under its warm skin as he rubbed, dust rising in tawny billows around him, his father nearby.

Just when he feared his spine could not endure one more jolt, the bus stopped and the driver called out, "Majok."

There was nothing around. Lion watched the bus growl away in a belch of exhaust and red dust. They were almost home. Kintu insisted on carrying the bag. As they walked along the trail, pausing beneath solitary trees to drink water, a kind of panic began to creep up on Lion. His mouth went as dry as the ground, his thoughts buzzed like evening insects. He was back in the world's cradle, his own cradle. His feet remembered the land and began to move faster. Kintu, weighted by the bag, stalked behind.

Just ahead, a bony old cow stood in front of two thatched houses, each with a broad, brown cross baked into the clay beside its doorless entrance. He turned to the glowering Kintu. "The crosses," Lion said. "Is that wise?"

Kintu grunted and rolled his eyes. "Ma. She insisted."

Lion paused for a moment to pray that his heart be prepared for whatever he would find. As he did, his mother emerged from her tidy hut carrying a big earthen bowl on one hip. She saw him, put her hand to her mouth, then walked toward him, tears streaming down her face.

"Ma." Gently Lion took the bowl and placed it on the ground. When he stood up, she hugged him fiercely to herself and wept.

A slender young woman, tall and adorned with hundreds of orange beads, who could only be Eulalia, rushed from inside and joined the embrace, jumping up and down in happiness, unbalancing everyone. "Come, Kintu," and she made room for him in the circle.

Kintu swaggered forward but stood slightly apart, formidable and unbending. Eulalia, took his hand and tugged him into the communal embrace.

Everyone but Eulalia began to relax. Bubbling with happiness and energy she pointed to the farther hut. "Kintu built the men's sleeping hut where you will stay with him. He is so clever. Come, Kori. See." She grabbed Lion's hand, needing to touch him.

Kintu argued, "You mean Ma built it."

"You did all the labor," his mother said. "But I had the knowledge, and now I've passed it to you, so I can rest." She spoke to him cautiously as to an unpredictable child.

Lion ran his hand over the broad cross. "The crosses, Ma. Very brave of you, but do you think it wise?"

"We're free now." His mother swayed in satisfaction. "Free from Khartoum. We can be who we are. Besides, I now have two strong sons to protect me—and the good Lord, of course."

Lion winced.

Noticing this, she asked, "Are you back to stay, Kor?"

"You know I came for the wedding, Ma."

She digested that for a moment, then said, "We can talk about it later. You're here now and that is miracle enough for one day. Tonight at the fire you can tell us all about Amrika." She spoke with maternal assurance. "You've been gone so long, Kori, I hope you're not uncomfortable. Do you remember anything of our Dinka ways? How we live?"

"I had two of the best teachers, you and Father. No matter where I go, I'm branded Dinka forever."

She took Lion's two hands in her own, possessively. "Son, you must teach your brother everything you know of men's skills. He was younger when he was taken."

Kintu's eyes widened in defiance, the whites glowing. "Do you think I'm stupid, Ma."

"Not stupid," she said. "But you were only a baby. And if someone has something good to teach you, why not learn it? You're a fast learner. Show Kor how clever you are. Show him the sorghum field and the strong corral you started."

Lion laughed. "A corral for that old cow?"

The electricity of Kintu's disdain crackled. "Do not mock us, Brother. We'll soon be rich."

Their mother explained, "Eulalia's bride price is quite impressive because of her beauty and education."

Eulalia laughed,. "It seems I'm worth many cattle. Two hundred."

Their mother's pride was endearing and comical, poultry-like with a puffing of the breast and ruffling of feathers. "Her husband-to-be is the eldest son of a chief and a very important district administrator for the United Nations. Their clan is twenty kilometers away. Eulalia will wear a big white wedding dress. Mine is pink lace. Her husband's great aunt is holding them. She has a house in Juba with closets, doors and windows. You will see. They're a good family."

Eulalia said, "I'm going to start a small school. Kori, you must come and be my first guest lecturer, tell the children about the wonders you've seen. Give them great hope."

"I'd like that." He feared as he said it, that it would never happen.

Kintu, who had shed his shirt, led him to the sorghum field. Lion noted his brother's many scars, the old lash marks on his back, similar to his own, like a ritual tribal scarification.

"It's a good crop," Kintu said. "Easy to grow, drought tolerant. We get paid cash by the U.N. to plant food crops. I also put time in every week building a community irrigation system, for which the U.N. also pays me."

Lion looked out on the fledgling plants in neat weed-free rows. "This is good, Kintu. Very good."

"Soon we won't need aid from anyone." Tremendous resentment decorated his words.

Their mother came up behind them and looped her arm in Kintu's. "I'm saving to buy a big iron wok and I'm going to pop the sorghum kernels like popcorn and sell little bags of delicious 'popghum' in the market. I got the idea from a woman in the refugee camp where we were. Nobody here is doing that yet. See, Kori, we have many plans."

Before darkness descended, Kintu helped Lion gather broad banana leaves for his bed, shake them and wipe them clean. "If you want, tomorrow we'll build you a proper cot because you've grown accustomed to a bed." His tone was accusatory.

"This is fine. Don't worry about me."

The family ate dinner around the fire, a simple meal of fish with millet porridge and milk. Nobody asked Lion about America. Their interests, it seemed, were more immediate: rainfall, rebels, safety, the impending nuptials. "It's going to be a very grand wedding," Eulalia said, nibbling around fish bones. "We'll be married in Saint Theresa's Cathedral in Juba—by the bishop, I'll have you know. Then we'll have a fancy party in a hotel—can you believe it. You'll love it, Kori. I'm almost finished my bead corset, thanks to Ma."

They talked about their father and Mayom, the days when they were all together, when their cattle were numerous and fat, and how in the night their lowing comforted them. After a while, the fire died down and one by one they said their good-nights and retreated to sleep.

By then it was too dark for Lion to read his breviary, and the bed of leaves in the hut did not invite him to kneel beside it, so he went back outside to say his evening prayers beside the cross his mother had baked into the wall of the dwelling. He knelt in the dirt and wearily crossed himself. "Thank you for delivering me safely, but it is not well with my soul, Abba. I'm a foreigner in my own home, struggling with my own language. Where are you? All I hear are insects and the nocturnal screeching of animals in the bush."

Lion thought of his bed of leaves and decided to pray some more, outside in the moonlight where the air moved in the night. He prayed in anguish and confusion about the direction of his life.

*Am I now too good for a dirt floor, a bed of leaves? Am I so self-indulgent? Do not turn from me, Father. I'm not turning from you, only resisting a path toward you that I find deadening. Do not let my body be torn apart by jackals or my soul by regret. Let me not be repulsed by the lack of comforts I only yesterday took for granted. Help me deal with Kintu. I find myself subtly sparring with him. I know he's glad to see me, but he already resents me. It's sort of like you and me, Lord. All is in flux. Help me navigate. Guide my feet along the path you would have me walk.*

He noted, in dismay, that his prayers sprang from him in English. *I do this for you, Abba, to serve your neediest. But who am I to say who is neediest? Is it my people living in huts, sleeping on banana leaves, or comfortable Americans adrift in their abundance? Help me. My soul is downcast within me. It seems I have not outrun my confusion.* He crossed himself again, got up from the dirt, brushed off his legs, and added one last prayer: *Since I'm already here, you might whisper in Bishop Binda's ear. Perhaps he has an assignment for me here.* When

Lion went inside, Kintu was already asleep, or pretending.

A bed never smelled better nor felt so uncomfortable. Lion missed his pillow, a blanket, even the electric fan, the handy bathroom. He could get used to the deprivation. Missing things was better than missing people. Through the doorway he looked up at a brilliant tapestry of stars and recognized their pattern from long ago. Mintaka, Ainilam and Ainitak. He felt a visceral connection with the spot where he had been born. "Thank you, Abba." He reached out his hand beyond his leaves and placed it upon the earth. *To dust you shall return. In Africa, a man lives close to the earth, close to his death, to the deep, organic mysteries of existence.*

# Chapter 29
## THIS DAY YOU WILL BE WITH ME IN PARADISE

Lion awakened as the first streaks of dawn lightened the sky. As soon as he stirred, Kintu whispered, "You awake?"

"Yes."

"You must miss your bed and your house and all your fine things in Amrika."

"I'd be lying if I said I didn't."

"And priests don't lie?"

"They do. They—we—are human. We sin."

"Priests die well. I give you that."

Lion waited several minutes before speaking. "Do you want to talk about it?"

"I dealt with all that. I'm excellent. How are you doing back here, living rough like this again? Ma says that you were sold as a slave. What was that like, to be bought and sold like an animal? How did your master treat you?" A hint of derision lurked in the questions. "Did he use you for himself?"

"My master was an evil man and so were his sons, God have mercy on their souls."

"Mercy? God damn them to hell." Kintu simmered a moment, then said, "I suppose God brought you back here to save us?"

"Perhaps he brought me back to save myself."

"I was never a slave. I was a soldier, a leader of men. I had a a big price on my head, dead or alive. I wasn't afraid of anything."

"Why did you turn yourself in? What made you do it?"

"I wanted a different life for myself. I wanted to go to bed at night without a gun beside me. I want what our father and mother had. A home. A place that's mine by right. I want children who won't be soldiers or slaves."

Lion accepted what he knew was a partial truth. The rest might come later. "It's good you're home, Kintu. Ma needs you."

"I know."

Kintu did not say in return that Lion, too, was needed.

At that moment, their mother peeked in on them. "Am I hearing my two sons awake in there?"

"We are."

"Kor, I'm going to market. Come with me." She turned to Kintu. "Darling, will you fish this morning?"

"I'll add it to my list, Ma."

"I know I can count on you, Son."

The sprawling market stood on the north-south river road where it intersected with a road going toward the Imatongs. Neither road was paved. "Kintu doesn't like to go to market," his mother said. "It was at this very market that he and Mayom were kidnaped. It was a terrible day. Many were killed. Shot, hacked to death. "

"Do you know how or when Mayom died?"

"Kintu said he was killed trying to escape." His mother paused at a basket of red rice, but bought none. "He was so small, so smart that one. My baby."

A woman sitting on an overturned bucket called to her, "Tereze. Yoo hoo."

They walked over to the woman's little plot of market ground where she had spread out a tattered cloth holding old plastic Coca-Cola bottles filled with cooking oil .

The woman grinned broadly, missing many teeth. "Yah, I see your Kor come back from Amrika. The Lord hears us, yah?" She held up a bottle. "You want? I give you. For celebrate."

His mother gently slapped Lion's hand when he reached for his wallet, then thanked the woman and accepted the oil.

As they walked away Lion said, "Ma, you know she can't afford to give you that oil."

"She needs to be able to give." She turned her attention to a display of vegetables. "Besides, she'll charge me a tiny bit more for every bottle of oil I buy in the future until the gift is paid for." They moved on. "You want to spend your money, Kori? There's something I really want. It's a silly thing, but I can't help myself from wanting it."

"Show me, Ma." Lion was confident he could afford anything here.

She led him to a far corner of the market where old furniture, doors, chipped crockery and odd pieces of mysterious machinery were piled. She pointed to a pink plastic chair. Immediately, a thin unshaven man, bent in posture and knobby in joint, materialized. "You like?"

When he quoted them a price, Tereze shouted at him in a fury. "That is not the price you asked one month ago. You're a thief because my son from Amrika is with me. That chair is one month older now. Your price should be lower, not higher."

"Ma."

"No, I don't want such a chair, a chair that has accommodated the ass of a thief."

After several more minutes of fierce acrimony, a price was agreed upon and Lion picked up the pink chair and carried it away, while his mother, at her own insistence, carried her basket laden with pawpaw, mango, okra, cabbage and the Coca-Cola bottle, balancing it on her head as she walked with great dignity down the dirt road toward home.

As they approached their compound, they heard Kintu bellowing incoherently. Lion dropped the chair and raced ahead, smashing through the banana plants. He saw Eulalia curled on the ground crying out as Kintu kicked her. "Stop," Lion commanded. "Kintu, in the name of Jesus, stop."

Eulalia ran to her mother while Kintu stood his ground, howling in rage, every muscle in his body taut, the veins in his neck bulging. All the rage of a lifetime of violence, the loss of what could never be regained, years and years of resentment, frustration and self-hatred spewed into the cosmos. Finally, Kintu fell to his knees, exhausted, sobbing.

Lion quietly approached and knelt beside him. "Breathe, Kintu. Take a deep breath."

Kintu sucked in air with heaving gasps, then collapsed, head to the ground. "I am a terrible man. I've done unspeakable things. Run from me, Kor, run while you can, for God has turned his back on me."

"God always seeks the lost soul. You are God's son, his beloved. If you were the only man in the world, Kintu, he would have died for you."

"I was a little boy crying for help and he didn't listen. He stood by while they robbed me of my childhood and turned me into a monster, until I did horrible things, until I did something so terrible I can never be forgiven."

"God forgives all our sins and puts them as far from us as East is from West." Lion noted how easily the words fell from his lips. He didn't even have to think or feel sincerity. He'd said them thousands of times before. He felt only a great inner weariness, a hesitation completely at odds with his brother's raw emotions.

"You don't know." Kintu looked up from the dirt, his face contorted, his voice broken. "If you knew, you, too, would curse me. I am the lowest of men. I cheated the gallows, and find I cannot live with myself. The evil crouches in me. I'm not fit to live among good people. Look how I just treated my own sister because she didn't come fast enough when I called her."

"Are you sorry for hurting Eulalia?"

"I am now, but not while I was doing it." He became calm and cold. "I felt that old familiar power rise up in me and feed me its red meat. And it tasted so succulent." He turned to Lion, his hands balled into fists. "Why?"

"That's the nature of violence, of evil. It's pleasurable, or we wouldn't do it. Kintu, have you been to confession since you returned from the bush?"

"Yes. In the rehab camp they have for us, the so-called lost boys." Kintu sagged into himself. "But there's one thing I never confessed, the thing that God will damn me to Hell for."

"When Jesus hung on the cross, he said to the thief crucified beside him, 'This day you will be with me in Paradise.' He even forgave the men who tortured and killed Him. Would you like to confess that sin now and receive God's absolution?"

"No. If I tell you what I did, you'll no longer be my brother. You'll turn from me in disgust."

"I will not." Lion prayed that his own words were true, and made the sign of the cross over his brother. "Let us begin. How long has it been since your last confession?"

Kintu spoke barely above a whisper. "Eight months ago. In the camp." He began to rock back and forth. "I can't do this, Kori. I can't say it out loud."

Years of experience in the confessional had taught Lion that this was a crucial moment for his brother, when he was remorseful, on his knees, humiliated at what he had done to his sister. The vulnerability might not come again for a long time. He pressed him, "You must speak the evil out of yourself and be free. Confess, Kintu. God is reaching out to you in this moment. He wants to free you."

The words issued from Kintu in anguish, "I committed the oldest sin in the Bible. I killed my brother. I killed Mayom."

Lion was not expecting this. *God help me. Give me words of peace and healing. Help me save this brother who is before me when I cannot save the one already gone.* "Kintu, see, I'm not turning away. No. I still love you. God loves you. Tell me what happened. Please."

It took minutes before Kintu was able to speak and then it was with a grave calm. "We, Mayom and me, were forced into the Lord's Resistance Army. Imagine that name given to the savages we became."

He glanced up to see if it was safe to continue. "It was a few months after we were captured, the night before we were to raid a small village. For the new soldiers, like me and Mayom, it was a testing; our first raid with the Resistance. Mayom wanted me to run away with him, but I was too afraid, and worse, I actually wanted to prove myself." He laughed bitterly. "I was so twisted, I wanted to prove myself to men I hated. I begged Mayom not to leave. I knew they'd capture him. But he crept away while I slept." Kintu took a deep breath and plunged on. "He didn't get far. The sun came up and we didn't attack the village. Instead, Commandant tied Mayom to a tree and tied me to a tree opposite him. All the new boys were made to beat him with sticks while I watched. He was so brave. Then they untied me and handed me a bayonet. 'Kill the worthless toad.' When I hesitated, Commandant said, 'Kill the toad or you'll suffer the same fate, only we'll leave you here, with no eyes, your genitals in your mouth, and you'll die slowly, crying for your mother like a baby.' Commandant cut a small slice in my neck." Kintu looked at Lion. "I was very frightened."

"You were only a child. " Lion wanted to run and never stop, shedding sin as he sped, becoming lighter until he could fly into the sun and be immolated—the ancient desire of men, to be consumed by something greater then themselves and no longer be responsible.

"Mayom begged me to kill him. He did that for me. Commandant laughed at us, so I grabbed that bayonet and I killed my little brother."

Before Lion could respond, their mother emerged from her hut and walked straight to Kintu. He crouched away from her as she knelt beside him in the dirt. "Kintu, look, at me."

"Go away."

"Look at me," she commanded.

He covered his face and turned from her.

Lion placed his hand on his mother's arm to restrain her.

She ignored him, but spoke more gently, "Look at me, Kintu. Please. I couldn't help hearing you." He turned his face cautiously toward her. She said, "Tell me about Mayom. Tell me about his last days. I want to hear how he was, what he said, what he ate, everything you can remember. Tell me now. Please."

Kintu looked at her in disbelief, then clutching at the hope she held out, began, "We always slept beside each other. We talked about you, Ma. All the time. We missed you and we knew you missed us, that you worried about us. We were just kids."

"I know you were. And I did worry. I prayed for you constantly. Go on. Tell me more." She made Kintu talk about Mayom until he wept,

261

then she said, "I am your mother and I am Mayom's mother and I forgive you. And if I forgive you, no one can hold it against you. Not even God."

Tereze stood up quickly before there could be any physical contact. "I'm going away now to live with Eulalia's husband's people. Not because of Mayom, but because you're not well yet and Eulalia is afraid of you. I'll pray for you unceasingly, Kintu, and I know, with the help of God, that one day you'll be restored to yourself."

Kintu hugged her feet and kissed them.

She backed away. Eulalia emerged from the women's hut and stood rigidly beside a sack filled with her belongings. Her gaze was fierce.

Lion embraced the women then watched as they hoisted their bundles, including the pink chair, on their heads and walked away toward the road. Banana leaves closed around them, shielding them from view.

Kintu called after them, "I'm sorry, Eulalia, I'm sorry. Sorry." He continued to sit in the dirt.

Lion felt utterly drained, but knelt beside Kintu and made the sign of the cross over him. "You have received absolution from God and from Ma. Now, go in peace, the peace that passes all understanding."

"How can a man like me ever find peace?"

"You were only a child, Kintu. None of it is your fault."

"I chose to do those awful things. I'm doomed."

"Do you know the three requirements for serious sin?" Lion didn't wait for an answer. "First, the act in itself must be wrong, which it was. Second, you must know that it's wrong."

"I did."

"Third, you have to consent to do it, freely, without fear or intimidation."

"You sound like God's lawyer."

"God doesn't want you walking around with a load of guilt weighing you down."

Do I get a penance?"

"Your life has been penance enough." Seeing that Kintu looked a little disappointed, Lion said, "On second thought, here's your penance. You have to come with me to Eulalia's wedding."

"Kor, I can't. She won't want me."

"You know Eulalia. She's a good person. Swallow your pride. Man up. No one wants a split in the family. We Majoks don't parade our troubles for everyone to see."

Kintu wiped his brow and leaned against the fence he was building. Since the day of his confession, he worked silently, almost violently, from morning to night. When he spoke, it was meekly with an economy of words. "I suppose you'll be wanting the land, Kor. You're the oldest, so it's rightfully yours."

"You're the one who's been taking care of things. Our father would be so proud of you." Lion grinned. "Soon you'll get your cattle. Then you can seek a wife."

"What if I do to a wife what I did to Eulalia?"

"You won't. You confessed. You're a new person, redeemed. Do you accept that?"

Kintu pulled firmly on the twine he had been knotting at the fence joint. "I think I do. I do."

"Pray that God removes from your mind the memory of those terrible years. Pray for the strength to live your new life in peace. Do good things."

"And what will you do, Kor?"

"Go to confession, myself. Then we'll see. We'll see."

Lion's Way

# Chapter 30
## THE BRIDE PRICE

The brothers continued to build the corral together. They walked about naked and covered with ash against the sun and insects. Lion reveled in the physical work, the freedom and simplicity of it, as he and Kintu built fences, water troughs and shelter for themselves at the far end of the large enclosure. They tended the sorghum crop, fished for food and kept their compound swept clean. Lion even enjoyed his exhaustion at the end of the day, when he was too tired for much conversation with God. At night, he crawled upon his bed of leaves saying the rote prayers of the rosary, grateful in the morning for having fallen into deep sleep before completing the mysteries.

The day they finished the corral, Kintu suggested they go into Juba and celebrate. "I've got money."

"I'm too tired."

Kintu flared up, seized one of Lion's hands, turned it over. "You're not used to hard work anymore. Your hands are delicate, lady hands. Shall I buy you gloves?"

A chill crept along Lion's skin.

Two days later, two hundred head of cattle arrived, ceremoniously led by Eulalia's fiancé, Joseph Garang, resplendent in the traditional Dinka male corset of pink and purple glass beads. Joseph carried a spear in one hand and with the other led a magnificent white bull whose horns grew as wide as half the world. Two cousins, both armed with semi-automatic guns, accompanied Joseph. The dust didn't settle for hours.

The men brought prepared food, a bottle of Soko, and stayed the night. It was obvious from Joseph's hearty camaraderie that he hadn't been told of what Kintu did to Eulalia.

Joseph had been introduced to Eulalia by Bishop Binda himself. He was an educated man, a lawyer, with aspirations to politics and asked Lion many questions about America, how the country was run, how disputes were settled and divisions accommodated.

Lion liked him, thought he was a good match for Eulalia.

Before the guests departed in the morning, Joseph presented one of the guns and some ammunition. "I hope you don't need this, but, as you know, wealth breeds envy, and our country is far from peaceful and law abiding."

When Kintu didn't reach for the gun, Lion did. "Thank you." He had never held a gun before, and felt the hard, repulsive thrill of it.

The wedding was scheduled for the following week. In the interval, Lion taught Kintu all he remembered about caring for cattle. He instructed his brother in the daily milking and ashing of the animals, and the placing of dung fires to ward off mosquitoes at night. He showed him how to cut the horns to encourage growth into a distinctive design to identify his own cattle. "Not only do you cut the horns, but every time the calf looks at you, you have to mimic with your arms, how the horns are supposed to grow. Like this." He did a little dance with his arms angled crazily. "It's the end of the dry season now, but when it comes around again, you'll have to drive your herd to a cattle camp in the Sudd. There's always plenty of water there."

Kintu said, "The U.N. irrigation system should be finished by the next dry season, so we'll have adequate water right here."

Lion laughed. "You go to the cattle camps not only to find water, but quite possibly a wife. Can the U.N. find you a beautiful wife?"

"I may have found a wife for myself. Our neighbor offered me his daughter. She's only sixteen, but very pretty and she's used to this kind of life. She's not a school girl."

"When did this come about?"

"When her father saw my cattle."

Kintu arranged with this neighbor to care for his new herd in his absence. He also left him the machine gun.

Lion saw the daughter peering shyly from the doorway. Her father did not invite her to come forward.

As they walked out to the road, Lion asked, "What's her name?"

"Akech."

"She looks sweet."

"She has a child. She was raped during the civil war. She won't cost me much."

"Is that why you're thinking about her?"

Kintu stopped walking. He shook his head in disgust. "You say you've forgiven me, that I am redeemed, but you don't act that way."

"I'm sorry. Please forgive me."

"I'm thinking about her because she knows suffering and humiliation, and she's come through. We're two of a kind; damaged people. We both like the traditional Dinka life. The dirty towns are not for us."

"You've spoken to her?"

"Yes."

"And?"

"Her father and I must agree on a bride price. We're almost there."

"Good. A wife will be good for you, Kintu."

"I think I'll be good for Akech."

In Juba, Kintu and Lion rented suits for the wedding and stayed in the home of Joseph's elderly Aunt Nyandeng, where their mother now resided. Tereze's pink plastic chair sat in the garden beside a bird bath. She rose to greet Kintu as soon as she saw him. "I was afraid you wouldn't come, Son."

"I'm not sure I should be here."

"It's your duty."

Lion noted the guardedness that precluded any expressions of affection between the two. It would take time.

Tereze warned, "No one knows of the trouble between you and Eulalia. If Joseph's family knew, they'd kill you."

The day of the wedding, music and people spilled from the church and when the Dinka sing, they cannot help but dance. They filled the aisles, the pews, and sang with such joy that the building seemed about to lift from its foundation. Many of those celebrating had taken refuge there from the slaughter of civil war only a few months before, so there was nothing timid or reserved about their hymns. These people were the survivors. They were here. They might not be here tomorrow, because the shadow of war was near. But now they sang. They had dressed in their finest clothes and carried gifts. The rhythm and robustness pierced Lion to the core. It was the pain of loss. All this culture, this music and way of life, had been taken from him and it could never be wholly his again. He could sing, he could dance and sway, but a part of him stood aside as the observer. The sense of loss was profound.

The hymns ended. At a signal, everyone decorously resumed their places. Bishop Binda sat on the altar surrounded by a phalanx of priests and deacons in immaculate white soutanes. He had become quite hunched and grey, with curly little tufts of hair above each ear. The organ played softly as Ma in her pink lace dress processed regally down the aisle on the arm of Kintu, who walked with a touching pride, though perspiring profusely. Ma smiled softly from beneath a coif of upswept curls, each curl bleached golden at the tips, an effect once achieved by using cattle urine and now purchased in a salon. No one would guess what lay between mother and son.

The mother of the groom, also with golden curls and escorted by a son, swept forward in an iridescent gown topped with an elaborate matching hat. She inspired a grave caution in the bride. Next, the six bridesmaids flowed down the aisle in a stream of flashing rhinestones and turquoise satin, their solemnity barely suppressing their innocent self-importance. Joseph waited stiffly at the altar in white trousers and a heavy white mandarin jacket with silver studs.

Lion tenderly took his sister's arm. "Ready?"

Eulalia grinned from beneath her veil. "I can't wait." Then she bit her lip. "Is it terrible to be so eager, Kori?"

"Joseph is a lucky man. You are beautiful."

The organ rolled into Mendelssohn's *Wedding March* and every head turned to see the bride on the arm of her brother, the one returned from America. As the two approached the altar, Bishop Binda nodded somberly at Lion. He swayed back and forth for several seconds, each sway smaller than the one before until he was still again.

Lion lifted Eulalia's veil, kissed her on the cheek, and retreated. After Mass, everyone went to the hotel for an outdoor reception in the hotel's huge walled garden. White canopies billowed from the trees and long buffet tables gleamed with silver chafing dishes. Lion nervously approached Bishop Binda. "Excellency —"

Before he could say more, the bishop glanced at him, not unkindly, and said succinctly, "Tomorrow morning, ten o'clock in the cathedral."

Amidst all the festivities, everyone danced traditional Dinka dances, bending, swooping, jumping. Lion had never seen his mother and sister happier. Kintu leaned over and said to him, "This isn't my world. It isn't our culture."

"Lighten up, Kintu. It's just for today."

"I can't get out of here fast enough."

Lion raised his glass of beer. "To you, Kintu. May the next wedding be yours." They both drank. "Aren't you sweating in that jacket?"

Kintu smoothed the lapels. "Yes, but I want to get my money's worth. I'll never wear such clothes again."

Ma personally served them wedding cake. She said to Kintu, "Look around, Son, there may be a wife for you here," and to Lion she said, "I hear you are meeting with our Bishop Binda tomorrow. Maybe he has a church for you. Nearby."

"Did he say that?"

"No. But why else? It would be the answer to a mother's prayer." She paraded away barefoot in a flounce of pink lace and blonde curls while her silver shoes lay askew under the table.

Bishop Binda was already at the church, seated in the first pew, when Lion arrived. He did not turn although he must have heard Lion's footsteps on the stone floor. Lion genuflected, then sat beside the bishop at a small distance. He began with an apology: "I'm sorry, Your Excellency. I should have called on you immediately."

"Father will do."

"I'm sorry, Father, but my mind is in great turmoil concerning my vocation, and it has been for a long time. I had hoped to be more clear before calling on you."

"And are you more clear now? Do you wish to leave the priesthood?"

Lion had not ever considered the last question, and found himself hurt by the suggestion, that he could be dismissed so easily. "I would not go that far."

The bishop's voice was calm and parental. "Tell me what has you so troubled in your soul."

"If you haven't heard, I've acquired a reputation in Hawaii as the Black Confessor." Once Lion began, the words poured from the depths of his spirit. "I am sent from parish to parish, listening not to glorious litanies and testimonies of faith, but to an endless dirge of sin. I walk everywhere, thinking I can lose evil like I lose pounds. Other priests perform weddings, baptisms, organize silent retreats, youth groups, fun runs. I sit in the confessional."

"Do you think that is an inferior assignment? Do you imagine God's grace is insufficient for you?"

"Oh no. Our Lord always gives me enough grace to hear the next confession. And the next. He will pour enough grace upon me that I can spend my whole life mired in other people's sins—and my own.

"I'm tired, Excellency. I feel at times that God saved me, gave me a new life, called me to the priesthood, and then, like a bored lover, he's on to other things. I'm a speck in the universe. But the Evil One—he always has time for me. He stalks me."

"A fallen priest is a great prize."

"All I want is peace and to be of service."

"Where do you think you will find this elusive peace? Here? You weren't here during the worst of the civil war when this church was filled with five thousand refugees from the massacres. Oh, no. You do not escape evil by coming home. That would be too easy."

"I think I might do some good here."

"Do you imagine that Africa cannot manage without you?"

"I imagine that Hawaii can manage without me. Bishop Carroll in Honolulu wants to assign me a wealthy suburban parish. When I try to imagine myself in such a position, ministering to people who have blessings beyond counting, I want to run away."

The bishop sighed impatiently. "Do you think these people are not dear to Our Father? I tell you, Kor, these people you consider unworthy, stingy, haughty, demanding, unlovely and unloving, they, too, are his beloved sons and daughters. Do you imagine that he does not yearn for them?"

"What am I to do?"

"Only you can answer that, you and the Holy Spirit. For myself, I find that if there's something I don't understand intellectually, it is because I am ignorant. Therefore I must employ intellectual curiosity and seek science, facts, knowledge." The bishop paused, swayed a bit, cleared his throat. "And if there is something I don't understand spiritually, it is because there is something I am unwilling to do. It's axiomatic that if I want to grow spiritually, the path is not through my intellect, but through obedience. Duty. Faithfulness to one's word. The accumulated wisdom of the ages has taught us this. Otherwise, left to our own proclivities, we are in danger of becoming eccentric, crazier than a bedbug, our words mere bushwa." The bishop fell silent. The two men sat beside each other beneath the cross. Finally, with a shrug of good humor he turned to Lion and said, "I find it rather ironic that in the past, missionaries from the West descended on us, converting us, and now it is Africa sending priests to the West to save the churches. I can't help feeling a bit satisfied by that twist." He smiled and swayed almost imperceptibly. "Do you wish a blessing, my son?"

The interview was over and Lion felt more burdened than before. He had hoped for some kind of affirmation or encouragement. Maybe even a command. He bowed his head.

Bishop Binda raised his right hand over Lion's brow and rested his left hand on his shoulder. "Father, Son and Holy Spirit descend on this, Your beloved son. You formed him tenderly in his mother's womb. You know his innermost thoughts. You know the number of his days. You have a perfect plan for his life. Mary, mother of graces and patron of priests, comfort your weary child. Illuminate his path with the light of your tender love. Amen."

"Amen."

They left the church together, chatting about family, the wedding, the weather. The bishop retired to the rectory and Lion walked to Aunt Nyandeng's house. Kintu had already left for home, anxious to get back to his cattle. Their mother bustled about making tea and offered moist lemony baseema cake. "I wish your father could see us now. He would be so happy."

"He does see us."

"I hope so. I've staked my life on that belief."

"Ma, I leave for America day after tomorrow."

"Why, Kor? This is your home. You are needed here."

He echoed Bishop Binda, "Am I so arrogant as to imagine Africa can't survive without me? The priesthood is like the military. You don't get to go where you might want. You go where you are sent. But I promise you I will ask the bishop of Honolulu to release me. If he does, I will be on the first plane home."

# Chapter 31

## INAPPROPRIATE RAINBOWS

It was Lion's first morning back in Honolulu and the rainbows of Nu'uanu Valley stood in great columns of color, the red, orange, yellow, green, blue, indigo, violet; bleeding into each other. The prophet Ezkiel wrote that blue was God's favorite, that his throne was made of the finest lapis lazuli. Lion walked briskly with Michael as he headed for the bishop's office. He got there in time to see Bishop Carroll drop his telephone with a clatter and clench his hands together to stop the shaking.

Lion stood still. "What is it?"

A moment of silence passed before the bishop spoke. "It's Dan, my son. He's been badly hurt, very badly. As we speak, he's being airlifted from Kabul to a military hospital in Germany."

"What happened?"

"I don't know all the details. He's critical." The bishop glanced at his trembling hands, and put them together in a grip that might have passed for prayer but for the way his knuckles turned white and fingertips red with the pressure. Guttural sobs suddenly wracked him. "My God, my God, my son has lost both his legs."

"I'll stay with you. I'll change my Lanai flight."

The bishop composed himself. "No. The whole island is expecting you, Protestants and all." He added, "There's not much entertainment there. I'll be alright. Just pray for Daniel."

They looked out the window instead of at each other. The valley was still beautiful, the rainbow curtain of color still draped on the brow of the hills. The eye discerned no change, yet everything had changed and become bright and mocking. "Prayer," the bishop sighed, "the last refuge of the powerless." The rainbows faded and a fitting gloom descended on the landscape. "According to his mother, Dan has a lot of anger toward me. Here I thought our meeting went so well."

"That's probably why he's angry. He met you, he felt your love and it made him aware of what he missed. If you had been a reprobate, he would have been grateful for your absence."

"I've kept you long enough, Lion. You have your Lanai flight to catch." He rummaged on his desk. "Ack, here it is, the report on Saint Anthony's School in Kailua. It's not a sure thing yet. There are other contenders for the post, but just have a look at the report while you're on Lanai and we'll talk again when you return."

"I'll call you from Lanai to see how you're doing."

When Lion telephoned him that evening, the bishop had nothing more to report about Dan Johnson.

Later, as Lion climbed into bed, he reflected on his day, and specifically on pain and wickedness. *They are intrinsic to our human condition, and the more clever and complex we humans become, the greater havoc we can inflict on one another and our world. Barbarism is not behind us, but just below the skin.*

*In the rainbow-drenched heights of Nu'uanu Valley where I walked just this morning, the invading army of King Kamehameha the Great once drove the defenders of Oahu over the cliffs to their deaths, four hundred men and women in a single sunny afternoon, spears glinting, red and yellow feather capes fluttering as if on their original wings. We forget the people, the blood, the past, as we drink in today's beauty. Was the beauty any consolation as the men and women plunged downward to death? What will console us as we die? Is there anything great enough for that moment when we release all certainties but death itself?*

*There is one thing: the light toward which we fly.*

# Chapter 32

## DEVIL ISLAND

Polynesian legends say that flesh-eating demons once made their abode on the island of Lanai. Tales of their cunning and prowess terrified the settlers of the other Hawaiian islands, so they left little Lanai alone for hundreds of years. Some people claim to this day, that if you peel back the two resorts, the three golf courses, and the one town, you will find that Lanai's red soil is still warm to the touch because hellfire crackles so close to the surface.

Three men and three dogs sat around a campfire on a rugged lava promontory at Kaunolu, claimed by many to be the finest fishing grounds in all Hawaii. It was a lonely, wind-scoured place, wild with stars.

Father Lion leaned back on his elbows, the glow of the flames burnishing his ebony face. He had come fishing with Eben Silva, who told the tale of the demons, and Kainoa Parker, Eben's lifelong friend and distant cousin. "That's quite the story, Eben. It reminds me of my father's tales when I was a child in Africa. All those old stories taught us lessons, usually about good versus evil, how cunning evil is and how strong and vigilant we must be against it."

"I thought you'd like that one, Father."

A clammy chill descended on Lion, first on his back which was away from the fire, and then his whole body. The fine hair on his arms stood up as he recognized his Enemy drawing near. Faintly in the shadows he detected the distinctive rank odor of something corrupt and old and it had come this night for him, of that he was sure.

"My friends, it has been a most glorious day. This afternoon I saw a niche in the lava, down close to the sea. I'm going there to sleep and pray."

"You sure? Some of those caves are old burial sites," Eben said. "It's even rumored that the bones of our great king, Kamehameha, rest in one of them. This was his favorite fishing spot. See that rock wall? One of his temples."

"I'll be careful, and respectful."

Kainoa asked, "Did we offend you, Father?"

"Nothing of the sort. My prayers are long and I am in the habit of praying aloud."

Eben handed Lion a flashlight. "Take this. The lava can be dangerous in the dark. Stay away from the edge of the cliff. It crumbles."

Lion tied his dog to a kiawe tree and put down a thick towel for him to sleep on. He explained, "I don't want Michael digging for bones in one of those caves, or running over the cliff in the dark." The real reason Lion was leaving his dog was to spare the poor animal the coming confrontation. Animals recognize evil immediately and in their innocence and bravado, might put themselves in danger. He patted Michael's head and turned to his friends, "I'm grateful for the light. I'll see you in the morning, God willing."

The priest clambered down to the shallow cave he had spotted earlier, rolled out his bedding and knelt on it to pray. He prayed so fervently that the words streamed forth in a language he didn't know, pouring straight from his spirit. He felt himself carried up until he floated among the myriad of stars. So much love flowed into him he could not hold it, so he stretched out his arms as if he were flying, as if more stars, super-novas, galaxies could flow from his hands, and he glimpsed the mystery of creation. The big bang was like a cosmic orgasm, love pounding forth seeking release in more love.

Then he heard the sly confident whisper, "Abeed," and he was back to Earth, on his knees in the dark. "We've been waiting for you, Abeed."

"Jesus, Jesus," he prayed. Suddenly he was thrown violently to the ground, his face in the dirt. He heard laughter, high, gleeful giggles. He lifted his head and tasted blood. His teeth had cut into his lip. He slid his hand in the direction of his backpack and a rock fell on it, nearly smashing his knuckle.

"Jesus have mercy," he shouted. "Defend me, Lord."

"You let that man do things to you, didn't you, Abeed? Things you like. You let the son of your master enter your body. We love him. You love him. Abeed is precious to us." The Adversary's voice dripped syrup, "Lion, I have big plans for you. Big. Maybe even Rome. Would you like that? The chair of Peter?" The very words had a sulfuric stench to them. "Or perhaps you prefer a wife? A voluptuous young wife, even two or three of them. Tell me, my darling. What do you want? I'm lis-tening."

Lion felt as if he were made of concrete, his tongue a stone.

The Adversary sat heavily on his chest and bent low, close to his face, his eyes burning. His breath reeked. "Have you heard from your brother? Kintu, he is my special project. You may have freed him for the moment, but I'll be back for him. You can count on it. Kintu is very weak and he has tasted my many pleasures. Yes. Did you know he drank Mayom's blood?"

"That's a lie." Lion had just made his first mistake, debating the ene-my. He could not stop shivering, even under the suffocating weight on his chest.

"Do you want me to leave Kintu alone and never trouble him again? I can do that. It's all up to you."

Lion recognized the snare into which he had been lured. In desperation he commanded, "Go away. Depart from me, Satan, and from my family, in the name of Jesus."

The Adversary flinched. "Ouch. Fine. I go, but before I do, I have an attractive proposition for you. Here it is: I promise—on my dishonor—that I will leave Kintu alone and never return for him, if you offer yourself to me in exchange. Your soul for his. Oh, nobody has to know. Shh." His sibilance was phlegmy.

"You will still look like handsome Lion, you will still be a priest, if you choose. Your master, whose name I cannot speak, gave his life for you on the cross. Can you do less than offer yourself for your brother? And I don't demand a cross, Lion. I'm not that kind of guy. No. I give you all your desires.

"Do you think Kintu will be nice to others, smile at babies, become a good farmer, a gentle husband? That's entirely possible. It's all up to you, Lion. Just say the word. Otherwise, I'll be back for him, and he will take me in. Yes, and he will be seven times worse than before. You'll see. Unless you give your life for his, as your master did for you."

"Michael the Archangel defend me in battle. Jesus come to my aid." Lion wasn't sure if he prayed aloud or in silence. He kept saying the name of his savior over and over, until he heard a burst of bitter laughter.

"I'm going, my pet, but I will return for you and your brother. In the meantime, I give you a friendly warning, Lion, because I am so very fond of you: Eulalia must always be on her guard with Kintu, never turn her back on him. He will kill her as he killed Mayom. Also, in parting, beware the oily clutches of those Kamanas. Oh, how they love you, love you so much they smother you. They want to replace your true family, to blot them from your heart. Those jealous leeches.

"Best of all, you may someday defy the authority of the harlot church. Those simpering priests and fat bishops think they have you, that you will slave for them all your days. But think of all the good you can do in Africa. You want to feed the hungry or start a school, like your sister? Or a clinic? Will you become a governor of men? I can arrange that. Just tell me. I can give you what you want. Oh, I know you don't want power for yourself. You only want to help your fellow man, don't you? Yes, I can see hospitals and schools and a shining Juba. If you want tree-lined streets and tennis courts, no problem. Just say the word. I see the future, how everyone will admire and love you. You're so wise, so benevolent. I see all this for you: statues of you in every schoolyard, your face on the front of the one hundred pound note. I spread it all out before you, whatever you want. The other one, whose name I cannot speak, only promises you a cross. I give you the world. The world, my darling Kor. Do you want it? Just nod your head. That's all it takes. Just a little nod."

"Jesus." Lion wasn't sure if he said it, so he said it again, and again, until the Adversary, with a sneering smile, leaned toward him as if to caress and kiss him, then abruptly vanished.

Shaking violently Lion lunged for his backpack drew out his breviary and crucifix. Clutching the crucifix to his breast and grabbing the flashlight, he opened his book, shone his beam on it and began his compline, the evening prayer: "O God come to my aid. O Lord make haste to help me." As he continued, howls rose up in the dark at the mouth of the cave.

He broke into loud song for the canticle: "Now that the daylight dies away, by all the grace and love, thee, maker of the world, I pray to watch my bed. Let dreams depart and phantoms fly, the offspring of the night. Keep me like a shrine beneath thine eye...."

He prayed and sang with all his being, as if his life depended on it, hearing in his pauses, behind his breath, from the darkest corners, mocking laughter and the taunting whisper of his despised name, "Abeed."

Lion kissed the crucifix. "Jesus," he prayed aloud, "You are my inheritance, all I could ask for. I will not run to alien spirits, for their sorrows are many. I will not share in their libations of blood. Their names will never pass my lips. My soul and my body will lie down in calm and hope. Jesus, I am yours, heart, soul, body, breath. All that I am, all that I was and will be, are yours."

Then, as if the decision was wrung from his tortured soul, as if the words burned and singed his throat, he cried out, "I forgive Yusef." The name of the son of Ali El Mum Nhom, the name he thought he had forgotten, snaked out from his deepest memory. "I forgive Yusef."

Lion collapsed onto his bedroll and wept as he never had before. He wept for all the years of his slavery, for his lost childhood, for his father, for his own exile.

First light began to seep across the sky, gently vanquishing the cold night. The land grew warm and the tidal voice of the ocean gladdened the air with promise. Lion fell asleep.

It seemed only minutes when the smell of cooking sausage awakened him. "Praise God." He grinned as he gathered up his things and climbed up the cliff.

"Whoa, what happened to you?" Eben immediately got out his first aid kit. "You look like you been in one beef." He handed Lion a cup of water. "Here, wash your lip." He dabbed at it with disinfectant. "Hoo, the nasty one."

"Thanks, brother."

"Look the hand, too. You took one bad fall."

Kainoa unhooked Michael who was whining and straining at the leash. He said, "The dogs were really spooked last night. I could have sworn I heard a pack of wild dogs howling."

Lion flinched from the sting of disinfectant. "Are there wild dogs on the island?"

"Not that I know of."

"Hmm." He ruffled Michael's fur. Reassured, the dog ran off to attend to his morning necessities, and seek out hapless quail.

Eben, now intent on scrambling eggs, claimed he slept so soundly he heard nothing. "Must have been the deer barking. They bark, too, you know."

"No deer ever sound li' dat." Kainoa warmed his hands near the fire although the morning had no chill. "What you think, Father? Some demons still here? You think there's some troot to the old tale, that Lanai was the isle of demons?"

"The Bible says that the devil prowls the world like a hungry beast seeking victims to devour."

Eben divided the eggs and slid them onto paper plates. "There's no such thing as the devil. All the evil what we see in the world comes from inside us. We do it. That's the trouble today. Nobody takes responsibility. Everything someone else's fault. The devil made me do it. No disrespect, Father, but you really believe in one guy wit horns, a tail and a pitchfork?"

Lion responded, "If you believe there's a force for good in the world, why not a polar opposite, a force for evil and destruction? Yin and yang. As for the horns and pitchfork, the evil one is much too clever to come for us in such a ridiculous costume. He comes for us disguised as our desires, our pride, our self-righteousness. He's the great illusionist. So don't go by appearances, but weigh all things well."

Kainoa asked Lion to bless the food, then he said quietly, "I know what I heard last night and it was the devil. He was prowling for one of us. That's my *mana'o*. You tell me, Father, am I wrong?"

"The strategy of our Adversary, according to the great saint, Ignatius of Loyola, can be compared to the tactics of an army commander. The commander explores the fortifications and defenses of the fortress he faces, and attacks at the weakest point. In the same way, our enemy stealthily examines us from every side, looking at our virtues, our theology, our morals, looking for the weakest, softest spot to insinuate himself. Well, let him do his worst, he cannot enter except by the door of our consent."

Eben opened a stash of brownies and offered them around. "Like I said, Father Lion, it's our own weaknesses and conniving what bring us down, not some devil."

"The evil one's greatest, most successful illusion is to make us think he doesn't exist."

"This is the spookiest story of all. You get the prize, Father."

Lion climbed down to the ocean, jumped into the cold sea, feeling it tingle along his skin and scalp, swam a few strokes then turned to float, his face to the morning sun. The wild salt of mercy washed over him.

# Chapter 33

## THE DEVIL'S DUE

Lion left Lanai with a great lightness of being, stunned by the awe and happiness known only to newly released captives. The elation stayed with him even as he reported to the bishop's office and learned about the bishop's son.

Lieutenant Colonel Daniel Johnson was burned so badly his face would have to be reconstructed through a series of skin-grafting surgeries that began almost immediately in the army's burn trauma center in Germany. He was lucky to be alive, although he might have argued that point had he not been in a medically induced coma for the first two weeks. He was also fortunate to be left with two functioning thighs that could be fitted with prosthetic legs.

After a month in Germany, he was transferred to Tripler Army Medical Center, the huge rosy-pink military hospital built during World War II on a green hill on Oahu. Now that his son was back in Hawaii, Bishop Carroll knew that some duty, some weight, like what he imagined love to be, would fall on him. It would either crush him or call him to some deeply affecting action.

"I wish I could comfort you," Lion said, "but I can only remind you that God did not spare his own son."

"The cross. Christian life always returns to the cross, doesn't it? What is your cross, Lion?"

If Lion had been completely honest, he would have said, "You are," or even, "My sacred vow of obedience," but, he gave the more remote, least offensive answer, "Exile."

Bishop Carroll looked at him as if for the first time. "Is your mother comfortable?"

"Very. She's living in Juba with my sister's family."

"Good. Good. If you ever need anything…" He left the sentence unfinished.

Lion headed for his next assignment, a retreat at Saint Anthony of Padua Church in Kailua, the parish where the bishop threatened to send him for good.

The prow of a great Polynesian voyaging canoe was how he thought of the interior of this unusual church. The distinctive architecture suggested a journey, water-borne and bound for distant lands. Everything swept upward to the cross as the mast, drawing the pilgrim onward as a sail pregnant with wind. The wood of the church seemed to groan with a remembrance of the forest from which it came. Lion knelt in prayer.

A Maryknoll missionary priest, imprisoned and then forgotten in the tumultuous Communist sweep of China, had stayed sane by designing this church in his mind, with all its bold thrust and detail. When the Communists finally released him from prison, Father Henry was an old man, broken in body, but with a mind eager for labor in the Lord's fields, and a heart full of love for the Chinese people for whom he prayed until his last breath.

When he arrived at Kailua, the growing parish of Saint Anthony of Padua needed a larger church, so Father Henry, with great zeal, got to work. He took his dream church to an architect who translated it into stone and wood. Lion tried to imagine the first time Father Henry, now deceased, lifted the bread above the altar and raised the chalice of wine.

All his prison chains slipped away. To see such victory this side of the grave was almost too much to contemplate.

The church door creaked open behind him, the clatter of a woman's shoes approached then stopped. "Excuse me, but this has to be the one and only Father Lion." The voice was deep, confident. He looked up into her face, strong, slightly jowly with middle age. Huge complicated earrings tugged at her lobes, dark hair swept upward from her face into a chignon. She was costumed to seize the day in a red blazer and navy skirt.

"Yes?" He rose to greet her.

"Sit, sit, Father. I didn't mean to disturb you. I just stopped in for a quick visit to ask the Lord what on earth he's thinking of these days, because I, for one, haven't a clue. And here you are—the famous Black Confessor. Have you got a year or two to listen to my problems?" Bristling with energy, she sat beside him in the pew.

Lion caught himself before a weary sigh escaped his lungs. He sat back down. "How may I help you?"

Her laughter was high-pitched, operatic, mocking as she plunged into her story with theatrical gestures, great shoulder shrugs, and eyes that flashed and flirted ostentatiously. She modulated her voice carefully, slipping in an occasional British accent. "My name's Paris Parnell. She reached into her commodious purse and pulled out a little silver case, snapped it open and handed Lion a business card. "I'm a freelance travel writer for the *New York Times, National Geographic, Modern Bride,* whoever writes me a check."

"That sounds exciting, going on journeys for a living."

"Well it was. But it's not. Magazines are folding, newspapers are laying people off and all those staffers become freelance writers pitching to a shrinking market. I'm taking a course in real estate. Ha-ha. Special today, a foreclosed house. Step right up, observe the loving care show-ered on this house by its previous occupants, who are now jobless and homeless at River of Life Mission." She shook her head. "I don't know what else to do. My husband's a history teacher with incipient Alzheimer's. I need a drink," she said. "Got a little wine? A cup of blood? Ha-ha. Father, I am stretched so thin." She stood up and ran her hand down her body. "Well not exactly thin. Hello there, God, I've got a few more pounds you can horrify off me. What else do you have in store? Cancer? A dirty bomb? Macular degeneration? Fleas?" She sat back down.

"I have to bring in the hula moolah because I've been presented with my brother Keenan's three children to raise because he shot himself in my kitchen one morning over two fried eggs and a bran muffin. God, the mess. I thought an omelet pan was hard to clean. Keenan lost his shirt and everything else he owned in the economic downturn. Then his gorgeous wife, and I mean drop-dead gorgeous - I should have her looks - ran off with the garbage man and now she's a crackhead in Las Vegas. She's crazy. But who can commit her? She has rights. Thank you ACLU. I suppose I could look at these three children as God's amusing way of replacing the two children I've lost. No, no, I didn't misplace them. My daughter Brooklyn died of breast cancer two years ago."

Lion said, "I'm so sorry. It is so much tragedy for one life. "

"They say you grow through your pain. Well, it just makes you a bigger target. I'm sorry for you, Father, because I'm not finished yet. I haven't told you about my son, London, who died of a drug overdose six months ago.

"Please, Mrs. Parnell, is all this true?"

"Not to worry, I have a surviving son, Oslo. He's alive and well in Budapest studying Crimean-Gothic and assorted Slavic tongues. God knows what he'll do with such an esoteric specialty. Go live in some Balkan village. I can see it all now, him in Lederhosen, the wife in babushka with missing sweater buttons and teeth. I suppose I should be grateful that I've got three replacement parts for my family." She glanced at her watch. "If you're free for dinner, come join my circus."

"I'm afraid I have the retreat here at church tonight. Would you like me to pray with you before you go home?"

"No. But you can pray for me. Ask God for a new cleaning lady. My last one quit to become a dog groomer. I can get you a discount flea bath for your dog. Is that the famous Michael by the door?"

"That's my buddy." Lion walked to the church door with her.

"Toodle-oo, Father. God how I date myself. Toodle-oo." She beeped the lock on her car door and turned to Lion. "I'll call you about dinner for another night. I'll throw together a little do. A hundred of my closest friends. Ha ha. Just joking. But I do want you to bless my house. There's some bad juju vibes in there. I'll invite Cynthia the dog groomer with her buckets and shampooches. Bring your dog. She'll tie a little neckerchief around him when she's finished. He'll look like my future Crimean-Gothic daughter-in-law. God help us all. *Au revoir.*"

Lion, exhausted, hugged Michael.

The Parnell house was right on Kailua Beach. Lion stood on the lanai facing out to sea. The trade winds sweeping in from the ocean blasted him. He was not good at parties. In fact, he dreaded them, the noise, the small talk, everyone preening. People usually exhibited a momentary interest in his novelty, then dropped him when he didn't keep up his end of the repartee. Tonight he also felt guilty and false.

He had visited his Waimanalo family that morning and Lili avoided him, leaving to go grocery shopping as soon as he arrived. She had the bloodshot eyes and slack mouth of the insomniac. He didn't know how to help her.

Barney Parnell joined him on the lanai "Lot of hot air in there." With a degree of amusement, Barney tilted his head toward the house. I don't know who most of those people are. Paris is always bringing home a new cast of characters. I don't know where she finds them—Maui, France, Safeway. I can't keep track. Some hang around for years. Others come and go.

"Ah, there you are, Father Lion." Paris burst from the house with her gold caftan billowing, a turban wrapped around her head and huge yellow plastic hoop earrings bobbing. "I was beginning to think you had run off with the dog groomer. Do I look African?" She posed with arms out. "I tried to get Uncle Barney here into a leopard loin cloth with a submachine gun, but he wasn't having any of it." She kissed her husband. "Perhaps we should do the blessing thing before everyone is too sloshed, shouldn't we, darling?"

Paris led the way indoors where the party buzz had grown to a convivial din. "Can you do the blessing in African?" she asked.

"I usually do house blessings in Hawaiian."

"But Hawaiian blessings are so overdone. I was thinking of something a bit more exotic, like ritually decapitating a chicken; something with a little oomph and feathers."

"Darling," Barney intoned with calm forbearance, "let Father Lion bless the house in his own way. Besides, whatever demons are lurking in our rafters probably don't speak Swahili."

She patted her husband's arm while addressing Lion, "Uncle Barney is always so pragmatic. Father, do the blessing as you see fit. Besides, I don't happen to have a live chicken handy. Or even a box of frozen thighs for that matter." She turned to go. "Do you have a turban or a shrunken head you can use? Ha ha. Just joking."

Her showmanship carried everyone along. It takes a large heart to decorate every ordinary moment with such extraordinary energy.

Lion filled the wooden calabash with water and poured salt into a smaller wooden bowl. He had already de-ribbed the ti leaf so he put his stole about his neck and announced he was ready. "But I'll need some-one in the family to assist with sprinkling salt."

Paris immediately called out, "Satchel. Where's Satchel? Oh, there you are, darling." She dragged a reluctant little boy through the crowd. "Satchel loves to throw things around, don't you, Satchel? He'll make an excellent salt tosser. Now do what the nice priest says, darling." She whispered to Lion, "He's the youngest of my brother's children. He saw it all."

The boy peered truculently from beneath a thatch of stiff, straw-colored hair. Lion bumped fists with him. "My name's Father Lion." His name always won children over.

"Really?"

"Really."

"Cool."

"We're going to go from room to room, praying. Now every time you see me dip the ti leaf in the bowl and sprinkle water, you take a little pinch of salt and fling it like this. Got it?"

Satchel nodded solemnly and took the bowl of salt in his two chubby hands.

Paris called everyone to attention with a huge Tibetan bronze gong hanging by the back door. She announced, "I bring you the famous Black Confessor, straight from the savannas of Africa. Ta-dah. Take it away, Father Lion."

He felt he should be in tights and sequins. "Peace be with this house and all who live within and all who cross its portals." He made the sign of the cross over the assembled guests. "We're going to bless each room, starting with the farthest from the front door."

"That will be Satchel's room," Paris said. "Lead on to chaos, Satchmo."

The child's room had barely an inch of floor space not strewn with tossed clothes and resting toys. Satchel stood proudly.

"You will be an excellent assistant with the salt," Lion said. He then ordered any unclean spirits dwelling within the room to depart in the name and power of Jesus. He dipped the ti leaf in water, nodded at Satchel, and the boy, with great flourish, tossed a handful of salt into the room as Lion sprinkled the water.

Lion bent down and whispered in his ear. "Good job. But let's use a little less salt on the next room or we'll run out before we get back to the kitchen."

"My room had a lot of unclean spirits and unclean clothes. It needed a lot of salt."

"Good. Good job."

Satchel cupped his hand and whispered in the priest's ear. "It used to be my cousin London's room. But London's dead, like my dad."

"My dad's dead, too, Satchel. It's hard, isn't it?"

"You're big, though. You don't need a dad."

"How old are you, Satchel?"

"Seven."

"I was exactly seven when my dad died. Let's talk about this later. Okay? Show me the next room so we can fling some more water and salt."

Followed by the crowd, they went from room to room, praying, chasing demons. In the kitchen, Lion experienced resistance, an entrenched, powerful and defiant presence that sent chills up his legs. Three times he repeated his command for the spirit to depart in the name of Jesus, felt it give ground and drove it before him toward the door. Satchel threw an extra measure of salt over his shoulder and looked to Lion for approval, his upturned face radiant. The child had great potential.

"We needed more salt there, Satchel. I'm glad you knew that."

The procession ended at the open front door. With a sweeping gesture, Lion ordered all unclean spirits to depart the house and never return because this home was now a sanctuary, a place of peace, a colony of the kingdom of Heaven.

Michael, who had been pacing anxiously outside, began to howl, setting off every dog in the neighborhood. The effect was chilling. People looked uneasily at each other. Lion thought that most of the guests probably believed in some form of supreme being, but few accepted a personified presence of evil. Even vampires and werewolves, traditional fiends, have become today's sex symbols. Evil has become simply misunderstood, a form of spiritual gender-bending.

Paris whispered, "The howling dog's good, a very good trick."

Lion asked Barney, Paris, and the children to stand by the door. "Do you invite Jesus, the Lord of Love, into your home and hearts?"

"Aloha, Jesus," Barney said. "Come right in."

"Would you like an apple-tini, Lord?" Paris turned to her guests, "Just joking. How about you, children? Shall we let Jesus in?"

They nodded. Satchel said, "He can sleep with me."

"You'll have to clean your room, first, darling. Cleanliness is next to godliness."

Lion concluded with the sign of the cross and a resounding "Amen," echoed by the assembled people who then dispersed to the comforts of the buffet and sofas.

Lion invited Satchel to a quiet corner of the lanai and told him, "My dad liked to sing. He carried me on his shoulders. Tell me about your dad."

"My dad blew his brains out. Some got on me."

Gently, Lion said, "My dad's blood got all over me when some bad men killed him."

"Gross."

"Yeah. I was scared."

"Me, too."

"Are you still scared, Satchel?"

"Sometimes."

"Me, too. But you know what I do? When I'm scared, I close my eyes and picture my guardian angel standing right next to me, watching over me. He's exceptionally large and has beautiful wings. His name is Michael."

"Like your dog?"

"I named my dog after my angel."

"What's my angel named?"

"Well, I don't know. But let's close our eyes and picture your angel. You can ask the angel what his name is and he or she will tell you in your heart."

The boy scrunched his eyes closed. Suddenly a smile bloomed on his eager face and he opened his eyes. "He's pretty big and he's got this really cool light saber. He said his name is Sparky." Satchel then asked, "Where's my dad now?"

"He's up in Heaven with my dad. They're both with Jesus and they are like new, no blood no wounds showing. They are perfect. Can you see your dad like that?"

The child squirmed in his seat, closing his eyes. Finally he said, "Yep, he's there all right. God glued him back together so good you can't tell."

"Now you know how to think of him, because that's how he is."

"Maybe your dad and my dad can play golf. My dad loved golf."

"He'll have to teach my dad."

"He never has time."

Lion shrugged. "In Heaven he has lots of time."

"Do you want another meatball?"

"I'm ready."

Satchel stuffed a whole meatball in his mouth, then joined the other children working a video game on the television monitor.

"He's a fine little boy," Lion said to Barney. "We talked about our fathers."

That evening, back in his room at the rectory, Father Lion stayed up into the night, praying. The Saint Anthony retreat was draining him. He had spent at least two hours a night for four nights, listening to sins and had one night to go. He felt sins weighing him down. He was caked in them, his pores clogged in grime, their thick oily taste in his mouth.

*If Bishop Caroll has his way, this will be my life, right here, in this rectory. Is this why you made me, Lord, rescued me from slavery?*

Africa lay fresh in his mind. He could still smell its fecund essence, hear throaty voices calling to one another in his first and dearest language and feel the familiar heat of home slowing him down, calming him.

# Chapter 34

## ALL RACHEL'S CHILDREN

As Lion prepared his morning coffee, the telephone interrupted. It was Lilinoe. "Lion, did Mom or Moses call you yet?"

"Not today."

"Momi had her baby at two a.m. this morning. A beautiful, healthy baby boy."

"That's wonderful. Is everyone okay?"

"Everyone but me. Lion, I need you. I'm going crazy. I have a hole in my heart as wide and deep as the ocean and I'm drowning in it. It's not supposed to be like this. They told me it was no big deal. That I'd feel relief. But I wish it was me who died on that table, not my babies. Please help me."

He hesitated, hardly daring to say the word. "The abortion?"

She shrieked into the phone, "God, why did I do it? I'm doomed, Lion. I have nightmares. I hear a baby crying. My soul is hemorrhaging. Help me."

"I will. I love you, Lili. Calm down. I'll come right away. Are you at home?"

"Yes. Please don't tell anyone. They don't know I was even pregnant."

"I'll pick you up." He looked in his breviary for the phone number the bishop had given him, and telephoned Sister Felicia Jenkins in Kaneohe, apologizing for calling so early.

"It's okay, Father. We have to tend to the lost sheep as they show up. Is the young woman Catholic?"

The question stopped him cold. "Does it matter?"

Sister Felicia spoke calmly to his indignation. "All that matters is the healing, the reconciliation. I ask only so I know how best to lead her in prayer."

"Yes. She's Catholic. And she's my sister, my *hanai* sister. I'll be bringing her myself."

"My only requirement, Father, is that the woman call me before coming. She has to take that first step herself. I'll be waiting in prayer, beginning this very minute."

Just as Lion was preparing to leave, Moses called to tell him about the baby. "We name him Jacob Lion Kealiimaikaiokaakamu Kamana, but we call him Cubby Boy. Like our Lion cub."

Deeply moved, Lion thanked Moses for the honor, and agreed to officiate at the baptism.

When he got to Waimanalo, Lilinoe was waiting at the gate. She got into the car and threw her arms around him.

"Where are we going?" she asked, as Michael bounded from the car to join the Kamana dogs.

"I have a plan, but it's all up to you." He told her about Project Rachel and Sister Felicia in Kaneohe. "The whole experience is designed by the Church for spiritual and emotional healing after abortion. Lili, you have no idea how loved you are, how much help is out there."

"Will you be there?"

"If you want. If you prefer privacy, I can wait in prayer somewhere out of earshot."

"I want you there."

"Do you have your cellphone? Call Sister Felicia." He reached into his shirt pocket and handed her the piece of paper with the number. "She's waiting for your call."

"You call."

"You need to take that first step yourself, Lil. It's part of the process. Besides, I'm driving."

"I'm scared."

"If you don't want to...."

"No, I do. Well, I don't, but I know I have to do something." She took a deep breath and punched in the number. The call was brief.

"She sounds so nice," Lili said. "I feel a little better. We should bring pastries."

"I'm ahead of you. I stopped in Kailua for coconut bread."

"Thanks for dropping everything and coming."

The convent on Kaneohe Bay was a private estate willed to the order of the Sisters of Divine Mercy. They had their own dock with a red kayak resting upside down on it. A statue of Mary presided over a garden of blue ginger, periwinkles and plumbago. Lion assumed it was Sister Felicia standing in the doorway dressed in a long denim skirt and faded shirt. Since giving up their habits, nuns dressed like orphans. Sister Felicia was smaller, slighter, more bird-like than he had pictured from her voice. Short mousey hair curled forward on a thin, sharp face. She radiated efficiency.

A golden retriever ambled over to greet the car, barking happily, its lavish tail swinging.

"That's Ignatius Loyola," Sister called out. "He's harmless. Iggy. It's okay, boy."

Sister Felicia introduced herself and held out both her hands to Lili. "I'm so glad you're here, and so is God. You've come to the right place."

She accepted the loaf of bread with thanks and led Lion and Lili straight to the chapel. "This used to be the master bedroom," she said. "But we converted it and enlarged it by taking out the bathroom. Oh, I hated to see that Jacuzzi go." She wrung her bony hands together.

A simple altar with a starched white cloth stood at the end of the room. A crucifix hung on the wall behind it. The floors were bare wood. Loose rows of folding chairs faced the altar. Sister Felicia settled them into the first row, already easing into the ritual, saying, "Our Father loves us simply because he created us and has bound himself to us forever. We, who are human, tend to love people when they're nice to us, and we're indifferent at best to those who don't like us. Even with the people we love, we have our clever little ways of punishing them if they displease us, don't we?"

Lili smiled nervously. Lion knew that Lili was desperate to be this meek.

"God's love isn't subject to these ups and downs." Sister Felicia continued in a talk she must have given many times. "He loves us no matter what. Divine love doesn't depend on our behavior. And he has all eternity to wait for us. Shall we come to him now in prayer?"

Lion and Lili nodded and they all crossed themselves. Sister Felicia opened her Bible and read from a card: "Eternal Father, source of all mercy and love, you sent your son to us, and you will that blood and water flow from his side to cleanse us of sin and restore lost innocence. Hear the cry of each woman who mourns the loss of her child to abortion. Forgive her, restore her to your grace and still the terror in her heart with a peace beyond all understanding. Through the intercession of the Blessed Virgin Mary, our mother, strengthen Lilinoe's faith in you. Give her the consolation to believe that her child..."

Lili softly interrupted, "Two. Two of them. I had twins."

Sister Felicia nodded thoughtfully then went on: "Give Lilinoe the consolation to believe that her children are now living happily with You, Lord. We ask this through Christ, who conquered sin and death. Amen."

Lili and Lion echoed the amen.

Sister Felicia then read the gospel of Luke wherein Jesus is criticized for associating with sinners and tells his critics the story of the shepherd with a hundred sheep who loses one and leaves the ninety-nine to search for the lost one until he finds it and sets it on his shoulders with great joy, calling out to his friends, "Rejoice with me because I have found my lost sheep."

She read from Jeremiah and the Psalms about God's compassion and how he forgives our sins and remembers them no more. "Our days are like the grass; like flowers of the field, we blossom. The wind sweeps over us and we are gone and our place knows us no more."

Lion heard the familiar passage as if for the first time. The words sucked all strength from him and he sat as if a mortal blow had been delivered. *Mayom, my brother. The wind sweeps over his unmarked grave. My father's bones lie bleaching in the African sun. When I die, I want my bones to nourish the soil that birthed me.*

Beads of perspiration gathered on Lion's brow and upper lip.

Without a pause in her reading, Sister passed Lion a box of tissues which she had at the ready.

Lion fumbled in his backpack for his own Bible, quickly found the passage and read along with Sister Felicia, "You are my shelter, from distress You keep me; with safety You ring me 'round."

He tried to hear the message as Lili might receive it but heard it only for himself. He felt like an obstacle in the path of her journey and was relieved when Sister Felicia quietly closed the book and asked Lili, "Are you familiar with visualization prayer?"

"Are you kidding? That's Lion's specialty. When I get to Heaven, or Hell, I'll know my way around because I've pictured it so vividly so many times, thanks to him."

"That's good. Lilinoe, do you know if your children were boys or girls?"

The mood of the moment changed instantly, went still, and became expectant. Lili bit her bottom lip and her brown eyes filled with tears. "I saw them on the ultrasound. Girls."

Gently Sister asked, "Do you have names for your daughters?"

Lili's mouth twisted in anguish. "Maleka and Malia—Martha and Mary."

Lion was surprised at the depth of her connection to her aborted children, that she had names for them, and he was chagrined at his ignorance of his sister's true emotions.

"Beautiful names. God bless them." Sister Felicia leaned toward Lili in a way that announced a crucial juncture had been reached. She was being the bird that sets the migration date for the flock in spring and this was the moment. Her entire being focused on Lili. "We're going to ask our Blessed Mother, in our visualization prayer, to bring Maleka and Malia to you and place them in your arms. Would you like that?"

Lion expected brass-knuckled sarcasm at the blatant manipulation, but Lili merely nodded.

"You can hold your children and say the things in your heart. Father Lion and I will sit in the back of the chapel and be in prayer. When you're ready to let your children go back to Heaven with Mary, just turn around and let us know, and we'll rejoin you. Take as long as you like." Still focused on Lili, Sister said softly, "Mary's coming now. Do you see her? She's carrying two beautiful babies."

Lili was rapt, transported.

Sister Felicia and Lion, with a minimum scraping of chairs, got up and sat in the back of the chapel. The nun quietly read her Bible, closing her eyes occasionally, so intense were her prayers. Lion felt bereft, shaken to the core of his beliefs, hating the arrows of fear festering in his heart, hating more his concern with himself. If he went back to Africa, he would never leave it. It would capture him. . He yearned to go anyway. He silently begged: *Give me a sign, Lord. Show me the way.*

Sister Felicia whispered, "I sense a spirit of disquiet in you, Father. Are you well?"

"Quite honestly, Sister, I'm having a vocation crisis." The words were out before he realized he had spoken. He plunged on, "I feel disoriented, perhaps even alienated."

"Have you spoken to our bishop?"

"He's part of the problem."

"I see."

He took a risk and trusted her: "I have come to believe I should be harvesting more fruitful fields."

"Hmm. More fruitful fields. Yes. Well, perhaps we who have given over our lives to Christ shouldn't be concerned about our audience, or about the fruits we bear. All we need concern ourselves with is the will of God. Lord, what wilt thou have me do today?"

"Today is easy, Sister. Today, he wants me here."

"Every day is today. And every day you are invited to share in Christ's suffering."

"It always comes back to Gethsemane, doesn't it? The trick is discerning his will."

"Gaze upon the crucifix."

"I do. I have. I don't always like what I see. I am afraid I may have caught the spirit of individualism."

Her sharp little features went rigid with satisfaction, as if she had snapped in the last piece of a jigsaw puzzle. "It sounds to me, Father, as if you have been given a priestly assignment to which you consider yourself unsuited, perhaps even—how shall I say it—superior? This is your hour of isolation. I will leave you in it and turn my thoughts and prayers to your sister. I gently suggest, Father Lion, that you do the same."

Her words stung. Lion turned his focus toward Lilinoe sitting in the front of the chapel holding her aborted children and prayed for her.

Twenty long minutes went by before Lilinoe turned and nodded to Lion and Sister Felicia to rejoin her. Sister Felicia sat on one side of her, Lion on the other. "Lilinoe," Sister Felicia began. "You didn't know that you could take care of these babies. You know it now, but you didn't know it then."

"Yes."

"I want you to ask your children to forgive you."

Instinctively Lili pulled her arms to her breast as if gathering her children closer and she sobbed. "I'm so sorry. I didn't know what to do. I was weak and frightened. I thought I was doing what was best. Can you forgive me? Please." Then she looked up, first at Lion and then Sister Felicia, pleading.

Sister Felicia hugged her and rocked her. "Your daughters do forgive you. They want you to know how happy they are in Heaven and that they will see you when you get there. Our Blessed Mother will now take Maleka and Malia back to Jesus." They sat for a few minutes before Sister Felicia turned to Lion. "Will you officially offer Lili absolution?"

Lion made the sign of the cross over his sister. "You are forgiven in the name of the Father and of the Son and of the Holy Spirit. Amen."

Sister Felicia closed her Bible with a final snap and said, "Lilinoe, you have acknowledged and named your children. They are part of your family and they sit before the throne of the Almighty, ready to intercede for you. You can now give them little spiritual chores from time to time. They'd like that."

"Thank you. Thank you both. I am so grateful."

"Would you like to stay for lunch?" Sister invited. "I've prepared a small salad and we have the bread you brought."

Lion answered, "I have to be going."

"Please, Lion," Lili begged. "Can't we stay? It's so peaceful here."

"I…" He sighed and put down his backpack. "Okay."

Sister Felicia put Lili to work setting the table while Lion wandered outside. A big cowbell clanged, calling him back in for lunch. Two more sisters, young Sister Mei Ling and old square-faced Sister Modesta joined them. The older nun, quite pleased with herself, said, "I made cookies. It's not Lent."

Sister Mei Ling sighed. "I'll have to paddle an extra hour in the kayak to work off those calories."

Lunch proceeded in just that chatty vein until Lion thought he would jump out of his skin. He excused himself as soon as he finished and waited outside. The beauty of the bay reflecting the mountains did nothing to calm his inner turmoil. Lili came out and put her arm through his. "I'm sorry, Lion. I'm keeping you and you've done so much for me. Let's go."

As they headed back to Waimanalo, Lili tried to engage him in conversation, "You know, I thought I would come here today and have a spiritual reckoning and leave all of it behind and get on with my life. Now I realize it will always be part of me, but in a whole new way. I'm so grateful, Lion."

He wanted to punch the dashboard in utter frustration, and felt horrible about his anger. "Glad to be of service."

She detected the formality and did not speak again. She would not let him rob her of her joy.

# Chapter 35

## PEOPLE WITH WINGS

"I've got one more assignment for you, Lion, before I settle you down at Saint Anthony's." Bishop Carroll smiled widely, almost smugly.

"Settle me down?"

"Don't look so distressed. It's a plum parish." He kept smiling, as if expecting Lion's dismay.

"I know and I appreciate your confidence in me. It's just that you know I hoped to settle down back in Sudan."

"We've been through this before. You are trying my patience. I need you on Molokai for two weeks. We'll have a formal announcement about your Saint Anthony appointment when you get back."

Molokai lies unnoticed, a mere mote on the vast blue blanket of the Pacific. A Cessna 404 turboprop, with Father Lion in the co-pilot's seat, droned across the Ka'iwi Channel from Honolulu toward the island. When he was assigned to Molokai after ordination five years ago, Father Lion was intrigued by the island's ancient name, *Moloka'i Pule O'o*, Molokai of the Powerful Prayer. If he ever needed a powerful prayer, he needed it now.

As the island slipped under the plane's wing, Lion felt his spirit soar in spite of himself. For him, Molokai was God's own cathedral with its green mountain spires and waters of life extravagantly tumbling everywhere. From the air, he saw that nothing had changed except that the cattle were back. He spotted them dotting the lush meadows of the east end and browsing the scrub of the west. He remembered the anguish occasioned by the cattle eradication program during his first tenure on the island.

The Cessna pilot, a man who looked more like a bookkeeper than someone who held planes aloft, soared above clouds, then dipped down along the ramparts of the north shore where dozens of waterfalls tumbled four thousand feet from green sea cliffs into remote valleys, eventually flowing into the ocean. The cascades splashed on ledges and soared upward in wind-tossed veils. The pilot grinned and shouted above the engine, "That there's Kahiwa. Sacred, they say." He pointed to a string of sylvan cascades. "There's Oloupena, and Hipuapua and Papalaua."

"Praise God," was all Lion could say at the splendor arrayed all around him. He gazed upon flowing water, crashing surf, rich land with a litany of ancient names.

The pilot seemed pleased. "They do praise God, don't they, Father. How many years since you been back here?"

"Too many."

"Lotta changes. Midnight Inn burned down, Sheraton closed, post-nine-eleven airport security, a new pizza place."

"Traffic lights?"

"Not yet."

"Movies?"

"No."

"Giraffes?"

"Gone. They broke their necks in the gulches."

The giraffes and other African browsers had been brought to Molokai to eat the *kiawe* scrub encroaching on Molokai Ranch's pastureland, and they became a tourist attraction.

Lion turned around to check on Michael in his kennel, which was strapped to an empty seat in the last row. The dog, a veteran flier, appeared to be dozing.

The first time Lion arrived on Molokai, the oil of anointment still damp on his head and hands, the entire congregation of Saint Sophia Church greeted him on the tarmac, singing, playing their ukuleles, and dancing hula. They draped him in leis up to his ears, and drove him to the church enthroned in the bed of a flower-bedecked pick-up truck as if he were the son of a chief. They welcomed him with a luau that had taken weeks to prepare.

This time, the welcome committee consisted of two members of Saint Sophia's altar guild, old Maria Espinola and brisk, gossipy Lourdes Banimbang, who drove him in her Honda straight to the rectory in Kaunakakai.

Father Kalawai, the current pastor, had left the day before for a final meeting in Honolulu before departure to Rome for the canonization of Father Damien. It was Lion's mission to fill in for the two weeks Father Kalawai would be away, and to get the leprosy patients from Kalaupapa onto the plane, making sure everything was in order for their comfort and wellbeing on the pilgrimage.

"How's Philomena Fong?" Lion asked.

"Not so good," the ladies chorused, fussing over a lunch they had prepared for him.

Mrs. Espinola, the shorter of the two, added, "Izzy, her son, move back home."

"The girlfriend with him." Mrs. Banimbang, thin as a stick, sliced banana bread with a disapproving thwack. "She's one fundamentalist, that girlfriend. Church of Joy of Resurrected Jesus. They use tambourines. What? An organ not good enough for dem?" Mrs. Banimbang obviously disapproved of tambourines in general and especially in church. "You want ice cream with your banana bread, Father?"

"No thank you on the ice cream."

"Better with ice cream, you know." She was already scooping some onto his plate.

He smiled in resignation. "Okay. The works."

"Dog, too?"

"Give him just a little." It was useless to object.

Mrs. Banimbang sat down, tugging at her blouse. "That girlfriend tell Philomena the Catholic Church is the church of Satan." Mrs. Banimbang had taken the accusation as a personal affront when Philomena told her that.

"Poor Philomena, no can do notting, she so weak." Mrs. Espinola shook her head. "They bring the whole Church of Joy of Resurrected Jesus to the house and pray over Philomena." Mrs. Espinola folded her arms against the outrage.

"Those holy roller tambourine bangers try snatch Philomena's soul away from the true church." Mrs. Banimbang grabbed at the air as if at an insect in flight. The bones of her hand gleamed white beneath her thin skin.

"They already got Izzy." Mrs. Espinola's spoon clattered into her empty ice cream dish. "But Philomena, she one rock. She stand firm in the faith, Faddah."

"Funny thing, Faddah…" Mrs. Banimbang paused to lick her spoon. "You remember that bull the Fongs had? Sir Lancelot? Well, 'bout this time last year, that bull all the sudden turn up. After all these years. Everyone thought that bull *ma-ke* die dead."

Father Lion kept his eyes on his ice cream. "Has Waynette Fong been home?"

"That's the really peculiar ting. That bull turn up when Waynette come home to visit the mom. She's one hot shot TV news reporter in Chicago now. She interviewed Brad Pitt. But her head no turn, she still one Molokai tita."

Herding everyone back on topic, Mrs. Espinola reminded them, "That Waynette loooove her Sir Lancelot."

"Like her own child," Mrs.Banimbang added. "Biggest bull 4-H ever saw."

The bull had been the subject of one of the first confessions Father Lion heard as a priest.

Years ago, when the state of Hawaii ordered the slaughter of all cattle on Molokai because of an outbreak of bovine tuberculosis, the decree devastated the small ranchers on the island. Many, like the Fongs, never ran livestock again. The large ranching operations were able to ride out the one-year ban on cattle, then restock.

The only condemned animal on Molokai not slaughtered was Sir Lancelot, the Fong's prize bull. It disappeared, and after an exhaustive search by the Department of Agriculture marshals, was presumed dead.

At the time, Father Lion, as the new pastor of Saint Sophia's, made the rounds of the ranches, calling on Catholics and non-Catholics alike, offering what comfort he could. Where needed, he helped with funds from his own small stipend and food from his pantry. On one of his visits to the Fong ranch, way out on the East End, Isaac and Philomena's daughter, Waynette, invited him to go riding. "I have something I want to show you, Father, something I know you will find interesting."

"I'm not much of a rider, I'm afraid."

"Our old mare Queenie is nearly dead. You'll love her."

Philomena had packed them a picnic lunch and off they went across the lush green hills and into the rainforest where the land rose toward the green mountains of the North Shore. Waynette snapped off a *hau* branch for a whip so Lion could keep poor Queenie plodding ahead.

The forest was deep and quiet with damp, lacy *haupu'u* ferns growing as high as the horses' heads. Banana *poka* vines fingered Lion's face and shoulders. He commented on the beauty of the flowers.

"Banana poka's an alien species," Waynette pointed out. "It chokes the native flora."

"Ah, the sword of beauty," he said.

They reached a clearing at a mountaintop where the land fell away into shadowed ravines. The sun felt good and a small wind blew about them. Waynette dismounted. "Over here, Father."

His knees buckled when he slid out of the saddle.

Waynette smiled indulgently, then parted some tall grasses, bending them over to reveal a red rock festooned in pale green lichen and etched with petroglyphs.

"The people have wings," he said, reverently. "Angels." He traced his hand over one figure. "How old are these?"

"I don't know. But I think they're from ancient times when people lived in Pelekunu Valley. Before the missionaries, before Western contact."

"How did people get to Pelekunu back then? I thought the only way was by boat."

Waynette laughed. "Maybe they flew."

"I've never seen petroglyphs quite like these. What do they mean?"

"In my Hawaiian studies class at UH, a professor lectured on the petroglyphs in Moanalua Valley on Oahu. There are winged people there, too. Nobody knows what they mean. They even brought in petroglyph experts from India. It just makes you wonder what the ancients were trying to tell us."

Lion walked over to what looked like the start of a trail. "Maybe they were warning us about the dangers of this trail. 'Watch out, folks, or you'll become angels, too.' Is this really a trail and if so, where does it go?"

Waynette spoke hastily, urgently, "Father, I want to make a confession."

He waited.

"An official one. So you can't tell anything."

He sat down in the grass beside the rock carved with angels, and she sat beside him. She was lovely and touchingly sincere as she bowed her head and crossed herself. "Bless me Father for I have sinned." She confessed and poured out her story.

"It was at the time of the cattle eradication program, and I knew they'd be coming for our herd, and for Sir Lancelot, so I got up in the middle of the night when everyone was asleep. I took water and a flashlight. No one heard me. The moon was so full and bright you could read by it. My dad once told us that on nights like that, they used to drive the cattle from the high pasturelands down to the shore because if they did it in the heat of day, the animals lost too much weight. At dawn, they'd mount their Percherons and herd the cattle into the surf. They'd tie them to shore boats and tow them out to the barge that would transport them to market in Honolulu. Now we've got the pier in Kauanakakai. Good thing. Sharks once made hamburger out of a Strickland Ranch herd."

Lion brought her back to her confession by asking, "What did you do when you got up in the middle of the night?"

"Sorry. I've always been a storyteller. Well, basically, I rustled our herd. I drove them out of the pasture. I was going to take all twenty-two of our cattle, including my Sir Lancelot, and keep them all from being slaughtered. But I kept losing animals along the way. They'd wander off in the dark. By the time I got to the rainforest I was down to eighteen head, and by the time I got here at the trail to Pelekunu, I decided all I could handle was Sir Lancelot. If I could save him, Dad could restart his herd."

"So, there is a trail and this is it."

"No one knows about it but me and my brother Izzy, and now you, and you can't tell because it's confession. Izzy and I found the ancient trail by accident when we were kids going exploring. It's really danger-ous and narrow along that mountain ridge over there, so of course we loved the thrill. Anyway, that night, just as I got close to the narrowest part of the Pelekunu trail with Sir Lancelot, it started to rain, *ka ua loko,* the fierce wind-driven rain. At one point, I thought we'd all die. It was so dark, wet and slippery that I couldn't find the trail. I was really scared, but I figured it was better for Lancelot to die falling down a ravine than in a slaughterhouse.

"I confess another sin, Father. When I was scared, I prayed to my an-cestors. I figured they knew the old trail to Pelekunu. Is that really bad? Like idolatry?"

"We have many spirits to guide us, Waynette. Father Damien once helped me find my way. He came to me in a dream. As Catholics, we have this great communion of saints who are our extended family. We can call on them anytime."

"Spiritual *ohana.* Awesome." She continued. "Right after I prayed, I found the trail again. It made a right angle turn that I had missed. Well, I made it all the way to Pelekunu, me, my dog, my horse, and my bull. I left Sir Lancelot there, Father, in Pelekunu, where nobody will ever find him. He's still there, but you can't tell because this is official, right?"

He nodded. "The seal of the confessional is sacred and binding."

At the time, he was new at the confession business. He had to offer guidance, reprimand, hope and love all at once. He began with the easy part, reprimand. "You know that what you did is against the law, don't you?"

"Yes, but is it a sin?"

"The lies are sinful. Waynette, you aspire to a career in television. As a journalist, you must have a commitment to truth. If you don't have integrity, you'll be just another talking head, as they say, reading a teleprompter."

"My father quoted Jesus from the Bible, 'Render unto Caesar that which is Caesar's, and to God that which is God's,' meaning we had to obey the law, like it or not."

"You can't have better advice than that which comes from the mouth and heart of Jesus. And your father."

"I don't have to tell the board of health folks about the Lance now do I? Because I won't, even if I burn in Hell for it."

Father Lion silently prayed for wisdom, and when he received an answer, he wasn't sure where it came from. "The cattle inspectors are experienced, intelligent men, cowboys, and trackers. If they can't find a huge bull on a small island, that is hardly your fault."

Father Lion and Waynette watered the horses and ate their lunch in companionable peace beside the ancient people with wings.

Before they rode back to the ranch, Lion glanced with longing at the trail to Pelekunu and prayed silently. *Where the clamor of the world dies in the wind, and the wild holds your secrets in its valleys, there, my friend, my God, my everlasting love, I yearn to sing my old songs to you, alone with you at last, save for the abiding birds and the chants of the ocean. Then I will know I am clean.*

That was five years ago. Mrs. Espinola and Mrs. Banimbang put the dishes away and wiped the kitchen countertops. "You can catch Waynette on CNN, Father," Mrs. Banimbang said. "Waynette Fong. You watch for her. That girl going places."

Mrs. Espinola puffed up with pride. "You know, for one small place, Hawaii has a United States president, an Olympic champion, a canonized saint of the church, and our own Molokai Oprah, Waynette Fong."

Mrs.Banimbang said, "Not to forget Sir Lancelot, biggest bull 4-H ever had, sole survivor of the cattle holocaust." She sat down next to Father Lion, close enough for him to whisper any tidbit of gossip he might offer, and asked, "How the Fongs do that, Father? I hear they hide that bull somewhere. Break the law? Hmm?"

Father Lion got up, scraping the chair back. He laughed, clapped his hands, and thundered, "That rumor is pure bull."

# Chapter 36
## A SHORTCUT TO HEAVEN

From two thousand feet up, the ocean lay flat like a sheet of plate glass. The only sounds in the hot morning were the creaks of leather saddles and the clopping of the mules' feet as they picked their way carefully down the switchback trail to Kalaupapa and the leprosy settlement, now grandly called Kalaupapa National Historical Park.

The twelve tourists on this day's excursion, who, fifteen minutes ago had been happily joking and snapping pictures of each other mounted on actual mules, were now as muted as the distant sea below; too alarmed to talk, clinging to reins and saddle horns as they lurched single-file down the perilous cliff face. This was far more than they had bargained for when they plunked down their charge cards and signed the liability waivers for the Molokai Mule Safari. One said, "I shoulda gone on the macadamia nut tour."

Another commented, "I'm texting my agent to make sure my life insurance is paid up." He laughed heartily but did not take his hands off the saddle horn.

Lion had done the mule ride many times before, although it had been a few years. The priests of the island had a standing invitation to take this transport when ministering to the isolated colony below. Lion knew enough to sit back and let the mule pick its sure-footed way on the narrow rock-strewn trail. These animals had been trained in the Grand

Canyon in Arizona and were steady, reliable plodders..

The mule train had traveled a quarter of the way down the treacherous descent when a woman's sunhat suddenly blew off, hovered momentarily like a flying saucer, and landed directly on the face of the mule behind it. The animal reared up in terror, almost throwing its rider, a tattooed girl from Los Angeles, over the edge. The sudden commotion spooked every mule in the train. Inexperienced riders screamed or yelped "Whoa," further inciting the mules. The panicked animals kicked each other, bit and attempted a stampede to the bottom as if toward a fire exit. Petrified, but calm of manner, Lion spoke softly to his mount while the two guides, one in the lead and one in the rear, tried to quiet the animals. Disaster was averted when a tourist from Montana, providently positioned in the middle of the mule train, snatched the sun hat from the mule's face. He grabbed its bridle and spoke gently but firmly to the animal while expertly preventing the other mules from bolting past him on a trail much too narrow for such choreography. The incident lasted only a few minutes but left everyone's heart pounding. "God!" the L.A. girl said. "Like I was almost friggin' killed by a sunhat."

The woman who owned the offending hat muttered an apology and tucked it, rumpled, into the elastic waistband of her pink slacks.

As the chastened band continued its descent, the pounding surf grew louder, until finally and with profound relief, the riders felt the wind-whipped sea spray in their faces. They relaxed in their saddles and let the mules pick their way sedately along a rocky lava shoreline. The L.A. girl turned and said to the man from Montana, "Can you believe this? It's like *Hawaii Five-O* on steroids. That friggin' trail is more dangerous than the Santa Monica Freeway."

"It's God's country."

"Yeah, well, God shoulda made a road down here. What's with the cliffs? I mean, like, were they necessary?" She smiled, "You saved the day, mister. You some kinda cowboy?"

He was young and gangly and blushed at the attention. He nudged his mule to ride beside her.

Lion was glad to be back at Kalaupapa. The wild beauty exhilarated him, filled him with its magnificence. He always felt at home amidst its tragic history.

In 1868, desperate at the swath leprosy was cutting through his realm, King Kamehameha V decreed that this isolated peninsula become a place of quarantine for victims of the frightening new disease. The Hawaiians called the disease *mai pake* for the destitute Chinese plantation laborers who had inadvertently brought leprosy to the Islands. Another name, *mai ho'oka'awale,* meant the separating sickness because it fractured families. They said, "Prepare for Molokai as for the grave." No one sent to Kalaupapa ever returned.

Surrounded on three sides by a rugged coast and raging surf, and on the fourth by the rampart of sea cliffs, the peninsula was a natural prison. Lion often wondered if the beauty was any consolation to the wretched exiles forced to live here. He tried to imagine how it must have looked to Father Damien, arriving aboard the *Kilauea* in May, 1873. At that time, Kalaupapa was a lawless place; its people, hungry and horribly disfigured were dying of one of mankind's most feared diseases. The strong preyed upon the weak. Death was sheriff, judge and jury. It is recorded that Damien slept that first night under a hala tree. He refused to sleep indoors until every exile had shelter. He became a pest to the Church and government in Honolulu, haranguing them for building supplies, medicine and basic necessities. It had been expected that the exiles would take care of themselves, fishing and farming as

Hawaiians had always done. The authorities had not factored in their weakness and despair.

Damien was a robust man, a Belgian farmer's son, skilled and resourceful. The first building he repaired was the church, and he moved the sickest patients there until he built an adequate hospital. He built homes, a school, orphanage, and a water system that still works today. He planted a thousand fruit trees. Most importantly, he visited the sick, bringing food and tending to their sores. He fed their souls with the sacraments, and he buried the dead, six thousand of them. He even built their coffins.

While Father Lion admired these spectacular accomplishments, he felt that Damien's greatest contribution was joy. He strewed joy like confetti, deluging the sufferers with it, distracting them with festivals and holy days and all the incumbent preparations. Even though leprosy attacks the vocal chords, Damien organized choirs. It sometimes took two organists to make up the ten fingers needed to play, but little Saint Philomena's Church rang with music. Damien organized processions and rituals, great and frequent occasions for adorning the church with leis and fragrant flowers. He carved holes in the floor of the church so the patients could expectorate without getting up and leaving.

Damien once said, "Leprosy is a shortcut to Heaven," and rejoiced when he, himself, was stricken. He died of leprosy among his beloved flock at Kalaupapa at age forty-nine.

When the mule train came to a halt in a grove of ironwood trees, the tourists didn't know whether to kiss the ground or the mules. As they dismounted, they were ushered aboard an old school bus for their tour of the leprosy settlement and a picnic lunch.

Lion waved to his friend, Kalau Ball, waiting in his ancient blue truck at the edge of the grove.

Kalau and ten other leprosy patients, along with a doctor and two nurses, were going to Rome for the canonization of Father Damien. In all, six hundred people from Hawaii were making the pilgrimage, with Bishop James Carroll heading the delegation.

Kalau drove Lion to his neat, white cottage. "How have things been?" Lion asked.

"Leimomi next door finally *ma-ke*. Ninety-two years old."

"A ripe old age. God bless her."

"Bless her? Ninety-two years with the *mai pake?*"

They parked near a stunted poinciana tree decorated with hundreds of painted eggshells and tin can lids spinning in the breeze. Kalau's late wife, Mary, had spent years adding decorations to the tree to cheer it up because it never bloomed. In thoughtful silence, the two men ate sandwiches on the front steps of the cottage.

Lion inquired, "All the time I've known you, Kalau, you never told me how you came to be here."

The man leaned back against the steps. "I'm a Kaneohe boy. The disease caught me when I was seven. The Board of Hell," he paused, drank soda, "that's what we called the Board of Health, came to our house in an official car. All the neighbors came out to look. Oh, the shame for the family. They took me to Leahi Hospital first and then they sent me to this place." He shook his head as if to shed the memory. "Agh, that was a long time ago."

"Seven," Lion said. "That's the age I was when I was kidnaped and sold into slavery."

"We robbed, Father. We sure robbed of our *hanabata* days. When I think about it, I still hate the trouble I had with this disease. Yes, you might say I am bitter about my life."

"I pray that Damien will take that bitterness from your heart on his canonization day."

"How 'bout you, Father? What do you say about your suffering in your life?"

Lion struggled for something that would be both honest and uplifting. "My life happened the way it did. It can't be helped. It is the way of the world. Do I wish it had been different? Of course. Can I do anything about it? I can look back in anger, or look back at that slave boy who was me and marvel at that little fellow's tenacity, his faith in goodness or some form of love. I didn't know what I had faith in at first, but my father, before he was murdered, always told me that God loved me, so I talked to God. I survived. My owner called me Filth, but that marvelous little guy inside me never forgot his name was Lion. I love that little boy. Look, my cherished friend, here we are today, survivors, eating a nourishing meal together under a bright blue sky on the steps of your home. I ask you, do we have our fair share of the world's goodness?"

Kalau laughed. "A big easy Cadillac would sure be nice." He relaxed into somberness. "I never thanked little Kalau. I never thought about my childhood that way. Little Kalau was so scared and not once did that kid cry. When they took me, I walked out with my head high. I never let my mother see me cry when she visited me at Leahi. They took me away to Molokai without notice. When the boat brought me here, I remember thinking that it was a very beautiful place. There were nuns waiting to take me to the orphanage."

Kalau took a deep breath. The long exhale could never be long enough to carry away the sorrow and anger of his disease. They had to be willed away and Kalau was weary of the effort. "You know, they smelled very nice, those nuns. Like soap. I still remember those things. Funny thing is, now they have the drugs for this disease, we're free to go. But we use-ta to this place. I love it here." He lifted his soda can.

"Here's to little Kalau and little Lion, two great kids." He then asked, "How you lose your fingers, Father? You got the *mai pake,* too?"

"I don't have your shortcut to Heaven. My owner sawed them off to teach a little slave boy a lesson."

"I'm sorry, Father. We all wonder and no one want to ask. But I think a slave has a short cut to Heaven, too."

"I hope so, because I sometimes have a rebellious heart."

"What? You want to get married or something, Father?"

Lion squashed his soda can. "Just the opposite. I often have an overwhelming desire to be completely alone." He didn't speak of his other conflicting desire, to return to Africa. It seemed disloyal.

"You come here and I promise we neglect you." Kalau smiled, rendering his ravaged face poignant.

Lion looked away. "My heart is torn between solitude and righteous action."

"Living here, with this damn thing, this disease, you learn to love loneliness. It becomes your spouse. I understand where you coming from."

"Thank you." The men were silent for a while, listening to the sound of the surf coming to them on a new breeze that spun the tin can lids dangling from the tree into a tinkling, glittering concert of the wind. Lion asked, "You coming to Mass and confession tonight, brother?"

"Flying all the way to Rome? Ho, you bet I am. My soul going to be spotless for the pope and Saint Damien. And in case of airplane crash or terrorism, I'll be ready to meet the Lord. No *mai pake* in Heaven, I hear."

Lion folded his paper napkin into a precise neat small triangle. "It's amazing how many Catholics caught leprosy."

"Father, it's the other way around. The people who caught leprosy became Catholic. Whatever Father Damien was, that's what they wanted to be. If Father Damien was a Hindu we would all be Hindu. Or Jew or Gnostic, whatevah. If he walked on fire or handled snakes or faced Mecca, we're right behind him doing the same. But he brought sweet Jesus and the gospel of love and he lived it and died for it. And we be right behind him to this day. That's the kine mark that man made. When President Roosevelt said Father Damien had to be dug up from Kalaupapa, from his grave next to the church, and his body go back to Belgium, oh, the people wailed and cried and pleaded. But nobody listen. The government body snatchers just took our Kamiano away with no regard. The people were very bitter about the move. Damien was always our saint."

"They brought his right hand home from Belgium at the beatification," Lion said. "That was something."

"This time," Kalau said, "we bring home a piece of his heel bone." He slapped his thigh and laughed. "Little by little we get that man back. We Hawaiians never give up. We look like we're in low gear, but we got one powerful prayer going on."

That night at Mass, Father Lion told the little band of patients, doctor, nurses, and nuns how Father Damien had visited him in a dream when he was a slave and told him to leave his master. "He is still delivering us from bondage, tending our wounds, leading us home."

After hearing confessions, he retired to his immaculate, bare room in the Kalaupapa guest house. In his prayers he reflected on how Damien had willingly embraced suffering, while he himself had run as far from his misery as he could, clear across the world. Hurl a spear into the earth in Africa and it will come out the other side of the globe in Hawaii. *Perhaps I am that spear.*

The thought of years in a suburban church made him shiver. At Saint

Anthony's he'd be just fifteen minutes away from Bishop Carroll's office in downtown Honolulu, expected at a moment's notice to join him for nine courses of gourmet food while being reminded that he was earning money for the starving by eating another rack of lamb. "How am I to do this?" he pleaded with almighty God.

Lion recognized the resentment clouding his attitude toward his superior. As the bishop became more involved with his son's family, he seemed to need Lion less, which was at once hurtful and a relief. He felt disposable.

Then there was the matter of the trip to Rome. Lion had assumed he would be chosen to go since Bishop Carroll was well aware of Lion's special devotional relationship with Father Damien. His disappointment must have shown on his face, for the bishop immediately apologized, "I wish I could bring every priest in Hawaii on the pilgrimage, but I can't. I'm counting on you, Lion, to take care of Damien's own island of Molokai so Kalawai can accompany his congregation to Rome. You'll go to Rome another time. I'm sure of it."

He prayed for Bishop Carroll and for the success of the pilgrimage. After an hour on his knees, he got into bed and noticed, with some peevishness, that his pillow was lumpy. He punched at it a bit, then laughed at himself.

*See what I mean, Lord? If you don't help me, I'll become choosey, and then it's only a small step to being demanding and imperious. I, who used to sleep with goats, am now vexed when my pillow is not up to standard. I lift up to you tonight, all the people around the world sleeping in dirt, on hard floors or banana leaves, in the cold or rain or on prison stones and ask you to watch over them.* He reflected on the leprosy patients and wondered what they might have become had they not been singled out, perhaps randomly, to suffer this dreadful disease. *How many millions of people never get a chance to bloom, are mowed down like weeds and lost, their gifts unused, their names unknown?*

*If all the sorrows of the world were piled into one mass, how high would the mountain be? As high as the moon? And what are the gradations of pain? The spectrum runs from extreme physical torture to moral anguish and uncomfortable social outrage, from pure evil to overwhelming futility.*

*And what of joy? If all the happiness and love in the world were gathered and raked into one garden, could the blooms blanket the world? If joy were clouds, ephemeral, swiftly passing before the face of the moon, could joy rain down sheets of drenching happiness? Could we drink it? Would we share it? Amassed, would joy be a higher mountain than sorrow?*

*Are they balanced? Which do we choose?*

# Chapter 37
YES

Kamakou, festooned in clouds, sheltered one of the few remaining pristine rain forests in the Islands. A parishioner had taken Lion there during his first Molokai residence as a priest. The silent harmony had filled him with peace. He had loved it immediately, and now he was back. For him, Kamakou harbored the innocence and holiness of Eden before the fall. The soaring heights of the old trees, the delicate ferns and damp mosses, the clean, sweet greenness of the air, the clear, exquisitely piercing bird songs were all of one fabric, woven by one hand. Some of the songs could not be heard any place else on Earth for the birds existed only here. The balance was delicate.

Lion reached out and placed his hand on a magnificent old Koa tree. *I wish I had your patient strength. You are rooted deep in the earth and you drink the sun in every leaf as you stretch toward the light. What do you know of life's storms and languor? How fitting it is that a tree held all the hidden knowledge of good and evil and grew in the very heart of Paradise, dripping such alluring fruit that it altered the plans of the Divine. Did your leaves stand frightfully still as that delicate hand of Eve reached out, desiring, what?* He paused under the weight of the answer. Power, of course.

He proceeded somberly. The trail winding through the rain forest was laid out as a narrow boardwalk raised just above the ground, defining the boundaries of human intrusion. All else existed as if man did not. Overhead in the green and silver canopy, the endangered *oloma'o* and the *kakawahie* flitted unseen, singing happily, not realizing Kamakou was their last stand on Earth.

The blessed serenity, an awareness of the immutability of time permeated Lion's soul. It was just what he needed as he flayed himself with options and consequences and tried to discern where his selfish desires ended and his selfless calling began. He had entered the priesthood almost as a sleepwalker, accepting the invitation, barely considering what else he might do. It had all unfolded rather miraculously as if destined from the outset which, he believed, it was.

He never ceased to be humbled by the thought that God had called him and given him mysterious gifts to heal and forgive sin, to change bread and wine into the actual body and blood of the Savior and feed his lambs. The Lord gave him these things not to be above or apart from other men, but to become the servant of all. And now when Lion thought of need, he turned slowly away from the tentacles of love and duty and felt Africa's throbbing heat, the familiar fear, the taste of his own death. "I belong to it all."

At the top of the mountain, the slatted path opened to the montane bog of Pepeopae, a Liliputian landscape where perpetual dampness miniaturized the forest into a perfectly ordered bonsai garden. Here the lavish red *lehua* ridiculously bloomed full-sized on ohia trees a foot high. Clouds sped in and out, dispensing rain, bringing darkness then light with the swiftness of a blade.

"In Kailua, Michael, my life will become a bonsai; well-tended and small, my roots bound up in wires of obligation, my years pruned into a shape that will be a small echo of what I might be." In that moment, Lion made a decision. It was an unremarkable moment in which he took an ordinary unmeasured breath, his heart beat and beat again, his eyes blinked. He stood still, shocked at the recognition of his martyrdom and the audacity of his surrender to it.

He fell to his knees there at the top of the mountain and whispered a fragment of Psalm Forty: "Sacrifice or oblation you wished not, but ears open to obedience you gave me." Lion then wept for Africa, for himself, for his life. He was Christ on his way to his personal calvary, to Kailua and the kind of martyrdom he most dreaded. Suddenly he laughed out loud at himself. Kailua? Martyrdom? Really?

The kind of martyrdom he had sought was suspiciously grand with more than a hint of glory. *Our desires come to us cloaked in virtue, hiding our deep, unrecognized malignancies, the ways in which we commit treason against our truths.*

He resumed his prayer, and as he did, the face of Christ became the scabby, methamphetamine-ravaged faces of Kailua teens, the broken body of Megan Roy, the sorrow of the father of her killers, the homeless campers at Nohili, the elderly betrayed by their children. *Jesus, you looked like a complete failure being taken down dead from the cross. How many people there on that hill outside Jerusalem believed your message of love and forgiveness would survive at all, much less spread across the world. Give me the grace to live out my priesthood always with honor and obedience. Obedience. Yes. That's it. Obedience—the most disagreeable of virtues. Lord, rain on me, shine your light on me so I may feed your people with my life.*

*I am just a passing shower, but behold, I come.*

# About the Author

Multi-award-winning author **Rita Ariyoshi** served as editor of Hawaiian Airlines inflight magazine for three years, then became the the founding editor of Aloha, The Magazine of Hawaii and the Pacific, and served as editor-in-chief of the magazine for ten years. She left the magazine to devote her time to a freelance writing career. She has guest-lectured at several schools in Hawaii, including the University of Hawaii, and was a speaker at the Maui Writers Conference. She lives in Honolulu with her husband, Joseph and dog, Miki.

Consider these other fine books from **Savant Books and Publications** and it's imprint **Aignos Publishing**:

*Essay, Essay, Essay* by Yasuo Kobachi
*Aloha from Coffee Island* by Walter Miyanari
*Footprints, Smiles and Little White Lies* by Daniel S. Janik
*The Illustrated Middle Earth* by Daniel S. Janik
*Last and Final Harvest* by Daniel S. Janik
*A Whale's Tale* by Daniel S. Janik
*Tropic of California* by R. Page Kaufman
*Tropic of California* (the companion music CD) by R. Page Kaufman
*The Village Curtain* by Tony Tame
*Dare to Love in Oz* by William Maltese
*The Interzone* by Tatsuyuki Kobayashi
*Today I Am a Man* by Larry Rodness
*The Bahrain Conspiracy* by Bentley Gates
*Called Home* by Gloria Schumann
*First Breath* edited by Z. M. Oliver
*The Jumper Chronicles* by W. C. Peever
*William Maltese's Flicker - #1 Book of Answers* by William Maltese
*My Unborn Child* by Orest Stocco
*Last Song of the Whales* by Four Arrows
*Perilous Panacea* by Ronald Klueh
*Falling but Fulfilled* by Zachary M. Oliver
*Mythical Voyage* by Robin Ymer
*Hello, Norma Jean* by Sue Dolleris
*Charlie No Face* by David B. Seaburn
*Number One Bestseller* by Brian Morley
*My Two Wives and Three Husbands* by S. Stanley Gordon
*In Dire Straits* by Jim Currie
*Wretched Land* by Mila Komarnisky
*Who's Killing All the Lawyers?* by A. G. Hayes
*Ammon's Horn* by G. Amati
*Wavelengths* edited by Zachary M. Oliver
*Communion* by Jean Blasiar and Jonathan Marcantoni
*The Oil Man* by Leon Puissegur
*Random Views of Asia from the Mid-Pacific* by William E. Sharp
*The Isla Vista Crucible* by Reilly Ridgell
*Blood Money* by Scott Mastro

*In the Himalayan Nights* by Anoop Chandola
*On My Behalf* by Helen Doan
*Chimney Bluffs* by David B. Seaburn
*The Loons* by Sue Dolleris
*Light Surfer* by David Allan Williams
*The Judas List* by A. G. Hayes
*Path of the Templar*—Book 2 of The Jumper Chronicles by W. C. Peever
*The Desperate Cycle* by Tony Tame
*Shutterbug* by Buz Sawyer
*Blessed are the Peacekeepers* by Tom Donnelly and Mike Munger
*Bellwether Messages* edited by D. S. Janik
*The Turtle Dances* by Daniel S. Janik
*The Lazarus Conspiracies* by Richard Rose
*Purple Haze* by George B. Hudson
*Imminent Danger* by A. G. Hayes
*Lullaby Moon* (CD) by Malia Elliott of Leon & Malia
*Volutions* edited by Suzanne Langford
*In the Eyes of the Son* by Hans Brinckmann
*The Hanging of Dr. Hanson* by Bentley Gates
*Flight of Destiny* by Francis Powell
*Elaine of Corbenic* by Tima Z. Newman
*Ballerina Birdies* by Marina Yamamoto
*More More Time* by David B. Seabird
*Crazy Like Me* by Erin Lee
*Cleopatra Unconquered* by Helen R. Davis
*Valedictory* by Daniel Scott
*The Chemical Factor* by A. G. Hayes
*Quantum Death* by A. G. Hayes and Raymond Gaynor
*Big Heaven* by Charlotte Hebert
*Captain Riddle's Treasure* by GV Rama Rao
*All Things Await* by Seth Clabough
*Tsunami Libido* by Cate Burns
*Finding Kate* by A. G. Hayes
*The Adventures of Purple Head, Buddha Monkey...* by Erik/Forest Bracht
*In the Shadows of My Mind* by Andrew Massie
*The Gumshoe* by Richard Rose
*In Search of Somatic Therapy* by Setsuko Tsuchiya
*Cereus* by Z. Roux
*The Solar Triangle* by A. G. Hayes
*Shadow and Light* edited by Helen R. Davis
*A Real Daughter* by Lynne McKelvey
*StoryTeller* by Nicholas Bylotas
*Bo Henry at Three Forks* by Daniel Bradford

*Kindred* edited by Gary "Doc" Krinberg
*Cleopatra Victorious* by Helen R. Davis
*The Dark Side of Sunshine* by Paul Guzzo
*Cazadores de Libros Perdidos* by German William Cabasssa Barber [Spanish]
*The Desert and the City* by Derek Bickerton
*The Overnight Family Man* by Paul Guzzo
*There is No Cholera in Zimbabwe* by Zachary M. Oliver
*John Doe* by Buz Sawyers
*The Piano Tuner's Wife* by Jean Yamasaki Toyama
*An Aura of Greatness* by Brendan P. Burns
*Polonio Pass* by Doc Krinberg
*Iwana* by Alvaro Leiva
*University and King* by Jeffrey Ryan Long
*The Surreal Adventures of Dr. Mingus* by Jesus Richard Felix Rodriguez
*Letters* by Buz Sawyers
*In the Heart of the Country* by Derek Bickerton
*El Camino De Regreso* by Maricruz Acuna [Spanish]
*Prepositions* by Jean Yamasaki Toyama
*Deep Slumber of Dogs* by Doc Krinberg
*Navel of the Sea* by Elizabeth McKague
*Entwined* edited by Gary "Doc" Krinberg
*Critical Writing: Stories as Phenomena* by Jamie Dela Cruz
*Truth and Tell Travel the Solar System* by Helen R. Davis
*Saddam's Parrot* by Jim Currie
*Beneath Them* by Natalie Roers
*Chang the Magic Cat* by A. G. Hayes
*Illegal* by E. M. Duesel
*Island Wildlife: Exiles, Expats and Exotic Others* by Robert Friedman
*The Winter Spider* by Doc Krinberg
*The Princess in My Head* by J. G. Matheny
*Comic Crusaders* by Richard Rose
*I'll Remember* by Clif McCrady
*The City and the Desert* by Derek Bickerton
*The Edge of Madness* by Raymond Gaynor
*'Til Then Our Written Love Will Have to Do* by Cheri Woods
*Aloha La'a Kea* edited by Robert "Uhene" Maikai
*Hawaii Kids Music Vol 1* by Leon and Malia
*William Maltese's Flicker - #2 Book of Ascendency* by William Maltese
*Retribution* by Richard Rose
*Shep's Adventures* by George Hudson

*The Immigrant's Grandson* by Vern Turner
*Source* edited by Rudiger Ruckmann

Coming Soon
*I Love Liking You A Lot* by Greg Hatala
*Hot Night in Budapest* by Keith Rees
*World Wakers* by Britton E. Brooks
*The Power of Dance* by Setsuko Tsuchiya
*Weaving Our Stories* edited by Luanna Peterson

http://www.savantbooksandpublications.com
*Enduring literary works for the twenty-first century*

Made in USA - Crawfordsville, IN
26110_9781737643128
10.02.2022 1648